COMANCHE MOON

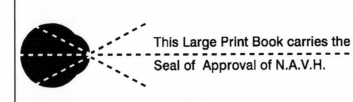

This Large Print Book carries the
Seal of Approval of N.A.V.H.

COMANCHE MOON

CATHERINE ANDERSON

WHEELER PUBLISHING

A part of Gale, Cengage Learning

GALE
CENGAGE Learning

Detroit • New York • San Francisco • New Haven, Conn • Waterville, Maine • London

GALE
CENGAGE Learning™

The publisher does not have any control over and does not assume any responsibility for author or third-party Web sites or their content.
Wheeler Publishing Large Print Hardcover.
The text of this Large Print edition is unabridged.
Other aspects of the book may vary from the original edition.
Set in 16 pt. Plantin.
Printed on permanent paper.

LIBRARY OF CONGRESS CATALOGING-IN-PUBLICATION DATA

Anderson, Catherine (Adeline Catherine)
    Comanche moon / by Catherine Anderson.
       p. cm. — (Wheeler Publishing large print hardcover)
    ISBN-13: 978-1-59722-828-2 (alk. paper)
    ISBN-10: 1-59722-828-1 (alk. paper)
    1. Orphans—Fiction. 2. Mute persons—Fiction. 3. Comanche Indians—Fiction. 4. Indian captivities—Fiction. 5. Prophecies—Fiction. 6. Large type books. I. Title.
PS3551.N34557C66 2008
813'.54—dc22   2008026378

Published in 2008 by arrangement with NAL Signet, a member of Penguin Group (USA) Inc.

This book is in memory of the Comanche Nation, a proud, noble, and often misunderstood people whose population was nearly annihilated by the white men who invaded Comanche territories. As I wrote this book, I felt sad that such a wonderful way of life had to end, and I hope that someday humankind will begin to learn from its mistakes — namely that we are all brothers and sisters. With ancestral ties to the Shoshone, the parent tribe of the Comanche, I felt such a great affinity for the "True People" as I wrote this tale. I will never walk through the ponderosa forests of Central Oregon, their seasonal hunting grounds, without hearing their voices whispering to me on the wind, saying, "Suvate"; it is finished.

ACKNOWLEDGMENTS

Looking back over the years, every writer realizes that certain people played key roles in his or her success. I will be forever grateful to my mother, Eleanora Clark La May Son, who was a writer, gave me my love of words and story, and always believed in me. Following in her footsteps, my husband, Sid, supported me with unflagging enthusiasm as I struggled to become published and then build my career. During that time, my sons, Sidney and John, selflessly endured deadline crunches, never berating me when my work took center stage. To this day, they cheer me on and celebrate my successes with me. Also crucial to my career is my longtime editor, Ellen Edwards, whose support, respect for my writing style, and deft editing have enabled me to consistently produce good books with unique and memorable plots. I also want to thank my agent, Steven Axelrod, who has been my cornerstone. Last, but never least, my wonderful readers have my eternal gratitude, for without them my writing journey never would have begun.

THE PROPHECY

From the place where the sun rises, there will come to the People a great warrior who will stand tall above his brothers and see far into the great beyond with eyes like the midnight sky. This Comanche shall carry the sign of the wolf upon his shield, yet none shall call him chief. To his people shall come much sadness, and the rivers will run red with the blood of his nation. Mountains of white bones will mark where the mighty buffalo once grazed. In the sky, black smoke will carry away the death cries of helpless women and children. He will make big talk against the White-Eyes and fierce war, but the battles shall stretch before him with no horizon.

When his hatred for the White-Eyes is hot like the summer sun and cold like the winter snow, there will come to him a gentle maiden from *tosi tivo* land. Though her voice will have been silenced by great sorrow, her eyes shall speak into his of a morning with new beginnings. She will be golden like the new day,

9

with skin as white as the night moon, hair like rippling honey, and eyes like the summer sky. The People will call her the Little Wise One.

The Comanche will raise his blade to slay her, but honor will stay his hand. She will divide his Comanche heart, so his hate that burns hot like the sun will make war with his hate that is cold like the winter snow, and the hate shall melt and flow out of him to some faraway place he cannot find. Just as the dawn streaks the night sky, he will chase the shadows from her heart and return her voice to her.

When this is done, the warrior and his maiden shall walk together to a high place on the night of the Comanche moon. He will stand on the land of the Comanche, she on the land of the *tosi tivo*. Between them will be a great canyon that runs high with blood. The warrior will reach across the canyon to his maiden, and she will take his hand. Together they will travel a great distance into the west lands, where they will give birth to a new tomorrow and a new nation where the Comanche and the *tosi tivo* will live as one forever.

PROLOGUE

Texas, August 1859

As pale as fresh cream, a full moon shone against the midnight sky, casting a silver aura across the star-studded blackness. A killing moon, some called it, and tonight that seemed fitting. The screams of dying women and children rang no more, as if, like the wind, they had come to this place only briefly and now were gone.

In the distance a coyote howled, the sound rising in a mournful crescendo, then trailing off into a wail that made Hunter of the Wolf shiver. He knelt alone on the bluff, his indigo eyes fastened on the trampled ground below the promontory. Judging by the swath of hoof marks, the Blue Coats had fled southeast after their attack on his village earlier that day.

He clenched his hands into fists. His wife's name rang like a litany inside his head, calling out to him for vengeance. Willow by the Stream had been heavy with his child. He

11

wished he could gather his war gear and set out immediately after her killers, but he and the other young men were needed here to tend the injured and bury the dead. Soon, though, he would make war as he never had before. He would hunt down the Blue Coats like the animals they were and return the pain they had wrought a hundredfold.

Hunter was no stranger to grief, but never had he experienced this terrible feeling of emptiness. Even as children he and Willow had been a pair, their laughter ringing across windswept grasslands. No other's hand had ever felt right in his. No other's smile had made a glad song within him. He had thought to have her always at his side. And now she was gone, leaving behind a canyon within him as vast as the plains that stretched forever into the horizon. Despite everything he had done to save her, she had lost their child and slowly bled to death in his arms. Her injuries, the result of vicious and repeated rape, had been inside of her where they couldn't be seen. Up to the last, he had kept hoping she would recover.

He could almost feel her spirit leaving him, see her running gracefully across the stepping-stones made of stars into the land of the dead. His gut tightened as he contemplated the path she might take. She had never been good at finding her way, depending always upon him to guide her. He prayed the

Great Ones held her hand to show her which direction to go. If she was all alone, she would surely get lost. The thought made unwanted tears well in his eyes.

The night wind had dried her blood on his hands and buckskin breeches. Hunching his broad shoulders, he emitted a keening cry of sorrow that echoed in the air around him. Drawing his knife, he hacked off his mahogany hair close to the scalp. Then he lifted his razor-sharp blade and slashed himself from the outside tip of his right eyebrow to his chin, his sign to all the People that Willow by the Stream would live forever within his heart. His blood stained the blade crimson. He wished it were the blood of a *tabeboh,* any *tabeboh.*

A movement to his left caught his attention, and he turned to see his mother approaching, her moccasins touching softly upon the ground as if she trod upon his grief. He made a quick swipe at his cheek, ashamed for her to see his tears.

An apologetic look crossed her face. "My *tua,* I know I should not approach you now," whispered Woman with Many Robes, "but I must talk with you."

She came to kneel with him. A tight, suffocating ache centered itself in his throat. Her smell was familiar and dear, reminiscent of his childhood when her gentle hands had soothed all his hurts. He yearned to bury his

13

face in her ample breasts, to cry as only a child could. "She trusted me to protect her," he whispered raggedly. "It was my promise to her in the song we sang together. I should never have left her."

Woman with Many Robes clucked her tongue, much as she had done years ago when he had come to her as a boy spouting foolish stories. "You wish to walk backward, *tua,* and it cannot be. I know it is hard to accept, but your wife has been taken because the song you sang with her was meant to be sung with another."

"The blood of my woman is still warm on my leggings, yet you mention the prophecy? You have sung the words to me all my life, and I have listened like a dutiful son. I won't tonight."

She stared into the distance. A cloud drifted across the moon, shadowing her face. "In a few hours, you will ride out. I must tell you something first, that you are the Comanche of the prophecy. You came to me from the place where the sun rises — from the loins of a Blue Coat twenty-six winters ago."

The air gushed from his chest as if she had struck him. "No! I have asked my father many times. Always he said I was his son! You will not speak such a lie."

He made as if to rise, but she grabbed his arm. "It is no lie. You have indigo eyes, not black, and you stand a head taller than your brothers." With her other hand, she caught hold of his medallion, turning the stone so he could see the image carved there. "You bear the sign of the wolf, yet none call you chief."

For a moment he could only stare at her in frozen silence. "You, the mother that I love, and a Blue Coat?"

"I did nothing wrong. It happened during an attack, much like the one today. The men were gone hunting. I tried to run, and the Blue Coat saw me." Her voice went reed thin. "He raped me and left me for dead. When I found I was with child, your *ap* claimed the babe was his and sang with me at the central fire."

"Why are you telling me this? So I won't avenge my wife?" His voice grew thick with rage, and he jerked his medallion from her grasp. "I will reclaim her honor. I must."

"Find her killers, yes, but don't take part in the bloodbath I've heard the others planning." Her tear-filled eyes implored him. "Your life is not your own. The fate of your people rests on your shoulders. You must find the honey-haired woman with no voice, bring her to us, and honor her as you never will another."

"I'll honor her with a quick death."

"Do not speak such a thing, for then it must be." She sighed and pushed to her feet. Placing her hands on her hips, she made much of the horizon for a long while. Then she

15

touched his bowed head. "I will not ask you to strike the hate from your heart, for that too is foretold in the prophecy. As for love, it wells up like a spring from a hidden place, and you cannot command that of anyone. But, *tua,* for the sake of your people, you must find the honey-haired woman and bring her to us."

His answer was taut silence.

"I know it is a hard thing. That is why you were chosen, because you are strong. The People will go the way of the wind one day soon. The Great Ones have chosen you to sing our song and keep our ways alive."

He threw her an incredulous glance. "Do I look weak like a woman? I am a warrior, not a storyteller."

Her smile was filled with sadness. "There are many ways to fight the great fight. The bravest warrior of all is the one with no shield. Your people need you to fight the *last* fight, the most bitter battle of all. And you must do it alone. When the time comes, you will see the path the Great Ones have chosen for you and walk it with courage."

"The Comanche of the prophecy must leave the People. I would never do that, especially not with a white woman. I'm afraid you underestimate my hatred, *pia.*"

"Remember one thing. I have cause to hate the *tosi tivo,* too. The dreams about the Blue Coat will haunt me always. But I took a *tosi*

16

tivo into my buffalo robes. I held him to my breast and called him son. And my love for him burns like the brightest star in the heavens. You are that *tosi tivo*. Strike it from your heart, deny it as you will, there is a place within you that is not Comanche."

CHAPTER 1

Texas, June 1864

The midafternoon sun slanted through the lone pecan tree's green leaves, spangling the ground with bright shimmers of gold. To Loretta Simpson's way of thinking, that tree was the only appealing thing on Henry Masters's farm. As she latched the smokehouse door and glanced over her shoulder at the familiar setting, all else seemed bleak and colorless. The squat little house and its naked dirt yard was a blemish on the rolling grassland, as disfiguring as a jagged scar on a pretty woman's face. The scraggly, parched rosebushes next to the porch were all but leafless, their branches casting skeletal shadows on the dwelling's log walls. Blistered by the sun day after day, the bushes would eventually die, casualties of the endless and futile war between her aunt's husband and the land.

That Henry Masters had chosen this location to erect his crude buildings and sagging fences said much about the sort of person he

19

was. If he had situated his farm closer to the nearby Brazos River, where scrub oak and pecan and willow trees formed a dark, low line, the shade and gentle breezes might have made life more bearable. Instead he had taken his stand in the open to save himself the work of uprooting trees.

Holding her bloodied hands away from her skirts, Loretta watched the little puffs of dust that mushroomed in front of her shoes as she walked from the smokehouse to the well. She didn't want to think about the doe she had just skinned and quartered but was at cross-purposes with her twelve-year-old cousin, Amy, who skipped along beside her.

"With that much milch in her udder, she was nursing at least one fawn," the girl fumed. "But did Pa care? No, not him. We've got to do somethin', Loretta. If we just leave them out there to starve, we're as guilty as he is."

Loretta increased her pace. As the older of the two, it was up to her to be practical. Two girls traipsing through the wilds in search of fawns would be asking for trouble, and Loretta figured she had troubles enough. Less than a month ago, a neighboring farm had been attacked. The bloody aftermath still haunted her dreams. Besides, that doe's fawns would be far too old to tame.

Amy heaved a defeated sigh. "I guess they'd be too big to bring home, not to mention the fit Pa would throw. Do you reckon they're old enough to forage for food and make it on their own? It's early summer. They're probably pretty old, aren't they?"

Swallowing a tight knot of anger, Loretta nodded with far more certainty than she felt.

"Pa could've hunted a few more days," Amy declared in a quavery voice. "Can't tell me there ain't bucks aplenty in those woods. He's just too dad-blamed lazy."

Pretending she hadn't noticed Amy's bad language, Loretta reached for the pulley rope above the well. Amy needed to vent her anger, and it was best she do it out here. There was enough friction in the house, especially between Amy and her stepfather.

Amy angled a peek at Loretta's face. "Ma must have been plumb desperate after Pa died to take up with the likes of him."

Loretta hauled up the bucket and concentrated on washing her hands. There was no point in letting Amy rile her. There were some things a person couldn't change, and Henry Masters was one of them. It would take someone bigger than Loretta, at any rate. Grasping the bucket by its rim, she gave it a brisk swish and tossed out the pinkish water with enough force to have laid Henry flat had he been standing there.

"Fill the bucket again, would ya?" Amy ran the tip of her tongue across her upper lip. "I'm dry as jerked venison."

Loretta hefted the bucket onto the edge of the well and, wetting her fingers, flicked the little girl in the face and flashed her a smile.

"That feels good. If that bucket was big enough, I'd jump right in. If it weren't for those durned Indians, I'd be goin' swimmin'." Lifting the ladle, Amy gulped, her throat making plunking sounds until she stopped to get some air. "Want some?"

Shaking her head, Loretta leaned against the well and swiped her forehead with her sleeve. Amy was right; a swim would be nice. In her homespun dress, she felt like a hen simmering in a pot, but it would be too risky to venture far from the house. A few days ago she and Amy had seen Comanches down by the river. One of the Indians had grabbed Loretta's braid and hacked off some of her hair. She could have been scalped; no telling why the Indian had spared her, but she wasn't about to tempt fate again. Uncle Henry had seen sign that unshod horses had been on his land several times since, so the Comanches might still be in the area.

Glancing down at Amy's flushed cheeks, Loretta was surprised to see the girl dipping more water. Instead of drinking from it, though, Amy upended the ladle over her honey-gold head. Water spiked her dark lashes and ran in rivulets down her lightly freckled nose. Loretta was reminded of herself at that age, all legs and arms, so skinny her blue eyes looked big as flapjacks.

Amy sighed and tossed the ladle into the bucket. "You goin' back in? Or are you gonna stay put here so old toad-face can't stare at ya?" She squinted against the sun, trying to see Loretta's face. "I'm sure glad I'm not twenty yet. Pa don't know squat about pickin' husbands. That Bartlett fella with the big nose would be better than Tom Weaver."

Loretta glanced at the log house. A string of smoke drifted from the catted chimney, trailing along the peak of the barkslabbed roof. Rachel was probably stirring the stew right this moment, wondering if their neighbor would be staying for supper. Just the thought knotted Loretta's stomach. She didn't blame Uncle Henry for wanting to find her a husband. Providing for a wife and stepdaughter was burden enough. But Tom Weaver? Amy was right; he made the Bartlett boy look like a prince. A constant dribble of tobacco juice ran from the corner of Weaver's mouth into his beard, and his unwashed body stank up the whole house. The thought of kissing him made her want to retch.

"You don't have to marry him," Amy said. "You earn your keep. Sometimes when ya ain't lookin', Pa eyes ya with downright fondness. Really! He never seemed to mind havin' ya here before. You're so pretty. Some handsome rancher'll come callin' soon."

What handsome rancher? Loretta glanced at

the endless stretch of open country beyond the farm, lifting a dubious brow.

A twinkle of devilment crept into Amy's eyes. "We could up and run off." She leaned forward, her small face aglow. "Back to Virginia, just you and me. Hire on as cooks on a wagon train! Once we got there, we could find jobs and save to send for Ma.

"Just imagine! You and me, in Virginia. Socials, barn dances, and church on Sunday, just like Ma tells about. We could sew pretty dresses and look so fine! You'd be married quicker'n a flea can jump. To somebody grand. Tall and handsome with a beaver hat and spit-shined shoes."

She twirled once more and then dipped low in a graceful curtsy. "Come on, Loretta, it's just for pretend. Show me how to dance. You recollect what Virginia was like, and I don't."

Images flashed in Loretta's mind of Virginia's thick forests and velvety green hills. She was too old for make-believe, but sometimes at night, she lay awake remembering, wishing. . . .

Doing a jig across the dirt, Amy cried, "Well? You gonna play or not?"

Unable to resist, Loretta snatched up her skirts and did a waltz step, imagining she had a partner. She tried to picture what he'd look like and decided his being tall or handsome wouldn't matter if only she felt happy when she was with him. Someone like her pa, strong yet gentle, assertive but thoughtful, a man who'd see beyond her silence and love her in spite of it.

Warming to the game, Amy stopped dancing to clasp her hands. "Let's make him rich, shall we? Rich enough to buy you a great big slate so you could write notes whenever you wanted. He wouldn't be ornery about it like Pa."

Loretta's feet dragged to a stop. Mention of Henry brought reality crashing around her. She stared at the dust covering Amy's pantalets to midshin, at the faded, worn folds of her skirts. They weren't in Virginia, never would be again, and even if they were, a man who could afford a beaver hat wouldn't give a mute woman in homespun more than a cursory glance.

"What's that?"

Alarmed by the brittle tension in Amy's tone, Loretta glanced over her shoulder. A red cloud rose against the powder blue sky. She shaded her eyes against the sun. Horses, judging by the dust, a number of them. It might be the border patrol from Fort Belknap, but she doubted it. The war had taken its toll. There were no troops in Palo Pinto County, so the border regiment was stretched mighty thin trying to control the Indians.

Amy stiffened, clutching Loretta's blue skirt. "What is it? Oh, Loretta, you don't think it's Indians, do you?"

Loretta hugged the girl's shoulders with a protective arm. Indians had been the first possibility to cross her mind, too.

"What if it's them? Maybe they liked our yellow hair, and they're comin' back to get it. . . . It is Indians," Amy cried. "I can see 'em."

Giving the girl a push, Loretta lifted her skirts to run. *Pray God it isn't a war party.* Her heart slammed with every step as she shooed Amy to the house. She could hear the muffled thrumming of horses' hooves. She longed to call a warning to Uncle Henry and Tom Weaver. Her throat strained, her lungs ached. Never had her muteness frustrated her so. Though she tried to block them out, pictures of the Samuelsons' farm flashed through her mind, old Bart nailed to his barn with Indian lances, his grown sons scattered across the yard like lifeless rag dolls.

Amy started to scream. "Indians! Indians comin'!"

A frenzy of motion erupted in the cabin, boots resounding on the puncheon floor, furniture scraping on the planks, Rachel yelling. Loretta hit the steps in a leap, grabbing Amy's arm to haul her up. Surely they moved in a dream, each leaden second stretching into eternity. She butted her shoulder against the door, throwing it open and jerking Amy inside. Slamming the door behind them, she whirled to drop the bar into its niche.

"Tom, take the left window," Henry barked. "Rachel, let Loretta tend Amy. You git the spare rifle and cover the back."

Herding Amy across the room, Loretta seized hold of the bed to move it. Beneath it was a trapdoor. Barring fire, Amy would be safe under the house. She lifted the hatch. A damp, musty smell assailed their nostrils.

"I don't wanna," Amy sobbed. "Please, Loretta, come with me."

For a frozen instant, Loretta was swept back in time. She was thirteen again, straining against her father's arm as he shoved her into the storm cellar to hide her from the Comanches. *Please, Papa. Let me stay with you and Ma. Please, Papa.*

Her father had slammed the door closed, yelling at her through the cracks: *You shush, girl, and mind what I say. Don't you make a sound, you hear? No matter what happens, don't you make a sound.*

Loretta, eyes riveted to the cracks in the cellar door, teeth embedded in her lip to keep from screaming, had witnessed the atrocities. But she had obeyed her father and uttered not a sound. Seven years later, she was still silent.

The thundering approach of horses brought Loretta back to the present. Catching Amy's arm, she pulled her to the opening and forced her down the steps. Amy looked over her shoulder, her small face pinched and white. Loretta slammed the trap closed and repositioned the bed. If this was an attack, God forbid that those animals should get their hands on a twelve-year-old.

Visions of her mother's violated body spun in her head.

Dust filtered through the windows, burning Loretta's throat. The Comanches were all around the house. She could feel them, smell them. *Not Amy. Please, God, not sweet little Amy.*

"Holy Mother," Henry exclaimed, "must be a hundred of 'em!"

Weaver agreed with a grim nod, kneeling at the other window. He tugged the collar of his brown shirt, stretching his neck for air, and steadied his rifle. "Don't git jumpy and shoot."

"Oh, mercy," Rachel screeched from the back window, "there are so many! We don't have a prayer."

Loretta stood motionless in the center of the room. The aroma of venison stew floated to her. Everything looked so normal, the lid half-off the salt barrel, the flour sack loosened, two mugs on the planked table where the men had been sitting. Aunt Rachel's patch work lay on the rocker seat. How could things be fine one moment and smell like death the next?

Moving to the window, she looked out over her uncle's shoulder at the scores of warriors on nervous horses. The face of her mother's murderer had been dark and angular, the nose long, the forehead sloped sharply to a high hairline. She never saw Indians that she didn't search for that face. Was he out there? There were far too many faces, all dark, all with high foreheads. Brown, oiled skin gleamed. Lean muscles flexed. Feathers floated from deadly, poised lances. She closed her eyes, then opened them. A pall of silence covered everything, broken only by the musical tinkling of brass bells that dangled from the Comanches' moccasins. The loosened doeskin membranes that usually covered the windows flapped in the sudden breeze.

"Don't shoot," Tom cautioned again. "That brave in the lead has a crooked lance with a white flag. Whatever it is they're wantin', it ain't a fight. You speak any Comanch'?"

"Not a word," Henry replied.

"I don't know much. If they do a lot of tradin', they can probably talk English, but if they don't — all we can do is hope my Injun will get us by." Tom spat a glob of chew onto Rachel's bleached floor. Then he bellowed, "What do you want?"

Loretta's nerves were strung so taut, she leaped. Nausea surged into her throat as the brown tobacco juice soaked into the floor. Was she losing her mind? Who cared if the puncheon got stained? Before this was over, the house might be burned to the ground. She heard Rachel crying, a soft, irregular whimpering. *Terror.* The metallic taste of it shriveled her tongue.

"What brings you here?" Tom cried again.

"Hites!" a deep voice called back. "We come as friends, White-Eyes."

The lead warrior moved some twenty feet in front of his comrades, holding the crooked lance high so the dusty white rag was clearly visible. He sat proudly on his black stallion, gleaming brown shoulders straight, leather-sheathed legs pressed snugly to his mount. A rush of wind lifted his mahogany hair, wisping it across his bronzed, sharply chiseled face.

Loretta's first thought when she saw him was that he seemed different from the others. A closer look told her why. He was unquestionably a half-breed, taller on horseback than the rest, lighter-skinned. If not for his sun-darkened complexion and long hair, he might have passed for a white man. Everything else about him was savage, though, from the cruel sneer on his mouth to the expert way he balanced on his horse, as if he and the animal were one entity.

Tom Weaver stiffened. "Son of a — Henry, you know who that is?"

"I was hopin' I was wrong."

Loretta inched closer to get a better look.

Then it hit her. *Hunter.* She had heard his name whispered with dread, heard tales. But until this moment she hadn't believed he existed. A blue-eyed half-breed, one of the most cunning and treacherous adversaries the U.S. Army had run across. Now that the war had pitted North against South, the homesteaders had no cavalry to keep Hunter and his marauders at bay, and his raiders struck ever deeper into settled country, advancing east. Some claimed he was far more dangerous than a full-blooded Comanche because he had a white man's intelligence. As vicious as he was, there were stories that he spared women and children. Whether that was coincidence, design, or a lie some Indian lover had dreamed up, no one knew. Loretta opted for the latter. Indians were little better than animals, killers, one and all.

"What do you want?" Henry cried. "The cow's a good milcher. There's two mules and a horse out back."

A stench of fear rose from Uncle Henry's sweaty shirt, the smell sharp and sticky. The Indian reached to his belt and pulled something loose. Lifting it high, he stared straight at the window where Loretta stood. She had the uncanny feeling he could see her. Something golden streamed from his fingers, shimmering in the slanting sunlight. *"Pe-nan-de,"* he yelled. "Honey, you call it. Send me the

31

woman whose hair I hold."

"Oh, sweet Jesus," Tom whispered.

Unable to drag her eyes from the strands of gold trailing from the half-breed's brown fingers, Loretta pressed a trembling hand to her throat. This isn't really happening, she thought fuzzily. In a minute I'll wake up. It's just a bad dream.

"We're outnumbered fifty to one," Henry said. "What in hell we gonna do?"

Tom shifted at the window. "Ain't no matter if it's a hundred to one, you can't send him the girl."

"Better just her than all of us." A trickle of moisture dripped off Henry's nose, and he made a quick swipe with his white sleeve. "I got Amy and Rachel to think of. You know what those savages would do to Amy, Tom."

"And what about Loretta?"

Loretta reached to the wall for support. He wanted *her?* Fear turned her legs to water. No, I won't go, she thought. Then she remembered Amy's white face as the trapdoor closed. A hundred Comanches against three rifles? Everyone in the house would die, including Amy. And she knew beyond a doubt that the girl's death would not be swift. Uncle Henry was right; better one life than five.

Loretta turned to her aunt. Rachel's skin had blanched to alabaster. Their blue eyes locked. Then Rachel glanced toward the bed.

That look gave Loretta the push she needed. She stepped toward the door, a haze of unreality surrounding her. The last seven years had come full circle. This time, she wouldn't be a coward. She'd do for Amy what her parents had done for her. A second chance. How many times in her nightmares had she found the courage to open the cellar door, to go out and help her mother? How many times had she awakened from those nightmares, asking God to forgive her because she could be brave only in dreams? Now she could absolve herself.

As Loretta drew near the door, Tom cried, "No! You miserable coward, Henry. You send that girl out there, and you'll never sleep a whole night through the rest of your life."

Loretta touched the door planks and froze. Through the cracks she heard bells tinkling, a merry sound, as out of place as cheerful music at a funeral. She made the sign of the cross and squeezed her eyes closed, trying to remember how to make an act of contrition, but the words jumbled in her head.

"Henry, no," Rachel pleaded. "Loretta, don't open that door. If they want a woman, I'll go."

"It's not *you* they're wantin'," Henry snapped. "One of 'em spotted Loretta down by the river the other day, and he's come back for her. They'll shoot ya down where ya stand."

Rachel whirled on her husband. "That girl's my sister's daughter. I'll never forgive you if you let her go out there!"

"Ya don't have to do it, Loretta," Tom argued. "There's some things worse than dyin', and this is one of 'em."

Loretta hesitated. Then the door squeaked on its leather hinges, swinging open a crack. A shaft of light fell across her face. She stepped across the threshold. *Better just me than everyone.* Another step. *Better the Comanches take me than Amy.* It wasn't so hard, now that she was doing it. She took a deep breath and walked out onto the porch. The door slammed shut behind her, and the bar thudded home with an echo of finality.

Staring at her with impenetrable blue-black eyes, the warrior on the black nudged the animal a pace forward. With that relentless eye-to-eye contact, he held her pinioned where she stood. For what seemed a lifetime, he studied her, not moving, not speaking, his lance still held aloft.

Loretta's courage disintegrated, and a violent tremor swept the length of her. He noted the shudder, and his observant gaze trailed up her body in its wake. His attention fell to her hips, lingered there with an insulting contempt, then traveled upward to her breasts. Humiliation scorched her cheeks.

"Keemah." He hissed the word at her, but it

34

seemed sharp as a rifle shot rending the air. Loretta jumped, confusion and mindless terror contorting her features. She understood no Comanche and hadn't any perception of what he wanted. She only knew he would kill her if she angered him. Her shaking knees beat a tremulous tattoo against each other. His lips twisted in a sneer. "Come forward, so this Comanche can see you."

Too frightened to feel her feet, Loretta stumbled on the steps, nearly falling before she regained her balance. Her skin prickled from the two hundred eyes that watched her. As she drew near the Comanche, he wheeled his mount to one side. Cone-shaped brass bells sparkled against the stripped leather of his moccasin. His stare was a tangible thing, reaching to touch her.

"Lift your face, woman."

She tilted her head back, keeping her expression carefully blank. He seemed to tower atop the stallion, his bare shoulders broad, his arms well muscled. The breeze swept his dark hair from his cheek, revealing a thin scar that angled from his right eyebrow to his chin. Brilliant white teeth flashed as he spoke.

"What do you call yourself?"

Loretta parted her lips, and the prolonged silence pulsated.

"Answer, *woman,* or die." Lifting his lance tip, he caught her braid, tugging it loose from its coronet. Slowly uncoiling, it snaked to her shoulder.

"Loretta!" Rachel screamed from a front window. "Her name is Loretta. Oh, please, don't hurt her, please." A horrible, gut-wrenching sob punctuated the plea.

The Indian pressed the tip of his lance against Loretta's throat. "Have you no tongue, *herbi?*"

"No-oo-o," Rachel wailed. "She can't talk! It's the truth! Oh, please. She's a good, sweet girl. Don't hurt her."

To Loretta's left, an Indian on a pinto began to babble in excitement and pointed a finger at her. The lead Comanche's arm went taut, causing the lance to prick her skin. He leaned forward, the thick, veined muscles bulging in his upper arm as he tensed to drive the lance forward.

"Ka!" roared the Indian on the pinto. Then he let loose with another garbled string of words.

Loretta closed her eyes and braced herself. Whatever it was the other Indian was saying, he was clearly arguing in her behalf. There hovered in the air a charged expectancy, turbulent, tingling along her nerve endings to the core of her, so that, for a suspended moment, she felt a peculiar sense of oneness with the man above her, perceiving his tumultuous emotions, his indecision, as if she were an integral part of him. He wanted to spill

36

her blood with a primal ferocity, but something, perhaps the Almighty Himself, stayed his hand.

Sensing reprieve, grasping for it with eager disbelief, she lifted her lashes in confusion to see the same emotion reflected in his cobalt eyes.

He began to tremble, as if the lance weighed a thousand pounds. And suddenly she knew that as much as he longed to murder her, a part of him couldn't, wouldn't throw the lance. It made no sense. She could see nothing but hatred written on his chiseled face. He had surely killed hundreds of times and would kill again.

Slowly he lowered his arm and stared at her as if she had bested him in some way. Then, so quickly she couldn't be sure she saw it, pain flashed across his face. "So you're sweet?" His smile dripped ice. "We shall see, woman, we shall see."

He said "woman" as if he were spitting bile and slid his lance arrow to her chin. She had heard of women being disfigured by Indians and expected him to slash her as he outlined her mouth and the slope of her nose. Breathless fear brought moisture to her brow. Black spots danced, blurring her vision.

She blinked and forced herself to focus on him. Laughter twinkled in his eyes. She realized that since he had decided not to kill her, he was, for some reason she couldn't imagine, playing a hideous game, terrifying her to test her mettle. She caught hold of his lance and shoved it aside, lifting her head in defiance. Chuckling low in his chest, he leaned over his thigh, making a fist in her hair. His grip brought tears to her eyes.

As he turned her face to study her, he said, "You have more courage than you have strength, Yellow Hair. It is not wise to fight when you cannot win."

Looking up at his carved features and the arrogant set of his mouth, she longed for the strength to jerk him off his horse. He wasn't just taunting her, he was challenging her, mocking her.

"You will yield. Look at me and know the face of your master. Remember it well."

Riding high on humiliation, Loretta forgot Amy, Aunt Rachel, everything. An image of her mother's face flashed before her. Never, as long as she had life in her body, would she yield to him. She worked her parched mouth and spat. Nothing came out, but the message rang clear.

"Nei mah-heepicut!" Releasing her, he struck her lightly on the arm. Wheeling his horse, he glanced toward he windows of the house and thumped his chest with a broad fist. "I claim her!"

Loretta staggered, watching in numb disbelief as Hunter pranced his stallion in a circle around her. *I claim her?* Warily she turned, keeping him in sight, unsure of what he might do. He rode erect, his eyes touching on her dress, her face, her hair, as if everything about her were a curiosity.

A taunting smile curved his mouth. His attention centered on her full skirt, and she could almost see the questions churning in his head. He repositioned his hand on the lance. The determination in his expression filled her with foreboding.

He rode directly toward her, and she sidestepped. He turned his mount to come at her again. As he swept by he leaned forward, catching the hem of her skirt with his lance. Loretta whirled, striking out with her forearms, but the Indian moved expertly, his aim swift and sure, his horse precision-trained to the pressure of his legs. He was as bent on seeing her undergarments as she was on keeping them hidden.

The outcome of their battle was a foregone conclusion, and Loretta knew it. His friends encouraged him, whooping with ribald laughter each time her ruffles flashed. She snatched the dirty peace flag from the wooden shaft and threw it to the earth, grinding it beneath the heel of her shoe.

After fending off several more passes, exhaustion claimed its victory, and Loretta realized the folly in fighting. She stood motionless, breasts heaving, her eyes staring fixedly at nothing, head lifted. The warrior circled her, guiding his stallion's flashing hooves so close to her feet that her toes tingled. When she didn't move, he reined the horse to a halt and studied her for several seconds before he leaned forward to finger the bodice of her dress. Her breath snagged when he slid a palm over her bosom to the indentation of her waist.

"Ai-ee," he whispered. "You learn quick."

Raising tear-filled eyes to his, she again spat in his face. This time he felt the spray and wiped his cheek, his lips quivering with something that looked suspiciously like suppressed laughter, friendly laughter this time. "Maybe not so quick. But I am a good teacher. You will learn not to fight me, Yellow Hair. It is a promise I make for you."

In that moment, what she felt for him went beyond hate, a black, churning ugliness that made her want to seize the lance he brandished and skewer him with it. *I claim her.* He planned to take her, then? Her gaze traveled from his woven wool belt of army blue to the muscular tracks that rippled in his belly. The hilt of his knife protruded from a leather scabbard on his hip. How many soldiers had he killed? One, a hundred, perhaps a thousand?

Her hair hung from his belt, trailing in a spray of gold down the dark leather of his pants. She felt certain she had never seen him before. Yet he had her hair. The Indian down by the river must have given it to him, and he had come from God only knew where to get her.

With a start, she noticed the warrior had stretched out a hand to her. A wide leather band encircled his wrist to protect him from his bowstring. Staring at his dark palm and strong fingers, she shook her head in denial.

"Hi, tai," he said in a low voice. Guiding his stallion closer, he bent to touch her chin. Her eyelid quivered when he brushed at a tear on her cheek. *"Ka taikay, ka taikay, Tohobt Nabituh,"* he whispered.

The words made no sense. Puzzled, she met his gaze.

"Tosa ehr-mahr." Raising his hand, he showed her the glistening wetness on his fingertips. "Silver rain, *tosa ehr-mahr.*"

He compared her tears to silver rain? She searched his eyes for some trace of humanity and found none. After a moment he straightened, raising his lance in what looked like a salute.

"Suvate!" he yelled, his glittering eyes sweeping the line of encircling riders.

A low rumble of answering voices replied, *"Suvate!"*

He seemed satisfied with the response and, with a mighty thrust, drove the lance into the earth. Again, he thrust out his hand. "Take it, Yellow Hair, in friendship."

She was afraid he might drag her onto his

41

mount if she touched him, but his eyes compelled her. Besides, if he was set on it, he'd have his way, with or without her co-operation. She lifted a quivering arm, expecting the worst, and placed her fingers across his palm. His callused hand tightened on hers, the warmth of his grip shooting to her shoulder.

"We will meet again. I will come to you like the wind, from nowhere. Remember the face of this Comanche. I am your destiny."

With that, he released her and rode his horse in a circle about the yard, one arm raised high, his head thrown back to emit a shrill cry that sent shivers up her spine. Moments later a cloud of dust rose in the yard, and four hundred hooves beat a deafening staccato of retreat.

CHAPTER 2

After the Indians departed, Rachel bolted from the cabin and wrapped her arms around Loretta. Woodenly she returned her aunt's embrace but kept her eyes on the cloud of dust that drifted toward the river, the Comanche's words echoing. *I am your destiny.* Despite the heat, a clammy chill washed over her.

"You're all right," Rachel crooned. "You're all right."

Tightening her arms around her aunt, Loretta closed her eyes. She had stood face to face with a Comanche warrior and was still alive.

From inside the house came the sound of furniture dragging the floor, and a moment later Amy flew outside, her small face pinched with fear. "I thought they'd kill you."

Loretta pulled away from Rachel and took the child into her arms, pressing her cheek against her braids.

"I ain't never gonna hide again," Amy

whispered shakily. "Not ever. Oh, Loretta, now I know what it was like for you that day when they killed your ma and pa, how sick you felt inside. I ain't gonna go down there ever again. I swear I ain't."

Loretta swayed back and forth, massaging the tension from the child's shoulders. The smell of damp earth clung to Amy's clothes. It called to mind the never-forgotten mustiness of her own hiding place in the cellar. She alone knew the agony Amy had just lived through, and the girl was right, it made a person sick inside. As horrible as it had been for Amy, though, Loretta knew she would do it again, protect her little cousin, no matter what.

With sudden clarity, Loretta at last understood why her parents had hidden her during the Comanche attack. At the time, she had been only six months older than Amy. If she had found the courage to open the cellar door, what could she have done? Nothing, save dying. Rebecca Simpson would not have wanted Loretta to reveal herself. Knowing her child was safe had probably been her only comfort those last torturous minutes. The realization eased the ache of guilt within Loretta that had been her constant companion for seven long years. She took a deep, cleansing breath, and tears she had never before been able to shed came streaming down her cheeks. A sob ripped up her throat.

Amy stiffened and pulled back. "Loretta, you're cryin'!" Her eyes grew round. "Ma, Loretta's cryin'."

Rachel put an arm around each girl. "And well she should. If anybody ever had call, it's —"

Amy shook her head. "No, Ma, *really* cryin'. I heard —"

Rachel, unnerved by the close proximity of the Indians, didn't seem to register what her daughter was saying. "Come, let's get in the house. You never know with those savages. They're just as likely to double back to catch us unaware."

The door to the cabin stood open, and Loretta followed the others inside. Turning, she faced the men, her eyes full of questions. Henry leaned his rifle against the wall. "Ain't no rhyme nor reason to what them critters do sometimes. I don't reckon they'll be back."

Tom, still standing by the window, frowned and shook his head, his gaze fastened on the lance in the yard. "I ain't so sure. A Comanch' don't leave his mark just anywheres. Couldn't have said it plainer. Loretta's just got herself betrothed."

Amy giggled, a high, shrill laugh that echoed Loretta's own feeling of unreality. "You mean he wants Loretta as a squaw? Why, that'd be worse than her marryin' up with Mr. Wea—" Amy's eyes bugged, and her cheeks flamed. "I mean . . . well . . ."

45

"Hush, Amy!" Worrying her apron, Rachel shot Tom a questioning glance. "What makes you say such a thing?"

"We all heard him lay claim to her and say he'd be back." Tom avoided Loretta's gaze. "Comanches don't make false promises. My guess is he'll bring a couple of blankets and a horse or two in trade. That's the way they do things amongst themselves when they buy a wife. Not to say he'll stay so polite if you don't accommodate him and turn her over."

Rachel clamped a hand over her heart. "Oh, mercy, we've got to get Loretta out of here then, to Fort Belknap, perhaps."

"Ain't no use, Rachel," Tom said softly. "They'll have sentries posted. You try to leave with her, and they'll run you to the ground. Ain't nobody gonna take a Comanche's woman."

Hearing herself referred to as a Comanche's woman made Loretta recoil. She backed up until she stood beside the table.

"No Indian's taking my sister's daughter, and that's that," Rachel cried. "I'd sooner see her dead."

Henry put a comforting arm around his wife's shoulders. "Now, woman, don't get yourself in a dither. Chances are Tom's wrong and they won't never come back. It don't make a lick of sense to me. Why would a no good Comanche worry about bein' polite? Why, if he'd had it in mind to take her, she'd be bouncin' around on the back of his horse right now."

"You got a better explanation?" Tom challenged.

Henry shook his head. "Nope, but like I said, what them heathens do don't always figure."

Rachel leaned weakly against her husband. "Oh, Henry, I think Tom's right. He's going to come back and try to take her."

Loretta's legs buckled. She crumpled onto the planked bench and braced an elbow on the tabletop. A horrible fluttery feeling attacked her belly, the wings of terror batting upward into her chest. Were the Comanches still out there, hidden from sight but watching? Was that lance a message from Hunter to his people?

I will come to you like the wind. I am your destiny. She visualized the Indian returning with a dirty blanket or two, a scrawny horse he no longer wanted, perhaps a battered pot. And Uncle Henry, coward that he was, would waste no time in handing her over. Loretta Simpson, bought by a Comanche. No, not by just any Comanche, but Hunter himself. It would be whispered in horror all along the Brazos and Navasota rivers. *Hunter's woman.* She'd never be able to hold her head up again. No decent man would even look at her. If she lived . . .

With a whining intake of air, Loretta lunged

47

to her feet and ran to the door. Before anyone could stop her, she was across the porch and down the steps. She'd show that *heathen*. If this was a message that she belonged to him, she'd destroy it. Grabbing the lance, she worked it free from the earth.

"Loretta, you fool girl!" Tom came after her, catching her arm to whirl her around. "All you'll do is rile him."

Jerking free, she headed for the front gate. Rile him or not, if she didn't refute the Comanche's claim, it would be the same as agreeing to it. Maybe he *would* come back for her, but if he was out there watching, at least he'd know he wasn't welcome.

She walked beyond the yard fence, then turned and swung the lance against the top rail. The resilient shaft bounced back at her. She swung again. And again. The lance seemed to take life, resisting her, mocking her. She envisioned the Comanche's arrogant face and bludgeoned it, venting her hatred. *For Ma, for Papa.* She'd never belong to a filthy redskin, never.

Sweat began to run down her face, burning her eyes, salty on her lips, but still she swung the lance. It *had* to break. He might be out there watching. If his weapon defeated her, it would be the same as if he had. Her shoulders began to ache. Each lift of her arms became an effort. Beyond the realm of her immediate focus, she saw her family standing around her in shocked horror, staring as if she had lost her mind.

Perhaps she had. Loretta fell to her knees, gazing at the intact lance. Willow, *green* willow. No wonder the dad-blamed thing wouldn't break. Furious, she snatched the feathers off of it and ripped them into shreds, sputtering when the bits of down flew back in her face. Then she knelt there, heaving for air, so exhausted all the fight in her was drained away.

He had won.

Willow leaves swayed before Hunter's eyes, but his gaze held fast, riveted on the slender girl as she tried to break his lance. With each swing of her arms, he clenched his teeth, growing angrier. Then the absurdity of it hit him, and a reluctant smile tugged at his lips. She knew he was out here. Grown men quivered in fear at the sound of his name, but a frail girl dared to defy him? He recalled how she had looked when she walked out to face him, golden head held high, big blue eyes meeting his in defiance. How dare she spit at him, not once but *twice?* He wavered somewhere between outrage, disbelief, and admiration. She might not look like much, but she had courage, he'd give her that.

His brother, Warrior, hunkered beside him and snorted with laughter, clearly pleased with the situation. Above the roar of the river, he said, "If she knew who you were, she wouldn't defy you like this."

Hunter never shifted his gaze from the girl.

"Once she knows who she's up against, this nonsense will stop. If there's anything I'm an expert on, Hunter, it's women. They push only when they think they can get away with it. You shouldn't have let her spit at you. Next time, slap her."

Hunter arched an eyebrow. Given the fact that his brother's wife was the most spoiled female in the village, he found this bit of advice amazing. He studied Warrior's solemn expression. "Is that so?"

"Trust me. She'll never try it again."

"How many times have you slapped Maiden of the Tall Grass?"

"I haven't. She knows who has the stronger arm."

Hunter bit back a grin. "Yes, she certainly does."

Returning his attention to the girl, he scowled. He would teach her some respect or kill her trying.

At last the girl's strength gave out, and she fell to her knees in defeat. A spray of feathers flew up around her. As the white plumes floated downward, her shoulders sank with them. *Suvate,* it was finished. She had to face her fate and learn to accept it, just as he must. Destiny knew no foe.

"It isn't too late!" Hunter's cousin, Red

Buffalo, rode into the small clearing. He leaped off his horse and trotted toward them, his bow and an arrow outstretched in one hand. "She's the woman you've been seeking. Kill her, Hunter, while you still can. You know how your mother is about the prophecy. Once she sets eyes on her, it will be too late."

Hunter eyed the proffered weapon, then shook his head. "No. I must remember my duty. It would be madness to kill her. The wrath of the Great Ones would rain down on us. I can't think only of myself."

"You despise her! If the prophecy comes to pass, you will one day leave the People." Red Buffalo's scarred face twisted with disgust. "How can you bear the thought of taking her back with you? After what the Blue Coats did to your woman? To mine. And my little boy? Has it been so long that you've forgotten?"

Hunter's face hardened, and a cold glint crept into his eyes. "I will never forget."

Loretta had no appetite for supper. She joined the others at the table, but the aroma of venison stew and blackberry-and-maize bread made her stomach roil. Amy's eyes sought hers across the table. Henry was tipping the mescal jug, and he got ornery when he drank. Poor Amy usually took the brunt of it.

Loretta sympathized, but tonight she was preoccupied. Plans of escape flitted through her mind, all of which she considered, then discarded. She pictured the plains that surrounded her, feeling as hemmed in by the endless space as she would have by a barred cell.

Desperate to keep her hands busy and thus stave off panic, Loretta split her wedge of bread and took a bite. It got bigger and drier as she chewed. Tom Weaver fidgeted on the bench beside her. Then she saw his hand flash under her chin. Glancing down, she spied a slice of buttered bread on the edge of her trencher. She gave him a cautious smile, and his crusty lips curved in a shy grin.

"I think one of us ought to ride to Belknap and get Loretta an escort to the fort," he said softly. "Better me than you, Henry, 'cause I got no womenfolk. It'll take time, but the border patrol is there, and I've heard tell that several families have built houses with picket bastions. Loretta would probably be safe enough if we could get her there."

"Question is, how many men could you get?" Henry's cheek bulged. He chewed and swallowed. "Half the time, they're out ridin' Indian patrol, and what happens if that there Indian *does* come back? If he don't find Loretta here, he's gonna be hoppin' mad."

"My gawd, Henry!" Tom cried. "You ain't seriously sayin' you'd keep her here?"

A flush crept up Henry's neck. "Of course not."

Rachel glanced uneasily at her husband, then back at Tom. "How long would it take for you to round up men and get back?"

"I figger a day, ridin' hard and barrin' trouble. It'd give us a fightin' chance, Henry." Tom shrugged. "She wouldn't have to stay there for an unbearable long time. Hunter is bound to start ruttin' after some purty little squaw sooner or later and forget Loretta. Just a matter of waitin' him out."

"And if the Indians return before you get back?" Not a trace of color showed on Rachel's lips.

Henry shoved his trencher to the center of the table. "You just git out your beads, woman, and pray that don't happen. Ain't no way I can hold off a hundred Injuns alone."

Tom gave Loretta a pat. "Don't you worry. I'll git back. You're almost my promised. A man takes care of his gal if he's worth his salt."

"Whether or not she's your promised is still undecided," Henry inserted. "I ain't spoke to her about it yet. If there's Injuns out there — and I ain't so sure there is — don't go riskin' your neck 'cause you think it'll gain you favor. I'm not so averse to Loretta stayin' on that I'll marry her off against her will. She's got a home here if she wants."

Loretta stared at her uncle. For weeks she had been living in dread, afraid he would make her marry Tom. Now that she knew he wouldn't, she felt off balance. She turned her attention to Tom's gnarly profile. If he tried to get her an escort and the Indians guessed his intent, his life would be at risk. Until tonight she had seen only his filth and ugliness, but there was more to him than that. He was a good man, too good to end up dead over a woman who didn't care for him. But she knew Tom was her only hope. She would be the world's worst fool if she discouraged him from riding to Belknap.

As if he sensed her thoughts, Tom swung his legs over the bench and stood up, avoiding her gaze. "Well, I should head home if I'm leavin' out at dawn."

Loretta rose with him, wiping her palms on her skirt. Tom shuffled to the door and took his hat off the peg. Placing the hat at a jaunty angle upon his head, he flashed a smile at her and reached for his rifle. "G'night, Miz Masters. Fine meal you served up there." With a cursory nod, he said, "Amy, Henry."

Knowing what she had to do, Loretta followed Tom out to the porch, closing the door behind her. He ignored her for a moment, tightening his horse's saddle cinch and stowing his rifle. When he turned to look at her, the brim of his hat shaded his face, so she couldn't read his expression even in the bright moonlight. He propped a boot on the top step, draping his arms on his knee.

"I'd like to think you came out to say good-bye, but I've got a hunch that ain't it. Am I right?"

A hundred words gathered in Loretta's throat.

"Honey, if you're wantin' to tell me you don't love me, I already know. I've got a few years on ya, but I ain't senile." He chuckled and nudged his hat back so he could see her better. "And if you're out here to tell me I shouldn't go to Belknap, that you won't marry me anyways, then don't bother. I'd go if you was ugly as a post and had three husbands. Understand?"

Loretta felt a rush of tears welling in her eyes. Angrily she dashed the wetness from her cheeks.

Tom sighed, and before she knew what he was about, he stepped onto the porch and took her in his arms. "Ah, Loretta girl, don't cry. I've got hide thicker'n a buffalo's, and I'm twice as ornery. Ain't no dad-burned Injun gonna get the best of me. I'm goin' to Belknap because it's gotta be done. When I git back, we'll take up right where we left off, me bein' a pest, no obligation on your part. I understand that, and I'm goin' anyways. Clear? Take a herd of horses to stop me."

Loretta wrinkled her nose. The smell of his shirt stifled her. His hand on her back was gentle, though, reminiscent of her father's when he had held her this way. She twisted her face to one side to get some air, her cheek to his chest.

He gave her a fierce hug, then grasped her firmly by the shoulders and set her back from him to study her face. There was a curious gleam in his eye that made her uneasy. Catching her chin, he tipped her head farther back. As if reading her mind, he said, "Don't be afraid of me, Loretta Jane. I'd never set out to hurt you."

His voice rang with such sincerity that Loretta relaxed. She no sooner did than she saw his head bending. Here it came, the dreaded kiss. . . .

CHAPTER 3

Loretta clamped her lips together. The next second, Tom's beard touched her skin, coarse as a wire scrub brush, and from its bushy center protruded hot, wet lips that smacked down on hers with bull's-eye accuracy. His arms tightened and pulled her flat against him. Then he darted his tongue past her lips and licked her teeth. Was this how people kissed? He tasted of sour tobacco, and her gorge rose. By the tense way he held her, she knew he was trying to elicit a response. She hated to hurt his feelings but couldn't pretend she liked any part of what he was doing. What little bit of dinner she had managed to swallow earlier was working its way back up her throat.

Just when she feared her convulsing stomach might humiliate them both, Tom gave her a pat and turned her loose, smiling as if he had done himself proud. His eyes glowed with fondness. "I thank you for that, Loretta. It was mighty fine, and even if you don't

never marry me, I'll have it to remember."
He gave her a little push toward the door.
"You git on back in the house now."

As revolting as she had found his kiss, Loretta hesitated. At times, her silence rose around her like a wall.

"I'll be careful, and there's no need for thanks." He flashed a grin. "Don't stand there lookin' silly. You only think you can't talk, girl. Them there eyes of yours never shut up. Now, go on, git. I can't leave with you standin' out here."

In a swirl of skirts, she turned back and hugged his neck, surprising herself as much as him. Before she lost her nerve, she kissed his cheek. Then she dashed into the house, her heart pounding like a kettledrum. Through the door cracks, she heard Tom chuckle. She swiped the back of her hand across her lips to get rid of the tobacco taste. Only then could she smile.

As soon as the dishes were washed, Loretta climbed the ladder to the loft where she and Amy shared a bed. The fading light of the downstairs fire shone through the cracks of the planked floor, shooting shafts of muted gold clear to the rafters. Amy's soft, regular breathing whispered in the semidarkness. She slept in a sprawl with the gray down quilt thrown off her hot little body, the hem of her nightdress riding high on her skinny thighs.

Loretta went to the foot of the bunk and unfastened the doeskin membrane on the window to let in some air. The child sighed in her sleep and muttered something.

A breath of coolness touched Loretta's bare limbs when she peeled off her clothes. It felt so good that she lifted her arms and turned a full circle, allowing the night air to wash over her before she hung her dress on the hook and slapped at it to get the wrinkles out. Every little crease showed on homespun. Remembering better times, mostly in Virginia, but some here in Texas when her parents had still been alive, Loretta sighed and went to the nightstand. Sloshing water from the pitcher into the washbasin, she added a dash of lavender, then carried the bowl and her washcloth to the windowsill.

Leaning her head back, she began her nightly ritual, wringing the rag to trickle the scented water along her throat and over her breasts. In summer, the customary week between tub baths seemed like an eternity. Running the cloth slowly over her body, she closed her eyes. Lands, it was so hot. A female could cook in this country, wearing all those clothes.

She had finished bathing and was rinsing her drawers in the leftover water when a coyote wailed. She poked her head out the window to watch the full moon. A wisp of cloud drifted across the moon's milky face, casting ghostly shadows on the ground. *A Comanche moon.* Uncle Henry said it was called that because the Indians often raided on moonlit nights. Good light to murder by, she guessed.

Comanches. She backed from the window and clasped her soppy bloomers to her chest. Was she insane, flitting around naked?

"Loretta Jane Simpson!" Henry yelled. "Damn, girl, you're pourin' water through the ceilin' like it's a bloomin' sieve!"

Leaping back to the window, Loretta knocked the bowl over as she held her underwear out the opening. *Oh, blast!* She watched the bowl go bumpety-bump down the bark slabs. And stop. Right at the edge of the roof.

"What in hell?" Footsteps thumped. "Quiet it down up there, or I'll come up and shush you good."

Loretta swallowed. The pitch of the roof was steep. How could she retrieve the bowl without telling Henry? He'd be a wretch about it. She just knew he would. Amy moaned and murmured. Tomorrow, she'd find a way to get the bowl tomorrow.

After throwing on her nightgown, she hung her underwear over the sill to dry and sat on the edge of the bunk to brush and plait her hair. On the bedside table was a portrait of Rebecca Adams Simpson, her mother. In the dim light, her features were barely discernible, but Loretta knew each curve of her face by heart. Sadness filled her, and she traced the scrolled frame with a fingertip. If her father had yelled about water dripping through the floor, Rebecca would have said, "Oh, pshaw, Charles, don't get in a fuss." Not that Charles Simpson would have yelled. He had been a small man with a quiet manner.

Loretta opened the nightstand drawer. Inside, arranged upon a fold of linen, were her mother's diamond comb and her father's razor. Two mementos and a portrait, all she had left of her parents. Her mouth hardened. The comb had been one of a pair, her mother's most prized possessions. Now, only this one remained, the other taken by a Comanche along with Rebecca's scalp. Tears filled Loretta's eyes again, making her wonder what had come over her since Hunter's visit. Seven years, and she hadn't shed a single tear, and now she couldn't seem to stop crying. It didn't make any sense. The time for grief was long past, and Loretta didn't cotton to weepiness.

She closed the drawer with a click and wiped her cheeks with the heels of her hands. As she stretched out by Amy, she pulled her rosary from beneath her pillow. Kissing the cross, she whispered her soundless prayers, comforted to know that God could hear her.

It seemed a long while before the pressure in her chest subsided and an uneasy sleep stole over her. Then, suddenly, she awakened, not knowing why but glad to have an end to her dream. She lay rigid in the bed, her nightdress wringing wet, her throat aching with unvoiced screams, and remembered the Indian of her nightmare. With trembling fingers, she clutched her rosary and stared at the window. Had she glimpsed a shadow there, or was that more of her dream?

The night wind whispered, rattling the bark on the roof. She strained her ears. A footstep? A rustle of leather? She set her rosary aside and crawled to the window. Silver light shifted in the swaying trees along the river, and she felt a cool breeze.

Oh, Lordy, her pantalets were gone!

She clutched the sill and eased her head through the square. What she saw didn't surprise her. Hunter sat astride his horse, right out in the open, bold and challenging. The wind caught his hair, whipping it about his carved features. He lifted a powerfully muscled arm to her in silent salute, his fist clutching her wet drawers. For several endless seconds they stared at one another, then he wheeled his horse, his arm still held high, her ruffled underwear fluttering like a flag of glory behind him. Loretta watched long after he rode from sight.

I'm dreaming. He wasn't really there. I've just been dreaming. She had nearly convinced herself when her gaze fell to the edge of the

62

roof. Where was her bowl? Had the heathen lowlife swiped that as well? Then she spotted it sitting under the window. She knew then that the Comanche had been there and had stared at her while she dreamed of him. She couldn't make herself touch the bowl. *He* had touched it. Oh, mercy. And now he had her drawers. Had he spied on her while she bathed? The thought made her feel naked as sin.

She began to shake. She sank back onto the bed and hugged herself, trembling so violently that she was afraid she might wake Amy. Her dream came back to haunt her. She stared at the uncovered window and wondered if she should refasten the membrane and pull the shutters closed. Picturing his huge knife, she rejected the idea. If he wanted in, it would take more than wood to keep him out.

Her thoughts flew to Tom Weaver. He had to make it back in time. He simply had to.

Loretta awoke the next morning to find Amy's face hovering above hers. The girl's blue eyes were wide with questions, her bow-shaped mouth agape. It was barely dawn, that eerie, quiet time when the sun still strained to peek over the horizon. Shafts of blue-gray light slanted through the loft window, but beyond their anemic glow, the room was still dark. Loretta scuttled deeper under the quilt.

"You woke me up," Amy accused in an emphatic whisper. "You talked out in your sleep and woke me up."

Loretta stifled a yawn and blinked.

"You talked! Dad-blast if you didn't!"

Dad-blast? If Aunt Rachel got wind of the language Amy was using, she would scour her mouth with lye soap. Coming wide awake, Loretta rolled over on her side. Amy shifted on her knees, pressing her face so close that Loretta's eyes crossed.

"Do it again," she insisted. "Say somethin'. I *knew* I heard you make a noise yesterday. Boy, won't Ma have fits? Talk, Loretta. Say my name."

Nonplussed, Loretta decided that she wasn't the only one who had been dreaming.

"Come on, Loretta, you ain't tryin' by half. Say my name." A determined glint crept into Amy's eyes. "Say something — or I'll get Ma's hatpin and give you a poke."

A tense silence followed. Then, in a hoarse, terrified whisper, Amy cried, "Jumpin' Jehoshaphat, there's Injuns in the yard!"

Loretta catapulted upward and landed on all fours in the middle of the bed. Peeking out over the windowsill, she looked at the yard and saw — just that: the yard. Not an Indian in sight. Amy reared back, her eyes the size of cow pies. Loretta skewered her with a murderous glare.

"Well, it might've worked."

Relief made Loretta giddy. She flopped down on the mattress and hugged her pillow. Her heart felt as though it might pound its way up her throat. *Hunter.* When Amy had said Indians were outside, Loretta had pictured him as he had looked yesterday, high atop his horse with a hundred warriors behind him, his broad chest and corded arms rippling in the sunlight. She had never seen such fierce, burning eyes.

"I — Loretta, I'm sorry. I didn't mean to give you that bad a turn, honest. I was just funnin' you."

Loretta clenched her teeth and burrowed her face deeper into the pillow. She wanted to throttle Amy for her foolishness.

"Loretta, please, don't be mad. I never thought you'd believe me. Where's your sense of humor? You don't really think that ol' Injun will come back? What would an Injun want with a skinny runt like you? They like fat, brown girls who smear bear grease all over themselves. You're probably downright ugly to his way of thinkin', the drabbest-lookin' female he ever saw. No gee-gaws. Stinky, too, with that lavender smell on you. And no creepy-crawlies in your hair."

Loretta kept her face buried, determined not to laugh.

"And sayin' he liked you? There ain't no such thing as a polite Comanche. He wouldn't *buy* you! He'd just steal you. He

65

came to look at you, that's all. Maybe he thought he had a hankerin' for ya and decided different once he got here."

Turning her head, Loretta cracked an eye, smothering a grin.

"Come to think of it, you do look sort of pitiful," Amy teased. "That's probably why he rode off. He took one look and got such a fright, he still ain't stopped runnin'."

Springing to her knees, Loretta grabbed her pillow and whacked Amy over the head. Amy, well aware that Henry would tan both their fannies if they woke him, smothered a shrill giggle, dove for her own pillow, and came up fighting. For several minutes they pummeled one another. Then exhaustion took its toll, and they collapsed upon the bed in a heap, their gowns damp with perspiration, their cheeks rosy from suppressing laughter.

When she caught her breath, Amy whispered, "I guess maybe I dreamed you was talkin'. You reckon?"

Nuzzling her cheek against the quilt, Loretta smiled and nodded. With the golden streaks of dawn behind her, Amy looked like an angel, her hair a molten halo about her heart-shaped face, her eyes big and guileless. What an illusion.

Amy fiddled with the corner of her pillow, her small, freckled nose wrinkling in a frown. "You ever heard tell of blessed release?" she asked softly.

It was Loretta's turn to frown. Talk about out of the blue. Who had told Amy about such a thing?

"Last week after we run into them Injuns by the river, Ma was talkin' to old lady Bartlett, and they was sayin' a decent woman was better off seekin' blessed release than bein' took by Comanches. What's that mean? It's somethin' bad, ain't it?"

For an instant Loretta considered lying. Then she forced herself to nod. This was hard, cruel country, and young or not, Amy should know certain things.

"If them Comanches come back and steal you, is that what you'll do, seek blessed release?" Fear chilled the blue depths of Amy's eyes. "It's killin' yourself, ain't it?"

Loretta's neck felt brittle when she nodded this time.

For once, Loretta was glad she couldn't talk. Amy would demand answers if she could, and Loretta wasn't sure there were words to describe the horrors she had seen.

"I know they did bad things to your ma. My ma wouldn't never tell what, but she looked funny when I asked her about it. You saw, didn't you." It was more statement than question. "That's what you have nightmares about. Not about your ma dyin', but about what they did to her." Amy seemed to ponder that a moment. "I wonder why they do such mean things? How would they like it if we did the same back?"

Loretta closed her eyes, appalled by the thought. White men would *never* retaliate in kind against the Indians. And therein lay the difference between human beings and animals. A picture of Hunter's dark visage flashed in her mind, his blue eyes glittering. For a moment such an overwhelming fear swamped her that she couldn't breathe. Oh, God, what did he want with her?

The sun was setting that same evening when Henry stomped in from the fields and announced that Loretta could take care of the horse and mules for him that night. Loretta clanked the lid back on the pot of beans and whirled from the hearth. She wasn't afraid of work, but it was liable to get dark if she started the chores so late. This morning she had written a message on Amy's slate about Hunter's nocturnal visit. Had Henry forgotten?

"You can't send her out alone," Rachel cried. "Those Indians might be nearby."

Loretta made fists in the gathers of her skirt and pulled the material taut against the backs of her legs.

"If there was Injuns out there," Henry hissed, "they'd have showed themselves by now. Tom's got you girls all upset over nothin'. Loretta had a nightmare last night, that's all. I checked the yard below her window for hoof marks, and there ain't a sign of nothin' out there. I'm flat tuckered. You got no idea what it's like workin' them dadburned fields in this heat."

Rachel glanced out the window uneasily. "Couldn't we leave the animals in the pasture for tonight?"

"And have 'em git stole?" Henry snorted with disgust. "That'd be dandy, right when Ida's finally gonna foal. And what would I do without them mules? You think I'm gonna pull that plow by myself? It ain't gonna hurt that girl to pack a little water and pitch some straw. That mare could drop anytime, and I want her in a clean stall when it happens."

"I'll go along and help." Amy, who was laboring over her nightly spelling lesson, glanced up from her slate with an eager smile. "I'm almost as good as Loretta with the pitchfork. And if we see anything, I can holler and she can't."

"Some help hollering would be," Rachel said. "Those Indians'd be after you girls like bears after honey."

"I just said there ain't no Injuns out there," Henry growled. "Don't you listen, woman? Lord A'mighty, I been out there all day! If there had been a Comanche within a mile, I'd be a dead man. I got Loretta's welfare at heart, too, you know. I wouldn't send her if I thought she'd come to ill."

Not wanting to be the cause of a fuss, Loretta headed for the door. Her aunt Rachel would get the worst of it if tempers flared. There was nothing to be scared of. The barn wasn't *that* far from the house. Besides, if Hunter wanted to kill her, he had already had opportunity last night while she lay sleeping. No, he had other plans for her. Probably something far worse than dying, but she wouldn't think about that right now.

"Loretta, you wait," Rachel called. "I'll get the rifle and come along."

"Oh, tarnation!" Henry exclaimed. "Damned fool woman, you'll work me into my grave yet." Reaching to the door peg for his hat, he dusted it on his trouser leg and clamped it on his head, falling in behind Loretta as she stepped over the threshold. "I'd like to have my dinner sometime before midnight, if it's all the same to you. I'll go with her. At least it won't take so long with her helping."

"Oh, thank you, Henry."

Henry grunted and turned to shut the door. "You jist be sure my dinner's ready when I git back. If it ain't, there'll be hell to pay."

Aware of how fast the sun was disappearing, Loretta crossed the porch and descended the steps. As she walked across the yard, she searched the dust for the hoofprints the Indians had left yesterday. Nothing. The wind had obliterated them. Which explained why Henry had found no evidence of Hunter's visit last night. Her uncle was many things, but smart wasn't one of them. *Nightmare, my foot.* Since when had she been one to raise an alarm over nothing? It infuriated her that Henry thought she was such a dimwit.

Since they had only two buckets in which to haul water, Henry's offer to accompany her was suspicious. He was the most economical man she knew when it came to work and too big a coward to come along as protection. She sneaked a glance at him. He looked harmless, but Henry was at his most dangerous when he was acting nice. She went out behind the chicken shed to fetch the pails and then returned to fill them with water from the well.

To her surprise, Henry offered to carry one. His loose-hipped gait caused water to slosh over the bucket's rim as he walked beside her in the wagon ruts that led out behind the barn. Loretta kept her head down and darted glances at him as he opened the gate to the barnyard. Ida, the barrel-bellied mare, whinnied and pushed her nose through the fence rails. Since Henry had been giving her grain each evening, she was far more anxious than usual to be let in from the pasture. The mules, Bessy and Frank, didn't appear to share in her enthusiasm and continued grazing.

After they had emptied the pails into the trough, Henry said, "I'll pack the second round of water by myself. You stay here and start tossin' the straw."

Loretta relinquished her hold on the bucket and gazed after him as he strode out the gate and around the corner of the building. It seemed she had misjudged him. She shivered and rubbed her arms.

One of the mules snorted, and the sound gave Loretta such a start that she jumped. Bessy had both ears thrown forward and was staring at a thicket along the left perimeter of the fence. Loretta made a dive for the pitch-fork where it leaned against the hay wagon. She studied the riverbank. To avoid having to haul water out into the fields to the livestock, Henry had fenced the acreage at an angle, the back closer to the river than the front, the grazing pastures bordering the stream. That put the barn less than a stone's throw from the thick line of trees. In this poor light, she wouldn't notice someone coming until he was on top of her. With the aid of the pitchfork, she vaulted into the wagon to see better.

There was nothing out of the ordinary lurking in the shadows. With a sigh, she forked some straw and threw it in a wide arc over her shoulder, long practice taking it to her mark inside the lean-to stall. The mules relaxed and lowered their heads to eat again. A moment later Ida ambled over to join them. The sound of their grinding jaws was soothing, but even so the hair on the back of

Loretta's neck tingled. She paused in her work to check the trees again. She felt as if someone were watching her. Detecting no sign of movement, she forced herself to stop dawdling and get back to work.

Henry took so long getting the second load of water that Loretta was nearly finished pitching straw when he returned. He emptied the buckets into the trough, set both on the ground, then stepped into the wagon and smiled at her. Taking off his hat, he dropped it on the tailgate and asked, "Need a hand?"

Uneasiness washed over Loretta. As he stepped toward her, his teeth flashed in another broad grin. She angled a puzzled glance at his shadowed face as he took the pitchfork from her. To her surprise, he tossed it over the side of the wagon.

"Sure you need a hand, sweet thing, sure you do."

His tone made a shudder run up her spine. He used that same syrupy-sweet voice trying to catch a chicken for supper. Loretta had watched him do it a hundred times, tiptoeing around in the pen and wriggling his fingers as if he were dropping seed. When an unsuspecting chicken ran up to peck the ground at his feet, he grabbed it by the head and wrung its poor fool neck. Loretta shrank back. Whatever it was he had in mind, it was sure as rain going to be ornery.

His gaze swept slowly down her body, then

returned to her face. "You're ripe for pickin', and that's a fact," he said in that same chicken-killing voice. "Have been for a good long spell. Yesterday when those Injuns came, all's I could think about was that I should've had you whilst I could. Tom callin' you his promised last night cinched it. I'll be damned. I didn't bust my ass raisin' you so somebody else could reap the crop. The only reason I let him come around was so you'd see how good you got it here."

Even in the dusky light, Loretta could see the wicked gleam in his eye. She threw a frantic glance in the direction of the house. The barn loomed in the way. Even if Aunt Rachel looked out a window, she couldn't see them. Henry took advantage of her distraction to snake out an arm and catch her around the waist.

Jerking her full length against him, he crooned, "Ain't no call to worry. I told Rachel we found a section of fence down and that we'd be an hour or so fixin' it."

Loretta felt as though someone had shoved a pillow down her windpipe. He laughed hoarsely and clamped his free hand on her rib cage right below her breast, his palm and fingers inching upward for softer purchase.

"I'm right glad that you can't talk, you know it? You won't start squallin' and bring Rachel runnin' to see what's wrong. Gives me time to enjoy you like you ought to be

74

enjoyed. Oh, yeah, Loretta, anytime I want you, for as long as I want you."

Laughing again, he pressed his hips forward, grinding a strange hardness against her. Images flashed in her mind of the Indian men who had violated her mother, and she knew exactly what that hardness was.

CHAPTER 4

Loretta threw back her head. For a moment she felt as if she might be able to scream. Then Henry's mouth clamped down on hers, and what sound she might have made was smothered by his grasping lips. Nausea clutched her stomach, and she wrenched herself from his embrace only to lose her footing. As she sprawled backward, he grabbed her wrists and followed her down, his thighs clamped around her hips. She overshot the straw and landed on her back on the wagon floor with him astraddle her.

He chuckled, inching forward. Then, with an ease that horrified her, he pinned her arms to the floor with his legs. Pain shot to her shoulders as the sharp ridges of his shins dug into her wristbones. Jackknifing her legs, she kneed his back, but he made a game of the blows, rocking to and fro, landing on her stomach so hard that her spine nearly snapped. Her throat strained, but with all her air gone, she couldn't have screamed if she'd had a voice. He continued to bounce on her even after she ceased struggling. Her tongue swelled, gagging her. Black dots swam before her eyes.

When she lay limp, he sat back on her belly and smiled, reaching for the row of tiny buttons on her bodice. She twisted her face aside and gulped for air, her windpipe whistling.

"I been eyein' these here sweet bosoms for a long spell," he whispered, slowly peeling her dress apart.

She could feel his calloused hands fumbling with the ribbons on her chemise as cool air seeped through the thin fabric. *Oh, God, help me. Somebody — please, help me.*

Suddenly a dark hand appeared and partially obstructed her view of Henry. She studied the hand, wondering where it had come from and to whom it belonged. Not to Henry. It was too square and brown. The hand turned slightly, and she saw a knife held to Henry's chin. Henry threw up his head and sprang to his feet. Scurrying backward, he staggered. A shadow leaped over the wagon board to follow him.

Fighting to breathe, Loretta rolled onto her side and hugged her middle. When at last her head began to clear, she twisted her neck to see Henry slithering backward on the balls of his feet to escape his attacker, his heavy boots plowing a trail through the straw. As he inched toward the end of the wagon, he kept his chin up, his eyes rolling to see the knife that gaffed him.

"Don't kill me," he mewled. "I know you laid claim to her — and you can have her. Take her — go on — just don't kill me, for the love of God, don't kill me."

With her eyes on her rescuer, Loretta pushed to a sitting position. Hunter? She had prayed for help, and God had sent her the Indian?

Henry clasped the Indian's broad wrist. "Please — I got a wife and child." Glancing downward, he cried, "Do somethin', you damned fool girl! He's gonna kill me, sure. Do somethin'. The pitchfork — git the pitch-fork!"

Loretta rocked dizzily to her knees and glanced around her. The pitchfork? Oh, God, where was it? Henry, still retreating, took one too many steps, ran out of wagon floor, and hit air. Windmilling his arms, he gave a cry and toppled. Hunter tipped his knife so the blade rode the curve of Henry's chin as he fell and sliced him to the cleft. Henry hit the dirt, then scrambled to his feet. Clutching his bleeding chin and squealing like a stuck piglet, he ran for the house, never once look-ing back.

Loretta knelt there and hugged her stom-ach, her mouth agape. Hunter turned slowly. He wore only a breechcloth, knee-high moc-casins, and the blue wool belt, so she had an expansive view of thigh and hip before he faced her. She had never seen a naked man before — and this one was as near naked as he could get. In all the places she and Aunt Rachel were round and soft, he was flat and hard, and where they were slim, he bulged with muscle. His legs were as sturdy and brown as tree trunks, his thighs roped with thick sinew.

His eyes glittered as dark as polished obsidian, routing through the twilight to find her. The touch of his gaze sent a shock coursing through her. Never had she seen such smoldering anger. As he stepped toward her she shrank back, her attention falling to the bloodstained knife he held in his hand.

Throwing out an arm behind her, she groped for the wagon board. If she could vault over it and run, she might have a chance. Her hand met air. She stared at the knife and imagined how it would feel plunging into her body. The Comanche glanced down. When he saw what she was looking at, he sheathed the weapon and held his empty hands out to his sides. There was no mistaking the gesture, but she wasn't reassured.

He advanced another step, and she slithered in retreat, slamming her back against the wagon board. He was too close for her to get away now, and he kept coming, his moccasins touching soundlessly on the floor. When he dropped to one knee on the scattered straw in front of her, Loretta flattened herself against the wood behind her. When he reached for her, she wriggled sideways into the corner. She heard a shallow panting sound and realized dimly that it was her own breathing. He slid his hand inside her unbuttoned bodice and pressed his palm against her ribs. The heat of his touch through the thin cloth of her chemise took her breath as effectively as Henry's bouncing had. She jerked away, clamped both arms around herself, and hunched her shoulders. He whispered something — a Comanche word — and locked gazes with her. Poised there as he was, he blocked any route of escape. Loretta began to tremble.

"Toquet," he whispered again.

She had no inkling of what the word meant, only that the sound of it was inexplicably soft, completely at odds with the harshness of his expression. His dark hair hung loose, wisping like a curtain around his powerfully muscled shoulders, its only decoration a long, thin braid on the left side of his head. The long hair alone made him seem frightening and foreign. The scar that slashed his cheek, unquestionably inflicted by a knife, emphasized his savagery even more.

He seized her wrists and pried her arms from her belly, forcing them to her sides before he released her. Then, so quickly she couldn't react, he clamped one large hand on her shoulder, anchoring her so she couldn't move, and slid his other back inside her bodice. When she started to struggle, he snarled something in Comanche that left her in no doubt he wanted her to be still. Terror proved a powerful persuader. She tried not to recoil as his fingers traced each of her ribs, pressing and probing, from the center of her chest around to her spine. By the time she realized he only wanted to check her for injuries, he had already finished and let go of her.

He sat back on his heel, arms draped on his bent knee, shoulders forward. As relaxed as he appeared, power emanated from his body, electrifying the air around her like the building intensity of lightning right before a storm. The smell of wood smoke, musk, and leather mingled with the straw and surrounded her.

He was staring at her. . . .

Loretta's mouth went dry as dust, and she did the only thing she knew to do, which was stare back. His eyes rested first on her hair. From the contempt she read in his expression, she got the feeling that he found her as revolting to look at as she did him. Next, he studied her face. Pride lifted her chin a notch. She was no raving beauty, but he was no prize either. She returned his regard, searching his features for flaws. With a shock, she realized she couldn't find any. Minus the scar, his face might even be handsome, if it belonged to a white man.

After what seemed an interminably long while, he unsheathed a small knife that hung from the back of his belt. She forgot all about her pride and shrank from him. He tossed up her skirt and grabbed her right ankle. For a moment she thought he meant to steal her only remaining pair of underwear — this time while she was still wearing them. Instead he slipped the knife inside her boot. Her skin tingled where his fingers had pressed. She stared at the hand-carved hilt of the weapon lying against her white drawers. What in Hades had he put it there for?

He rose in one fluid movement and placed a hand on the sideboard to vault out of the wagon. Turning, he held out his arms to her. Pushing unsteadily to her feet, she stepped back. He glanced over his shoulder toward the house, then looked at her again, clearly growing impatient. Before she could react, he grabbed her by the waist and swung her to the ground, steadying her until she had her balance. He was at least a head taller than Henry, so tall that, standing close, she had to crane her neck to see his face. Their eyes met for a moment. Then, as if he were made of shadows, he sprinted across the barnyard, jumped the fence as if it weren't there, and disappeared into the trees.

Numb with shock, Loretta turned to run.

The moment she moved, she felt the cold metal of his knife pricking her ankle. She lifted her skirt and jerked the disgusting thing from her boot. With a shudder, she tossed it next to the wagon and walked backward for a moment, rubbing her fingers clean on her dress.

"Loretta!"

She turned to see Aunt Rachel running around the corner of the barn, skirts flying, a rifle in one hand. Rachel skidded to a stop next to the wagon and threw the butte of the Sharps carbine to her shoulder, scanning the woods. "H-Henry t-told me. Where the devil are they? Get behind me, Loretta. Hurry."

Loretta hesitated, but only for an instant. As Uncle Henry had said, there was no rhyme or reason to what Indians did. Hunter might let her live one moment, then hack her to death the next. She got behind her aunt, and the two of them backed through the gate and followed the wagon ruts to the house.

When they got inside, they found Henry lying on the bed moaning. Loretta hung back by the door to button her bodice, her attention riveted to her uncle's bloody shirt. Surely his chin hadn't bled that much. The way he was carrying on, a body would have thought — Loretta stepped closer, staring in puzzlement. The left side of his shirt was hanging off him in shreds. Through the slitted cloth, she could see shallow cuts in the flesh over his ribs. Amy was at the stove, moistening a rag with water from the kettle. Her small face was pinched and pale when she looked at Loretta.

"You okay? They didn't —" Amy's gaze dropped to Loretta's half-buttoned dress. "Wh-what did they do to you?"

"Hush, Amy, and get me that rag over here." Rachel leaned the Sharps against the wall next to the bed and dropped to her knees beside her husband. With trembling hands, she grabbed the front of his shirt and ripped it open, gasping when she got a good look at his cuts. "Oh, Henry, you could've been killed."

Henry ran his hand over her tousled hair. "Now, now, I'm fine, and Loretta's fine. That's what counts."

"Only because you —" Rachel's voice caught. "Oh, Henry, can you ever forgive me for how I acted yesterday? Only a brave man would have stood alone against that many Comanches."

"I done no more than any man would've done." Henry's blue gaze lifted to Loretta's, and he smiled. Coldness washed over her. "I wasn't really brave. When them Injuns jumped out, I stood my ground because there weren't no choice. The first chance I got, I ran like hell. We didn't stand a prayer without a gun. To save Loretta I had to get up here to the house. Wasn't till I was halfway here that

84

I even realized they'd cut me. It was plumb scary, I'll tell ya, three of 'em comin' at me, and me with nothin' but my skinnin' knife to fight 'em off."

"Well, thank God you aren't cut deep. It's nothing short of a miracle."

It was more like a fantasy, but Loretta couldn't say so.

Henry glanced down at his lacerated ribs. "From the blood, I thought it was worse." His gaze lifted. "You okay, girl? Did your aunt Rachel git there in time to stop —" He glanced at her bodice. "They didn't — violate you, did they?"

Loretta shook her head and averted her face. Henry had slashed his ribs with his own knife? Knowing Henry, the cuts were superficial, but it was still an act born of desperation. If it hadn't been so horrible, it would have been funny.

Amy came up to Loretta and hugged her waist. Loretta tried to return the hug, but after what Henry had just done, being touched, even by Amy, made her skin crawl. Pulling away, she scurried up the loft ladder and threw herself on the bunk. Burying her face in the pillow, she pounded the ticking with her fists. She hated Henry Masters — hated him — hated him. Life out here on this godforsaken farm was bitter enough without having to watch her back every second. Now she wouldn't dare even take a walk by herself for fear he might follow her.

Her anger spent, she rolled onto her side to stare out the window. Minutes passed before she noticed something lying on the sill. She sat up to see what it was. Disbelief swept through her. *The Comanche's knife.* She curled her fingers around the hilt. The carved wood felt warm against her palm as if the heat of his hand still lingered upon it. Remembering the mocking gleam she had seen in Henry's eye, Loretta clutched the knife to her bosom. She wouldn't throw the weapon away again. She didn't dare.

The following morning, dawn was heralded by approaching riders, and every member of the Masters household hit the floor in a mad dash. There was no time to dress before a deep voice resounded from outside. "White-Eyes, we come as friends." The words froze Loretta midstride, her pulse thundering in her temples. Tom hadn't made it in time.

"Oh, my God," Henry croaked. "Rachel, can you see my boots? Dammit, load the rifles."

Loretta scrambled down the loft ladder, so scared she didn't even think about Uncle Henry seeing her in the skimpy summer nightgown. She lunged for the rumpled bed so she could hide Amy. Even as she did, she knew it was useless. There wasn't time.

Henry swore when he saw her wrestling

with the bedstead. "Forgit that. Git to the other window, girl. Rachel! You're in charge of loading."

"Come out, White-Eyes," the voice called. "I bring gifts, not bloodshed."

Henry, wearing nothing but his pants and the bandages Aunt Rachel had wrapped around his chest the night before, hopped on one foot as he dragged on a boot. By the time he reached the window, he had both boots on, laces flapping. Rachel gave him a rifle. He threw open the shutter and jerked down the skin, shoving the barrel out the opening. "What brings you here?"

"The woman. I bring many horses in trade."

Loretta ran to the left window, throwing back the shutters and unfastening the membrane to peek out. The Comanche turned to meet her gaze, his dark eyes expressionless, penetrating, all the more luminous from the black graphite that outlined them. Her hands tightened on the rough sill, nails digging the wood.

He looked magnificent. Even she had to admit that. Savage, frightening . . . but strangely beautiful. Eagle feathers waved from the crown of his head, the painted tips pointed downward, the quills fastened in the slender braid that hung in front of his left ear. His cream-colored hunting shirt enhanced the breadth of his shoulders, the chest decorated with intricate beadwork, painted

87

animal claws, and white strips of fur. He wore two necklaces, one of bear claws, the other a flat stone medallion, both strung on strips of rawhide. His buckskin breeches were tucked into knee-high moccasins.

Her gaze shifted to the strings of riderless ponies behind him. She couldn't believe their number. Thirty? Possibly forty? Beyond the animals were at least sixty half-naked warriors on horseback. Loretta wondered why Hunter had come fully clothed in all his finery with wolf rings painted around his eyes. The others wore no shirts or feathers, and their faces were bare.

"I come for the woman," the Comanche repeated, never taking his gaze from her. "And I bring my finest horses to console her father for his loss. Fifty, all trained to ride." His black sidestepped and whinnied. The Indian swayed easily with his mount. "Send me the woman, and have no fear. She will come to no harm walking in my footsteps, for I am strong and swift. She will never feel hunger, for I am a fine hunter. My lodge will shelter her from the winter rain, and my buffalo robes will shield her from the cold. I have spoken it."

Aunt Rachel crossed herself. "Holy Mary, Mother of God, pray —"

"We don't sell our womenfolk," Henry called back.

"You sicken my gut, *tosi tivo*. After you had

88

bedded her, you would have sold her to that dirty old man." With a sneer twisting his lips, he lifted Tom Weaver's wool riding blanket from his horse's withers and tossed it to the dirt. "Better you sell her to me. I am young. I will give her many fine sons. She will not wail over my death for many winters."

"I'd rather shoot her, you murdering bastard," Henry retorted.

"Then do it and make your death song." The Comanche wheeled his horse, riding close to the window where Loretta stood. "Where is the *herbi* with such great courage who came out to face us once before? Does she still sleep? Will you hide behind your wooden walls and let your loved ones die? Come out, Yellow Hair, and meet your destiny."

Sweat trickled down Loretta's spine. Her destiny? Her eyes flew to Tom's blanket. They had slain him. She refastened the doeskin with shaking hands, remembering how gently Tom had hugged her the night he left.

The rifle Aunt Rachel had loaded for her rested against the wall. The temptation to use it was almost overwhelming. With her heart in her throat, Loretta looked at her uncle, knowing before he spoke that he would send her out there.

"They'll kill us," was Henry's response to her pleading expression. "I got to think of my family. You ain't one of us, not really. I have

Rachel and Amy to think of first."

Rachel and Amy? Looking into her uncle's eyes, Loretta read cold, crawling fear, and it wasn't for his womenfolk. It was one thing to sacrifice her life to save the others, but it was another to be sold. Dying was quick, at least. *Many winters.* Dear Lord, belonging to that Comanche would mean a lifetime of slavery, groveling for mercy from an animal who didn't know the meaning of the word.

Loretta shook her head and cast her aunt a beseeching glance. Surely if the Comanche was willing to trade fifty horses for her, he sought a peaceable purchase, not a battle. He would have no guarantee that his arrows wouldn't find her as a target.

Henry leaned his rifle against the wall. "You gotta go. Ain't no choice." He walked toward her. "And don't get it into your head to make a fuss, or I'll backhand you good. Hear?"

"No!" Rachel threw herself at her husband. "Don't you dare send her out there! So help me, I —"

With a sweep of his arm, Henry knocked Rachel aside. She fell backward, hitting the wall with such force that her head cracked against the logs. Loretta retreated, watching her uncle, groping for the table behind her. He planned to toss her on the steps like so much baggage. Panic blocked out any rational thoughts she might have had about the safety of her aunt and cousin. When he lunged, she whirled to run — but his hand snaked out and grasped her arm. The next instant, bright spots flashed before her eyes, and the side of her face exploded with pain. She staggered, dimly aware of Henry's fingers biting into her arm, dragging her. From far away she heard Aunt Rachel scream Amy's name. Then she felt Henry's grip loosen. She stumbled and blinked, trying to clear her vision. When the room came into focus, she froze. The door was wide open.

Amy stood on the porch, Henry's rifle held unsteadily to her small shoulder. "You Injuns get out of here!" she cried. "You can't have Loretta. Go away, or I'll shoot you. I mean it!"

Beyond the child, Loretta could see Hunter. She thought she saw admiration flicker in his eyes, but it disappeared so quickly that she couldn't be sure. He sat his horse loosely, his face an unreadable mask, deathly calm. "I am here," he challenged.

The blast of the gun sent Amy reeling. A spray of dust rose two feet wide of her mark. As she staggered to get her balance, Hunter threw himself forward along his horse's neck, and the stallion lunged up the steps, hooves thundering. The Comanche leaned sideways, curling an arm around Amy as he rode past. She screamed and dropped the gun. The Indian threw her across his thighs and smacked her on the bottom when she kicked.

There was no time to think. Loretta ran for the door, grabbing the gun propped against the wall. Her gown snapped taut around her ankles as she bounded across the porch and down the steps. The Comanche rode in a wide circle around the frightened, riderless horses and tossed Amy into the arms of a fellow Indian who waited in the ranks. The little girl's indignant screeching filled the air. Loretta lifted the Spencer carbine to her shoulder, leveling the sights on the Comanche as he circled back to her. The bells on his moccasins tinkled merrily with each movement of his horse.

"Let me go!" Amy screamed. "You stinkin' savage!"

Loretta glanced toward the child. A young brave struggled to keep Amy atop his pony. He laughed uproariously when she tried to scratch him. The girl caught a handful of his black hair and pulled with all her might.

"Ai-ee!" the boy exclaimed. "She tries to take my scalp."

Whoops of laughter spiraled among the men. Loretta dragged her gaze back to Hunter. He had halted his mount some fifteen feet from her.

"Where will you spend your cartridge?" he asked. "If you love her, shoot her. It is wisdom."

Amy's screaming turned to pitiful sobbing. Loretta's aim wavered, and she glanced toward the other Indians, trying to see her cousin. What was Henry doing? Why didn't he back her up? How long could it take to load a rifle? The miserable coward.

"You have time for one shot," Hunter went on. "If you waste it on me, my friend will take your sister and avenge me. Your father hides behind his wooden walls. You stand alone."

Sweat ran into Loretta's eyes. She turned slightly and leveled the barrel of her gun at Amy. Blinking, she snugged her finger around the trigger. Tears sprang to her eyes as she recalled Amy's queries about blessed release. *It's something bad, isn't it? It's killing yourself, isn't it?* Not always, Loretta thought. Sometimes it was death by a loved one's hand.

"Think long on this, Yellow Hair," Hunter cautioned. "I came in peace to buy a woman, not steal a child. She is too skinny to bring this Comanche pleasure. You are not." He leaned forward, stretching an arm along his horse's neck, his hand open to her. "Come to me, and I will send your sister back to her mother unharmed."

Loretta stared at him. Did he mean it? His eyes pierced hers. The scar on the side of his face flickered as his jaw muscle tightened. If the tales about him were true, he might spare Amy. On the other hand, he might take them both captive if given half a chance. She remembered how gently he had touched her last night, and her confusion mounted.

"Drop the weapon and come," he urged. "It is a fair trade, no? She goes free. I have spoken it."

In the background, Loretta heard laughter ringing. Already the braves made sport of Amy. The child screeched again.

"You will do this, no? You have courage. It shines in your eyes. If you fight the big fight, you cannot win. It is best to hold the head high and surrender with dignity. Put down the gun."

CHAPTER 5

Loretta's shoulders slumped in defeat. With numb hands she lowered the rifle to the dirt.

A nasty grin twisted Hunter's mouth. "So it is a trade? You are my woman?"

For once, she was glad she couldn't talk.

"You can make sign language, herbi." His eyes locked with hers, glinting, watchful.

Amy cried, "No, Loretta, no, don't do it!"

Lifting an eyebrow, the Comanche waited. The tension mounted, reminding Loretta of the lull right before a storm, thick, heavy, unnaturally quiet. She caught the inside of her cheek between her teeth and forced herself to nod. His eyes flickered with satisfaction.

Nudging his mount forward, he closed the distance between them and leaned down to encircle her waist with a steely arm. With little effort he lifted her onto his horse, positioning her sideways in front of him so her shoulder pressed against his chest, her bottom wedged between him and the ridge of his stallion's neck. Never had she felt such quivering, helpless fear. He was going to take her. The reality of it sank home now that he had her on his horse.

"Tani-har-ro," he said softly.

She turned her head to find that he was sniffing her hair, his expression quizzical. The moment their eyes met, her insides tightened. Up close, his face seemed even harsher than it had the night before, features chiseled, lips narrowed to an uncompromising line, his skin baked brown by the sun. She could see in minute detail the tiny cracks in his grease paint, the thick sweep of his lashes, the knife scar that slashed his cheek. His eyes were without question the darkest blue she had ever seen and seemed to cut right through her. If she had been entertaining the thought of pleading with him, it fled her mind now. She remembered what he had said to her that first day. *Look at me and know the face of your master.* She supposed, by his standards, he had a right to smell her hair since he had paid dearly for every strand.

A flush slid up her neck. In nothing but a nightgown, she would have been embarrassed in front of any man; with Hunter her humiliation was tenfold. He swept his gaze over her with no sign of guilt, no hesitation, his attention lingering on whatever drew his interest. When he traced her collarbone with a fingertip and gave her arm a squeeze, she felt like a head of beef at auction.

"You are too skinny. Your father should feed you more." Catching hold of her chin, he tipped her head back and forced her mouth open to check her teeth. "Hmph-hh," he grunted, returning his arm to her waist. "This Comanche paid too many horses. Without your *pitsikwina* to cover you, you are all bones."

She flashed him a glare, only to discover that his eyes were filled with laughter. He slid a hand up her side, his fingers firm and warm where they hugged the curve of her ribs. She stiffened when he cupped the underside of her breast, but she didn't resist his touch. "Maybe not all bones. What do you have there, *herbi?* Do you try to hide the sweet places your mother promised me?" He watched her for a moment, as if trying to predict what her reaction might be to such outrageous familiarity. Then his mouth twisted in a mocking smile. "You do not spit when your sister may suffer my wrath. I should keep her, I think. She is a brave warrior, no?"

Loretta's heart caught. *Fool!* Her eyes flew to Amy. She should have shot the child while she had the chance.

"Ah, but I have said she will go back to her mother, no? And you have said you are my woman." Tightening his grip on her breast, he leaned forward and brought his mouth so close to her ear that shivers raced down her spine. "Your heart pounds, woman. It is a lie you speak? You will fight this Comanche when your sister is out of danger?"

She knew he was testing her, daring her to resist him, glorying in the power he wielded. Knowing that gave her the strength to be still. She shook her head in reply, praying Comanches used the same gesture to say no.

"It is a promise you make?"

He rasped his thumb across her gown, teasing her nipple. The shock of feeling that spiraled from her breast to the hollow of her belly nearly took her breath. Keeping her face carefully blank, she nodded.

"This Comanche thinks you lie."

With a shake of her head, Loretta lifted pleading eyes to his. Endless seconds passed as his fingertips followed the path of his thumb, each feather-light caress more shattering to her pride than the last. She clenched her teeth. His features blurred, and she realized she was looking at him through tears.

Suddenly he began to laugh and dropped his hand to her ribs. "You do not lie so good, Yellow Hair. Your eyes make big talk against you. But that is okay. We have had this one moment together, no? And you did not spit."

Chuckling, he ducked his head and tightened his arm around her with such crushing strength that she couldn't breathe, let alone fight. Then he wheeled his horse, yelling gibberish. The young man who held Amy nudged his pony out of the ranks and galloped it toward the house. In a skid of hooves and flying dust, he dumped her none too gently onto the dirt and rode off. Amy scrambled to her feet, holding out her arms.

"Loretta, no . . . Loretta, please . . ."

To Loretta's relief, Rachel burst out of the cabin, grabbed Amy, and dragged her up the steps. After shoving the child through the door, she reappeared with a rifle in her hands. Lifting the stock to her shoulder, she took careful aim. At Loretta . . .

It happened so fast that even the Comanche was taken by surprise. His body snapped taut. For the space of a heartbeat, Loretta felt a shattering sense of betrayal, of fear. Then she understood. Aunt Rachel was going to kill her rather than see her taken by Comanches.

The blast of the gun and a roar from the Comanche came almost simultaneously. He threw his body forward, slamming Loretta against the stallion's neck. Pain exploded in her chest, a flattening, mind-searing pain. Insane as it was, the thought crossed her mind that the Comanche hadn't won after all.

The stallion reared, striking the air, then leaped forward, nearly tossing both his riders. Loretta was squashed between the long ridge of the animal's neck and the Comanche's chest. Sitting sideways as she was, her body was twisted at an impossible angle.

Instinctively she clutched the horse's mane to hold her seat. She was going to fall. The hooves of the other horses thundered all around her. If she lost her grip, the other riders would surely trample her.

Desperation filled her. She was slipping. At the last moment, when her fingers lost their hold and she felt herself falling, her captor's arm clamped around her ribs, pulling her back onto the horse. Then the weight of his chest anchored her, so heavy she couldn't breathe. Wind blew against her face. Slack-jawed, she labored for air, pressure building to a pulsating intensity in her temples.

The Indians rode a safe distance from the house before stopping. When Hunter finally drew rein and leaped off the horse, Loretta fell with him and landed in a heap at his feet. Dust plumed around her. Men dismounted, yelling, running in her direction. For a moment she thought they were going to swoop down on her, but they circled her captor instead, jabbering and touching his shoulder. There were so many legs, some naked. Brown buttocks flashed everywhere she looked. Hunter snarled something and peeled off his shirt. A furrowed flesh wound angled across his right shoulder.

Pressing a hand to her chest, Loretta glanced down in bewilderment. She had been so sure. . . . Laughter bubbled up her throat. Aunt Rachel had missed? She never missed when she could draw a steady bead on a still target. Loretta's throat tightened. *The Comanche.* She looked up, confusion clouding her blue eyes. He had shielded her with his own body?

Waving his friends away, Hunter hunkered down and scooped a handful of dirt, pressing it to the shallow cut on his shoulder. Loretta stared at the blood trailing down his arm. If not for his quick thinking, it could have been her own. Survival instinct and common sense warred within her. She knew death might be preferable to what was in store for her, but she couldn't help being glad she was alive.

As if he felt her staring at him, the Comanche lifted his head. When his eyes met hers, the fury and loathing in them chilled her. He stood and jerked the feathers from his braid, wrapping them in his shirt. Never taking his gaze off her, he stuffed the bundle into a parfleche hanging from his surcingle.

"Keemah," he growled.

Uncertain what he wanted and afraid of doing the wrong thing, Loretta stayed where she was. He caught her by the arm and hauled her to her feet.

"Keemah, come!" He gave her a shake for emphasis, his eyes glittering. "Listen good, and learn quick. I have little patience with stupid women."

Grasping her waist, he tossed her on the horse and scooted her to the back of the

101

blanket saddle. The hem of her nightgown rode high. She could feel all the men staring at her. Had he no decency? With trembling hands, she tugged at the gown and tried to cover her thighs. There wasn't enough material to stretch. And it was so thin from years of wear, it was nearly transparent. The morning breeze raised gooseflesh on her naked arms and back.

With a grim set to his mouth, her captor opened a second parfleche, withdrawing a length of braided wool and a leather thong. Before she realized what he was about to do, he knotted the wool around one of her ankles, looped it under his horse's belly, and swiftly bound her other foot.

"We must ride like the wind!" he yelled to the others. "*Meadro!* Let's go!"

The other men ran for their horses. Grasping the stallion's mane, Hunter vaulted to its back and settled himself in front of her. When he reached for her arms and pulled them around him, she couldn't stifle a gasp. Her breasts were flattened against his back.

"Your woman does not like you, cousin," someone called in English. Loretta turned to see who spoke and immediately recognized the brave who had encouraged Hunter to kill her that first day. His scarred face was unforgettable. He flashed her a twisted smile that seemed more a leer, his black eyes sliding insolently down her body to rest on her naked thighs. Then he laughed and wheeled his chestnut horse. "She won't be worth the trouble she will make for you."

Hunter glanced over his shoulder at her. The fiery heat of his anger glowed like banked embers in his eyes. "She will learn." With an expertise born of long practice, he lashed her wrists together with the leather. "She will learn quick."

Behind the large group of warriors stretched an endless carpet of green grass dotted with blue petals. Ahead lay a dense grove of pecan and willow trees. The men had been riding nonstop fourteen hours, making a great circle back to the Brazos near Loretta's home, an evasion tactic in case the *tosi tivo* tried to follow them. Come morning, if they felt certain they weren't being pursued, they would take a direct route to their village.

To the west, the sinking sun was a red orb, streaking the evening sky with wisps of dark gray and pink. Loretta no longer sat erect on the horse to keep her breasts from touching the Comanche's naked back. She slumped against him, her lolling head pillowed by the muscular cleavage of his spine. Pain shot up her cramped legs from the bonds of coarse wool braid. The rawhide around her wrists had cinched tight, cutting into her skin. Her tongue was a parched lump. One more mile, and she felt sure she would die.

She imagined herself sinking into blackness, escaping. It would be cool and dark in heaven. The water there would flow sparkling and icy. There would be no Comanche with cruel, midnight blue eyes.

Hunter's voice rumbled inside him, vibrating against her cheek. Loretta felt the stallion slowing down. Angry words in a language she couldn't understand ricocheted around her, high, low, growling, shrill. She fluttered her lashes, too miserable to care why the men argued, just thankful for the reprieve. She felt Hunter shift his weight backward, felt his hard hands fumbling with the tight band of leather that bound her wrists. The next second her arms were freed and fell like dead weights to her sides. Hunter's strong back disappeared. She slumped forward on the horse, not caring about anything as long as she could rest.

Something cold touched her left ankle. In some distant part of her mind, she realized that someone was cutting the wool braid that bound her feet. She kept her eyes closed, her cheek pressed against the horse's sweaty neck, her arms hanging. A moment later her right ankle was freed as well.

And then came a new kind of pain. Not fire, but thousands of needles pricking her legs, the agony shooting to her hips. She gasped and bolted upright. When she did, she pitched sideways. The world turned upside down. Arms caught her. The sky spun above her. Someone yelled.

Torture. She was being carried, but the arms that cradled her were made of white-hot fire, singeing her wherever they touched. She didn't think there could be any pain more excruciating. Then cruel hands lowered her to a soft mat of grass, but the blades of the grass turned to sharp spikes, piercing her flesh.

Loretta closed her eyes and gave herself up to the pain. Someone held her and rocked her — someone strong with a deep voice that whispered like silk through her mind. The words were sometimes strange, but the few she understood made the meaning of the others absolutely clear. She was safe where she was, *sure enough safe — forever.*

Ice. Loretta sucked in a whine of air as the shock of water washed over her body.

A warm arm encircled her waist. A large hand clamped over her ribs. She twisted her neck to see, then froze. The Comanche.

Instinctively she thrashed and squirmed in his arms. She tried to throw herself away from him. But it was all to no avail. Hunter held her fast with one arm hooked through her elbows behind her and walked deeper into the water until it hit her chin high. A convulsive shudder ran the length of her. *Cold.* Oh, mercy, it was so horribly cold.

He ran a hand down her belly. The touch was slow, effortless, leaving her in no doubt that he could explore any part of her he chose, at his leisure. "Ah, *mah-tao-yo,* you are so hot. Even where you are not burned. *To-quet,*" he whispered. "You will not fight."

Something about his voice seemed familiar, oddly comforting. Her father, she realized, somehow his voice put her in mind of her father. She fought back tears. Shivers racked her. *So cold.* The freezing ache of it blocked out everything else. Her teeth began chattering nonstop. When she could bear it no longer, she made one last attempt to get free.

"It will pass," he promised. "You will be still. It is a burn, no? From the sun. You have fire inside you. The cold will chase it away. You understand?"

She tried to nod. When she did, she took a mouthful of water and choked. He exclaimed under his breath and turned her so her chin rested on his shoulder. The shock of his body heat against her breasts and belly made her gasp. In the moonlight, the cut in his flesh from Rachel's bullet was a black line.

"Toquet, mah-tao-yo, toquet." His arms tightened around her, hard, powerful, yet strangely gentle. "Close your eyes, eh? Trust this Comanche. We will make war tomorrow."

Time ceased to exist. There was nothing but the night, the water, and the Indian. Loretta floated into a dream world. She was sick, so awfully sick. Too sick to care what happened. Too sick to fight it.

CHAPTER 6

Hunter spread his hand under the cloth of the woman's gown and stared at the clear outline of his fingers. As incredible as it seemed, the sun had gone right through the thin material and cooked her fair skin. Comanches sometimes got sunburned, but never like this. With a snort of disgust, he wadded the gown into a ball and tossed the useless thing on the fire. From now on he would dress the girl in leathers.

The material ignited explosively, and the light from the heightened flames played upon her body, flickering on her small breasts, shadowing her curves. He stared down at her, more angry than he had ever been, with himself. No matter how he tried not to think of it, his mind circled back to his behavior tonight, immediately after stopping to make camp, then later down at the river. How could he have treated a White-Eyes so kindly?

Rocking her in his arms had been unforgivable enough, but then he had caught himself calling her *mah-tao-yo,* little one, a name he had once used to address his wife, Willow by the Stream. It was the ultimate betrayal, not just of Willow by the Stream, but himself. Try as he might to justify it, there were no excuses.

He couldn't imagine what had come over him. What bothered him most was that it was impossible to forget, even in the dark, that this woman was his enemy. Unlike some of her kind, she didn't bear any resemblance to one of the People. Her hair was honey gold, as blinding as sunshine when the moonlight hit it right, and her skin shone as white as sun-washed silver. Every time he looked upon her, shock coursed through him. The woman of the prophecy? His woman? He yearned for a plump, comfortable female with beautiful brown skin and long curtains of black, shiny hair. Instead he got skin the color of buffalo fat, stretched taut over spindly bones, and hair the same yellow brown as parched grass.

The girl's screams during her delirium had convinced him that she was indeed the woman of the prophecy. Just as the Great Ones had foretold, her voice wasn't gone, only silenced by great sadness . . . the massacre of her parents. Long ago, Hunter had known another girl whose voice had been stolen from her in such a way. After examining that girl at length, the *puhakut* in the village had claimed that her heart had been laid upon the ground by seeing her family killed and that one day, when joy returned to her, she would speak again. Many winters later the mute girl had married a kindly man, and after the birth of her first child, which brought her great gladness, she regained her voice, just as the *puhakut* had predicted. This white girl would as well. How or when, Hunter couldn't begin to imagine, but he knew it would come to pass. Beyond that, he refused to think. According to the song of the Great Ones, he was to be instrumental in her recovery.

With a shaky sigh, he reached for the grease pouch and loosened its drawstring. Like it or not, he had to take care of her. If she died, the Great Ones would be displeased. If he had had only himself to worry about, he might have walked off and left her. After all, what could the Great Ones do to him that would be worse than this? But he must think of his people, of how his actions might affect them.

The hot flare of anger within him condensed into a hard little knot in the pit of his stomach. He dipped his hand into the grease and leaned forward to smear it on the woman's tortured skin. His hand hovered above her leg. He couldn't help but remember how jealously she had guarded her ruffled breeches that first day or how painfully ashamed she had been this morning when

110

the hem of her *pitsikwina* had ridden up on her thighs. If she had any idea that she was lying here naked, he felt sure her face would turn redder than the sunburn had already made it. And if she knew he was about to run his hands over her? He could only guess what her reaction might be. Terror, probably. Accompanied by a good deal of spitting if her past transgressions were an indication. Stupid girl. Grown men had dared less and died for their trouble. Perhaps his brother was right, and she didn't know who he was. Hunter was well aware of the fear he inspired in the *tosi tivo.* Most whites recognized him the moment they saw the scar on his cheek and looked into his indigo eyes.

A suppressed smile made the corners of his mouth twitch. Perhaps he would be wise not to tell her who he was. As much as he disliked her spitting, the thought of her being obedient and too easily cowed appealed even less. Something about her — he had no idea what — evoked confusing emotions within him. Anger blanketed those emotions, prevented him from having to deal with them. Ah, yes, he liked her much better when she was spitting. Much better. Sick and helpless as she was now, he found himself feeling sorry for her.

He glided his greased hand up her thigh to her hip, acutely aware of how hot her skin was and how fragile her jutting hipbone felt against the leathery surface of his palm. She tossed her head and moaned, her sooty lashes fluttering on her flushed cheeks. He studied her face for a moment, then lowered his gaze to her breasts. The tips were the delicate pink of cacti blossoms. In all his life, he had never seen such nipples. The anger in his gut tightened into a knot, fiery and churning. Skidding his hand along the ladder of her ribs, he cupped the underside of her breast, then feathered his fingertips over its crest and watched the pebbled surface go taut and eager, thrusting upward for more. She moaned again and tossed her head, her forehead wrinkling in a bewildered frown. Clearly he was the first ever to touch her there. His smile, no longer suppressed, lifted one side of his mouth into a mocking grin. She was not so haughty when asleep, he thought. Her body, the body he had paid so many horses for, betrayed her and responded to him. It gave him a perverse satisfaction.

His smile quickly disappeared when he realized with something of a shock that hers was not the only traitorous body.

Dawn came in wisps of pink against a blue-gray sky. Through the trees, shafts of misty sunlight formed luminous motes of warmth along the river. Birds sang. Squirrels chattered. The low rush of the water was ceaseless. Loretta woke slowly, aware before she

112

opened her eyes that something was horribly wrong. Amy wasn't this big. The arm around her was hard and heavy, the warm hand that cupped her breast distinctly masculine. She frowned and wondered where the hairy blanket touching her cheek had come from. Where was the gray down quilt? Why did she hurt everywhere? Through the spikes of her eyelashes, she stared at a gnarled tree root. A breeze stirred the leaves overhead. The moldy floor of the forest blended its musty smell with the rich, tantalizing aroma of coffee. Then the sound of men's voices drifted to her, the tones conversational, interspersed with an occasional chuckle. Friendly voices. Normal-sounding voices — except for one thing. She couldn't understand the language.

With a start, she remembered. Her sudden gasp of alarm woke the Comanche who held her in his arms. She knew without looking that it was Hunter, the most horrible. His hand tightened reflexively on her naked breast, and his arm hardened to steel around her. He grunted something and nuzzled her neck.

Loretta's first instinct was to grab his hand, but she no sooner tried than she realized that her own were bound behind her. He pressed his face against her hair and took a deep breath. She could tell he was only half-awake by the slow, lazy way he moved. His thumb grazed her nipple, teasing the sensitive tip

113

into an unwilling response. Her body sprang taut as well, jerking with every flick of his fingers. He yawned and pressed closer.

Oh, God, help me.

Lowering his hand to her belly, he pressed his palm against her spasm-stricken muscles and kneaded away the tightness. She felt like a sensitive harp string, thrummed by expert fingers. Horrified by her body's reaction, she tried to twist free, but he threw a damp, buckskin-clad leg over both of hers and pinned her to the fur. Her back stung each time she moved, the pain so sharp it made beads of sweat pop out on her brow. Her thighs felt as if they were on fire.

"M-mm-m, you are still hot," he mumbled. His hand lingered on her belly. "Not too bad where the sun did not touch, though. The fever is better."

No man had ever dared touch her like this. She tossed her head from side to side, strained to get her arms and legs free, then shuddered in defeat.

"Do not fight." His voice was so close, it seemed to come from within her own mind. "You cannot win, eh? Rest." His sleepy whispers invaded her whole being, slow, hypnotic, persuasive. He rubbed her in a circular motion, pausing in sleep, then coming awake to rub some more. "Lie still. Trust this Comanche. It is for the burn, no? To heal your skin."

As he slid his palm slowly downward, she realized she was slick with some kind of oil. Her heart drummed a sensual alto, off-key to the soprano shrills of fear emitted by her nerve endings. *No, please, no.*

He molded his hand to the slight mound between her thighs, searching out its external softness, his fingertips undulating in a subtle manipulation that shot bolts of sensation to the core of her. Nuzzling her hair again, he sighed, his warm breath raising goose bumps on her neck.

"Ah, Blue Eyes, your mother did not lie. You are sweet."

He gave the conjuncture of her thighs a farewell caress, then traced the curve of her hip with a hand that skimmed the painfully burned flesh there so lightly that she scarcely felt it. The pressure of his palm increased when it gained purchase on her ribs where the sun had not reached. His hand tightened its grip, squeezed, and released so rhythmically that it seemed to keep time with the strange, blood-pounding beat inside her. It was as if he had begun the rhythm within her, as if he somehow knew the thrusts, the lulls, better than she.

Held captive now by more than bonds and strength of arm, she turned her face to study his, fascinated by the sleepy innocence that clouded his half-closed eyes. The merciless killer was gone, replaced by a drowsy, mischievous boy who stroked her as if she were a newly acquired pet. A slow smile curved his mouth, a dreamy smile that told her he was more asleep than awake. He moved closer to whisper something unintelligible against her cheek. Her lips tingled, then parted. She found herself wondering how it might have felt if he had kissed her, then cringed at the wayward thought. Comanches didn't kiss, they just took. And her time was running out.

With the tip of his tongue, he outlined her ear. *"Topsannah, tani-har-ro."* The words came out so slurred, she doubted he even knew he was saying them. "Prairie flower," he muttered, "in springtime."

He fell silent. His arm around her waist went lifeless and heavy. His breathing changed, becoming measured and deep. The mahogany fringe of his eyelashes rested on his cheeks. Loretta stared, incredulity sweeping over her in waves. He was fast asleep. And she was pinned beneath his arm and leg. She wrinkled her nose. The fur of the buffalo robe tickled, and it smelled sharply of smoke and bear grease. Probably full of lice and fleas, too, she thought with disgust, then promptly began to itch, which was sheer torture because she couldn't scratch.

His hand rested on her ribs like an anchor. Though escape was impossible, bound as she was, being so close to him made her feel claustrophobic. Slowly, ever so slowly, she tried to ease out from under him, only to have him go tense again and pull her back into the crook of his body. "Sleep," he murmured. "We will make war tomorrow, no?"

Loretta strained her neck to see over the fur. Some distance away, the other Indians stood in groups around small fires, some yawning, some wide awake with tin cups in their hands. One man was staring in her direction. She quickly ducked her head under the robe, but not fast enough. Moments later she heard the faint whisper of moccasins approaching. Leather swished. She sensed the presence of someone beside her and slitted her eyelids. Through her lashes, she saw obsidian eyes looking down at her from a dark face framed by blue-black hair. She recognized this Indian. He was the one who had spoken in her behalf that first day, the one who had not wanted her killed. It didn't make her fear him less.

To her horror, the man lifted the edge of the robe to look at her shoulder. Frantic, she jerked at the leather that held her hands behind her. This was her worst nightmare. *Comanches.* Not one, but two. And she couldn't even fight them. If he yanked the robe off her, there would be nothing she could do but lie there in shame.

Hunter stirred and yawned, then rose up on one elbow to bark in Comanche, "What is it, *tah-mah?* Can't you see I'm trying to sleep?"

"I just came to check the woman."

Hunter squinted at the sun and sighed. "So, how does she look?" He sat up and drew the robe farther down her shoulder, taking care not to uncover her breast, laughing softly at the horrified expression on her face. Of all the men, his brother, Warrior, would be least likely to harm her. He was a fierce fighter but otherwise gentle, more apt to defend her than attack her. "It seems better to me. The grease, maybe. Not such a deep red. Old Man was right about the cold water chasing away the fever, too. She's hot, but nothing like she was."

Warrior pressed a palm to her skin. "Old Man says if you don't keep her cool, the fever will come upon her again."

"Not another bath?" Hunter propped an elbow on his upraised knee and rubbed his forehead. All trace of laughter fled. He didn't relish the thought of the battle he'd have with her. "Don't wake me with news like that. Bring me coffee first."

"Not another bath, but no traveling in the heat. We'll have to stay here a few days."

"You're willing to risk that? What about the *tosi tivo?*"

Breaking open a mullein leaf, Warrior laved his fingertips with healing juice and applied it to the frightened girl's cheeks. She shrank

118

back — only to run into Hunter, which made her flinch. "We're probably safer here, right under their noses, than we would be miles away. When we circled back, we covered our trail well. You have to remember how stupid the *tosi tivo* are. They will follow the trails the others laid and never even think to look for us here, so close."

"Yes, but —"

"She's your woman. If the situation were reversed, you would risk it."

Hunter grew impatient with his struggling captive and caught a handful of her braid to hold her still. "There, I've got her. The nose is worst. On the end where it curves up. Her forehead, too, *tah-mah*."

Warrior dabbed juice and smiled. "She doesn't like me. Come to think of it, she doesn't seem any too fond of you."

Leaning farther forward, Hunter took another look at her face. Her eyes were as big as a startled doe's. Twinkling laughter lit up his own. "She doesn't look as if she wants to spit today, eh? Give me a week, and she'll be broken to ride."

"You blow like the wind." Warrior raised a sarcastic eyebrow and tossed aside the used mullein. "You taught me all I know about being a warrior, *tah-mah,* but when it comes to reluctant women, you are as clumsy as a new bear cub."

"That's because they're never reluctant."

"Oh-ho," Warrior said with a chuckle. "I seem to remember differently. Willow by the Stream didn't exactly race from the central fire to your tipi on your wedding night. You made her dance until she was so tired she wouldn't make a fuss." A tense silence rose between them, a silence heavy with memories. "I'm sorry, *tah-mah*. I spoke her name without thinking."

"It has been many winters. My heart is no longer laid upon the ground." Hunter rested a heavy hand on the girl's bare shoulder, his frown thoughtful. "So, we will camp here? Has anyone scouted the area? You're sure it's safe?"

"Swift Antelope and Red Buffalo checked for trackers last night and this morning. As crazy as it sounds, Red Buffalo claims the girl's *ap* hasn't even gone for help yet."

"He's such a coward, he's probably waiting to be sure we're gone. I'm surprised his women haven't ridden to the fort for help. They are by far the better fighters."

Scarcely aware he was doing it, Hunter feathered his thumb back and forth on the girl's arm, careful not to press too hard because of her burn. She was as silken as rabbit fur. Glancing down, he saw that her skin was dusted with fine, golden hair, noticeable now only because her sunburn formed a dark backdrop. Fascinated, he touched a fingertip to the fuzz. In the sunshine she glistened as though someone had sprinkled her with gold dust.

"Swift Antelope still hasn't stopped talking about the younger one," Warrior said. "Her courage impressed him so much, I think he may be smitten. I have to admit, though, once you get used to looking at them, the golden hair and blue eyes grow on you."

"Maybe you should take her across the river and sell her, eh?"

"I could double my investment." With a grin, Hunter pulled the robe back over her. She reacted by shrinking away from him, and he gave a disgusted snort. "She must think we're hungry and she's going to be breakfast."

"Speaking of which, are you going to feed her?"

"In an hour or so. If we're staying here today, I can go back to sleep." He drew his knife and cut the leather on Loretta's wrists. "Wake me if the sun gets on her, eh?"

"You'd better keep her tied."

"Why?" A yawn stretched Hunter's dark face.

"Because she's looking skittish."

"She's naked." Sheathing his knife, Hunter flopped on his back and shaded his eyes with one arm. "She won't run. Not without clothes. I've never seen such a bashful female."

"The *tosi tivo* truss up their females in so many clothes, it would take a whole sleep just to undress one. Then they have them wear breeches under the lot. How do they manage to have so many children? I'd be so tired by the time I found skin, I'd never get anything else done."

"You'd think of something," Hunter said with a chuckle.

"You know, once you fall asleep, she could go for your knife. You want to wake up with your throat slit?"

"She's more likely to kill herself than me. You know how they are." Hunter's mouth lifted at the corners. "Her honor is gone. A man has seen her naked. As *boisa* as it sounds, that's how they think."

"Want some help watching her?"

Hunter threw back his head and laughed. "Just wake me when the shade leaves, you horny old man. Come anyplace close and I'll tell Maiden of the Tall Grass. She'll burn your dinner for a month."

Loretta watched the other Indian leave, her heart slamming wildly with relief. It was short-lived. Hunter turned onto his side and snaked an arm under the buffalo robe, catching her around the waist. He was fully awake now, and she had no idea what to expect from him when he pulled her close. She scarcely dared breathe, she was so frightened. He snugged his hand beneath her breast and nuzzled his face against the back of her neck.

"You will sleep now, Yellow Hair," he

122

whispered. "I must rest. It will be a very long journey home."

Home. Loretta listened to the hum of the river and stared sightlessly into the woods. Oh, how she longed to be home. The morning fire would be warming the loft right now. And she would be snuggled under the gray down quilt with Amy, waking to the smells of coffee and pork slab in the fry pan. She recognized the Brazos River. The farm was so close. The Indians were clever, she'd give them that. The rangers would never think to look for them here, never in a thousand years. Tears filled her eyes. She tried to stop them, but they ran in rivers down her cheeks. Her stomach started quivering. Her chest heaved.

The Comanche rose on an elbow to look down at her, then touched her cheek. After staring for a long while at the moistness that came away on his fingertips, he sighed and lay back down, wrapping his arm around her again. "You will stop this."

Loretta held her breath. But she could only hold it for so long. The instant she drew air, a jagged sob knifed its way down her windpipe.

"You will stop," he hissed. "This Comanche will blow hard at you like the wind."

Loretta squeezed her eyes closed. She thought of her parents. She wondered if one of these men had taken her mother's scalp. Oh, mercy, she had to get away. . . .

As if he guessed her thoughts, he cinched his arm more tightly around her. "You cannot go back. You are my woman now. *Suvate,* it is finished. You will be quiet and sleep."

A hiccup caught crosswise in her throat. He groaned and gave her a light shake.

"You did not hear? You will stop the tears. I have spoken it. Don't test my temper, Yellow Hair. It is a warning I make for you, eh? Disobey me and we will fight the great fight."

Loretta again tried to stifle herself by holding her breath. She had no idea what "the great fight" was, but it was a foregone conclusion that he would win. When her air rushed out, it erupted, wet and shaky. She clamped a hand over her mouth.

Hunter snarled something at her and leaped to his feet. Running a hand through his hair, he stepped around in front of her and stared down at her contorted features with a thoroughly disgruntled expression playing upon his own. "You will have stopped this when I return. You understand?"

She nodded, averting her face to deflect her shame. *His woman?* The moment he touched her, she would be ruined forever. She'd never be able to go home. People would stare at her and whisper behind her back. Hunter strode off toward the other men. Loretta sobbed in earnest then. All the fear, the exhaustion, the tension of the last twenty-four hours, came pouring out of her. She cried until there were no more tears and no energy left with which to shed them. Then she fell into an exhausted slumber, her last thought being that she had to escape.

CHAPTER 7

Sporadic outbursts of conversation and the tantalizing smell of roasting meat tugged Loretta from the depths of an exhausted sleep. Slitting her eyelids, she peered at the bright orb of the sun, guessing by its position above the canopy of trees that it was nearly noon. Pain throbbed behind her eyes. A ceaseless burning sensation tortured her skin. Her tongue cleaved to the roof of her mouth, prickly and thick. She would have paid a king's ransom for one sip of cool water.

Acutely aware that some of the Comanche warriors were gathered around a nearby fire, Loretta was afraid to call attention to herself by moving. The buffalo fur was heavy, hot, and airless. She could hear the fire crackling, the hissing sound of fat dripping into flames. Occasionally the breeze picked up and rustled through the leaves overhead. Birds twittered, squirrels chattered, and in the background there was the constant rushing sound of water. If she closed her eyes, she could almost

126

believe she was down at the river with Amy, the farm and safety a short walk away.

Cramps shot up the calves of her legs, bunching her muscles into tight knots. An uncomfortable pressure grew in the pit of her stomach. Unable to lie in the same position a moment longer, she eased onto her back, clenching her teeth as the fur pallet touched her sunburned shoulder blades.

The guttural voices nearby rose and fell, their tones argumentative but friendly. Occasionally someone laughed. If the Indians had been speaking English, they could have passed for white men, swapping stories, poking fun at each other. But they weren't white men. She saw a war shield propped against a bush, its face painted with heathen symbols. Scalps hung from the bridle of a nearby pony, the long tresses of one a rich red, without question a white woman's.

Sweat popped out on Loretta's brow and trickled down her temples. She had to get away from here.

The sound of approaching footsteps set her heart to skittering. Loretta closed her eyes and pretended to be asleep. She could sense someone staring at her. Heat bathed her cheeks. It grew hotter, then hotter still. The sensitive skin inside her nostrils began to sear. *Smoke?*

She opened her eyes. A smoldering chunk of wood hovered in front of her nose, its embers red hot. Loretta jerked back, her gaze darting from the wood to the sturdy brown hand that held it.

"You do not spit, Yellow Hair?"

Broad brown shoulders eclipsed the sun, the features above them a grotesque blur of scar tissue. Loretta recognized the Indian who had urged Hunter to kill her that first day. The smoldering wood, wielded so deftly, inched closer to her nose. Grabbing handfuls of the fur and shoving with her feet, she slithered sideways, scarcely aware of the pain on her sunburned back. The Indian grunted and slammed a foot down on her chest.

His scarred face twisted into an ugly smile. "You are so good at spitting. Spit fast, eh? Drown the coals, before you are scarred and ugly like me."

Loretta's breath came in short, ragged gasps. The hair on her upper lip was singeing, the stench acrid in her nostrils. The Indian's black eyes glittered down at her.

"Your courage has flown, eh? There are no rifles to make you brave?" He leaned forward so that more of his weight rested on her. "I will put my mark on you, eh? When my cousin grows tired of you, he has promised you to me. It is fair, no? I will do to you what your *tosi tivo* friends did to me."

He shoved the wood forward. Just in time, Loretta jerked her face aside.

Suddenly another Indian appeared. He was

much older, his greasy hair streaked with gray. Dressed only in a breechcloth, his scrawny brown body looked as tough as uncured leather, his concave buttocks and thin legs stringy with muscle. Gesturing wildly and jabbering words she couldn't understand, he pointed toward the river. Loretta went limp with relief when he wrenched the chunk of wood from her tormentor's hand and threw it aside.

The younger Indian snarled a rejoinder. As he removed his foot from Loretta's chest, he slipped his toe under the fur and gave it a toss. She scrambled for cover, sick with shame when she felt cool air waft across her breasts.

Leering down at her, he said, "Old Man spoils our fun, but we will play another time. Very soon, eh?"

Loretta jerked the buffalo hide over her head. Perspiration filmed her body, yet she shivered. Even after the Indians walked away, she couldn't stop shaking. Animals, they were all animals.

Only a few seconds later, she once again heard footsteps. Long brown fingers clasped the fur and lifted it from her face. Expecting the worst, she stiffened and squinted into the sun. The dark, hulking silhouette of a man crouched over her. Sunblinded, she couldn't immediately make out his features, but the gleam of his mahogany hair and the breadth of his shoulders identified him.

He held a tin cup out to her, very like the ones Aunt Rachel had hanging in her kitchen. Tom Weaver had been right; these Comanches traded often with white men. Where else would they get coffee and tinware? No wonder they had such a good command of English.

"You will drink."

His deep, silken voice was expressionless, and that frightened her more than his anger or threats might have. His wide chest and powerful arms gleamed in the sunshine, muscle rippling and bunching beneath his burnished skin every time he moved. She stared at his stone medallion, at the crude wolf head etched on its face. More graven images decorated the band of leather on his wrist, a serpent intertwined with grotesque stick figures whose heads bore a resemblance to the sun and moon.

She rose up on an elbow, taking care to keep the fur clasped to her breasts. With a trembling hand, she took the cup, careful not to touch her fingers to his. Water slopped over the rim and ran down her neck as she drank. Cool, wonderful water. After only five swallows, it was gone. She ran her tongue across her cracked lips, savoring every drop, then handed the dented container back to him. She longed for more but didn't know how to ask for it.

Hunter set the cup on the pallet and leaned forward on one knee. The combined smells of smoke, beaver oil, leather, and sage emanated from him. *Injun smell.* It clung to the fur, her skin, her hair. A whole tub of lye soap and a bucket of lavender water would never get it off her.

His dark blue eyes cut into hers as he pressed his palm against her cheek. As he slid his fingers to the side of her neck, fear tightened her throat. He touched her with the same matter-of-factness that he might have a horse. Possessively, with arrogant superiority.

Glancing over his shoulder at the group of men behind him, he cried, *"Cho-cof-pe Ok-oom! Keemah, cah boon!"*

Loretta jumped; she couldn't help it. Hunter looked back at her, the corner of his mouth lifting in a contemptuous sneer. The old Indian who had championed her only moments before turned from the fire and strode toward them. *"Hein ein mah-su-ite?"*

"He-be-to. Heep-et?" Hunter nodded toward Loretta. *"Cona."*

Elbowing Hunter out of the way, the old man knelt and fastened his dark gaze on Loretta. Though she tried to keep her expression blank, her mouth quivered, and a muscle in her cheek twitched. Jabbing a finger at his chest, the old Indian said, *"Nei nan-ne-i-cut*

131

Cho-cof-pe Okoom." His wrinkled mouth spread in a snaggle-toothed grin to expose teeth blackened with decay. "In Comanche that say, 'My name Old Man.' You understand? *Cho-cof-pe Okoom* — Old Man."

Though Old Man had rescued her earlier and seemed harmless enough, Loretta didn't trust him. She didn't trust any of them. She shrank away when he tried to touch her. Hunter snarled something and grabbed a fistful of her hair. She tried to remember a prayer, any prayer. To her relief, the old Indian merely touched her forehead.

"Te-bit-ze!" he exclaimed to Hunter. He directed an accusing glance at the sun, then pointed toward the river, spouting more gibberish, which he punctuated with an emphatic, *"Namiso!"*

Whatever it was Old Man had said, Hunter appeared none too pleased. As Old Man walked away, Hunter released his hold on Loretta's hair and stood, motioning for her to get up as well. Disbelief welled within her. She had no clothes. Surely he didn't mean for her to — *"Keemah! Namiso!"* he hissed. When her only response was to stare at him, he said, *"Keemah,* come! *Namiso,* hurry! Do not test my patience, Blue Eyes."

Loretta clutched the fur to her chest and shook her head. She wouldn't parade stark naked before all these men. She wouldn't.

A dangerous glint stole into his eyes. "You

132

will obey this Comanche."

The bridled anger in his voice sent sheer, black fright coursing through her, but she set her jaw.

With a low growl, he leaned over and scooped her up, fur and all, into his arms. Before she could register what he had done, he slung her over his shoulder, one arm clamped behind her knees, his other hand holding the fur so it wouldn't fall. "Stupid white woman. You do not learn too quick."

A few moments later Hunter reached the river and waded thigh deep into the current. With a grunt, he gave her a toss, keeping a firm grip on the buffalo robe so that she spun out of it as she fell. There was no time to feel embarrassed. Iciness engulfed her, the change in temperature such a shock to her feverish body that she gasped. Water seared up her nose and down her windpipe. Darkness, everywhere darkness. For a moment she wasn't sure which way was up. Then she saw light shimmering. She shot to the surface, choking and coughing, arms flailing wildly.

A blur of movement, Hunter threw the fur onto the riverbank and waded toward her. She couldn't touch bottom and, despite the desperate pumping of her arms and legs, went under again, taking another draft of water.

Grabbing her by the hair, he dragged her to the surface and nearer to shore so her feet touched. Bringing his face close to hers, he tightened his grip on her braid. "You will obey me." He enunciated each word with venomous clarity. "Always. You are mine — Hunter's woman, forever with no horizon. The next time you shake your head at me, I will beat you."

A measure of the water she had inhaled surged up her throat. Unable to stop herself, she choked and then coughed. The ejected spray hit him square in the eyes. He blinked and drew back, an incredulous look on his face. Loretta clamped her palms over her mouth, angling her arms to hide her breasts, her shoulders heaving.

As angry as he appeared, she fully expected him to lay her flat with his fist. Instead he released her braid and caught hold of her arms. When she finally got her breath, he let go of her and returned to shore, his leather-clad legs cutting sparkling swaths through the water. After wiping his face dry with the buffalo robe, he turned to glower at her.

He sat on his haunches and rested his corded forearms on his knees. Glancing upstream and down, he said, "Your wooden walls are far away, Yellow Hair. If you try to slip away, this Comanche will find you."

Until that moment, the thought of swimming off hadn't occurred to her. She shot a glance over her shoulder at the swift current. If only she had clothes . . .

"You do not make like a fish so good. Save this Comanche much trouble, eh?"

She thought she detected laughter in his voice, but when she looked back at him, his gaze, blue-black and piercing, was as unreadable as ever. He studied her for several endless seconds. She wondered what he was thinking and decided, from the gleam in his eye, that she didn't want to find out.

"Your eyes say I lie when I call you my woman. This is not good. It is our bargain, eh?" He plucked a wisp of grass and ran it slowly between his fingers, watching her in a way that suggested he would soon touch her — just as slowly. "It was a promise you made for me, and now you make a lie of it? This is the way of your people, to say empty words. *Penende taquoip,* honey talk, eh? But it is not the way of the Comanche. If you make a lie, I will carve out your tongue and feed it to the crows."

The breeze caught his hair, draping strands of it across his chiseled features. For an instant, the knife slash that marred his cheek was hidden, and he seemed less formidable. Her attention was drawn to his lips, full and sharply defined, yet somehow hard, perhaps because of the rigid expression he always wore. Deep crevices bracketed his mouth — laugh lines, surely. Ah, yes, she could imagine him cutting out her tongue and smiling while he did it.

"You do not like me too good. That is a sad thing, eh?" With a sweep of his hand, he indicated the world around them. "The sky is up, the earth is down. The sun shows its face, only to be chased away by Mother Moon. These things are for always, eh? Just as you are my woman. The song was sung long ago, and the song must come to pass. You must accept, Blue Eyes."

Loretta yearned to break eye contact but found she couldn't. The silken threads of his deep voice wove a spell around her. She must accept? Already he was planning to give her away to his horrible cousin. She sank lower in the water, keeping her arms crossed to hide her breasts. Could he see through the ripples?

Still studying her with the same unnerving intensity, he said, "When the wind blows, the sapling bends, the flowers lie low against the earth, the grass is flattened." He thumped his chest with his fist. "I am your wind, Blue Eyes. Bend or break."

Bend or break. In all her life, she had never felt quite so helpless. Her attention moved to the knife on his hip. If only he would drop his guard — just for a moment.

As if he sensed what she was thinking, he smiled another humorless smile and lowered his gaze to her chest where the water lapped just above her splayed fingertips. She tightened her arms around herself. He said nothing more, but words weren't necessary. She couldn't stay in the river forever, and when she emerged, he would be waiting. She was trapped. Always, forever, with no horizon.

The seconds stretched into minutes. Loretta grew numb with cold. The Comanche grew tired of crouching and stretched out on the sandy bank, one knee bent, his upper body propped on one elbow so he could watch her. Loretta felt certain her blood had turned to ice. Shivers set in. Her teeth began to clack. And still he watched her, his mouth twisted into that mocking sneer she was coming to know so well.

When at last he sprang to his feet, she retreated a step, lifting her chin so the lapping water couldn't reach her mouth. He bent to retrieve the buffalo robe and beckoned for her.

"Keemah."

She knew by now that the word meant "come." She shuddered and looked longingly at the fur he held.

"Keemah," he repeated. When she made no move to obey, he sighed.

Sinking lower into the water, Loretta accidentally took a mouthful and choked.

He glanced skyward, clearly exasperated. "This Comanche is not stupid. You would run like the wind if I took my eyes from you."

She shook her head. Frowning, he studied her for a long moment.

"This is not *pe-nan-de taquoip,* the honey

talk. It is a promise you make?"

She nodded, her teeth chattering.

"And you will not make a lie of it?"

When she assured him she wouldn't with another shake of her head, he dropped the fur to the ground and pivoted on one foot. She could scarcely believe he truly meant to keep his back to her. She stared at the broad expanse of his shoulders, at the curve of his spine, at his long, leather-clad legs. Like the wild animals he hunted, he was lithe and lean, his large frame padded with sleek, powerful muscle. If she tried to run, he would be upon her before she had gone more than a few steps.

Plowing her way through the water to shore, she kept her eyes riveted to his back. A small rock cut into the sole of her foot as she scrambled up the bank. She bit her lip and kept going, afraid to hesitate even for a second. By the time she reached him, her heart was slamming. She grabbed up the fur and slung it around her shoulders, clasping the edges tightly to her chest.

Standing this close to him, she could see the sheen of oil on his skin, the dark hair that dusted the crease of his armpits. She didn't want to touch him. The seconds ticked past. Was his hearing so keen that he knew she was still behind him? She sensed he was waiting her out, testing her in some way she couldn't fathom, proving his mastery over her. She worked one hand free from the heavy robe. So fast that she scarcely felt her fingertips graze his skin, she tapped his shoulder and snatched her hand back.

He turned to look at her, his gaze lingering a moment on her bare feet and legs. Humiliation scorched her cheeks. He stepped toward her, stooping as he did to catch her behind the knees and toss her over his shoulder. As Loretta grabbed his belt for support, she realized two things: the cold water had eased her headache, and the hilt of the Comanche's knife was within her reach. . . .

Without stopping to think of the possible consequences, she reached out, imagining how it would feel to bury the blade into his back, to be free of him. Just as her fingers curled around the knife handle, he spoke.

"Kill me, Yellow Hair, and my friends will avenge me. The blood of your loved ones will be spilled as slowly as sap drips from a wounded tree." He kept walking and made no move to grab her hand. "My friends know the way to your wooden walls, eh? Make no grief behind you. It is wisdom."

Loretta jerked her hand from the knife, horrified by what she had nearly done. Her family. They could go back and kill her family. . . .

The other Indians crowed with laughter when Hunter carried her through camp. Through golden wisps of hair that had worked loose from her braid, Loretta spied the disfigured face of Hunter's cousin. He flashed her a grotesque smile and reached under his breechcloth to fondle himself, his eyes glittering. Some other men standing near him began to laugh and gyrate their hips. The obscenity shocked her. The fact that Hunter said nothing filled her with dread. He clearly had no reservations about sharing her with his friends.

After Hunter lowered her onto her fur pallet, which she was swiftly coming to regard as her prison, she clutched the buffalo robe around her and rolled onto her side. *Make no grief behind you.* She felt like an animal caught in a snare — awaiting the trapper and certain death.

The sun burned through her closed eyelids, red and hot. Loretta heard Hunter walk a short distance away, heard him murmur something. His stallion nickered in response. She lifted her lashes and watched the Comanche go through the contents of a parfleche. He withdrew her ruffled drawers, the buckskin shirt he had worn to the farm yesterday morning, and a drawstring pouch. As he walked back to her, he pressed her bloomers to his nose and sniffed.

He met her gaze as he drew the lavender-scented cloth away from his face. For the first time, he smiled a genuine smile. It warmed his expression so briefly that she might have believed she imagined it but for the twinkle that remained in his dark eyes as he knelt beside her.

He dropped the clothing onto the fur and held up the pouch. "Bear fat for the burn. You will lie on your face."

Their gazes locked, laughter still shimmering in his. Seconds dragged by, measured by the wild thumping of her heart. He wanted to rub her down? Oh, God, what was she going to do? She clutched the fur more tightly.

Hunter shrugged as if her defiance bothered him not at all and tossed down the pouch. "You are sure enough not smart, Blue Eyes. You will lie on your face," he said softly. "Don't fight the big fight. If my strong arm fails me, I will call my friends. And in the end, you will lie on your face."

Loretta imagined sixty warriors swooping down on her. As if he needed more of an advantage. Hatred and helpless rage made her tremble. Hunter watched her, his expression unreadable as he waited. She wanted to fly at him, scratching and biting. Instead she loosened her hold on the buffalo robe and rolled onto her stomach.

As she pressed her face into the stench-ridden buffalo fur, tears streamed down her cheeks, pooling and tickling in the crevices at each side of her nose. She clamped her arms to her sides and lay rigid, expecting him to jerk back the robe. Shame swept over her in hot, rolling waves as she imagined all those horrible men looking at her.

She felt the fur shift and braced herself. His greased palm touched her back and slid downward with such agonizing slowness that her skin shriveled and her buttocks quivered. So focused was she on his touch, on the shame of it, that several seconds passed before she realized he had slipped his arm beneath the fur, that no one, not even he, could see her.

Relief, if she felt any at all, was short-lived, for he laved every inch of her back with grease and then tried to nudge her arms aside to get at the burned skin along her ribs. She resisted him, but in the end his strength won out. When his fingertips grazed the swell of her left breast, her lungs ceased working and her body snapped taut.

He hesitated, then resumed the rubbing, diving his fingertips between her and the fur to graze her nipple. She wasn't burned there, and she knew he pressed the issue only to drive home his point. She belonged to him, and he would touch her whenever and wherever he pleased. A sob caught in her throat. Once again she felt his hand pause. His gaze burned into the back of her head, tangible in its intensity.

At last he withdrew his arm from under the fur and sat back. Loretta twisted her neck to look up at his dark face, not bothering to wipe away her tears, too defeated to care if he saw them. He set the leather pouch on the pallet beside her. For an instant she thought she glimpsed pity in his eyes.

"You rub the rest, eh? And put yourself into the clothes."

With that, he rose, presented his broad back to her, and walked away to crouch by the only remaining fire. Loretta clutched the fur to her breasts and sat up, not quite able to believe he had left her alone to dress.

CHAPTER 8

Hunter crouched beside the fire, a cup of coffee cradled in his palms, his gaze fixed on the shifting flames. He could see his yellow-hair from the corner of his eye and knew every time she moved, every time she looked at him. Somehow she had managed to stay covered with the fur while she pulled on his shirt and her ruffled breeches.

His brother, Warrior, squatted next to him and began tossing chips of bark onto the coals, watching them ignite. "The *tosi tivo* must be very poor lovers."

Hunter glanced up, more than a little bewildered by his brother's observation. Warrior was like that, though, the thoughts in his heart darting here and there like autumn leaves caught up in the wind.

"You don't agree?" Warrior pressed.

Warrior's voice and the musical cadence of the Comanche language fell sweetly on Hunter's ears. Talking *tosi tivo* talk to the yellow-hair had left a dirty taste on his tongue. "The *tosi tivo* are very poor at every-thing."

Warrior glanced toward the yellow-hair, squinting as a trail of smoke got in his face. "She still hides beneath the buffalo robe. Your shirt and her ruffles are not enough."

Hunter searched his brother's dark eyes.

"I think the *tosi tivo* teach their women such foolishness because they are afraid."

"Hm. And what would they be afraid of?"

Warrior grinned. "A woman who isn't well loved will seek solace elsewhere."

Hunter huffed at that idea. "With as many children as their women bear, how can you think they need solace? The trouble with the *tosi tivo* is that they have no honor. They will call a man friend, then borrow his woman when his back is turned. The many clothes make the wife borrowing a little more tricky, eh?"

A thoughtful frown settled on Warrior's forehead. He dumped the remainder of the wood chips he had collected onto the fire. The flames hissed· hungrily and flared brighter. "This is the truth? And what of the females? Don't they spurn the men who try to shame them?"

"The females have no honor, either."

Brushing his hands clean on his leggings, Warrior shot a worried look at the white woman. "You must teach her, eh? If you go down in battle and I have to take her into my lodge circle, I want to know her children are yours."

"She will learn. I will teach her honor if I kill her doing it."

Warrior plucked a blade of grass and began to nibble on it, his expression distant. Hunter recognized the signs. His brother's thoughts were flitting to yet another place. After a moment Warrior spat and said, "Old Man tells me that you may have to strike the girl to make her obey. That is their way. She may not understand anything else. This worries me. You have a heavy hand when you grow angry. Normally, I wouldn't be concerned, but with the yellow-hair I'm afraid your patience will snap like a wet bowstring."

Hunter scooped a handful of wood chips and tossed them into the flames. The flare of heat matched his mood. "She's my woman, *tah-mah.* Let me do the worrying."

"But her bones are like a bird's. If you lost your temper with her and used your fists, you would shatter them."

Hunter scowled and made no reply.

Old Man, who had been standing nearby and listening, joined them at the fire to pour himself another measure of coffee. Once his cup was filled, he stepped back from the flames. "*Ai-ee,* Hunter, are you planning to be our dinner? It's already so hot in these woods that I'm about to stifle."

Hunter had chosen to crouch by the fire

because he hoped no one would join him there, but he saw no point in telling Old Man and his brother that. "A warrior can find great truths by searching the flames."

"You have troubles with your woman, eh?" Old Man smiled. "You young braves! All too proud to seek advice. I lived with the *tosi tivo* for many winters, remember. I know things about them that you don't." A rakish grin slanted across Old Man's crinkled face. "Especially about the women."

Hunter wasn't in the mood for advice. "The girl is half my size. I think I can handle her without calling council."

"You disappoint me, Hunter. Where is the patience you show with the wild horses you train? Has it gone the way of the wind?"

"A horse is worth the trouble. A yellow-hair is not."

"I know men who greatly treasure golden women. Perhaps she will grow on you."

"I prefer a horse. A *black* one."

"Women, horses, there is little difference, eh? Well trained, they both give men smooth rides and much pleasure. What happens when you first rope a mustang?"

Hunter knew where this conversation was going and refused the bait. Warrior replied for him. "Every time he runs against the rope, he flips end over end."

"And what does he learn? Not to challenge your rope, eh? After that first lesson, he knows you are his master and allows you to gentle him with kindness. The white woman is the same. She is afraid and lunging against the rope. As soon as you break her of that, the battle is won, eh?"

Hunter wished it could be that simple. When a horse accepted the touch of his hand, joy filled him.

After swirling the dregs of his coffee, Hunter emptied his cup onto the fire. Rising to his feet, he said, "You are both very wise, and I am glad of your advice. I will handle the woman my way, though. She is *my* woman, eh?"

"Take care," Old Man warned. "The *tosi tivo* are unpredictable. Especially the females. Wisest-One had himself a yellow-hair once. After one night in his buffalo robes, she jumped into the Talking Water River and drowned herself. Not even Wisest-One could be that bad a lover."

Hunter gave a careless shrug as he ambled toward his camp. There was something different about his woman. As he approached the pallet, he realized it was the expression in her eyes. There was a feverish glitter in their blue depths. He stopped some three feet away and took a moment to study her. Despite himself, he felt uneasy. She had the crazed look of a warrior about to fight a death match.

He folded his arms across his chest. In his hunting shirt, she looked no bigger than a child, her narrow shoulders extending only inches beyond each side of the neckline, the sleeves rolled up to accommodate her much shorter arms. She was as helpless against him as a fledgling in its nest, unable to take flight, too small to fight back.

"We will take a walk now, to find some shade. *Keemah.*"

The girl didn't move.

He snapped his fingers. *"Keemah! Namiso!"*

The corner of her mouth twitched, but otherwise she sat motionless, her gaze leveled on his knees. He knew she heard him and that she understood. A hot band of anger tightened around his chest. It was bad enough that he had been saddled with her. He wouldn't put up with her obstinacy. Leaning forward, he made a fist in the front of the hunting shirt and hauled her to her feet so roughly that her head snapped back.

The softness of her breasts pressed against his knuckles. She tried to shrink away, but all the slack in the shirt was bunched in his fist, making retreat impossible. She grabbed for his wrist, her pupils flaring, her already flushed cheeks turning a deeper scarlet. He gave her a shake. "You will obey me."

Her eyes darkened to slate gray, as turbulent as a storm-swept sky. In that tension-packed instant, only for an instant, Hunter had to admire her. She would kill him if she could.

That thought no sooner registered than he

149

saw her arm coming up, but until her fist connected with his cheek, he didn't believe what he was seeing. She had little strength and even less weight to give the blow force, but her pointed knuckles hit their mark with a treachery all their own.

A frightened *tosi* captive never struck her captor. She cringed, she wept, she groveled, but never did she attack. He couldn't have been more shocked if the earth and sky had switched places. He blinked, but when his vision cleared, his cheek still smarted and his woman's blue eyes were still talking murder.

"You dare to strike me?" The words hung between them, lending credence to the impossible. He tightened his grip on the shirt and jerked her off the ground. "You —"

Before he could repeat the accusation, she threw another punch, this time at the corner of his mouth. Then she knifed upward with one knee, catching him at the apex of his thighs. His gut contracted on a dizzying surge of pain and shoved all the air from his lungs. Rage obscured his vision, painting her and everything around them in glowing red.

Emitting a snarl, he tossed her from him. She tumbled backward onto the fur. He followed her down, vising her slender hips between his thighs while he captured both her wrists in one hand. Bracing his other hand on the fur, he leaned forward. Her eyes widened. Then she twisted onto her side and threw back her head. With a feeling of unreality, Hunter watched as she sank her teeth into his arm. Pain shot clear to his shoulder.

His knife cleared its sheath before he realized he had drawn it. He held the razor-sharp blade to her throat, his body atremble with the effort it took not to kill her.

She had her eyes squeezed closed, awaiting death. Her fear clung to the air he breathed, so intense he could smell it, taste it. Yet she was biting his arm? Another tremor shook him. He wasn't sure whose body convulsed, his with rage or hers with terror.

And then realization hit him. She *wanted* him to kill her. The Comanches called it *habbe we-ich-ket,* seeking death. His little fledgling had found a way to fight back.

As the truth dawned on him, he began to tremble even more, his knuckles turning white around the hilt of the knife. With one flick of his wrist, he could grant her wish and be forever free of her. Sweat beaded on his face and chest. His breath whined down the restricted passage of his windpipe.

Slowly, the brittle tension flowed out of his body, bringing in its wake a muscle-draining wave of defeat. With great reluctance, he withdrew the knife from her throat. As if she sensed the ebb of his anger, she bit down harder, a final, valiant attempt to goad him into killing her. Maybe the *tosi tivo* weren't so stupid, after all. He would be wise to remem-

151

ber that the blade of his temper had a double edge, one that could be turned against him.

Steeling himself against the pain she was inflicting, Hunter stared down her, not quite sure how to get his arm away without knocking her loose with his fist. Suddenly it struck him how absurd the situation was — a Comanche warrior, kneeling over a white woman and doing nothing while she sank her teeth into him. Hunter, the fierce warrior and merciless killer, unable to control a girl half his size?

A reluctant laugh erupted from his chest. Then another. And the next thing he knew, he was laughing and couldn't, didn't want to, stop.

His guffaws startled her so badly that she forgot to keep her jaws clenched. He freed his arm and rolled off her onto his back. For days Hunter had kept his emotions under tight rein. Now all those feelings, the constant and ever-building tension, the anger, the resentment, and the burning hatred, poured out of him, interlaced in such a confusing tangle that they were as difficult to separate and control as dogs fighting over a bone.

The girl jackknifed to a sitting position. He knew it wasn't funny, and yet it was. A great joke on both of them. He draped his forearm over his brow. He heard her drag in a breath. And then, with a grunt that could only be born of fury, she flew at him. Her blows weren't well placed and rained upon parts of his body that were steely with muscle and impervious to something as harmless as a woman's fist. Her small face was twisted, her teeth bared, her eyes sparkling with tears. Hunter sheathed his knife, chuckling as he sat up to ward her off.

He felt her fingers graze his belt. Then honed metal flashed, arcing like blue death in the sunlight. She had his knife!

For just an instant he thought she meant to stab him. Then he saw the path of her thrust. She aimed for her own belly. With the same quickness that served him so well in battle, Hunter drew back his arm and knocked the knife from her hands. The weapon tumbled harmlessly to the dirt a few feet away.

Breathing heavily, he gaped at her. Until that instant he hadn't realized the depth of her hatred for him or the strength of her fear. She sank to her knees, her arms vised around her waist, her head hanging. Great, racking sobs tore from her chest. If there was one thing he understood, it was the importance of honor, even for his enemies. There was no shame in waging fierce war and losing.

He started to speak, but no words would come. The sound of her sobs worked their way down inside him. He had heard sobs like these before . . . on a night long ago and yet not so long ago.

For an instant he was swept back to that

moment, and the pain of remembering nearly bent him double. An image of Willow swam through his mind, her innocence destroyed, her life's blood pouring from her body. *Don't leave me, Hunter. The Blue Coats might return. Please, don't leave me.* The ache inside his chest became more acute. He had vowed that night never to make war on the helpless. Until now, it was a vow he had kept.

The past shifted into shadows and melded with the present. Hunter studied the girl's golden head, still hung low. Were she and Willow so different? If it were Willow here now, she would seek death to escape. And she would tremble in fear at the thought of being raped. Had hatred hardened his heart so much that he could no longer see as their eyes saw? Had he become like Red Buffalo?

When Hunter reached out to touch the girl's hair, trying in the only way he knew to make amends, he was reaching back through the years to another. Reaching out with gentleness, as he wished the Blue Coats had reached for Willow.

Hunter's hand quivered as he touched his fingertips to the wisps of gold atop the girl's head. When she felt the weight of his palm, she struck out at him and shrank away. Hunter rose to his feet and retrieved his knife, shoving it angrily into its sheath. This time, though, his anger was directed at himself.

"Come, Blue Eyes, we must take a walk and

get out of the sun," he said softly.

She ignored him. Hunter settled the matter by tossing her over his shoulder as he had before. As a precaution, he slid his belt around so the hilt of his knife pressed against his belly. She didn't struggle. Her sobbing had quieted. But her tears trickled down his back and burned into his skin as he carried her. He was relieved that the fight had drained out of her. If she defied him again within sight of his men, he would be left with no choice but to chastise her.

A grim scowl settled on his brow. *Habbe we-ich-ket,* seeking death. It was a black wish that she had in her heart. And it was one he could not grant her. Surrendering to him was the only choice she had, the only choice he could offer her.

The evening air was as thick as syrup, hot and sweet with smells of summer, not a breath of breeze to stir the trees. Loretta sat with her sensitive back pressed to the silvered trunk of a stunted oak and stared into the twilight, murky with smoke from the Indians' cooking fires. Though hours had passed since her confrontation with Hunter, she still shook when she thought of it. She realized now that she would never succeed in making him kill her.

She felt hollowed out, sucked dry, exhausted. Except for the fear, building pressure within her like steam caught under a kettle lid. The Indian with the burned face — Hunter's cousin — had been hovering at a distance all afternoon, a vulture waiting to feed on carrion. Every time Hunter left her alone, he watched her, an unholy gleam in his eyes as his gaze traveled slowly over her body. Once, he had unsheathed his knife, smiling at her as he tested the blade with his thumb. She had known what he was thinking. Driving *him* to murder would be easy enough. The problem was, she wanted to die quickly, not inch by inch.

For seven years Loretta had struggled to stay one step ahead of the memories. Seven years of running. Seven years of terror every time she saw dust on the horizon. Now, what she had dreaded most had happened. This was reality, and somehow she had to deal with it. No more running. No way to escape.

A blink away from tears, Loretta hugged her knees more tightly, determined not to cry. She wouldn't give Hunter the satisfaction. The miserable bastard. He had laughed at her. It had taken all her courage to hit him. Never in her life had she been so scared. Surrender with dignity, he had told her. Why wouldn't he let her die with dignity?

Comanches didn't have feelings like white people did. No compassion. They were subhuman, and even that was being kind. They disemboweled people. They bashed babies' heads on rocks. They stole and raped little girls, slowly burning off their noses and ears with hot coals. Only monsters did such things.

She and Hunter were enemies; that she understood. He hated her. She understood that even better. But deadly enemy or not, hated or not, Loretta never would have laughed at him if their roles had been reversed. She might have obliged him and slit his throat, dad-blame him, but she wouldn't have laughed.

She hated him more than she had ever hated anyone — so much that during the course of the afternoon, she had imagined murdering him in a dozen inventive ways. Not that she'd get a chance or that she would do it even if the opportunity presented itself. *Make no grief behind you.* She had her family to think of. Nothing could induce her to jeopardize Amy and Aunt Rachel.

At the moment, Hunter was gone, probably down at the river getting more water. As before, the others watched her during his absence. Some were preparing their evening meals. Others visited or tossed dice. But regardless of what they were doing, they kept her under constant surveillance. Guarding captives was routine to them, she supposed. The few they didn't butcher were traded to the Comanchero for goods and rifles. The Comanchero either sold the poor souls across the border or ransomed them back to their families for a tidy profit.

Loretta sighed. Though her luck couldn't last, she had to admit she had received far better treatment than she had expected. The Comanche's repeated applications of grease and mullein juice had made her sunburn feel better. Now, instead of burning everywhere, she itched. Probably from fleas.

She looped her arms around her knees again and shivered, a sure sign that her fever wasn't completely gone. Laughter floated through the air, falling softly around her. The sound made her feel so lonely. She missed Amy and Aunt Rachel. Had they gone for help? Or was Uncle Henry just waiting for a border patrol to happen by?

If a border patrol was out searching for her, it was probably en route to the Colorado River, following the false trail the Comanches had laid. Hunter knew the border patrol would think he had gone west or northwest, deep into Comancheria. So instead he was on the Brazos, almost in their laps.

A shadow moved to Loretta's left, and she leaped with a start. As the Comanche walked toward her, she let her gaze trail the length of him. The cut on his shoulder from Aunt Rachel's bullet looked almost healed, maybe because his skin was so burnished. His flat nipples were as dark as his hair. And she had never seen so much muscle.

He hunkered down and extended a cup to her. Having him so close made her feel claustrophobic — made him seem larger. She pressed her knees together. Looking at the water sharpened the ache in her belly. She couldn't drink another drop. But how could she tell him? She raised her left hand and, using the fore and middle fingers of her right hand, made a walking motion across her left palm. Then she pointed to the bushes.

Hunter watched her and grunted, *"Hein?"*

Stupid Comanche. She jabbed a finger at the cup, then placed a hand over her stomach and shook her head, trying to look pained, which wasn't too great a task. On top of her physical discomfort was the nagging realization that this savage ruled her every move.

"You would like to make a walk?" He lifted one shoulder in an eloquent shrug and shoved the cup toward her. "You will drink first."

She gave another emphatic shake of her head. A determined glint stole into his eyes. She sighed and took the cup from him. With a flick of her wrist, she emptied it on the ground.

She could tell by the ticking muscle in his jaw that he was furious. She set down the cup and pointed toward the brush again.

With what sounded like a weary sigh, he rose and offered her a hand up. Preferring not to touch him, she shifted her weight onto her knees and grasped the trunk of the oak. Her legs were stiff from sitting for so long, her muscles sore from the long horseback ride the day before. For a moment she thought her knees might buckle when she stood up.

He grasped her arm and, with no regard for her bare feet, led her a short way through the brush to a small clearing. Releasing her, he folded his arms across his chest and inclined his head at the ground, indicating that she should do her business there. She signaled him to turn his back.

Heaving another weary sigh, he looked around them. "You will make a promise of it? You will not run?"

Loretta nodded. She would have promised him just about anything in return for some privacy.

He studied her for what seemed an eternity, then turned his back. "Do not make a lie of it, Blue Eyes. If you do, the crows will be very happy birds, eh?"

Loretta stepped to the edge of the clearing and hid behind a bush. As quickly as she could, she did what she had to, wishing with all her heart that she was at home in the necessary house.

As she tugged up her bloomers, she saw something moving in the brush. Hunter's stallion had been left free to graze most of the afternoon, and his nose had led him into the thickets.

Loretta gaped. The horse was no more than twenty feet from her. Because of thick mesquite, Hunter hadn't been able to see him from the clearing. The stallion wasn't wearing the padded surcingle, but he wore a rope halter. She could ride bareback.

Her neck stiff with tension, Loretta glanced over her shoulder. Hunter still stood with his back to her. He had accepted her word and was therefore bound to trust her.

For an instant she stood there, rooted in indecision. She hadn't forgotten what he threatened to do if she broke a promise. Her tongue tingled, but that wasn't enough to stop her. Much more than her tongue was at stake if she didn't get out of here. Besides, the horse's appearance there had to be Providence. She would be a fool to pass up what was her only chance of escape.

Treading lightly, Loretta inched toward the horse. Two feet, three. Twigs and nettles cut into her feet; she scarcely felt them. Five feet, ten. She cast a look over her shoulder. The Comanche hadn't turned around. Two more feet, that was all. . . .

Then the horse nickered. The sound seemed as loud as a cannon boom. Wings of fright fluttered inside her chest. She made a lunge for the stallion's halter. As her fingers grasped the rope, the black sidestepped and snorted, eyes wild. For a moment she feared he might strike at her with his front hooves, but he sniffed the shirt she wore and quieted immediately.

"*Kiss! Mah-cou-ah, kiss!*" Hunter yelled.

Loretta knew the Indian was bearing down on her. Retreating two steps so she could get a run at the stallion, she swung onto his back, ignoring the pain of her sunburn. The horse quivered as her legs tightened around him. Hunter was less than four feet away. His murderous expression was all the impetus she needed. She slapped the stallion's rump with all her strength and sent him charging through the brush.

She didn't dare go home; Hunter would follow her there. Her only hope was Fort Belknap. The most direct route was along the river, but the Comanche would anticipate that. She headed away from the stream. Shouts rose behind her, and she knew the men were running for their mounts. Covering as much ground as she could before they gave chase was her only chance.

The black was magnificent. Never had Loretta felt such power under her. Wind caught her hair, undoing her loosened braid to stream it like a golden banner behind her. Exhilarated and half-dizzy with terror, she lay along the stallion's neck, urging him forward with her body and her heart. *Please, God. Please, God.* The words rang in her mind, over and over. If Hunter caught her . . . He wouldn't catch her, he wouldn't! God hadn't given her this chance to escape just to see her fail.

Hunter had told her yesterday that he rode like the wind, but it seemed to Loretta that she and his horse *were* the wind. The black gloried in speed and took his head, cutting his own trail, jumping obstacles as if they weren't there, cutting sharp turns, so fleet of foot that Loretta couldn't imagine anything catching him. Tree limbs passed above her in a blur. Freedom! She was going to get away. She was really going to do it.

The thought no sooner took root than Loretta heard another horse behind her. She craned her neck to look back and saw Hunter pursuing her on a roan, the other Comanches trailing him. Her chest constricted, and panic rushed her. She pressed her body closer to the stallion. Digging her heels sharply into his flanks, she urged him to run even faster, praying he still had speed to spare and that the increasingly uneven ground wouldn't slow him down.

Sweet, beautiful, wonderful horse. Loretta nearly wept when she felt his powerful muscles coil and spring forward in another mighty surge. He had more heart than any animal she had ever seen.

Glancing over her shoulder, she saw Hunter reining in his mount. Dust rose around him as the roan's hooves dug into the dirt. "No!"

he yelled. "*Suvate!* It is finished!"

Loretta nearly whooped with joy. He was quitting! He was giving up the chase! He was going to let her —

Suddenly the stallion pitched forward and emitted a horrible scream. An instant later she was flying through the air. Time seemed suspended, seconds stretched into eternity, as she sailed up in an arc. Then she hit the ground, and the world went black.

When Loretta regained her senses, she was surrounded by a cacophony of thundering hooves, shouts, and screams. Horrible screams. She knew what made the sounds . . . an animal in agony. She blinked and peered upward, trying to bring the world into focus. Hunter leaned over her, skimming his hands down her body. Then he was gone.

When the earth stopped pitching, Loretta pushed up on her elbows, her still dazed senses directed toward the screaming and a blur of movement. Slowly, the blur came into focus. The stallion. The poor beast was thrashing, trying frantically to stand. Even from where she lay, Loretta could see the odd angle of his right foreleg, broken clean in two. Her stomach felt as though it dropped a foot. Had he stepped into a varmint hole?

Oh, God, not the horse! Guilt slammed into her like a giant fist.

Slowly she sat up. About four feet from the

stallion, Hunter stood rooted, his face twisted, his fists clenched. His cousin approached and offered him a rifle, but Hunter knocked the weapon aside. The surrounding woods went eerily silent, the only sounds those of the horse, high-pitched and heartrending.

After a moment, the tension flowed from Hunter's body. Speaking softly in Comanche, he walked toward the crazed stallion. Loretta heard several of the other men murmur in disapproval, but they made no move to stop him. Was Hunter mad? The horse was blind with pain, dangerous. Loretta couldn't move, couldn't think beyond the moment. The other Comanches didn't move, either. Indeed, no one seemed to breathe.

"Pamo," Hunter whispered. *"Nei Pamo."*

The horse's screams changed pitch, took on a pleading note. He threw his head, seemed to focus on his master, and whinnied. Hunter dropped to his knees in front of him.

"Ah, my good friend."

The stallion quieted, grunting and nudging his master's belly. A wind came up, catching the man's long hair and the stallion's silken mane. Cast against the backdrop of trees and mesquite, the two formed a picture Loretta knew would be burned in her memory. Wild creatures, both, burnished skin and ebony.

Bending his head, the Comanche touched

his lips to the stallion's muzzle, breathing in, then out. The horse inhaled, tasted, and the fear seemed to leave him. With a great shudder, he stopped struggling to gain his feet and eased onto his side.

Loretta didn't need to understand Comanche. The body language of love was universal. Man and beast were one in a way she had never experienced, never dreamed could be. The Comanche moved closer, whispering, sometimes smiling, as if he spoke of long-ago moments he and his friend had shared. He stroked the horse's neck, shoulder, even his injured leg, weaving a hypnotic spell. The animal trusted the Comanche so completely that he at last lowered his head to his master's knees and heaved a sigh.

Hunter hunched his shoulders and knelt there for a long while, still speaking softly. Then, with no inflection in his voice to warn anyone of what he was about to do, he said, "*Erth-pa, pa-mo.* Sleep." The words no sooner passed his lips than he drew his knife and, with a mighty thrust, buried it to the hilt behind the unsuspecting stallion's shoulder. The large animal jerked, gave a death kick, then exhaled his last breath.

Silence cloaked the woods. Hunter didn't move, didn't speak. Loretta had never seen such pain etched upon a man's face. She felt as if she might be sick, wished that she could die. If she had known this would happen, she

166

wouldn't have chosen that moment to flee. And never on this man's horse.

At last Hunter looked up. In the dusk she couldn't be sure, but she thought a tear shimmered on his cheek. He strained to lift his stallion's head from his lap and lowered it gently to the ground. A muscle along his jaw spasmed when he grasped his knife and pulled it from the animal's heart.

Rising to his feet, he turned his eyes, which appeared almost black in the twilight, toward Loretta. He held the bloody weapon aloft in his left hand so she could see it.

Never taking his eyes from hers, the Comanche used the bloody knife to slash his right forearm from just below his elbow to the back of his wrist. Loretta flinched, for the blade ran deep. She stared at the blood, watched it stream down Hunter's arm, drip onto the dirt. The thought crossed her mind that if he had done that to himself, no telling what he might do to her.

The Comanche's cousin approached him and placed a hand on his shoulder. Hunter shrugged away, his gaze still fixed on Loretta. Heart in throat, she looked at Hunter's cousin. The man's twisted features were solemn. There was no doubt the horse's death distressed him, but in his eyes she saw something else — something that had nothing to do with sadness or regret. Satisfaction.

When Loretta drew her gaze back to

Hunter, she knew why his cousin appeared so gratified. She had finally succeeded in making Hunter so angry that he would kill her. And, judging from his deadly calm, her death would not be swift.

CHAPTER 9

As Hunter strode toward his yellow-hair, countless emotions welled within him, grief, rage, regret, but what burned most brightly was thirst for revenge. He had trusted her promise, and she had made a lie of it. All *tosi tivo* were the same, spewing honey talk, none of the words written upon their hearts. His beautiful Smoke had paid the price for Hunter's poor judgment.

Over the years the *tosi tivo* had taken many of Hunter's loved ones, his brother Buffalo Runner, for whom Hunter bore a mourning scar on his right palm, his sister, Rain, for whom he bore another scar on his left palm, and his beloved wife, for whom he had marked his face. There had been others in his village, friends, relatives, children. Now, even his war pony, Smoke.

The girl slithered backward on her rump when he reached to grab her arm. Disgust roiled within him. Everything about her was an affront, the flower smell, her golden hair, her wide blue eyes, her berry-red and peeling skin, her ridiculous breeches. Even the feel of her wrist in his hand set his teeth on edge. *Hoos-cho Soh-nips,* Bird Bones, that was what he would call her.

He jerked her to her feet and yanked her against his chest with so much force, her wind slammed out of her. He was aware that the other men watched, that they waited to see what punishment he would mete out. If Hunter was too soft with her, they would lose respect for him. So be it. At least for now. If he punished her when his heart was this heavy, he'd kill her.

The ride back to camp seemed interminable to Loretta. Hunter rode in grim silence, one bruising arm clamped around her waist, his other hand clenched into a white-knuckled fist in the roan's mane. She tried to imagine what fate awaited her.

Terror sluiced like ice water down her spine. She began to quiver, then to tremble. When she had contemplated death as a means of escape, she had hoped for something quick. Too late, she realized Hunter did nothing rashly.

When they reached camp, he rode the roan to the oak where she had been sitting all day. After dismounting, he hauled her off the horse and pulled her behind him to his pile of bags, where he made quick business of gathering stakes and lengths of rawhide. Gripping her arm, he made a circle of the camp until he found a rock. Their next destination was the pallet. With a snarl, he kicked what she had come to regard as her buffalo robe out of his way. Then he shoved her down on the other fur.

Loretta landed on all fours. Afraid to move, to breathe, she watched him drive the first stake. He glanced up at her, his eyes glittering. As he moved to drive another stake, she almost made a run for it.

Then she looked up. Indians stood all around her. To a man they stared at her, their faces dark with anger. Hunter's cousin was less than fifteen feet away. He alone was smiling. She knew that he and the others were waiting to watch her die. If she bolted, she wouldn't make it five yards.

When Hunter had driven the last stake, he straightened and said, "You will lie on your back. I warn you, woman, do not fight me. If you do, I will sure enough kill you. It is a promise I make, not your *tosi tivo* honey talk."

Loretta figured he would kill her no matter what, but it seemed a moot point. She was one woman against sixty men. Courage and prayer eluded her. Fear anchored her hands and knees to the fur. It took all her strength of will to move. Her arms shook as she crawled to lie down. Rolling onto her back, she clenched her teeth and closed her eyes.

Hunter seized her left wrist in a cruel grip and swiftly lashed it to a stake. *Her mother.* She forced her mind to go blank and was scarcely aware as Hunter tied her other wrist and spread her legs to secure her ankles. When he had finished, she felt him kneel beside her. Lifting her lashes, she saw he had drawn his knife. He leaned over and slowly brought the bloodstained blade toward her face.

He was going to cut out her tongue. A metallic taste coated the roof of her mouth and puckered her palate. Rage sparkled in his indigo eyes, brilliant and brutal. The razor-sharp edge of his knife lightly grazed her cheek.

"You made a lie of your promise, Blue Eyes. I said what I would do. You thought I was blowing like the wind, eh?" His white teeth flashed in a sneer. "The crows will be very happy birds and will fly far away with your lying tongue so it will never again lay my heart on the ground. That will be good, no? We will do it, eh? When the moon shows her face? Do not go away. You wait here for this Comanche."

Sheathing his knife, he rose and left her. Loretta turned her head to see that the other men were still standing there — watching, waiting. She heard Hunter go over to the oak, heard him speak, heard someone reply. Then the sound of hooves thrummed through the ground, and she realized he was riding away on the roan. The other Indians gathered their horses and walked off, clearly disappointed that their entertainment was delayed.

When the last of them had gone, Loretta stared at the darkening sky. The moon would come out soon. How long would Hunter delay her torture? An hour? Two? She should be praying, but for the life of her she couldn't think of the words. Images of Amy and Aunt Rachel passed through her mind, the good times they had shared and the bad. Uncle Henry wasn't so terrible, not really. She worked her wrists, trying to free them from the leather. The thin thongs cut into her skin but didn't loosen.

Time passed. She had no idea how much. It grew so dark that red-gold auras hovered over the fires. Hunter would return soon. *Pray, draw strength, make your peace with God.*

Hunter didn't return.

Loretta wasn't sure when it happened, but slowly her fear altered, focusing less on what Hunter might do to her and more on what could happen before he returned. Snakes, bears, wolves, cougars. She had wanted to die . . . but, please, God, not as an animal's dinner. Or slowly, from poisonous venom.

Blackness . . . Why had she never noticed how dark the nights were? Something rustled in the brush, and she craned her neck. Shadows shifted. An animal? Or only a breath of wind? She strained against the leather, oblivious of the pain as the strips bit into her flesh. Moisture filmed her face. She heard something slither in the grass. A snake? She fastened her gaze on the closest campfire, concentrating on the light. She couldn't see Hunter. Why hadn't he come back yet?

A hysterical urge to laugh hit her. Of course! He had chosen the worst torture of all . . . waiting. Alone in the dark to contemplate death, either at his hands or by some beast of prey. By the time he returned, she already would have died in her mind a thousand times and in as many ways.

Moonlight shimmered on the river, silver-white where it caught in the ripples, casting the untouched surfaces of water into glistening blackness. The night wind whispered, as sadly as lost souls searching for solace, and Hunter lifted his face to it.

His hands ached from gathering rocks for Smoke's grave. Flexing his fingers, he drew up his knees and rested his folded arms on them. He sighed and let his eyes close so his heart could drift along the path of memories, back to Smoke's birth, then forward, recreating the moments they had shared these many years. It hurt to remember, but he knew the pain would cut deep and leave a wound that would begin to heal. A man couldn't run from grief. In the end it always caught up to him. Better to face it now.

The muscles along Hunter's throat tightened. As had happened so many times in his life, his grief had to walk behind his responsibilities, like a woman behind her husband. He could mourn Smoke for only a few short minutes. The yellow-hair waited, and Hunter had to return to camp.

He gazed into the darkness at the flickering shadows. Above the tops of the trees on the opposite side of the river, he could see endless stretches of starlit sky. He longed for home where the plains stretched forever, where the wind sighed through the river canyons, sweet with the smell of grass and mesquite. If only his friends hadn't come across a mute yellow-hair and ridden to tell him.

Loretta heard something. A rustling sound. She dropped her chin to her chest and peered through the blackness, heart slamming. A black shape moved. She knew it wasn't her imagination this time. She strained frantically against the leather strips that bound her hands. Then the shape moved between her and the flickering light of the campfires, taking on the outline of a man, a tall man who moved with fluid strength. She went weak with relief.

He gathered wood for a fire, lighting the tinder with a fire drill. It was a long, tedious process. In the moonlight, she could see the constant play of muscle across his back as he pulled the small bow back and forth. At last, though, the friction created sparks, the tinder caught fire, and the parched wood flared to life, a brilliant yellow in the darkness. Loretta longed to be closer to the heat.

Hunter brushed his palms clean on his pants, turning to give her a long perusal. Her heart nearly stopped, she was so scared.

The fire cast its light over him. Outlined against the blackness, he looked more like an artist's carving than a flesh-and-blood man, his chest and arms burnished copper, his pants and moccasins muted gold. Flickering shadows danced across his face, obscuring his features.

With pantherlike grace he walked toward her, his feet seeming to skim the earth. As he neared the pallet, he pulled his knife from its sheath. Loretta jerked. As he knelt beside her, she strained away. His piercing blue-black eyes locked with hers.

Offering no explanation for his clemency, he bent over her and cut the leather that bound her wrists. Then, with the same quick precision, he slashed the leather that secured her feet and sheathed his knife, not speaking, not looking at her again. Scarcely able to believe he wasn't going to do something horrible, Loretta slowly sat up and rubbed her wrists, watching him. He walked to his leather bags and rummaged in them. When he returned, he tossed a piece of jerked meat in her lap, keeping another for himself.

Closing her hand around the meager fare, she bowed her head and blinked back tears. She was acutely aware of him as he crouched by the fire. The night air nipped at her feverish skin, but she didn't dare join him to warm herself. He tore off a piece of meat with his teeth and began to chew. At least she didn't need to worry that the jerky was poisoned. She had no idea what kind of meat it might be.

Thinking about food made her stomach growl. It seemed like a century since she'd eaten. She uncurled her hand and studied the meat. It looked pretty much like the jerked venison from home. Her mouth started to water. Hunter was gazing into the fire, either ignoring her or pretending he was. She sneaked a bite. A delicious smoke flavor filled her mouth as she rolled the tough fibers across her tongue. She glanced at him and thought she detected a glimpse of a smile, but when she looked again his mouth had settled into its familiar grim lines, his jaw muscle bunching as he chewed.

Loretta took another tiny bite. Then a bigger one. The meat tasted so good; she couldn't swallow fast enough. Her stomach growled again, so loudly that Hunter glanced over. She averted her face and stopped chewing, reluctant to let him know she was actually enjoying something he had given her. The moment he looked away, she stuffed the remainder in her mouth.

When he finished his portion, he retrieved the other buffalo fur from where he had kicked it earlier and stretched out on his back beside her. Snapping his fingers, he pointed to the space next to him. Loretta curled up on her side, as close to the edge of the pallet as she could. She jumped when she felt his hand in her hair. When she realized that he had wrapped a length of it around his wrist, helpless rage welled within her.

Miserable, Loretta hugged herself to ward off the cold, too proud and too frightened to seek warmth with him under the fur. He sighed and yawned, draping a corner of the robe over her. Accidentally? Or on purpose? She couldn't be sure.

Heat radiated from his body and immediately began to warm her back. Loretta fought against the desire to inch closer and hugged herself more tightly. It really wasn't that cold tonight. It just felt that way because of her sunburn. Oh, but she was chilled. So chilled she felt sick — hot on the inside, shaking on the outside. When she closed her eyes, her head whirled. If only he would throw more wood on the fire.

Seconds slipped by, mounting into minutes, and still Loretta huddled in a shivering ball.

The Comanche lay motionless beside her. Warmth seeped from his body, beckoning to her. She cocked an ear, trying to tell by his breathing if he was awake.

She'd be crazy to move closer unless he was asleep. If he was, he'd never know, would he? And she could warm herself, stop shivering. He had to be asleep. Nobody could lie that still otherwise.

She wriggled her bottom over just a little way, then held her breath. He didn't move. For a long while she lay there listening, waiting. Nothing. She moved in another inch. He remained perfectly still. Loretta relaxed a little, taking care not to lean so close she touched him. In a few minutes she would grow warm and ease away, and he would be none the wiser.

With no warning, he rolled onto his side. He threw a heavy arm across her waist, splaying his broad hand on her midriff just below her breasts. With an ease that alarmed her, he pulled her snugly against him, scraping her sunburned thigh on the fur. His well-padded chest felt as warm as a fire against her back. He bent his knees so his thighs cradled hers. For several seconds Loretta held herself rigid, not sure what to expect next, imagining the worst.

He nuzzled her hair, his breath warm on her scalp. Was he asleep? She stared at the fire, her nerve endings leaping every time he inhaled and exhaled, every time his fingers flexed.

Slowly the heat from his body chased the chill from hers. Loretta's eyelids grew heavy. The wind whispering in the treetops seemed peaceful now, not frightening. The shifting shadows that had terrified her for hours became just that, shifting shadows.

A branch cracked somewhere in the darkness. A large animal of some kind, she guessed. It didn't matter. Wolf, bear, coyote, or cougar, Hunter the terrible was beside her. Nothing would dare challenge him.

Her thoughts drifted and grew blurred. Sadness washed over her when she remembered the horse. She relaxed and leaned against her captor. A soot-black blanket of exhaustion settled over her.

A fly buzzed around Loretta's face. Dimly she recognized the sound, aware that morning had come and that the Comanche lay beside her. In another part of her mind, that dark, shadowy part where nightmares lurked, the buzzing magnified and carried her back in time, to another muggy morning, to the loud buzzing of other flies, and to horror.

She was in the storm cellar. . . .

It was strangely quiet outside. The cow didn't low. The chickens didn't cluck. The pigs didn't grunt. Just a heavy silence, except for the flies buzzing. Maybe that was why they sounded so loud, because there wasn't any other noise. One thing was for sure, the Comanches were gone. No more yipping. No more laughter. Pa wouldn't care if she came out now, would he? Even though he hadn't come back yet, like he promised.

Loretta pressed her palm against the rough planks of the door and pushed. The hinges creaked, and sunlight spilled across her face, the brightness blinding. She stumbled up the steps and out into the yard. The wind picked up, fluttering some blue cloth that was lying on the ground a few feet away. Loretta didn't look at it.

Instead she walked to the house. Up onto the porch, through the door, into the kitchen. The bottoms of her shoes felt hot, but she didn't pay them any mind. It was long past time for chores. She hadn't done her milching, hadn't fed the pigs or chickens. Pa would be mighty perturbed if he woke up and found her loafing.

He *would* wake up. Here shortly. He and Ma both. She'd just go on about the chores as usual. And pretty soon they'd wake up. They had to.

The handle of the milch bucket blistered Loretta's palm as she picked it up and carried it out of the kitchen, across the yard to the barn. At first she didn't notice, so intent was she on her own thoughts; eventually, however, the pain began to nag at the edges of her mind, tugging her back to reality. Then she heard the flies. The buzzing was so loud that she slowed her steps and turned. *Flies.* They swarmed all around her, landing, biting through the cloth of her dress, crawling everywhere her skin wasn't covered.

Ten feet from her, the blue cloth still fluttered in the breeze, calling to her. Unnerved, she forced her gaze back to the house — only the house had been reduced to cinders. Smoke trailed skyward in feeble wisps from the crumbled remains.

A terrible smell assailed Loretta's nostrils. She knew its source. She wouldn't look down at the blue cloth. She would keep her eyes lifted to the sky, block it all out. It would go away if she pretended hard enough. It would! Ma said anything could come true if a body wished hard enough. And Loretta was wishing harder than she ever had. She had to. Otherwise this would all be real. And her parents would be — they would be —

Despite her determination not to look, Loretta lowered her gaze to the blue cloth. The ground seemed to tilt. She couldn't breathe. No. That was what she tried to scream. *No!*

Loretta jerked awake and clamped her hands over her ears. *Flies.* For several seconds she remained trapped in that frightening limbo between reality and nightmare. Then she felt a callused hand on her bare midriff, fingertips grazing her breast. *The Comanche.* Dream and reality melded. Flies, Indians, blood. She couldn't breathe. She jackknifed to a sitting position, trying to throw his arm off her, but it was under her shirt. And he still had hold of her hair. Panting, she struggled to free herself.

"You went to a dream place, eh?" His fingers tightened, curling like warm bands around her upper arms. His gaze delved into hers, searching, reading. She yearned to look away but couldn't. "A bad place, no?"

Loretta's neck felt brittle. She couldn't nod, didn't want to. He was curious about her dream, but even if she had been able to talk, she couldn't have explained. Wouldn't have tried.

At last he dropped his hands and looked up at the sun. "*Nei te-bitze utsa-e-tah,* I am sure enough hungry. We will make a walk to wash the sleep from our faces, eh? Then I will get meat to put over our fire."

He pushed to his feet. Not wanting him to touch her, Loretta scrambled to stand before he reached for her. The effort availed her naught. The instant she gained her footing, he gripped her elbow and pulled her along beside him. As they passed the main circle of campfires, Hunter yelled something. Several of the other men glanced up, replying in Comanche.

Tightening his grip on her arm, Hunter

steered her toward the river. "My cousin made a kill this morning. He has fresh meat. You are hungry, no?"

In truth Loretta wasn't, but she nodded, afraid of angering him. Still shaken by her nightmare, she found the weight of his hand on her arm revolting. For all she knew, he might have been present the day her mother died. His was an extraordinary face, but she had been in shock that day and didn't remember everything as she should.

She guessed him to be in his early thirties, plenty old enough to have gone on that raid and maybe hundreds before that. Comanche boys became warriors at an early age, some of them participating in their first bloodbath when they were no older than Amy.

There was a ringing sound in her ears. The world around them seemed unnaturally bright. She was disgusted with herself for meekly following the guidance of his hand. As they walked, small rocks and nettles cut into the soles of her feet. She fell back once, hopping on one leg while she tried to pluck a sticker from her toe. She didn't expect him to stop, but he did. After she had rid herself of the sticker and they continued on their way, he seemed to pick the path more carefully.

When they reached the river, he turned left. "*Tohobt Pah-e-hona,* Blue Water River. You call it the Brazos, eh?" He pointed ahead of them. "*Pah-gat-su,* upstream." Jabbing a thumb over his shoulder, he said, "*Te-naw,* downstream. You will listen good, Blue Eyes, and learn. *Tosi tivo* talk is dirt in my mouth."

His tone set Loretta off balance. Dirt in his mouth? If he hated the whites so much, why on earth had he taken her? Upstream, downstream, she couldn't remember the words. She didn't want to. The language of murderers. All she wanted was to be free of the whole filthy lot of them.

Another rock jabbed her insole, and she winced, missing a step. He released her elbow and swept her off her feet into his arms. He took her so much by surprise that if she could have screamed, she would have. Their eyes locked, his mocking, hers wide.

Though he now bore Loretta's weight, her position was such that her back was in danger of breaking if she didn't loop an arm around his neck. He stood there, looking down at her and waiting. Her mouth went dry. She wished he would just toss her over his shoulder again and be done with it. Being carried like a sack of grain wasn't very dignified, but at least that way she didn't have to cling to him.

That determined glint she was coming to know too well crept into his eyes. He gave her a little toss, not enough to drop her, but enough to give her a start. Instinctively she hooked an arm around his neck. His lips slanted into a satisfied grin, a grin that said as clearly as if he had spoken that he would have the last word, always. He started walking again.

The firm cords of muscle that ran down from his neck undulated beneath her fingers, his warm skin as smooth as fine-grained leather. His hair, silken and heavy, brushed against her knuckles. Beneath her wrist she could feel the crusty cut on his shoulder from Aunt Rachel's bullet. Remembering the wound he had inflicted on his arm last night, she wondered just how many scars he had. Strangely, the longer she was around him, the less she noticed the slash on his cheek. His was the kind of face that suffered imperfections well, features chiseled, skin weathered to a tough, burnished brown, as rugged as the sharp-cut canyons and endless plains from whence he'd sprung.

He carried her to an outcrop of flat rock along the river's edge, then set her gently on her feet. They stretched out side by side on the bed of stone. When Loretta splashed her face, the cool water felt heavenly on her sunburned skin. Determined to ignore the Comanche's unwelcome nearness and take advantage of the few concessions he allowed her, she pushed forward on the rock. Dunking her head, she worked her fingers through her hair to remove the twigs and dirt that had gotten in it when she'd fallen off the horse. After wringing the water from her long tresses as best she could, she sighed and cupped her palms in the swift current, taking a long drink. When she lowered her hands, her reflection shimmered up at her, pale and golden in contrast with the bronzed, dark-haired man next to her. Seeing herself beside him made the nightmarish situation she was in seem all the more real.

She turned to look at him, and at the same instant he looked at her. For several heart-beats they simply studied one another.

"Even the water sings our song." He sighed and rose to his knees, glancing back down at their shimmering images.

Loretta stood, too weary to make sense of things. His songs and his gods had nothing to do with her. He sprang to his feet, and once again she suffered his hand upon her arm as they walked back to camp.

Hunter's cousin was crouched by their burned-out fire skinning a rabbit when they returned. Instantly wary, Loretta went to sit on the pallet. Pretending indifference, she began working the tangles from her hair. Hunter joined the other man, conversing with him in Comanche while they finished preparing the meat and skewered it on a spit. After building a low fire, they drove the spit into the earth at an angle so the rabbit was suspended over the flames to roast slowly.

When they finished positioning the meat,

both men turned to regard her. From their tone of voice, she guessed they were arguing. She continued to finger-comb her wet hair, wishing she knew what they were saying, praying her trembling hands didn't betray her.

A bead of water trickled from her nape down her spine, as chilling as her thoughts. After cutting her loose last night, Hunter hadn't pulled the stakes. Did he plan to tie her again? Using her long hair as a veil, she sneaked a glance at him. He was looking at her. His cousin threw up his hands, kicked at the dirt, and strode away.

The ensuing silence made Loretta's nerves leap. A shadow fell across her, and she knew Hunter had moved to stand over her. After several endless seconds, she dared to lift her head. The anger no longer played upon his face. Indeed, he appeared amused. He hunkered down before her, his indigo eyes sharp and assessing.

Disconcerted and uncertain what to expect, Loretta stared at his stone medallion. He touched a nearly dry tendril of her hair and rubbed it between his fingers to test its texture. Then he grasped her chin. His thumb and fingertips tightened on each side of her mouth, pursing her lips. When she looked up he met her gaze, searching, not speaking, all trace of laughter gone.

The heavy, sweet smell of the dead rabbit

clung to him. Repulsed, she tried to pull away, but his hold on her was relentless. He feathered his thumb across the chafed surface of her extended bottom lip, his dark face so close that their breath mingled, hers quick and shallow, his slow and measured.

As difficult as it was to admit, she knew that a few more days as Hunter's captive would see her focused entirely on her survival. She could almost see herself — jumping to do his bidding, suffering his touch without complaint, groveling for mercy when he grew angry. If she let that happen, how would she ever face people back home if she somehow managed to escape?

Indeed, how would she face herself?

As if he sensed what she was thinking, his expression took on a note of mockery. Relinquishing his hold on her, he rocked back on his heels and lowered his gaze to rake her body with an insolent slowness that set her cheeks aflame.

She was a possession to him, something he felt free to fondle and look at — as he might a trinket he had traded for. When would he become unsatisfied with merely looking? Her sunburn was better, her fever nearly gone. If he had held off taking her because she was ill, time was running out.

After a moment he rose to his feet, crooked a finger at her, and said, *"Keemah."*

Loretta started to get up, then caught

herself. A hot lump formed in her throat. If she obeyed him so easily now, she would find it even easier the next time, and soon she'd be scurrying about like his chattel. Was that what she wanted — survival at any cost? *No.*

The denial scarcely took root before his hand clamped down on her left arm. The next instant she was jerked to her feet. After staggering to get her balance, she threw her head back and glared at him. His response was to yank her to his side.

"Do not test my temper, Blue Eyes. My horse lies dead because of you. It is not too late to punish you, eh? *Keemah,* come. You know the word."

His voice coiled around her like a noose, coarse and relentless, the words enunciated with such exaggerated slowness and clarity that she felt like a dog being trained to lead. When he pivoted and tried to pull her toward his pile of belongings, she dug her heels into the dirt. With a strength she hadn't dreamed even he possessed, he tightened his hold and drew her inexorably forward. She tried to pry his fingers loose, but they were like steel talons.

When they reached his leather bags, he released her and fished through his possessions until he found a drawstring pouch. After loosening the ties, he grabbed her hand and poured a measure of dried fruit and nuts onto her palm. For an instant Loretta felt ashamed for giving him so much trouble when he only wanted to feed her, but the emotion quickly fled.

As hungry as she was, her choices were few, and compliance was not among them. She had few avenues of escape. Braced for his reaction, she tipped her palm and spilled his offering onto the dirt. He could make her do a lot of things, but he couldn't make her eat.

CHAPTER 10

By the time the rabbit finished roasting, Hunter was at a loss as to how to handle his captive and was having doubts about the wisdom of not punishing her last night. She had thrown his food on the ground. When he offered her water, she had dumped it out. Sooner or later he would have no choice but to punish her.

When Red Buffalo and two of his friends ambled over to enjoy their portion of the rabbit Red Buffalo had killed, Hunter kept one eye on the girl, hoping she had the sense to behave herself. Red Buffalo smiled as he knelt by the fire. He had either forgotten their argument over the girl, or he was regrouping for another round.

"Smells good, Hunter," Red Buffalo said. "Who needs a woman, eh?"

"All wives do is nag." Arrow Maker, one of Red Buffalo's friends, leaned over to steal a bit of meat from the rabbit's leg. As thin as the weapons he tooled, Arrow Maker scarcely cast a shadow standing sideways and was more in need of a woman than any brave Hunter knew. "I'd rather sneak under lodge walls. Why tug a rope and see the same old hags every night?"

"Just be careful some jealous husband doesn't catch you." Hunter removed the rabbit from the spit, shaking one hand when the sizzling meat scorched his fingers. "I like the thought of having women in my lodge circle. The winters can seem very long without someone to warm your buffalo robes."

Red Buffalo studied the yellow-hair. "If *that's* why you want her, you're a fool. White females lie under you like a slab of rock."

Hunter placed the charred meat on a piece of hide. Throwing a glance at the yellow-hair, he shrugged. "Even stone can be tooled to serve a man's needs. Maybe with a good teacher, she will be passable."

Red Buffalo spat into the fire and sent the woman a smoldering glare. "You're too soft with her. What she needs is a firm hand. Give her to me for a few days. I will teach her."

Rising to his feet, Red Buffalo walked over to the pallet. Though Hunter remained bent over the meat, he was very much aware of the girl's fear. Red Buffalo grabbed her by the hair, forcing her head back.

In English he said, "We will have a good time together, eh, woman?" With a low laugh, he swept his palm down her front, giving her breast a cruel squeeze through the soft leather of Hunter's shirt. "While I teach you how to play our games?"

Still in a crouch, Hunter turned on the balls of his feet, his knife held loosely in one hand. If anyone was going to mistreat the girl, it was going to be him. "Let go of her."

"Let go?" Red Buffalo gave her hair a jerk. "Cousin, surely you would not challenge me over a stinking yellow-hair?"

The girl's eyes were huge with fright. She sat with her shoulders hunched, her arms hugging her breasts to protect them from further abuse, her neck crimped to ease the pull of Red Buffalo's hand on her hair. "If you want a yellow-hair to play with, Red Buffalo, go steal your own. That one belongs to me."

Red Buffalo's gaze dropped to the knife in Hunter's hand. "Is it a fight you seek? We have always shared everything."

"Not our women."

"She's a slave, not a woman."

"The woman of the prophecy."

"Ai-ee!" Ishatay, Coyote Dung, strode around the fire to stand between the two cousins. "Have you two been guzzling stupid water? Let go of her, Red Buffalo. She isn't worth it."

When Red Buffalo released the girl, he gave her a shove that sent her sprawling. Hunter shifted his gaze to her face and saw tears shimmering in her eyes — involuntary tears, he felt sure, from having her hair pulled so viciously. She was too proud to cry so easily otherwise. A knot formed in the pit of his stomach.

Striding back to the fire, Red Buffalo snarled, "Serve me my meal. I want to get away from here. The stench sickens my gut."

Remembering how Red Buffalo's hand had clamped on the girl's breast, Hunter began to shake. The reaction was so inexplicable that he could concentrate on little else as he sheathed his knife and picked up a piece of the rabbit. "Take your share and go eat someplace else."

"You choose her over me?"

Ignoring the question, Hunter walked over to the pallet to give the girl her portion. The moment he extended his hand to her, she struck out with her arm and sent the steaming chunk of rabbit flying. The plop it made hitting the dirt seemed to resound. Hunter glanced at the meat, then back at the girl, more than a little astounded.

"If you don't punish her for this, I will!" Red Buffalo roared.

Hunter heard his cousin come up behind him. The girl shrank back, her eyes huge as Red Buffalo's hand closed on her arm. Hunter grabbed Red Buffalo's wrist. "She's my woman. I will handle her."

"Like you did last night?"

With his temper already on the rise, Hunter's patience had worn as thin as the sinew on his hunting bow. He shoved Red Buffalo off balance and tensed to carry through with his fist. "I said I will handle her!"

Red Buffalo shrugged and retreated a step. "It *is* my meat she wasted."

"And she's *my* woman. Therefore it is my place to discipline her. Not yours."

Hunter grabbed the girl's wrist and hauled her to her feet. Turning toward a nearby log, he jerked her along behind him. She balked and tried to pry his fingers from her arm. Hunter gave her another jerk, in no mood for her obstinacy.

Just as he started to sit down on the log, she flung herself away from him. He almost lost his hold on her. Small though she was, she was quick and slippery with grease. During the ensuing struggle, she smacked him alongside the head with her elbow and made him see stars.

Bent on teaching her a lesson, Hunter forgot about her sunburn, about Red Buffalo and his friends, about everything. He dropped onto the log and yanked her across his lap. When his knees slammed into her belly, her air *whooshed* from her chest.

"You will learn not to fight me."

She arched her back, eyeing his left arm. He knew what she was thinking, and that made him even angrier. Grabbing her by the nape, he shoved her head back down before she could sink her teeth into him. Clamping his right leg over both of hers, he vised them between his thighs. She swung wildly with her fists, squirming and trying desperately to kick, but Hunter had her exactly the way he wanted her, in an unbreakable hold, bottom up.

"*Samos,* one!" he counted as his palm connected with her rump. "*Wahat,* two! *Pihet,* three!"

Red Buffalo and his friends drew closer, hooting with laughter. Punishment like this was unheard of in their village.

"*Ai-ee!*" Coyote Dung placed his hands on his hips and leaned forward at the waist. He took up the count with Hunter, and as the fourth blow fell, he yelled, "*Hi-er-oquet!*"

The girl's slender body jerked, so violently that Hunter winced. Why didn't she stop fighting? Never had he laid his hand on softer buttocks. He could imagine how the clap of his palm must sting. Yet still she pummeled his leg and struggled to escape?

He struck her again. "*Mau-vate!* That is five, Blue Eyes. Stop the fight, and I will stop the punishment."

Her answer was to sink her teeth into his thigh. Hunter roared and grabbed her by the hair to break her hold. Did she think he could allow this in front of the others? He slapped

197

her buttocks again. Leaning to one side so he could see her face, he hissed, "You will *not* fight me!"

For an instant, blue eyes, brilliant with hatred, pain, and stung pride, clashed with his. Then she spat. The spray hit Hunter full in the face. He executed the sixth blow with more force than any preceding it. Leaning to one side again, he looked into her swimming blue eyes and said, "You want to fight? Eh?" *Kerwhack!* "Fine. That is good. We will fight. You want to spit?" He slapped her rump. "Still want to spit? Eh?"

Judging by the number of voices Hunter heard around him, he knew they were drawing a crowd. He no longer cared. All that mattered was making the woman yield. No one had ever dared strike him in anger and live to repeat the mistake. Except this girl. She wouldn't tread the same path again. He would see to that.

Intent on thrashing her until she ceased defying him, Hunter lost count of the slaps he meted out. And still she fought, squirming, kicking, awkwardly striking his leg and side with her fists. Didn't she realize he couldn't give her quarter when the other men watched? Through the thin cloth of her breeches, the skin of her buttocks felt red hot. She was not going to yield, he realized.

Raising his arm for yet another blow, Hunter hesitated. Her slender body jerked and tensed in anticipation. A wave of aversion washed over him. He had fought and killed many men. In that, there was at least a sense of victory, even of honor when the foe was formidable. But in this? The victory, when and if it came, would be dust in his mouth. As if from a distance, he heard the laughter of his friends, their voices cheering him on.

With a grunt of disgust, Hunter shoved the girl off his lap. She tumbled to the dirt and came up on all fours, her golden hair a wild mass of curls around her sunburned and tear-streaked face, her blue eyes glittering with impotent fury. Though she was outflanked by an overwhelming number and had little strength with which to do battle, she refused to surrender. The sons she bore him would be fierce warriors. For the first time, Hunter wondered if the Great Ones had not smiled upon him.

More furious than hurt, Loretta clenched her fists and stared up at her captor. The laughter of the other men became a roar in her ears, and the sound of it made her humiliation complete. Quivering rage swept through her. She staggered to her feet. *Away.* That was all she could think. Away from Hunter.

Wheeling, she broke into a run. She didn't think beyond placing one foot before the other. Not about Hunter chasing her. Not about the other men who surrounded her.

When she slammed face-first into a solid chest and felt hands grabbing her arms, she blinked to see, then struck out. The next instant something hard connected with the side of her head, and lights exploded before her. She reeled and hit the dirt in a full-length sprawl, her vision eclipsed by starlit blackness.

She tried to rise to her knees. Her body felt as heavy and limp as wet rawhide. She could hear angry voices — rising, falling, fading in and out. Again she attempted to get up and couldn't. Someone seized her by the shoulders and turned her over. A weightless sensation buoyed her. She peered through the swirling folds of darkness, trying desperately to see who touched her. *Please, God, not Hunter's cousin.*

As Hunter scooped his yellow-hair, dazed and at last subdued, from the dirt, his foremost emotion was rage that Coyote Dung had dared to strike her. His second was fear that the other man's fist might have done serious damage.

Looking down into the girl's disoriented eyes, his guts wrenched. She was finally broken. Only moments ago that had been his aim. Now he wished she was spitting and kicking and biting again. These last few days his feelings had become as insubstantial and difficult to grasp as snowflakes. Maybe he was more like his brother, Warrior, than he believed.

Snarling at the other men to leave, Hunter carried the girl to the pallet and laid her down gently, kneeling beside her. "*Hah-ich-ka ein,* where are you, Blue Eyes?"

"Hunter, is she all right?"

Hunter glanced up to see his young friend, Swift Antelope, hovering over him. The boy's expression was filled with alarm.

"I think so. Leave us, eh, Swift Antelope? If she comes around and sees another strange face, it will frighten her."

Swift Antelope nodded and began backing up. "Is there anything I can do? Get you water or something?"

"No, just leave us."

"She is very brave, is she not? Like her sister."

Hunter nodded and motioned the boy away. The girl's long lashes swooped low, casting dark shadows on her cheeks, then lifted to unveil eyes far bluer than the prophecy foretold. Blue like the summer sky, yes, but far more brilliant. Her tears caught the sunlight and shimmered, reminding him of distant heat waves. The corners of her mouth quivered as she tried unsuccessfully to rise up on one elbow.

"You will be still," he ordered in a low voice.

She frowned and blinked up at him. Afraid of what his fingertips would discover, Hunter leaned forward and gently probed her jaw and temple. Though she winced, he couldn't detect any broken bones, no telling redness. Coyote Dung's fist must have connected with the side of her head. Her senses were rattled, but no serious damage had been done.

Relieved, Hunter smoothed glistening wisps of golden hair from her damp cheeks, fascinated by the way the tendrils, now freed from her braid, learned the shape of his fingers. The spirals of gold caught the sun and ignited, flashing silver fire. Not the color of parched grass, after all, but sunshine. His gaze shifted to her face, trailing slowly from her delicately etched brows to the upturned slope of her small, sunburned nose. Downy hair shone in the shallow cleft of her upper lip, along the hollows of her cheeks. He didn't know why, but suddenly he felt like smiling.

As Loretta's vision cleared, she stared up at the Comanche's harsh face, bewildered by the gentleness of his touch. She was confused even more by the concern she read in his eyes. Passing a hand over her row, she blinked again. That Indian must have knocked her plumb senseless. It was the only explanation. She had done everything she could to enrage Hunter, insulting him, defying him, biting him, spitting on him. Yet he had retaliated by only giving her a paddling and then this concerned look? Uncle Henry had whipped her much harder many a time and for far less.

Hunter ran his hand into her hair, skimming her scalp with warm, callused fingertips. When he touched a tender place, Loretta flinched but was too dazed to pull away.

"It is not wise to fight when you cannot win, Blue Eyes. I have said these words to you before, eh? You do not listen so good." As he rocked back on his heels, one corner of his mouth lifted in a wry smile. "When no one watches, you fight your big fight with this Comanche, eh? *Only* when no one watches. Or I must punish you, yes?" His smile faded. "With me, never with Coyote Dung." He thumped his chest. "*Che kas-kai,* a bad heart. You understand? He is *mocho-rook,* a cruel one."

Loretta's attention was drawn to the other Indians who had gathered in groups some distance away. With a shock, she realized how dire her fate might have been if any other than Hunter had been her captor. Her mind reeled. How many times had she heard Hunter spoken of with dread? Merciless, cunning, a menace to the frontier. Those were only a few of the things she had heard about him. Yet he was cautioning her to fight her battles with him so she wouldn't get hurt?

After giving her a few minutes to recover her equilibrium, he stood and strode the few steps back to the fire to get his portion of the rabbit. As he returned to the pallet, he pulled his knife and sliced the meat into halves, extending one piece to her. Loretta knew he must be hungry, and his portion hadn't been that large to begin with. After the way she had been behaving, she couldn't believe he would offer her more food. If their roles had been reversed, she would have let him starve and said good riddance. She pushed up on one elbow. He leaned over and shoved the meat closer.

"You will eat" — unmistakable laughter played upon his face — "so you will stay strong. We cannot fight the big fight if you tremble from hunger."

Loretta lowered her gaze. A rush of conflicting emotions assailed her. She detested this man. She shouldn't care if he didn't get enough to eat or feel in the least guilty for having wasted his stupid meat. Yet she did. And for the life of her, she couldn't accept part of his meager portion only to toss it away. She hated herself for that and hated him for eliciting such traitorous feelings within her.

When she didn't take the meat, he hunkered next to her. Why wouldn't he leave her be? She was so tired, so awfully, horribly tired. Tired of being afraid. Tired of fighting him. Tired of fighting herself.

"*Hein ein mah-su-ite,* what do you want?" he asked in a low voice. "The little rabbit is good. The *tosi tivo,* white men, eat rabbit, do they not?"

Loretta kept her face averted.

He sighed. "Blue Eyes, you will see into me, eh?" Because he was still holding the two pieces of meat, he didn't have a free hand and nudged her shoulder with his forearm. "*Nabone*, look."

For the first time, she detected a note of entreaty in his voice, scarcely recognizable under his martial arrogance, but there.

When she looked up, his eyes caught and held hers. After a long moment he said, "You are *to-ho-ba-ka,* the enemy. That is so, eh? *Tosi mah-ocu-ah,* a white woman? And I am the enemy to your people, a *Te-jas,* a Comanche." He held his arm out in front of him, his forearm waist high and horizontal, and made a writhing motion around to his side. "Snakes Who Come Back, eh?" His mouth tipped into a grin that transformed his face. For a moment he not only looked human, but handsome. "You like that, eh? Comanche and snakes, all the same?"

The grin set her off balance, and again she averted her face. He shoved a piece of the meat under her nose.

"The rabbit, he is not *to-ho-ba-ka,* the enemy. He is *tao-yo-cha,* a child of Mother Earth, eh? You can eat him. It is not surrender when we eat the gifts of Mother Earth."

The smell of the rabbit wafted up Loretta's nostrils and set her mouth to watering. Against her will, her gaze riveted on the pink, juicy meat. Hunger pains knotted her middle.

She felt her resolve slipping. What did she hope to prove, anyway? That she would fight to the dying end? Even if she did, who would know? She would, of course, but pride wouldn't fill her belly.

Hunter pressed the offering closer. "You will take him? He belongs to no one."

The smell was nearly too much to resist. But, wincing as her sore buttocks touched the pallet, she sat up and once again refused the meat. He grunted in disapproval and sat beside her on the fur. In the ensuing silence she could hear his jaw popping as he chewed. Nothing on God's earth had ever smelled as good as that rabbit.

"You will eat nuts and berries?"

Loretta shot him a look and then glanced toward his collection of leather bags, recalling the mixture he had poured onto her palm earlier. Pride rose like gorge in her throat.

"You will walk backward in your footprints, eh, and go forward again a different way? My *ner-be-ahr,* mother, gathered the berries and pecans. Warrior, my brother, found the honey tree. Gifts from Mother Earth, eh? Like the rabbit."

The smell of the meat wafted to her nose. She stared straight ahead. She couldn't afford to give in.

As if he sensed how fragile her willpower had become, Hunter pushed to his feet and went over to his bags to get the pouch and a gourd canteen. When he returned he loosened the drawstring and set the bag on the fur between them. After scooping out a handful of the fruit-nut mixture for himself, he gestured for her to do the same.

When she made no move to acquiesce, he said, "Hm, it is good, eh? You will take a little. It will not sicken your gut."

Tears welled in Loretta's eyes. Who had said the flesh was weak? Not true. Needs of the flesh dictated. The thirsty drank. The cold sought warmth. And the starving ate.

She could almost taste the bittersweet pecans filling her mouth. She wished she could devour everything in the bag. He offered her the canteen of water. She hesitated, then declined. She knew it wouldn't be long before he realized she didn't intend to eat or drink. Not this morning, not ever. There would be a showdown. She dreaded that. But there were some things even he couldn't force her to do.

While he finished his meal, Loretta consoled herself by hugging her knees, acutely aware that he watched her. A meadowlark warbled nearby, its clear voice ringing sweetly. She focused on the sound and tried to pretend the Comanche didn't exist. It was an impossible feat. Leaves above them danced in the sunlight, casting flickering splashes of gold upon the ground. She studied the patterns, wishing he would leave. Wishing she were someplace else. Anyplace else.

When she could bear his silent perusal no longer, Loretta forced herself to turn her head. His indigo eyes met hers, reflecting the shadows and sunlight, shifting, elusive, impossible to read. His features, carved in burnished copper, offered no clues. The wind caught his hair and draped it in dark wisps across his face, catching it in his long lashes, but still he studied her with an unblinking intensity. No trace of laughter showed in his expression, but she had the feeling he was amused by her.

Her heart leaped when he suddenly stood up. He went to his saddle packs to put away the food pouch. A moment later he returned with a long rope. With deft hands he looped one end of it into a slip knot and lowered the noose over her head.

As he shoved the knot snugly against her throat, he said, "We will make a walk."

Loretta cast a horrified look at the leash.

"You do not surrender so good, Blue Eyes. The tether is wisdom. No fighting the big fight in the bushes, no honey talk, no lies, no happy crows, and no dead ponies." He gave a light tug. "*Keemah,* come."

Loretta wondered if he would strangle her if she sat tight. Peering up at his harsh countenance, she found she didn't have the courage to find out. She pushed to her feet and walked meekly beside him toward the brush.

Except for closely guarded walks into the bushes, Loretta spent the remainder of the day sitting in the shade of the oak, under the constant supervision of her captor. She suffered his ministrations to her sunburn with hopeless passivity, the possibility of escape gone from her mind. He was unfailingly kind, which, instead of soothing her, served to increase her trepidation. He had to be toying with her. She didn't know what to expect of him from one moment to the next.

Along about dusk the monotony was broken by a thunder of horses' hooves. Another dozen warriors rode into camp, dismounting in a cloud of dust. Loretta watched them with detachment. Surrounded as she was by so many savages, a few more or less didn't make much difference to her. One rider had remained on his horse. She focused on him, then straightened, her pulse accelerating. *Tom Weaver?* She threw a startled glance at Hunter, who had been feeding the fire. After returning her regard a moment with those unreadable eyes of his, he strode to greet the newcomers.

A dozen questions sprang to Loretta's mind. Why hadn't Tom been killed? If those other Indians had been holding him prisoner all this time, where had they been keeping him? And why had they brought him here?

To kill him? She clasped her knees and dug her fingernails into her skin. She couldn't bear it if they tortured him in front of her. Yet what could she do to stop them? She couldn't even save herself.

After conversing with the other Indians, Hunter seized Tom's horse's bridle and led both horse and rider back to his camp. Loretta studied Tom. A livid bruise slashed his cheekbone above his beard. An angry red rope burn encircled his throat. His shirt was ripped at the shoulder, the edges of the rent soaked with blood. He looked terrified — a weak, quivery terror that she understood all too well.

Hunter cut Tom's feet free and hauled him off the horse. Tom staggered and nearly fell. Hunter steadied him, then steered him to the fire, where he pressed down on his shoulder to make him sit. Tom fastened his attention on Loretta.

"You okay, girl? Have they —"

Hunter thumped Tom low on the back with the inside of his moccasined foot. Tom bit off the words, his blue eyes searching hers. Loretta knew what he was wondering. She started to signal a reply, but Hunter watched her. Even though she knew Tom would think the worst, she bent her head. If she angered the Comanche, he might retaliate by harming Tom.

"You filthy, slimy bastards!" Tom cried.

Scarcely able to believe her ears, Loretta looked up just in time to see metal flash. Hunter pressed his knife to Tom's throat and crouched next to him. Words weren't necessary. One more sound out of Tom, and Hunter would kill him.

She rose to her knees. The sound she made, slight though it was, drew the Comanche's attention. She lifted her hands in silent supplication. The air thrummed with tension. Then, very slowly and deliberately, Hunter withdrew the knife from Tom's larynx and returned it to its sheath.

Relief sapped the strength from Loretta's limbs, and she sank back onto the pallet. Hunter tossed another piece of wood onto the fire, sending up a spray of live coals, a few of which fell in Tom's lap. Tom scrambled backward and tried to shake them off, no easy feat with his hands tied behind him. In the process he lost his balance and toppled sideways.

Hunter squatted by the fire and draped his arms over his knees, his gaze fixed on the feeble flames while Tom struggled to sit back up. The Comanche's eyes shone with that peculiar light Loretta was coming to recognize as laughter. After a long while he said, "When the sun rises, we will leave. You will be set free, old man."

Tom didn't look as if he believed that.

His eyes still glowing with that somber

amusement she hated so much, Hunter glanced at her. "I make no grief behind me."

The muscles along Tom's throat stood out as he struggled to speak. When he finally did, the words came out in a squeak. "And what about her?"

"She goes with me."

"I'll b-buy her from ya. R-rifles, I can get rifles. And cartridges."

There was no mistaking the interest that bit of information sparked in the Comanche. Loretta's heart soared with sudden hope. "You have rifles?"

"I — um, no. B-but I can git 'em."

Hunter studied Tom at length, then slid his gaze to Loretta.

"Please," Tom whispered. "There's other gals you can steal. Don't take this one. Let her go home to her family." Breaking off, he licked his lips. "She ain't done you no harm."

After a long while, Hunter returned his attention to the fire. "This Comanche does not sell his women. Not even for rifles. She goes with me."

"Why this girl?"

Hunter tossed a sliver of wood onto the flames. "Another will not do."

Silence fell over the three of them, as heavy as the darkness that soon descended. Loretta pressed her back to the tree and stared across the clearing. Hopelessness welled within her. Indians, everywhere she looked. Tom was as helpless against them as she. And every bit as scared. Seeing him quake in fear cemented her belief that the Comanches were not only treacherous, but impossible to escape. It would take an army to rescue them, and the army was off fighting the Northerners.

Tom was untied only long enough to partake of a meager meal of water and jerked meat. After the two men finished eating, Hunter hauled Tom to the tree where Loretta sat. Pulling his arms behind him to encircle the trunk, Hunter lashed the older man's wrists with rawhide. Loretta was left beside Tom while their captor banked the fire for the night.

"We'll only have a few seconds, girl, so listen close," Tom whispered with feverish urgency. "They be Quohadie, the fiercest and cruelest of the lot. He'll take ya to the Staked Plains. And once he gets ya there . . . well, you know what that means."

Loretta nodded. Few white men ventured into that country. Few dared. Once Hunter got her that far from civilization, there would be no hope of rescue. Not that there was now.

"Tomorrow when they set out, they'll probably kill me. If they don't, they'll leave me without my horse. We're too close to Belknap for them to risk me ridin' for help." He leaned against the oak and sighed. "I wish to God I had a gun."

Acid coated the back of Loretta's tongue.

She knew what he was thinking and threw a frightened look toward the fire to be certain Hunter wasn't listening.

Tom made a hollow little plunking sound as he swallowed. "He's bent on keepin' ya. Ain't no way in hell I'm gonna talk him outa it." A brief silence settled over them. "You know what ya got to do, girl."

Loretta couldn't bring herself to meet his gaze.

"He'll never let ya get near a weapon, so's you can do it quick. That don't figger in the games they like to play. Ya got no choice, girl. No choice at all. Goin' without food and water is yer only way out. You know how I hate sayin' this, but it's better than —" He heaved a sigh. "Out there on them plains in this kinda heat, you won't last more than three days without water, maybe even less. If I'm left alive, I'll try to get help rounded up and reach ya before —" He peered at her through the gloom. "You understand what I'm sayin', Loretta Jane?"

Hysterical laughter bubbled in Loretta's chest. Did Tom truly believe she was that stupid? That she hadn't already considered her pitiful options and taken action?

"You got no choice, girl. Don't think ya do. He's not treatin' ya too bad right now, but as God is my witness, he will. Just pray you go before they start in on ya." He swallowed again. "I don't know why he's held off.

Maybe he's takin' you back to his village for some kinda ceremony or somethin' — to his squaws. Or maybe he just fancies a wife with golden hair. Either way, believe me when I say dyin' of thirst will be kinder."

Loretta hugged herself. She understood. She understood all too well.

Moments later Hunter came back and jerked the furs out from under Tom's legs. With his usual arrogance, he motioned for Loretta to follow him and walked away into the shadows at the far side of the fire. A flush stole up her neck as she rose to go with him. Tom was watching. That made her sleeping with the Comanche seem all the more shameful. She didn't dare balk, though. Tom might pay with his life.

Hunter spread the pallet and motioned for her to lie next to him. Keeping her back to him, she stretched out on the fur, putting as much distance between them as the pallet allowed. She felt him wrapping a length of her hair around his wrist and intertwining it in his fingers. She prayed he wouldn't touch her — not in front of Tom.

There was no God in heaven. A heartbeat later, Hunter's steely arm encircled her waist, and his large hand splayed beneath her breasts. The fur abraded her sunburned thigh as he slid her toward him, but that sting was nothing compared to the degradation. What would Tom think? Loretta knew well what he'd think, and she couldn't blame him. But what choice did she have?

Chapter 11

Long before dawn, the Comanches broke camp and prepared to ride out. Despite Hunter's assurance to the contrary, Loretta expected Tom to be killed before they left. Once again Hunter surprised her. Relieved of his horse and boots, Tom would have to walk home — a goodly distance in bare feet, but he wasn't harmed. Loretta was even allowed to bid him good-bye. Hunter stood nearby, ever watchful.

Tears filled Tom's eyes, catching the first anemic rays of sunlight, as Loretta walked through the misty ground fog toward him. He touched her hair, then groaned and pulled her into his arms for a fierce hug. "Ah, Loretta, I'm so sorry. If I was half a man, I'd be able to do somethin'."

Loretta clung to Tom and wished she never had to let go. He smelled even worse than the Indians, but he was her only link to home, to the people she loved. She had never been so frightened.

"Remember what I said," Tom whispered. "No food or water."

Already weak with hunger and beginning to dehydrate, Loretta nodded, wondering why Tom hadn't noticed her abstinence. Fear, she guessed. It had a way of consuming a person.

"I'll try to come get you." His voice thickened, and his arms began to tremble around her. "I'll try my best."

Again she nodded, even though they both knew the odds were against his making it in time.

Hunter's voice cracked like a whip. "*Meadro*, let's go."

Loretta gave Tom's neck a final hug and eased herself out of his embrace. She tried to smile at him but couldn't. Hunter seized her by the arm and drew her toward Tom's horse, which was now outfitted in Comanche riding gear. When he lifted her onto the mare's back, she wondered if he would tie her on, as he had before, and received her answer when he mounted behind her, encircling her waist with one arm.

Loretta craned her neck to keep Tom in sight as Hunter nudged the mare forward into a trot. A knot of tears swelled at the base of her throat. This was it, her last contact with home.

"Do not look behind you, Blue Eyes," Hunter murmured. "We go to a new place, eh? It will be good."

Loretta doubted that.

The Comanches rode steadily northward, fording both the Clear and Salt Forks of the Brazos within five hours, passing so close to Fort Belknap on the upper fork that Loretta could scarcely believe their temerity. The country quickly broke into high plains after that, stretching forever with nothing but rolling hills to break the monotony of the horizon. Hunter frequently offered her water, but each time she refused.

From the sun's position, Loretta guessed it to be around noon when the Indians at last stopped to rest. Dizzy with exhaustion and thirst, she slid off the mare and stumbled. Hunter kept her from falling and led her to a spot of shade under a bush. The combined effects of her sunburn, the inadequate amounts of food and water over the last few days, and the heat were already taking a toll. She sat down and bowed her head, steeling herself for the moment when Hunter offered her more water.

"Blue Eyes, you will drink?"

Loretta waved him away. A long silence settled over them. Then Hunter grasped her chin and forced her to look at him.

"*Habbe we-ich-ket,* seeking death, it is not wisdom." He wedged the canteen between his knees and caught her hand, placing it on his muscular upper arm. "*Ein mah-heepicut,* it is yours. No harm will come to you walking in my footsteps. You will trust this Comanche, eh? It is a promise I make for you."

Loretta stared into his indigo eyes, aware of the leashed power beneath her fingertips. For an instant she believed he truly meant it, that he would protect her, always. Then her gaze shifted to the scar on his cheek, to his heathen medallion, to the images carved into the leather of his wristband. Half-breed or no, she couldn't trust this man.

He sighed and released her hand to take a long, slow drink, calculated, she was sure, to make her yearn for one herself. He wiped his mouth and said, "We will see, eh? It is a hard path to walk, going thirsty in the sun. You will yield."

With that, he corked the gourd and set it beside her in the shade so she could help herself if her willpower wavered. Rocking back on his heels, he ran a finger along her cheekbone. "I must protect you from the sun, eh? So you do not burn."

Scooping a handful of dirt, he mixed it with a little water from the canteen to make a mud paste. It felt wonderfully cool when he smoothed it on her face. After he finished he sat back and studied her again, his dark eyes gleaming with that silent laughter that irritated her so. She must look like a blue-eyed bugaboo with her face streaked brown and her hair flying every which way. Well, he was no prize, either.

Far too soon to suit Loretta, the rest period ended and they mounted up again. Above her the sun burned like an orange orb, searing her eyelids, leeching the precious stores of moisture from her body, until the hours seemed to spin by in a dizzying, torturous endlessness.

In the early evening the Comanches took another short break at the North Fork of the Little Wichita. After climbing off the horse, Loretta sank down at the edge of the stream to bathe the cracked mud from her face. The temptation was great to take one small sip of water, but she knew she mustn't.

When Hunter told her it was once again time to ride out, Loretta would have cried if there had been any extra moisture left in her body to wring out for tears. Her limbs ached. Her head swam. And she was weak. All she wanted was to sleep. How could they press onward like this? How could the horses?

Less than ten minutes after they left the stream, Loretta began to nod and felt herself slumping. She jerked upright and blinked. Hunter tightened his arm around her and slipped a hand under her right knee to lift her leg over the horse's head. Gathering her against his chest, he cradled her crosswise in front of him.

"Sleep, *nei mah-tao-yo,* sleep."

His deep voice sifted through the exhaustion that clouded her mind. *Nei mah-tao-yo.* She had no idea what it meant, but it sounded so soft the way he said it — like an endearment. The hollow of his shoulder made a perfect resting place. She leaned into him, her cheek against his warm skin. He smelled of sage, smoke, and leather, earthy smells that were becoming familiar and somehow comforting. As she drifted into blackness, she no longer thought of him as an Indian, just a man. A wonderfully sturdy man who could hold her comfortably while she slept.

Dreams haunted her. Silly, stupid dreams, about Amy, Aunt Rachel, Tom Weaver. Wonderful dreams. Dancing with Amy by the well. Running through a field of red-gold daisies. Sitting at the table with Rachel and studying the fashions in a year-old *Godey's Lady's Book* that Uncle Henry had picked up in Jacksboro.

Then once again, she was standing out on the porch in the moonlight to bid Tom goodbye. She knew he meant to kiss her and braced herself. His whiskers and wet lips touched her mouth.

Then, inexplicably, the dream altered, and the mouth that claimed hers changed to wet silk, the pressure firm but somehow gentle. Heavy folds of dark hair brushed her cheeks, forming a curtain around her. She pressed a hand against the warm planes of a man's well-muscled chest and became aware that strong arms held her. Wonderfully strong arms.

"*Mah-tao-yo,*" a deep voice whispered.

Loretta focused on the dark face above her, realizing with a shock that dream and reality had blended. The wet silk on her lips was Hunter's fingertips, wet with water from the canteen. The curtains of heavy hair that brushed her cheeks were real, as were the muscled chest and arms. She stiffened.

"We have reached the *Oo-e-ta,* the Big Wichita," he told her in a low voice. "We will rest here. You will be awake now, eh?"

She straightened and cast a disoriented look around her. The shadows of stunted trees surrounded her, brushed silver with moonlight. The rushing sound of water told her they were near the river. Crickets and frogs serenaded, a gentle, pleasant cacophony that rose from the banks and rode lightly on the breeze. A medley of scents assailed her, summer grass and prairie blossoms, their perfume so sweet that she felt drunk from it. As she tipped her head back to breathe it in, wooziness overcame her. She clutched the mare's mane to get her balance.

Hunter dismounted and reached up to lift her from the horse. As his large hands encircled her waist, Loretta stared down at him, her senses still spinning. The Big Wichita was a good seventy-five miles from her home. She couldn't believe they had ridden so far. Even if Tom rounded up help and tried to follow, he would never catch up with the Comanches before they reached the Staked Plains.

Hunter swung her to the ground. Her legs nearly buckled, and she staggered. He caught her arm, leading both her and the horse to a level spot near the stream. She sat on a smooth rock while he pulled his packs off the mare and unsaddled her. Before he led the horse down to the river for a drink, he spread the buffalo robes for Loretta to lie down, but she was too exhausted to walk. Instead she slid off her perch onto the dirt and hugged the sun-warmed rock like a lover, resting her cheek against its smooth surface.

A fitful sleep overtook her. A short time later she heard footsteps nearby. Hunter, she guessed. She tried to open her eyes, wondering why he hadn't brought the horse back with him. Through the fringe of her lashes, she saw moccasins, bare legs. Not Hunter? Exhaustion weighted her eyelids, drew them closed. What difference did it make? One Indian, a dozen, as long as they let her be, she didn't care what they did.

When Loretta awoke to the crackling of a fire, she had no idea how long she had slept. More than likely a few minutes, but it could have been hours. Golden light fell across the small clearing, flickering on the bushes, throwing eerie shadows. The smell of burning mesquite wafted to her nostrils. Hunter crouched over the flames, coaxing them to burn more hotly by shifting the wood and blowing on the coals. When Loretta sat up, he glanced over at her.

"You did not like the robes?"

Her gaze slid to the pallet he had made for her. It lay in a mussed heap, as if she had lifted the furs and tossed them down carelessly. A prickle of unease ran up her spine as Hunter walked to the pallet and grasped the furs to straighten them. If neither of them had touched the bedding, then who had? A fleeting memory of moccasins and bare legs flashed through her mind.

As Hunter lifted the top fur, Loretta glimpsed something beneath it. Her breath caught. A huge rattlesnake lay coiled on the pallet, hidden from the Comanche's view by the other buffalo robe. As yet, the rattler hadn't buzzed a warning. Hunter didn't realize the snake was there. Loretta shot to her knees, her throat constricting.

In that fraction of an instant, it seemed that the Indian and the snake moved as slowly as cold honey dripping off a spoon. She reached toward her captor, her attention fixed on his wrist, on the bulging vein that ribboned his arm. A venomous bite so close to the heart might be fatal. She saw the snake lift its head, its fangs gleaming in the bright firelight. There was no time to think. Instinct took over.

"Snake!" she screamed. "Snake!"

Hunter reacted to her cry, not leaping away as she might have, but instantly offensive. Using the robe he held as a shield, he deflected the rattler's first strike and then lashed out with his other hand, catching it behind the head before it could recoil and strike again. The snake writhed and hissed as Hunter lifted it from the pallet. For a moment he held it aloft. Then he looked at Loretta. After what seemed an eternity, he pulled his knife, beheaded the rattler, and tossed it into the brush.

Loretta knelt in the dirt, clutching her throat. *Snake.* The word bounced off the walls of her mind, shrill, echoing and reechoing. She had screamed. . . .

Disbelief swamped her. Surely her ears had deceived her. She couldn't have screamed, she just couldn't, not after seven years of silence. And *never* to save a Comanche.

Sheathing his knife, Hunter walked toward her hesitantly. Loretta stared at him — at his long hair, his fringed moccasins, his buckskin pants, his medallion, the gods on his wristband. A *Comanche.*

She felt as if her insides were shattering into a million shards, slicing her apart. Visions of her parents flashed through her head, her mother lying in a pool of dried blood, her eye sockets and mouth crawling with black flies, her father tied to a tree, his body mutilated beyond recognition and obscenely rearranged in death. Those memories were burned into her mind, never to be forgotten, never. She couldn't have betrayed her parents like this. She couldn't have. . . .

"N-no," she croaked. "No."

Hunter knelt on one knee in front of her. As she stared at him, he became a blurred mass of muscle, heathen gods, and stinking leather. A suffocating, claustrophobic feeling hit her. Before he could grasp her shoulders, she swung blindly, clipping his cheek with her fist, the memories rising within her like bile. "Don't touch me! Don't *touch* me!"

Tightening his jaw against the pain that shot along his cheekbone, Hunter grasped the girl's shoulders. Even with nothing but firelight to illuminate her face, he could see the shock in her expression, the ache of betrayal in her eyes, her suffering all the more acute because she had betrayed herself. To save someone she hated . . .

Sobbing, she struck out at him again, then again, until she was pummeling his face, her own twisted with hysteria. She had saved his life. Hunter flinched but made no move to stop her or to defend himself. Her eyes had a glazed, unseeing look in them, and her sobs spoke of grief trapped within her for far too long. He knew it wasn't really him she was striking out at, but herself.

At last he drew her against his chest, and

she clung to him as if he were about to throw her off a cliff. He wondered if that wouldn't be kinder. "You're a murderer," she sobbed. "I hate you, don't you understand? I *hate* you!"

He tightened his arms around her, awash in painful memories of his own. She *didn't* hate him, not anymore. That was why she cried. The blood of her people called out to her for vengeance, as his did to him. And her heart had turned traitor. "*Toquet,* it is well."

"No!" she wailed. "My parents . . . oh, God, my parents. You killed them — butchered them." He ran a hand up her spine. Beneath his palm, she quivered. "You k-killed them."

"No, no, I did not. It is a promise I make for you, Blue Eyes. I did not kill them."

Beyond the light of their fire, Hunter saw shadows shifting. He lifted his head. Several of the other men, drawn by her screams, stood outside his camp. He recognized Swift Antelope and Warrior, thought he saw Old Man. Red Buffalo and his friends lurked off to the left, almost indiscernible in the darkness. Hunter waved them away. The girl had enough to contend with.

He understood how she felt, better than she knew. Oh, yes, he understood. . . .

Sweeping her into his arms, he carried her to the pallet. The moment he laid her down, she huddled in a ball, great sobs shaking her shoulders. Hunter knelt beside her. How could he comfort her when he couldn't comfort himself? They were sworn enemies, but somehow their hatred had become lost in the weave of their emotions like a single thread in cloth.

She buried her face in the crook of her arm. The sound of her weeping made him feel sick. He rose and walked slowly around the pallet, searching the ground for telltale footprints. *Nothing.* Had the snake slithered into his buffalo robes on its own? And if it hadn't, who had put it there? Someone who hated the yellow-hair. Someone who had hoped she would climb into the bed without looking. Hunter sighed and lifted a weary gaze to scan the darkness. Suspicion gnawed at him. The snake *could* have gotten into the bedding on its own, after all. It wouldn't be the first time such a thing had happened.

Hunter lay down on the pallet and pulled the girl into the curve of his body. She huddled with her back to him, shivering and sobbing. He wrapped a length of her silken hair around his wrist and covered her with the fur.

"Don't touch me. Please, don't. I can't bear it."

Her voice cut into him. He released her and rolled onto his back to study the starlit sky, wondering about her mother, her father, the horrors she must have seen. He was no stranger to the atrocities committed during raids. True, he had made a pact with himself to make war only on men, but he had ridden with hundreds of braves who had no such compunction.

After a long while the girl's sobbing subsided, and her breathing became slow, measured. In her sleep she scooted her rump toward him, seeking warmth.

He rolled onto his side and curled an arm around her. Slipping his hand under the shirt she wore, he pressed his palm against her feverish midriff and traced the ladder of her ribs with his fingertips. She was as soft as a pelt of ermine. He could feel the rhythmic thump of her heart, the warmth of her just beneath her skin. He closed his eyes. Her voice rang in his mind, as clear as a morning bird's. *I hate you, don't you understand? I hate you.*

When the sun rose, she would have even more reason to hate him. If she didn't drink soon, she would die. He couldn't allow her to go another day without water. Hunter took a deep breath and let it out slowly. Where was his anger? His hatred? He wasn't sure when it had happened or how, but the small woman beside him was no longer his captive; he had become hers.

Loretta was awake long before the first pink shafts of sunlight streaked the horizon. She lay on her back with the Comanche's arm

230

flung across her. His large hand cupped her breast, the warmth of his palm seeping through the leather of her shirt. His shirt. She didn't try to move. What difference did it make? Today, a week from now, sooner or later he would take her.

The dry lining of her throat protested when she tried to swallow, but even so, there was a different feeling down inside her, an alive feeling. She could scream if she wanted. The realization frightened her; she didn't know why.

The Comanche stirred beside her. She concentrated on the sky, her senses numbed to him and anything he might do. Death loomed before her, beckoning, peaceful. In heaven there wouldn't be any Indians. It wouldn't be heaven if there were.

Hunter sat up and swept back his hair. Smoke from one or two fires already drifted on the air. The morning was cool and crisp. He settled his gaze on the steel-blue horizon, relieved he was no longer hemmed in by trees and undergrowth. Out here a man could see his enemy coming.

Stretching, he glanced over his shoulder. The girl's eyes had a hollow look, and she seemed unaware of him. He passed a hand before her and was relieved when her gaze sharpened. He pushed to his feet. The others were beginning to stir. If he planned to get any water down her, he had to begin.

After fetching the canteen, he approached her. "You will drink, Blue Eyes?"

She gave her head a shake. Her sunburn was beginning to heal, and without the flush she was pale. Soon all the dead skin would be gone.

"You must drink."

Her voice came out in a hoarse whisper. "No."

Hunter dropped to his knees beside her. He didn't want to do this. . . . Laying the canteen on the fur, he launched himself at her. Before she realized what he planned to do, he seized both her wrists and straddled her waist.

"Wha— Let me go!" she croaked.

She bucked beneath him, but he had the advantage of weight. When she tried to knee him in the back, he remembered the night the cowardly White Eyes had attacked her in the wagon. He pinned her arms beneath his knees, hating himself for hurting her.

"You will drink." Picking up the canteen, he uncorked it and leaned forward. "My way or yours?"

She thrashed, trying to avoid his hand. "I — no!"

Grasping her chin, Hunter dug his fingertips and thumb into her cheeks. When at last her jaws parted, he held the canteen over her yawning mouth and began trickling water down her.

To his surprise, she went perfectly still. By breathing carefully through her nose, she was able to let him fill her mouth without swallowing. The excess water sluiced out onto her cheeks and ran into her hair. Hunter couldn't plug the canteen and lay it down, not without turning her loose. And if he turned her loose, she'd spit out the water.

"Warrior!" he yelled.

Several fires away, Warrior shot up from his bed. After looking around in befuddlement, he spied Hunter and broke into a run. Within seconds he was standing by the pallet, his sleepy brown eyes riveted on the yellow-hair.

"*Tah-mah,* what are you trying to do, drown her?"

"Yes. Squeeze her nose."

"What?"

"Do it!"

Warrior knelt at her head. "Hunter, are you —"

"Do I have to call Swift Antelope?"

Warrior pinched the girl's nose. "If she dies, it is your doing."

"She isn't going to die. I'm trying to make her drink." Hunter watched the girl's face turn red from lack of air. After a few seconds the muscles in her throat became distended. Then, at last, she swallowed part of the water and began to choke. "Turn loose. *Warrior,* turn loose!"

Warrior, who always seemed to be one

thought behind everyone else, finally released her nose and sat back on his heels. The girl gasped and sucked water the wrong way. Grimly, Hunter watched while she fought to get her breath.

When at last she stopped coughing, he said, "You will drink?"

Her eyes glittered up at him, so filled with hatred that a chill ran up his spine. Hunter grasped her chin again. "Her nose, Warrior. And this time, turn loose when she starts to swallow or we *will* drown her."

"*You* will drown her. I'm just helping."

The process was repeated. When she had stopped choking the second time, Hunter once again offered her the chance to drink on her own. She refused. Two swallows of water were not enough, and Hunter knew it.

By the time the tenth swallow had been accomplished, Hunter dripped sweat, Warrior looked sick, and the girl was limp with exhaustion. Yet still she fought. Hunter's admiration for her grew. She had great courage — Comanche heart, his people called it.

Hunter hoped ten swallows would suffice. He would stop midmorning and make her drink more. The thought made his guts clench. She would fight him again. And again. Perhaps when they reached his village and she saw that he would not allow the people there to harm her, she would give up. His mother, Woman with Many Robes, had a gentle, loving hand. If anyone could reassure the girl and bring her around, it would be her.

If he could get the yellow-hair there in time.

Echoing his thoughts, Warrior said, "She'll die if she won't drink. Half of what you poured into her got spit out."

"She isn't going to die," Hunter hissed. "I won't let her. I'll make her drink often. What I get down her will be enough."

A troubled frown pleated Warrior's brow. "Hunter, what if she isn't the woman of the prophecy? Have you thought of that? She doesn't seem to like you very well."

"She's the woman of the prophecy. I'm sure of it." Hunter lifted his knees off her arms and pushed to his feet. "She will stop fighting soon. No one can fight forever."

"How can you be sure? That she's the right woman, I mean?"

Hunter capped the canteen. "I know, that's all."

The girl rolled onto her side and hugged her belly. Warrior studied her, his expression unreadable. "We will have to ride hard if you want to get her home alive."

"Yes." Hunter sighed. "Go tell the others, eh?"

It seemed to Hunter that time became measured by the steady and ceaseless clop of his horse's hooves on the marbled earth. The sun hovered endlessly in one place, a burning circle that gilded the azure sky with silver. The girl rode cradled in his arms, her head lolling on his shoulder, her hands curled limply in her lap. As still as death. . . . He wanted to spur his horse forward so they could reach their resting place on the South Fork of the Pease River more quickly. This time he would make sure she drank enough that he wouldn't fear for her life.

Warrior rode to Hunter's right, Swift Antelope to his left. They seemed to sense his mood and spoke infrequently. Hunter didn't encourage conversation. Doubts tortured him. Should he turn back? What did the Great Ones expect of him? Would the girl die if he pressed onward? And if he took her home to her people, what then? What of the prophecy? What of his people?

As if he heard Hunter's thoughts, Warrior moved his pony closer and said, "You must trust the Great Ones, *tah-mah*. If you are certain she is the woman of the prophecy, then all will be well. The song cannot come to pass if she dies."

Hunter tucked in his chin to study the girl's mud-streaked face and found himself wondering how he ever could have thought her ugly. Could a shaft of sunlight be ugly? A sparkle of moonlight upon water? "I'm certain, Warrior. She is the woman. Already, part of the prophecy has come to pass, eh? Her voice has been returned to her."

"And she has stolen your Comanche heart, has she not?"

"She has great courage for one so small, but my heart is my own. As it will always be." Warrior leaned sideways to peer over Hunter's shoulder at the yellow-hair's face, his own creasing in a grin. "Yes, there is something about her, is there not? The mud, I think. It does something for her."

Hunter smiled in spite of himself. "She looks like She Who Shakes got ahold of her. Remember when Ki-was, Rascal, let her make his war paint?"

Warrior chuckled. "The time she mixed it too thin? The three red stripes on his chin dripped, and he rode into battle looking like a People Eater. Yes, I remember."

Hunter flexed his tense back, letting the sound of Warrior's laughter soothe him.

"She sleeps like a baby, Hunter. That's a good sign, no? She must be starting to trust you. She'll begin eating and drinking soon."

"She's just exhausted and weak from thirst. Too weary to be frightened. Or to give me trouble."

Warrior sighed. "We will stop soon. I'll help you get some water down her, eh? She will be all right."

Swift Antelope nudged his pony into a gallop and, hooking a leg through the strap on his surcingle, slid sideways to ride horizontal along the animal's belly so he could snatch

237

up a clump of snakeweed. After righting himself, he waved his prize in the air, yipping shrilly at Warrior.

Hunter smiled again. "Go show our young friend how to ride, eh? He grows bored."

"You need company right now."

"I am fine. Go."

A plume of dust rose behind Warrior's pony as he rode off to race with Swift Antelope. Hunter chuckled when his brother flipped sideways to ride beneath his horse's belly. Swift Antelope took up the challenge and did likewise, touching his sagging rump to the ground only once. Hunter could remember a time when the boy had been dragged while riding that way, one foot hung up in a sur-cingle strap. Now it wouldn't be long before he could accurately shoot his bow from that position.

Not to be bested, Warrior launched himself out of the saddle to stand on his horse's back while at full gallop. Soon, several other braves joined in the competition, the stunts becoming more difficult as the number of partici-pants grew. High-pitched voices echoed and reechoed over the rolling grassland.

Hunter felt the girl stir and glanced down to see that her eyes were open. The yipping and hollering had disturbed her. As if she felt his gaze, she looked up, her expression quiz-zical. He wondered how long it would take before she became accustomed to speaking.

"They play, no? There are no trees to hide the *toho-ba-ka,* the enemy. Our hearts are glad."

She cast a dubious frown at the men.

Hunter reached for his canteen. "You will drink?"

"No," she whispered.

Hunter uncapped the gourd and pressed it upon her. "You must drink, Blue Eyes."

"No."

Hunter retied the canteen strap to his surcingle, swallowing down a surge of anger. "You will not die. This Comanche has spoken it. It will be for nothing, this suffering."

She leaned her head against his shoulder and closed her eyes. Hunter tightened his hand on the reins, frustration and fear building within him. Last night she had saved his life. How could he watch while she ended hers?

When the Comanches reached a river, their play came to a halt. They forded the stream to travel along the rocky bank of a northward fork. Somewhat revived by the water she had been forced to consume, Loretta sat astride the mare, suffering the confines of Hunter's arm around her waist and the familiarity of his hand on her midriff. His broad chest served as a prop for her back; soon she leaned against him, letting her body undulate with his in rhythm with the horse's gait.

After about forty minutes of silence, he

bent his head close to hers. "*Mah-tao-yo.* My arm is strong, no?" He hugged her close to demonstrate. "A strong arm to lean upon, a shield against all that might harm you? You will trust this Comanche. Drink and eat. It is a good place where we go."

Loretta made a fist in the leather of her shirt and squeezed until her knuckles hurt. She didn't want to die. It would be so easy, so horribly easy, to believe him.

"You will be warm with me in my lodge? I have many buffalo robes. And plenty food. Meat, yes? And my strong arm will protect you, forever into the horizon. There is nothing to fear." He pressed his hand more firmly against her midriff. "My tongue does not make lies. It is the truth I speak, not *penende taquoip,* the honey talk, but a promise. I have spoken the words, and they are carried away on the wind to whisper to me always. You will trust? When I go away from you on raids and hunting trips, my brother's strong arm will be yours. No harm will come to you."

Loretta swallowed. His brother? The man who had helped pour water down her, she guessed. The one he called Warrior.

"You can seek death another time. *Te-bit-ze,* sure enough. But first, you will see what lies on the horizon. It is wisdom."

"I want —" Tension and disuse strung her voice so taut, it twanged like a harp cord. "I want to go home."

"That cannot be. You go with me — to a new place. You are my woman, eh? You have said it, I have said it. *Suvate,* it is finished."

"I'm *not* your woman," she cried. "You stole me from my family."

"I traded many fine horses."

"You bought me, then. And that's just as —" Loretta craned her neck and stared up at his carved features. "I'm a *person,* not a thing."

"The white men have slaves, and this is okay, yes? Your Gray Coats fight the great fight so you can own black men. Is this not so? This Comanche has a slave, too. It is good."

"No! It's not good. It's monstrous." She passed a hand over her eyes. "I'll die before I let you touch me. You hear me?"

"Ah, but Blue Eyes, I touch you now." He slid his hand up her ribs and gently cupped her breast. "You see? I touch you, and you do not die. There is nothing to fear."

He braced his arm against her and kept his hand firmly in place. For several seconds he held her thus. "This is what you fear? The touching?" Incredulity rang in his voice. "This is why you will not drink?"

Loretta shifted, trying to escape his hold, still clutching his wrist.

"You will answer this Comanche." He feathered his thumb across the leather, a coercive tactic she couldn't ignore, teasing her nipple into a prickly erection that made her breath catch. "You seek death to escape my hand?"

A sob caught crosswise in her throat. "Please . . . please, don't."

He bent his head so his lips feathered against her ear. "For this you fight the big fight? Blue Eyes . . ." His voice trailed off, as if he couldn't think what to say. Then he withdrew his palm from her breast and returned it to her ribs. "My touch has brought you no pain. I heap no shame upon you. I cannot see into you and understand. You will make a picture for me, no?"

A picture? The picture in Loretta's head was too horrible to draw with words. "Do you think I don't know what you monsters do to white women? I know! My mother — I —" She swallowed. "Your strong arm! Mine to lean upon until it turns against me."

His lips trailed to her temple, lingered there, his breath a warm mist in her hair. For a long while he was silent, and then he said, "My arm is yours to lean upon for always. Until snow comes to your hair, eh? For always, until I am dust in the wind."

He sounded so sincere. "I won't listen to this, I won't. Do you think I'm so stupid you can trick me with — with honey talk?"

"I make no tricks." His arm clamped tight. "I have no need, eh? If my heart talks murder,

I do it. If I want to play games with my woman, I play them. I need no tricks. I want, I take. It is a very simple thing."

Warrior rode up beside them, filling the air with dust. Loretta shifted her gaze to the scalps on his bridle, to a telltale strip of calico cloth tied to his surcingle. Helpless tears filled her eyes.

Chapter 12

The remainder of the trip was a blur to Loretta — stopping for the night, riding endlessly through the sun, fighting futile battles with Hunter to keep from drinking. With each hour her pride slipped further from her grasp and her hopelessness grew. *I am your wind. Bend or break. I want, I take.* His image hovered before her constantly, arrogant, powerful, and relentless. Her only consolation was that eventually she would slip away from him into the velvety blackness of slumber, never to awaken.

By the time they reached his village, Loretta had lost all sense of time and was uncertain how many days had passed. In her more lucid moments she was certain they traveled in circles, laying false trails. Late one afternoon they ascended a plateau overlooking a river valley, the rolling meadows that paralleled the stream a vibrant green, an occasional cactus or red yucca dots of color. Along the riverbanks, lofty cottonwoods swayed in the breeze, their silvered trunks and dappled leaves a camouflage for the countless lodges erected among them. Not the Staked Plains? With bitter disappointment, Loretta realized that her captor had not only made far better time than most white men would, but he had gone in a different direction than Tom had expected, foiling any attempt to follow him.

She stared down at the village through heavy-lidded eyes. She had no idea what river this was and didn't care. The village was here; that was all that mattered. And there were more Comanches in one place than she had ever seen. Hunter vised his arm around her waist, anchoring her to his solid chest. Bending toward her, he whispered, "Do not fear, *mah-tao-yo*. I am beside you, eh?"

The other Indians threw back their heads and gave long, shrill cries, like deranged coyotes baying at the moon. Within seconds hundreds of voices from below returned the call, and antlike figures scurried to and fro between the conical houses. Hunter urged the mare forward, leaning to distribute their weight as the horse plunged down the steep decline. Fear shot up Loretta's spine. The moment she dreaded had arrived.

The other horses hurried toward the village like cows toward oats. Tom Weaver's mare, less enthusiastic, ambled along, her ears cocked and flickering at the odd noises rising in the air. Given a moment's respite, Loretta watched the people swarming forward to greet the returning warriors, her heart racing as she imagined those same bodies swarming toward her. The yipping and laughter and garbled words ricocheted off the trees around her.

The men made a pass through camp, riding the paths between the lodges, greeting everyone. A gaggle of dirty, half-naked children trailed behind them, chortling happily. In the excitement two shaggy dogs got into a fight and, during the tussle, nearly knocked over a meat rack. A short, slender woman in a buckskin shift took after them with a stick.

Loretta had never seen so much confusion. People were emerging from the brush arbors in front of their tepees, waving and laughing. Squaws who had been cooking pulled their pots off the fires as they hurried out to greet their sons, brothers, husbands, and lovers.

Everywhere Loretta looked, she was reminded of where she was. Fur pallets were arranged around the low-burning fires. Garishly painted war shields perched on tripods outside most of the lodges. Tin pots dangled from spits. Buffalo stomachs distended with water hung on racks. A white woman's nightmare, a Comanche village.

Hunter rode straight into the swarm, his arm clamped around Loretta's waist, his body tensed. As throngs of people pressed in on his horse, she felt his broad shoulders hunch forward, as if to shield her. Sexless faces swam before her, a blur of brown, all hostile and evil. Hands shot out. Cruel fingers grabbed at her bloomers, pinching skin as well as cloth. Panting with horror, she shrank against her captor.

"*Ob-be mah-e-vah,* get out of the way!" Hunter snarled. With a sweep of one arm, he drove back several bodies. "*Kiss! Mah-ocu-ah, kiss!* Stop, woman, stop!"

Pain exploded on Loretta's scalp. A scream tore from her throat as she was jerked sideways. A woman had seized a handful of her hair and seemed determined to keep it. With a roar, Hunter rocked back and planted a foot on the woman's chest, sending her sprawling into the crowd. Some of Loretta's hair went with her.

Then Loretta heard a husky feminine voice booming above the din. The throng of bodies parted to admit a tall, plump woman. She brandished a long, wooden spoon above her, thumping an occasional head as she passed, her brown eyes snapping with anger. When she reached Hunter's side, she stood with her feet spread, arms akimbo, her attention riveted on Loretta. The chaos around her began to settle like stirred dust.

Loretta sensed that something momentous was about to happen, and that it had to do with her. She stared down at the woman, afraid to move, unable to swallow. The squaw's classic features struck a chord within her, familiar in some indefinable way. Thick braids rode her broad shoulders, strands of silver threaded through ebony. She was beautiful, yet not, her face too chiseled and arrogant to be entirely feminine. The shapeless buckskin dress she wore clung to the solid planes of her figure, revealing that hers was a generously rounded but well-shaped body. And her eyes . . . Direct, piercing, oddly familiar, they sized Loretta up and seemed to find her wanting. How many times had Hunter studied her just this way?

Realization slowly dawned. The chiseled features, the full, beautifully defined lips, the strong chin and proud bearing. Her captor's mother.

The woman met her son's gaze and smiled. Shifting her attention back to Loretta, she said, *"Ein mah-suite mah-ri-ich-ket?"*

"My mother, Woman with Many Robes, asks if you want to eat?"

Loretta gave an emphatic shake of her head, pressing closer to his chest. In a toss-up, she chose to stay with Hunter. He leaned forward so he could look into her eyes. "You will not be afraid. My mother will crack heads. Your good friend, eh? You will trust."

Loretta scanned the wall of leather-clad bodies and, for the first time, hugged her captor's arm more closely around her. The dark depths of his eyes shifted, warming on hers. A ghost of a smile flitted across his harsh mouth, and his fingertips tightened their hold on her ribs. Looking up, he said something in Comanche.

The woman nodded and turned to shoo the onlookers out of the way, her spoon tapping a hollow tattoo on slow-moving heads. Hunter chuckled, his chest vibrating against Loretta's shoulder blades as he steered the mare along the path his mother cleared. The crowd formed walls on each side of them, hanging back only when Hunter drew up before a lodge. When he began to dismount, Loretta clutched his wrist, terrified he might abandon her.

"Yo-oh-hobt pa-pi! Yo-oh-hobt pa-pi!" a small girl cried, dancing around the mare's legs, her button eyes gleaming, her plump brown bottom jiggling so hard that she was about to lose her breechcloth. *"Ein mah-heepicut?"*

Hunter pried Loretta's frantic fingers from his arm and slid off the horse. Smiling at the child, he leaned over and retied her breechcloth thong. *"Huh,* yes." Glancing up at Loretta, he said, "She is a yellow-hair, and she is mine."

The child looked fit to bust and ran to Hunter's mother. *"Kaku,* Grandmother! *Yo-oh-hobt pa-pi,* a yellow-hair! *Hah-ich-ka po-mea,* where is she going?"

Hunter lifted Loretta from the horse and into his arms, stooping to shoulder his way into the lodge. His mother and niece hovered behind him as he took measure of the room and headed toward a raised bed at the rear. Layers of fur, soft as eiderdown, sank beneath Loretta when he laid her down.

The opening to the lodge darkened as people pressed close to peer inside. Weakness and exhaustion clouded Loretta's thinking and made focusing difficult. She blinked and tried to sit up, afraid Hunter would leave her. If he did, those bodies would rush in and converge on her.

He placed a heavy hand on her shoulder. "You will be still." Turning toward the door, he yelled, "*Mea*, go!" Loretta jumped with every inflection of his voice.

The child bounded onto the bed, landing on all fours, her round face wreathed in a smile. *"Hein nei nan-ne-i-cut?"*

"What is your name?" Hunter translated, tousling the imp's hair as he hunkered beside the bed. "Loh-rhett-ah, eh? *Tohobt Nabituh,* Blue Eyes." To Loretta, he said, "Warrior's daughter, *To-oh Hoos-cho,* Blackbird."

Blackbird giggled and glanced at her grandmother, who stood watching from across the room. "Loh-rhett-ah!"

Loretta scooted toward the head of the bed to press her back against the taut leather wall. The little girl followed, reaching out with a small brown hand to lightly touch the flounces on Loretta's bloomers. Loretta stared at her. At last, a Comanche she didn't detest on sight. She was tempted to grab hold of her and never let go. Loretta guessed her to be about three years old, possibly four.

While Blackbird satisfied her curiosity about Loretta and examined her from head to toe, Hunter carried on an unintelligible conversation with his mother. From the gestures he made, Loretta guessed he was relating that his captive refused to eat or drink and that her voice had returned. A look of concern flashed across the older woman's dark face. Hunter rose and thumped the heel of his hand against his forehead, rolling his eyes toward the smoke hole above the firepit.

"Ai-ee!" Woman with Many Robes crossed the packed grass-and-dirt floor and leaned forward to peer at Loretta. After babbling shrilly for several seconds, all the while waving her spoon, she crooned, *"Nei mi-pe mah-tao-yo,"* and placed a gentle hand on Loretta's hair.

"My mother says the poor little one must have no fear."

Woman with Many Robes cast her son a suspicious glance. When it became apparent that he planned to say no more, she brandished her spoon at him.

With great reluctance he cleared his throat, eyed the people crowding the doorway, and said, in a very low voice, "You will have no fear of me, eh? If I lift my hand against you, I will be a *caum-mom-se,* a bald head, and she will thump me with her spoon." He hesitated and looked as if he found it difficult not to smile. "She will make the great *na-ba-dah-kah,* battle, with me. And in the end, she will win. She is one mean woman."

Woman with Many Robes stroked Loretta's hair and nodded, saying something more. She no sooner finished than Blackbird burst into giggles and rolled away from Loretta, planting a hand on her tummy. Whatever it was the woman had said, the child thought it hilarious.

"You must eat," Hunter translated. "And drink. Soon you will feel better, eh? And she will trade with the Comanchero for you a big spoon. If I ever again strike fear into your heart, you can do your own thumping."

Loretta concurred with Blackbird. She'd need much more than a spoon to do battle with Hunter. She planted the heel of her hand on the bed to hold herself upright. Her spine felt as if it had turned to water.

As if he realized that Blackbird wasn't aiding him in his cause, Hunter snatched the child off the bed and tucked her under one arm. He carried her to the door of the lodge and set her gently on her feet, shooing her outside and jerking down the lodge flap so the others couldn't see inside. Blackbird poked her ebony head back in and cried, "*Kianceta*, weasel!"

Hunter snarled and lunged at her. His unexpected ferocity startled Loretta, but Blackbird swung on the leather flap like a baby opossum, giggling and screeching, completely unintimidated. Her uncle pried her loose and, with a pat on her plump bottom, sent her away. Silence settled inside the lodge. An uncomfortable silence.

Loretta cast a dubious glance around the room, expecting . . . well, she wasn't sure what, but heathenish things, surely, bloody scalps and war paraphernalia, not furs and stacks of parfleche, cooking pots and spoons, or a clothing rod. Beautifully crafted buckskin shirts hung on its pegs, along with breeches and breechcloths. All male clothing. This must be Hunter's lodge, she decided, not his mother's.

"*Ein mah-suite mah-ri-ich-ket, Tohobt Nabituh?*" Woman with Many Robes asked.

Hunter turned from the lodge entrance. "You will eat? My mother will bring you very good food, eh?"

Loretta drew up her knees and hugged them. Beyond the leather walls voices rang out, the language foreign and frightening. Woman with Many Robes seemed kind, but Loretta couldn't forget the women outside who had attacked her, nor the fact that Hunter considered her his chattel. She shook her head, so weary she wanted to sink into the furs and go to sleep.

Hunter's expression clouded. His mother looked distressed. They conversed back and forth, then Woman with Many Robes exited the lodge. A decision had been reached, and Loretta had the feeling she wasn't going to like it. Hunter secured the bearskin flap so no one would enter and then walked slowly toward the bed, his gaze leveled on hers, his arms folded loosely across his broad chest.

After studying her until she wanted to ooze under the furs and hide, he sat beside her. "I will force you to drink and eat, and you will not die. All this suffering. Only to surrender in the end? It is *boisa*." He reached out and lightly rested his hand on her hair. "You will eat, eh, Blue Eyes? A little bit?"

"No."

A muscle along his jaw tightened. His eyes gave hers no quarter. "You cannot escape me. You are here. That is the way of it."

Glancing toward the door and the horrors she knew lay beyond, she whispered, "I have no choice."

"You choose where you place your feet, Blue Eyes. This path you walk is bad — very bad. This Comanche will show you, eh?" He leaned closer. "You will learn that my hand upon you is not a terrible thing."

Loretta's eyes widened. "N-not now?"

His fingers curled in her hair, making a

loose fist. "You will not eat. You fear my touch. You would die first. Your words, eh?"

Loretta's senses started to swim. She blinked to clear her vision. She tried to shrug his hand away. "Even if I ate and you let me be tonight, you wouldn't the next, or the next." Heat crept up her neck. "And — after you, all your friends. Do you think I'm so stupid?"

He had abandoned his grip on her hair to trace the too generous neckline of his hunting shirt, his fingertip burning a trail along her collarbone, up the slope of her shoulder, along her throat. She closed her eyes, too weak to shove him away.

"No friends, Blue Eyes. You belong to this Comanche."

"I'll fight you — until I draw my last breath." She swayed and righted herself. "Why bother with me? Why not find yourself an Indian woman?"

"It is you I want." He brushed his knuckles along the hollow of her cheek. "Your skin is moonlight. I am dark like night next to you." He slid his hand behind her neck and drew her toward him. "Sunshine in your hair, moonlight on your skin, this Comanche's bright one, no?"

"No," she replied in a raw voice.

"You will eat?"

"No."

He bent to taste the flesh at the hollow of

her throat, his lips silken, his teeth nipping lightly, his warm, moist mouth sending jolts through her. "Like ermine, *mah-tao-yo*. So soft. And sweet like flowers."

She wedged her fists between them, her knuckles knotted against the warm, solid planes of his chest. As she opened her eyes, the room spun. "Please — please, don't. I'm not even sure what your real name is. Please don't."

"Hunter," he whispered next to her ear. "Hunter of the Wolf, Habbe Esa. Lie on your back, Blue Eyes. You are weak, eh? Lie on your back and close your eyes. Let me chase your fear away. With nothing to fear, there is no need to die, eh?"

"No." She tried to push him away. "No."

He slipped an arm under her knees and drew her down the bed onto her back. She propped herself up on her elbows, trying to evade his lips as they nibbled their way down her neck to her collarbone. And lower. Panic welled within her. She couldn't fight him. Not when she trembled like this. Not when the world tipped sideways. He slid the tip of his tongue under the leather to trace wet circles on her chest — just above her breasts. Her nipples sprang taut, sensitized to the soft leather that grazed them when she moved.

Never before had Loretta actually felt the blood drain from her face; she did now. Sucking in a draft of air, she tried to twist sideways, but his arm, roped with muscle and tensed against her, blocked her escape. As she shifted position, his lips found her ear and, in unison with his teeth and tongue, learned its texture, its taste, its shape, discovering with unerring accuracy the sensitive places. His warm breath made chills run over her.

"Habbe . . ." Her voice trailed off. She wanted desperately to distract him, but instead it was she who couldn't seem to concentrate. "Your name, wha— what was it? Habbe what? What does it mean?"

"Habbe Esa, Road to the Wolf, Hunter of the Wolf. My brother the wolf showed his face in my name dream."

"Y-your name dream?" She wriggled away and shoved the heel of her hand against his chin so she could sit up. "Wh-what's a name dream?"

His eyes gleamed down at her as he drew back his head. "A dream a man seeks when he becomes a warrior. In the dream, he learns his name. A woman has no need. She is named by others."

He dipped his head and captured her thumb between his teeth. Mesmerized, Loretta felt his tongue flick across her knuckle. Dear God, she was going to faint. And while she was unconscious, he would — he would . . . She felt herself tip sideways. His arm caught her from falling.

He released her thumb. "Blue Eyes?"

Loretta licked her bottom lip, trying desperately to right herself, to stay conscious. She couldn't pass out — she just couldn't. His face blurred. And his voice seemed distant.

"*Hah-ich-ka ein,* where are you, Blue Eyes?"

Loretta blinked, but it did no good. Was this how it felt to die? All floaty and distant from everything? *Hah-ich-ka ein,* where are you, Blue Eyes? She tried to answer. Couldn't.

Meat broth? In heaven there were supposed to be angel wings, glorious songs of praise, streets lined in gold, and fluffy pink clouds. Loretta swallowed and surfaced to consciousness, becoming aware by degrees. A large hand clamped her jaw. Something warm and thick trickled into her mouth. Voices rang in her ears. She strained to escape the hand that held her. She mustn't eat. Bits of meat caught on the back of her tongue. Her throat convulsed. And then she strangled.

Someone held her head while her stomach purged itself. Hard hands. A damp cloth skimmed her face. A voice called to her. A very deep voice. Loretta spun away into darkness.

"If I don't take her back to her wooden walls, she will die." Hunter met his father's steady gaze across the leaping flames. "Then what will become of the prophecy? She emptied her belly of the meat broth and precious water as well. She will sure enough die if this continues."

Soat Tuh-huh-yet, Many Horses, drew on his pipe and blew smoke toward the peak of the lodge, then toward the ground. After taking another drag, he exhaled east, west, north, and south. The pipe then passed from his right hand to Hunter, who inhaled slowly and returned the pipe to his father with his right hand to make a full circle, never to be broken.

"My *tua,* you have only just arrived. Give her some time."

"She'll be dead in a day or two." Hunter spat a fleck of tobacco. Though he would never admit it, he detested the taste of his father's pipe. "I have tried everything, Father. I've been kind to her. I've promised my strong arm will be hers forever into the horizon, until I am dust in the wind. And I've tried bargaining with her."

"What bargains?"

Hunter shot a wary glance toward the shadows, where his mother sat listening. "After my mother left the lodge, I said that perhaps I would be a tired Comanche when the moon rose if she were to eat and drink."

"And if she didn't, and you were not tired?" Many Horses' dark eyes filled with laughter. He too shot a glance into the shadows. "The bargain did not please her?"

Hunter shook his head.

"Perhaps she is not the right woman," Many Horses said softly.

"She is the woman. I am certain of that."

"Has a spirit voice come to you during a dream?"

"No, my father." Studying the flames, Hunter grew thoughtful. "No man has a more abiding hatred for the *tosi tivo* than I. You know this is so. My heart burned with anger when I went to collect the yellow-hair. I wanted to kill her."

Woman with Many Robes leaned forward, her features dancing in the firelight. Hunter met her gaze. She was a woman with much wisdom. She observed the customs and seldom interrupted when men were speaking, but on those occasions when she did, only a stupid man ignored what she had to say.

He waited to see if she meant to share her thoughts. When she remained silent, he cleared his throat, which was afire from the pipe, and continued. "Now, I would not kill her. She has touched me. My hatred for her has gone the way of the wind. She saved my life." He quickly related the tale about the rattlesnake and how she had broken her silence to warn him.

"You would prefer that she live for always away from you?"

Hunter's guts contracted. In that instant he realized how much he wanted the woman beside him. "I would prefer that my eyes never again fall upon her than to see her die." His mouth twisted. "She has great heart for one so small. She makes war with nothing, and wins."

Many Horses nodded. "*Huh,* yes, Warrior and Swift Antelope have already told me."

"I would take my woman back to her land," Hunter said. "I know the words of the prophecy, eh? And I would not displease the Great Ones, but I see no other path I might walk."

Hunter's mother rose to her knees. "My husband, I request permission to speak."

Many Horses squinted into the shadows. "Then do it, woman."

She moved forward into the light, her brown eyes fathomless in the flickering amber. "I would but sing part of the song, so we might hear the words and listen." She tipped her head back and clasped her hands before her. In a singsong voice, she recited, " 'When his hatred for the White Eyes is hot like the summer sun and cold like the winter snow, there will come to him a gentle maiden from *tosi tivo* land.' "

"Yes, wife, I know the words," Many Horses said impatiently.

"But do you listen?" Woman with Many Robes fixed her all-seeing gaze on her eldest son. "Hunter, she did not come to you, as

261

the prophecy foretold. You took her by force."

"*Pia,* what is it you're saying? That she would have come freely?" A breath of laughter escaped Hunter's lips. "The little blue-eyes? Never."

His mother held up a hand. "I say she would have, and that she shall. You must take her to her wooden walls. The Great Ones will lead her in a circle back to you."

Hunter glanced at his father. Many Horses set his pipe aside and gazed for a long while into the flames. "Your mother may be right. Perhaps we have acted wrongly, sending you to fetch her. Perhaps it was meant for her to come of her own free will."

Hunter swallowed back an argument. Though he didn't believe his little blue-eyes would ever return to Comancheria freely, his parents had agreed that he should take her home, and that was enough. "What will lead her back to me, *pia?*"

Woman with Many Robes smiled. "Fate, Hunter. It guides our footsteps. It will guide hers."

Loretta snuggled deeply into silken furs, trying to escape the persistent hand that shook her shoulder and the voice that called to her. Not her name, anyway. *Blue Eyes.* What kind of name was that?

"Blue Eyes, you will be awake now. Home . . . you wish for home?"

262

Home. Amy and Aunt Rachel. The gray down quilt. Pork slab and eggs for breakfast. Coffee on the porch when the sun peeked over the horizon and streaked the sky with crimson. *Home.* To laughter and love and safety. Oh, yes, she wished for home.

"Be awake, little one. This Comanche will take you back. Loh-rhett-ah? Wake up, Hoos-cho Soh-nips, Bird Bones, you must eat and grow strong so you can go home. To your people and your wooden walls."

Loretta opened her eyes. She rolled onto her back and blinked. A dark face swam above her. Funny, but blinking didn't bring him into focus. She reached out, curious, then thought better of it.

"You will make the honey talk with me? We will make a treaty between us, one with no *tiv-ope,* writing. You will eat and grow strong, and I will take you to your people."

Honey talk. All lies, according to Hunter. Loretta peered up. She ran her tongue across her lips and tried to swallow. "H-home?" she croaked.

"*Huh,* yes, Blue Eyes. Home. But you must eat so you can live to go back. And drink. For three days. Until you are strong again." His fingertips grazed her cheek and trailed lightly into her hair. "Then this Comanche will take you."

"You will?" she rasped.

"It is a promise I make. You will eat and drink?"

Loretta closed her eyes. She had to be dreaming. But oh, what a lovely dream it was. To go home. To have Hunter volunteer to take her there. No need to worry that his wrath would rain upon her family. "No tricks. You swear it?"

"No tricks."

His voice echoed and reechoed inside her head, loud, then like a whisper. She fought to open her eyes. The darkness was surrounding her again. "Then I will eat."

Meat broth. Hunter cradled her in one arm and held a steaming cup to her lips. Loretta filled her mouth. Her throat refused to work. She rested her head against her captor's shoulder, then with great concentration managed to swallow. The broth hit her belly, resting there like a lead ball.

"No more. Sick, I'm going to be sick."

"One more," he urged. "Then you will sleep."

Loretta tried to focus. The rim of the cup pressed against her lips. She took another mouthful of broth and forced herself to swallow it. Then she felt herself floating down onto the furs. *Sleep.* Strong hands moved her about and covered her with a heavy robe. Strong hands, gentle hands.

"Home . . . you will take me?"

"*Huh,* yes, bright one. I will take you."

Loretta drifted. He would take her. It was only a dream, after all. She could trust his promises in dreams.

CHAPTER 13

Loretta woke slowly, disturbed by a sound that reminded her of hens clucking. The chicken coop? When she rolled onto her side and struggled to open her eyes, she felt fur against her cheek. Memory came spinning back, a confusing blur of images. The village, Woman with Many Robes thumping heads with a spoon, Hunter nibbling her neck. And then blackness. In the far reaches of her mind, she recalled someone waking her several times to pour broth and water down her.

The clucking sound seemed closer now and slowly became recognizable as husky giggles. With a jolt, Loretta came fully awake. She opened her eyes to find Blackbird's impish face hovering inches above her own. The next instant she realized the little girl was not alone. Two other children, a boy of about five and a girl of perhaps two, were on the bed as well, their button eyes wide with curiosity.

Loretta raised up on an elbow. She no

longer felt woozy, just horribly weak. Wary of the shadows, she shot a quick glance around the lodge but saw no adults. Children, no matter what their race, weren't particularly intimidating.

The little boy touched his dust-streaked hand to Loretta's hair and made a breathless "ooh" sound. He smelled like any little boy who had been hard at play, a bit sweaty yet somehow sweet, with the definite odor of dog and horse clinging to him. Blackbird concentrated on Loretta's blue eyes, staring into them with unflinching intensity. The younger girl ran reverent fingertips over the flounces on Loretta's bloomers, saying, *"Tosi wannup,"* over and over again.

Loretta couldn't help but smile. She was as strange to them as they were to her. She longed to gather them close and never let go. Friendly faces and human warmth. Their giggles made her long for home.

With a throat that responded none too well to the messages from her brain, Loretta murmured, "Hello." The sound of her own voice seemed unreal — an echo from the past.

"Hi, hites." Blackbird linked her chubby forefingers in an unmistakable sign of friendship. *"Hah-ich-ka sooe ein conic?"*

Loretta had no idea what the child had asked until Blackbird steepled her fingers.

"Oh — my house?" Loretta cupped a hand over her brow as if she were squinting into the distance. "Very far away."

Blackbird's eyes sparkled with delight, and she burst into a long chain of gibberish, chortling and waving her hands. Loretta watched her, fascinated by the glow of happiness in her eyes, the innocence in her small face. She had always imagined Comanches, young and old, with blood dripping from their fingers.

A deep voice came from behind her. "She asks how long you will eat and keep warm with us."

Startled, Loretta glanced over her shoulder to find Hunter reclining on a pallet of furs. Because he lay so low to the floor, she hadn't seen him the first time she'd looked. Propping himself up on one elbow, he listened to his niece chatter for a moment. His eyes caught the light coming through the lodge door, glistening, fathomless.

"You will tell her, *'Pihet tabbe.'* "

Trust didn't come easily to Loretta. "What does that mean?"

A smile teased the corners of his mouth. "*Pihet,* three. *Tabbe,* the sun. Three suns. It was our bargain."

Relieved that she hadn't dreamed his promise to take her home, Loretta repeated *"pihet tabbe"* to Blackbird. The little girl looked crestfallen and took Loretta's hand. *"Ka,"* she cried. *"Ein mea mon-ach."*

"*Ka,* no. You are going a long way," Hunter

translated, pushing to his feet as he spoke. "I think she likes you." He came to the bed and, with an indulgent smile, shooed the children away as Aunt Rachel shooed chickens. "Poke Wy-ar-pee-cha, Pony Girl," he said as he scooped the unintimidated toddler off the furs and set her on the floor. His hand lingered a moment on her hair, a loving gesture that struck Loretta as totally out of character for a Comanche warrior. The fragile child, his rugged strength. The two formed a fascinating contrast. "She is from my sister who is dead." Nodding toward the boy, he added, "Wakare-ee, Turtle, from Warrior."

Loretta didn't want the children to leave her alone with their uncle. She gazed after them as they ran out the lodge door. The sound of their laughter floated outside with them. Sensing Hunter's eyes on her, she swallowed, trying to organize her thoughts. Though he had treated her kindly during their journey and had been extremely patient with her, she couldn't forget his veiled threats upon their arrival here.

"Wh-where are your children?"

For an instant she thought she glimpsed pain in his expression. Then he smiled. "They play *Nanipka,* hiding behind the hill."

"Then you — have no children?"

"No." He bent over a neat pile of parfleche and leather boxes, the braid of muscle in his arm flexing and knotting with his every movement. "My woman was killed *mau-vate taum,* five years, ago. Our child was within her."

"Oh . . ." Loretta dropped her chin to gaze at her lap and twisted a length of the buckskin fringe on her shirt around her finger. "I — I'm so sorry."

He glanced over at her, his brow pleated in an inquisitive frown. Sensing his bewilderment, she looked up. "That is . . . very sad."

His frown deepened, but the confusion in his expression disappeared. "*Huh,* yes, very sad."

"How was she killed?" She whispered the question hesitantly, not sure he'd answer but feeling a need to know.

"It is a memory on the wind." After rummaging a moment in a parfleche, he withdrew a drawstring pouch. Returning to the bed, he sat beside her, his manner carefully nonchalant, as if he were trying to put her at ease. "Berries and nuts. You will let a little bit food say *hi, hites* to your belly, eh?"

Hi, hites. Loretta recognized the words as those Blackbird had said as she linked her forefingers in the sign of friendship. "Hello?"

"Yes. It says in Comanche, 'How are you, my friend?' "

He set the pouch between them on the fur, the top spread wide so she could help herself. Loretta stared down at the honey-glazed pecans and dried berries. Last night, when she had agreed to eat and drink, she had been

270

too ill and exhausted to think clearly. In the light of day, despite what he had said a few moments ago, it seemed entirely too likely that he might have been lying to her about taking her home.

She took quick measure of her strange surroundings. His war shield sat on a tripod nearby, the feathers that lined its circular edge fluttering in the breeze that came in through the lodge door. She could hear a multitude of voices coming from outside, the words garbled and foreign. His power over her was absolute. He could keep her here forever if he wished. Or kill her on a whim.

"Hunter of the Wolf, did you mean —"

"Hunter, if your tongue grows weary."

She licked her lips. "Hunter . . . did you mean what you said? About taking me home?"

"I have spoken it."

She studied his dark features, searching for some clue to his thoughts. *I have spoken it.* No inflection in his voice, his expression unreadable. What kind of answer was that? "I — I know what you said, but did you *mean* it?"

His mouth thinned. "I have spoken it."

She hugged her knees, deducing by the edge to his voice that he disliked having his word questioned. "I —" She dug her fingernails into her palms. "I want to go home very badly."

Loretta fixed her gaze on her captor's medallion. All around her, the smell of his world permeated her senses, leather, dust, smoke, and unidentifiable foods. She was probably out of her mind to trust him. But, oh, how she wanted to. *Home.* To Aunt Rachel and Amy. It was a fact that he hadn't lied to her — except for the time he had promised to cut out her tongue and hadn't. She couldn't very well hold that against him.

She scooped up a handful of nuts and berries, taking a small amount into her mouth. The sweet taste of honey washed over her tongue, activating her salivary glands. Her stomach growled in response. He heard the sound and cocked an eyebrow.

"It is good?"

"Mm," she said, taking another bite and brushing her palm clean on her bloomers. "Delicious."

"Dee-lish-us?"

For the space of a heartbeat she forgot to be afraid of him, and a smile spread across her lips before she realized it was coming. When he smiled back at her, the strangest feeling swept over her, an inexplicable warmth. He had smiled at her before, of course, but never like this.

"Delicious," she repeated. "That means *very* good, much better than just good."

His smile didn't fade, and she found herself fascinated. On a civilized man, that lopsided grin of his could have been heart-stopping. His sharply defined lips lifted lazily at one corner to reveal gleaming white teeth, deep creases bracketing his mouth. Not the face of a killer, surely.

The mood shattered when he reached out to touch her cheek. The sudden movement made her recoil, reminding her of who he was and what he was. That he considered her his property. Because she jerked away, he settled for capturing a lock of her hair, twining it through his fingers.

"You are dee-lish-us. Like sunshine, eh?"

Unnerved by the gleam that had stolen into his eyes, Loretta caught hold of his hand to disentangle it from her hair. Just because there were no scalps in his lodge didn't mean he was above taking one if the mood struck. "Only things you can *taste* are delicious."

The moment the words passed her lips, she recalled how he had nibbled at her neck. Heat crept up her nape. As if he guessed her thoughts, his gaze dropped to her throat. She found herself longing for her homespun dress with its mutton sleeves and high neckline.

Mischief danced in his eyes. Or was it a trick of the light? "This Comanche is not a Tonkowa, a People Eater."

"Tonkowa *eat* people?" Last year there had been a number of Tonkowa up at Fort Belknap. Loretta had seen several during a visit there. They had been friendly Indians and seemed harmless. They'd even volunteered their scouting services to the border patrol, helping to track Comanches. She had been within touching distance of cannibals? "Mercy," she whispered.

He thumped the heel of his hand against his forehead. "No mercy. They eat brave enemies to steal their courage. It is sure enough *boisa*. They are *to-ho-ba-ka*, enemy, to the People."

He rose from the bed and fetched the canteen. She drank the water he poured for her, then returned the cup to him with a satisfied murmur.

"You will drink more?"

"No, thank you."

She felt suddenly tired and wished he would leave so she could sleep. Instead he stoppered the canteen and sat back down on the bed. She drew up her knees and stared at him. He stared back. The silence grew heavy, and so did her eyelids.

"You grow weary," he said softly, bending forward to drop the canteen and cup onto the dirt floor. "You will lie on your back, eh?"

The thought struck her that he might lie down beside her, as he had during their journey. "No, no, I'm fine — really."

He clasped her ankle. The heat of his grip shot up her leg. Her breath caught at the familiarity. As accustomed to his touch as she had become, she didn't like it or easily accept it. At home a woman didn't even show her ankles, let alone allow a man to touch them. And this man touched her anywhere he chose, with no hesitation. He tugged lightly.

"You will lie on your back. No harm, eh? I will watch."

"Must you?"

"Hein?"

Hein? Loretta had no inkling what that meant. "Must you watch? It makes me nervous. I can't run away."

"Nuhr-vus?"

"Nervous." She shrugged one shoulder and then tried to pry his leathery fingers from around her ankle. "Nervous . . . uneasy." She gave her leg a shake. His hand moved with her foot, his grip unbreakable. "Would you let go? It's indecent, you touching me like this."

"In-dee-sent?"

"Indecent. Shameful. Would you *please* let go? It is my foot, you know."

"And you are my woman."

She threw her head back and sighed. He had a grip like an iron vise and outweighed her by a good ninety pounds, every ounce muscle. *His woman.* For a moment she had lost sight of that and let him lull her into a false sense of security.

He pulled on her leg and slid her toward him until she lay on her back. Then he released her ankle to loom over her, planting a hand on each side of her. Loretta stared up at his dark face, her heart pounding, her mouth dry.

After struggling with him so many times, she knew how easily he could pin her beneath his weight, how quickly he could capture her hands and render her helpless. The gleam of lust in his eyes terrified her. What was to stop him from taking her? If she screamed, no one would intervene.

Where were his mother and her spoon when she needed them?

"You will sleep." The low timbre of his voice vibrated through her. "I will watch."

With that, he left her and sat on his pallet. She heard a rapping sound and glanced over to find that he was chipping flint with a bone punch. On closer inspection she saw two flint arrowheads lying next to him — arrowheads that he would one day use to kill white people, no doubt. She huddled on her side and stared at him. Even from across the lodge he intimidated her. Yet she was completely dependent upon him. She would never relax enough to sleep with him sitting there.

A few moments later a shadow fell across the room. Hunter's cousin stood in the doorway. The sight of the man's disfigured features made her heart leap. Dressed only in a breechcloth and moccasins, he was nearly naked.

Not acknowledging her presence by so

much as a glance her way, he stepped inside, bringing with him a sense of evil, so tangible, so cold, that the air seemed thick with it. He looked at Hunter. To Loretta's surprise, he spoke English. "Your father tells me you will take the woman back. Cousin, this is *boisa*. Kill her. If you cannot spill her blood, I can."

Loretta knotted her hand into a fist and pressed it against her waist.

Hunter glanced toward her, then stood. "You will make no talk of killing, Red Buffalo."

Red Buffalo snorted with disgust. "I will make more than talk. I demand you bring her to the central fire."

Central fire? Loretta's breath stopped midway from her throat to her lungs. She could almost hear the flames sizzling.

Hunter spread his feet and crossed his arms over his chest. "She is my woman. She stays in my lodge."

"Yet you return her to her people? Beat her. She will eat. If you cannot make her, I will."

Red Buffalo advanced on the bed. Loretta threw Hunter a frightened glance. Captor or no, he was her only security, the one person who stood between her and death. His dark blue eyes met hers. Red Buffalo reached for her. His fingers were about to close on her arm. Loretta shrank away, her breath coming in shallow little gasps.

At the last second Hunter said, "Do not

277

touch her, cousin. My heart will be laid upon the ground if I must lift my hand against you."

Loretta closed her eyes on a wave of relief, then quickly opened them again.

"You challenge me?" Red Buffalo straightened and whirled. "For a yellow-hair? I am your blood! You would forsake me for she who hates you?"

The veins along Hunter's neck stood out, the only outward sign of his anger. "I forsake you? You think my eyes are blind? That I do not know how the snake came into her bed?"

Loretta scooted back against the taut leather wall, her attention shifting from one man to the other. Red Buffalo had begun to tremble, hands clenched at his sides.

"You say I put the snake there?"

"The words whisper in my heart. *Mea,* go. Until your loyalty to me is greater than your hatred."

"I have stepped between you and enemy rifles!"

"And now you make war on my woman. Do not test me again, cousin."

The muscles across Red Buffalo's back knotted and twitched. He stood there a moment, quivering with rage, then spun and spat in Loretta's direction, his black eyes livid with hatred. "Your woman," he sneered. "She sickens my gut. You forget your wife who died for a yellow-hair?"

With that, he stormed out.

A brittle silence settled over the lodge. A tremor shook Loretta as the aftershock set in. The snake had been planted? She stared at Hunter; he stared at the doorway. When at last he looked at her, his eyes churned darkly with emotion. He returned to his pallet and sat down, legs crossed at the ankles in front of him. With a sigh, he reclaimed his flint and bone punch, bending over the flat rock he used as a base for his work.

"You will sleep. I will watch."

The stony mask of anger that hooded his face did a poor job of concealing his pain. He loved his cousin, yet he had defended her against him. Loretta lay down, but sleep was beyond her. Seconds dragged by, mounting into minutes, and still the silence rang out, broken only by the report of bone against flint.

Loretta swallowed. "Hunter?"

His indigo gaze met hers.

"Thank you. For — defending me."

Almost imperceptibly, he inclined his head. "Sleep, Blue Eyes. It is well."

"I — I'm sorry for causing a rift — a big fight — between you. I truly am sorry." Afraid he might not understand, she placed a hand on her chest. "My heart is on the ground."

His mouth thinned, and he glanced outside. "Let your heart be glad again. The hatred came upon him long ago."

Something deep within Loretta knotted, twisted. She hugged her middle and tried desperately not to think, to deny the reality she could not accept, that Hunter, the legendary killer, was a man who thought, and felt, and loved — just like any other. He even mourned a dead wife.

He was also a man true to his word. He had promised to defend her, and he had.

The next three days passed in a blur. Most of the time Loretta slept, while Hunter watched over her. When she awoke he was always nearby, either inside the lodge or within sight beyond the doorway. Instead of feeling nervous, she drew comfort from his presence. When she thirsted he brought her water. When she hungered he provided her food. When the night grew chill it was his buffalo robes she huddled under. On those occasions when she needed to use the bushes, he accompanied her, and despite the hostile glances she received from other Indians in the village, none dared approach because he was beside her. She came to depend on him for everything.

Late the third day, Hunter took her for a walk. She had no idea why and began to feel uneasy when they had gone quite some distance from camp. The pale blue of the sky had already turned steely and pressed closer to the earth. To her left, down along the river, she could hear the birds twittering as they settled to roost for the night. Soon it would be dark.

Her imagination ran rampant. Had he changed his mind about taking her home? Had his cousin talked him into killing her? He was a man of few words, and when he did condescend to speak, his simplistic English often left her with more questions than answers.

"Where are we going?" she asked.

"You will see."

She cast an uneasy glance at the knife on his belt. Then her eyes trailed up his muscular torso to his face. The breeze caught his hair, pulling it back so she had an unimpeded view of his features.

She had grown so accustomed to the slash on his cheek, she scarcely noticed it now. Instead she saw the proud lift of his squared chin, the high line of his cheekbones, the chiseled profile of his nose and forehead. As she studied him, the conviction grew within her that for all his many faults, lying was not among them.

Sweat pooled in her palms. She averted her face and trudged along beside him, picking her path carefully so she wouldn't step on prickly grass or a drooping bull thistle with her bare feet. The bright pink blossoms on a stalk of crazyweed brushed against her calf, their scent wafting to her nose like delicate perfume.

He caught her arm to help her across a rocky wash that zigzagged toward the river. The unexpected weight of his hand would have taken her breath a week ago. What was happening to her? How had she come to regard a Comanche as someone she could trust? It was insane.

It was also undeniable.

Oh, she didn't trust him completely. That would have been foolish. They came from two different worlds, and his definition of harm was probably far looser than hers. She knew he still might force himself on her and that he would be brutal in the taking. If she angered him, he might beat her. But her life wasn't in danger. Not from his hand.

The whinnying of a horse gave Loretta her first clue to where they were going. As they crested a grassy knoll, her eyes widened. A broad meadow of yellow-green grass stretched before them, and it was chock-full of horses — sorrels, roans, paints, grays, and every other conceivable color. Hunter motioned for her to stay put while he walked into the herd. A few minutes later he returned, loosely holding a black stallion's line. The horse strongly resembled the one whose leg she had broken.

Hunter slowed as he drew near and held out the line to her, his dark eyes gleaming in that way she had once found so unsettling.

Now she realized the gleam was only a smile that had not yet touched his lips. As her fingers curled around the rope, she looked up. "He's beautiful."

"When the sun rises, we will ride for your wooden walls. He will carry you." Taking her hand, Hunter stepped to the stallion's head and lifted her palm to his velvety muzzle. "Give him your smell."

The stallion snuffled and nibbled her fingers, grunting a greeting.

"He's so beautiful, but after what happened to . . . I can't ride him. I'd never forgive myself if something went wrong. I felt so —" She broke off and licked her lips. It hit her that she had never apologized to him for killing his horse. She should now, but so much time had passed, and she wasn't sure what to say. "My heart is still sad about your stallion. I wouldn't want something to happen to this one."

"It is finished." His face tightened as he spoke. "This stallion says *hi, hites,* how are you, my friend." He ran a muscular arm around the black's neck, moving in close to his shoulder. "He is son to my friend who is dead. Breathe into him so he will know your smell and remember with no horizon."

The thought of kissing a horse wasn't particularly appealing, but after witnessing the Comanche's rapport with his other stallion, she couldn't argue that he knew better than she how to communicate with them. She bent over and exhaled close to the black's muzzle. The horse sniffed and nibbled her face, nickering and blowing. Loretta gave a startled laugh and reared back, scrubbing her mouth with her sleeve. She glanced up to find the Comanche smiling. Her laughter trailed away, and she felt suddenly self-conscious. His large, sandpapery palm still enfolded hers, and the contact made her heart skitter.

His fingers tightened. "You like?"

"I — um, yes, he's wonderful. His left ear isn't notched like so many of the others. Why is that?"

"The notched ear says a horse is gentled. He is not. If another puts hands upon him, he fights the big fight."

"Then how can I ride him?"

"You will be his good friend. Come close."

Loretta stepped back instead. "But he's wild."

Tightening his hold on her hand, Hunter tugged her forward. "He is friend to me and no other, eh? He carries me because he wishes it. Now, he will carry you."

With that explanation, which fell far short of reassuring her, he reclaimed the line and lifted her onto the stallion's back.

Loretta looked down. "I — I'm not too sure this is a good idea."

"It is good. You will trust, eh? I have said words to him. He accepts. Lie forward along his neck and whisper your heart into his ear. Run your hands over him. Tighten your legs around him."

Heart in her throat, Loretta did as he told her. She whispered, "Please, horse, don't get mad and kill me." The stallion nickered and sniffed her bare foot, the whites of his eyes rolling. Hunter chuckled. "He smells your fear and asks if there is danger, eh? He should run like the wind? He should stand? He is sure enough nuhr-vus, like the little blue-eyes is nuhr-vus when she thinks I will eat her and pick my teeth with her bones. You will say to him as I say to you — it is well."

Loretta jerked her foot back, afraid the horse might bite. "He m-may not understand. He's a Comanche horse, isn't he?"

"*Toquet,* it is well. Whisper your heart. The words are in your touch. Be easy and make him easy."

She ran her hands over the stallion's sleek coat, her fingers splaying on the powerful muscles in his neck and shoulders. When she began to believe the horse wouldn't rear, she relaxed. The stallion lowered his head and began to graze. Hunter handed Loretta his line.

"Let him carry you, eh? Whisper to him. Teach him your hands bring no pain — only good things. He will find sweet grass and listen."

"He's so beautiful, Hunter."

285

"Say this to him."

Loretta did. The stallion flicked his ears and nickered. While he grazed, she petted him. Just when she began to feel confident, Hunter lifted her off his back. When he took the stallion's line from her, he captured her hand as well, his long fingers curling warmly around hers.

"He is now your good friend." He looped his free arm over the stallion's shoulders. "If you share breath with him often, you can paint yourself and wear leaves on your head, and he will still know you. For always."

"Well, until I get home, at least." She swallowed. "I *am* still going home, aren't I?"

Something flickered in his eyes — a dangerous something. Loretta's legs felt as heavy as wet clay, and she watched helplessly while he pressed her palm to his cheek. "You wish to go?"

His jaw felt hard and warm. "I — yes, I wish to go."

He moved her hand from his cheek to his chest, forcing her palm flat against the vibrant muscle of one breast. His eyes held hers, relentless and piercing. Loretta yearned to move away but knew she had little hope of breaking his hold. She could feel his heart thumping, a steady, sturdy beat in contrast with the uneven flutter of hers.

"You will walk backward in your footsteps and go forward a new way?"

"I —"

He slid her hand upward so it rested on his shoulder, forcing her closer. His height was such that she had to tip her head back to see his face. If he had been a white man, she would have been worrying that he planned to kiss her. But he wasn't a white man. And she doubted gentle persuasion was what he had in mind. He seemed a yard wide at the shoulders, a looming wall of muscle. There was heat in the depths of his eyes as he studied her, a heat that had never been there before.

"I would have you beside me," he told her huskily.

"But you promised to take me home."

The stallion nickered and sidestepped, pulling both of them off balance. Hunter released the horse to catch her, his arm encircling her waist. Loretta snapped taut when his hard thighs pressed intimately against hers.

He bent his head and nuzzled her hair, his breath sifting through the strands to her scalp. A shiver ran through her. For a moment she struggled against him, but then she felt as if an invisible web were entwining itself around her, the silken threads binding her so she couldn't move, couldn't think.

She closed her eyes, wildly afraid, of him and what he was making her feel. She tried desperately to conjure an image of her mother, anything to break the spell. Perhaps he knew how to be gently persuasive after all. She knew she should pull away, yet an unnameable something held her transfixed. His mouth trailed to the slope of her neck, sending tingles down her spine. A treacherous languor stole into her limbs. Heat spread through her belly. For an instant she wanted to lean against him, to let his wonderfully strong arms mold her to his length.

The shock of his hand on her bare back brought her to her senses. Her eyes flew open, and she gasped. She tried to arch away from him and succeeded only in accommodating his mouth when her head fell back. He pressed his lips to the hollow of her throat, where her pulse beat a rapid tattoo. His callused palm slid slowly but inexorably to her side, his thumb feathering against the underside of her breast. Horrified, she groped for his wrist, her fingers finding feeble purchase through the leather.

"Ah, *nei mah-tao-yo*," he whispered. "You tremble."

His mouth continued its downward path, lips like silk nibbling her collarbone. Acutely aware that the generous neckline of her shirt provided little barrier against him, she abandoned her hold on his wrist and caught his face between her hands. Forcing his head up, she met his gaze, disconcerted even more by the longing she saw in his eyes. "You're frightening me."

"It is *boisa,* this fear." Beneath her shirt, his warm hand stilled on her ribs. "You are my woman."

"And that's exactly why you frighten me. You can't *buy* a woman." She twisted to one side, wedging one arm against his larynx. She had no delusions. If he pressed the issue, her strength was no match. "Why can't you understand that? A woman must come freely."

Lowering his hand to her waist, he leaned away from her, his dark eyes searching, thoughtful. "And when you come freely, you will have no fear?"

"I —" She stared at him. "I suppose if I — not that I ever would, mind you — but *if* I came to you freely, then, no, I probably wouldn't." Loretta knew she was babbling. He looked confused, and she didn't blame him. She broke off, and her gaze chased away from his. "It's so completely unlikely that I — but *if* I did, I don't suppose I would be afraid. I wouldn't come if I were."

His arm relaxed around her. After studying her for what seemed an eternity, he said, "Then this Comanche will wait. Until the Great Ones lead you in a great circle back to him."

The return trip to Loretta's home took five days. Despite her eagerness, at times she actually found herself enjoying the lazy pace.

The forty Comanche braves who rode with her and Hunter seemed to accept her, and she no longer felt threatened when her captor wasn't at her side, which was rarely. *Home.* The nightmare was nearly over.

Loretta worried about the reception she might receive. People weren't likely to believe her Comanche captor hadn't raped her. But she would face that when it happened. For now it was enough that she was going to see Amy and Aunt Rachel again.

Hunter made the time pass more quickly by teaching her things while they rode: how to find water by watching the birds and wild horses and by searching for certain types of grass that grew only near underground springs; how to track; and, most fascinating, how to read the signs left by Comanches to show which direction they had traveled.

"Hunter, if you leave signs for other Comanche bands, why do white men have so much trouble finding you?"

"They are not smart."

Loretta laughed softly. "I think I've been insulted. You think I'm stupid?"

He threw her a look that made her laugh again. "A little bit smart. Because I teach you."

"Ah, so I'm ignorant, not stupid? I suppose I can accept that." She scanned the endless expanse of golden hills, lined up ahead of them like loaves of fresh-baked unleavened bread. This harsh land was Hunter's general store, the shelves stocked with all he might need. To her it was an alien place and frightening, so immense it had the perverse effect of making her claustrophobic. She felt vulnerable out here, so terribly vulnerable. "In my world, you wouldn't be smart, either."

"That is good. The *tosi tivo* way is *boisa*."

"How so?"

He nodded toward a scrawny mesquite tree that had sprung up in a cluster of rock. "He plants dead trees in the earth, and the trees fall over. That tree does not."

Loretta's stallion did a restless sidestep. She shifted her weight and reined him back into line, stroking his neck as she squinted to see through the dust the other horses were stirring up around them. "No, it doesn't fall over, but it's not where it needs to be for a fence, either."

"A fence says the earth belongs to the *tosi tivo*? He will become dust in the wind, the fence will rot, and the earth will still be. Another *tosi tivo* will come, and he will plant more dead trees. It is sure enough *boisa*."

"But the *tosi tivo* buys the land. It belongs to him. He puts up the dead trees so others will know where his boundaries are, so his livestock won't run away."

"He cannot buy the land. Mother Earth belongs to the true People."

Loretta gazed after the other warriors, silent

and thoughtful. "The true People. Your people?"

"Yes."

"That is your belief. But according to ours, the land *can* be bought. And fenced. You understand? No one means to steal from you. They're just taking what's been given to them by the government or what they've paid for. You must learn to be open-minded. There's lots of land, plenty for all."

Hunter grunted. "Let the *tosi tivo* find the lots of land, plenty for all, and plant dead trees there. This is Comanche land, and it cannot be given or bought."

"And we say it can. As you're so fond of saying, it is not wise to fight when you cannot win. We are the stronger. We have better weaponry. When you're outnumbered and outflanked, you must surrender your ways and accept the new."

He looked over at her. "Strong is right?"

"Well, yes, I suppose you could say that."

"You say a woman cannot be bought. I say she can. I am strong. I am right."

Just when she started to relax around him, he jerked the rug from under her. "That's different."

"I say it is not." Mischief twinkled in his eyes as he slowly ran his gaze from her ankle to her waist. The way his attention lingered on her hips brought a flush to her cheeks. "You believe a different way. But I am strong;

you are not. I shall take what I have paid for. You will surrender, no? To my ways?"

"Never." She tugged down the hem of her shirt, once again painfully aware that her lower extremities were covered only with drawers. "It isn't the same thing at all."

"Ah, but it is. Your heart cries no. Our hearts cry no. Strong is not always good, Blue Eyes. To surrender and die inside, that is not good. Do not ask this Comanche to do what you cannot. It is wisdom."

A lump rose in Loretta's throat. She had never analyzed the situation from the Indian point of view. Their land? In a way, they had a right to think so. They were here first. She nibbled her bottom lip, loath to admit what she had difficulty accepting. "I'm sorry your land is being taken, Hunter."

"I am sorry, you are sorry. They take the land. They kill the buffalo. Our sorrow does nothing."

She leaned forward to finger-comb her horse's mane, still unsettled because he had turned the tables on her. She was anxious to change the subject. "My good friend grows weary. Will we stop to rest soon?"

"Yes."

"Your good friend is tired, too." She glanced sideways at the stallion he rode, an almost exact replica of her own. "Can I ask something?"

Hunter's mouth lifted at one corner. "If I

say no, you will be silent?"

"Are you saying I talk too much?" Loretta hesitated, realizing it was true. Silence had been her prison for far too long. And while she had the chance, she hungered to learn all she could about him — to put her ghosts to rest. "I was just wondering, of these two horses, why did you choose that one as your good friend? Is he superior to this one in some way?"

"Sup-ear-ee-or?"

"Better."

"Not better. He has a crooked front hoof, like my good friend who is dead." He paused and seemed to search for the right words. "He is his face on the water, no? How is it you say this?"

Loretta leaned sideways to see the stallion's tracks. His right front hoof left a notched-crescent print in the dust. "Reflection?"

"Yes, he is his reflection."

"The spittin' image of — What was your dead friend's name?"

"It is not to be spoken. He is dead, no? To say his name would not show respect. What is this to do with spit?"

"It's just a saying. When someone or something looks just like something else, it's called a spittin' image. I don't know why."

"You do not know, but you say the words? The words from your mouth say who you are, Blue Eyes. I make a lie; I am an *easop*, storyteller. I speak hate; my heart burns with hate. The People do not make talk if they do not know the words. If it is spoken, it must be. A man is what he speaks. This is not so with the *tosi tivo?*"

Loretta shrugged and bit back a smile. "I seriously doubt I'll become spit. It's just something everyone says."

"You will learn the meaning of this spit image, no? And say it to me. When we meet again?"

Loretta tightened her hand on the reins. "Yes, *if* we meet again."

He glanced over at her, his expression suddenly solemn. "We walk backward in our footsteps, eh? Maybe you will walk forward a new way when we reach your wooden walls. You could be a little bit happy as my woman, no?"

Loretta fixed her eyes on the horizon ahead of them. They were only a day and a half's ride from her home. A day and a half from real clothes, a chance to wash her hair, to eat her own kind of food. Yes, he had been kind to her. As reluctant as she was to admit it, she'd even come to like him a little. But not enough to belong to him. Never that.

"To be happy, I must be at my wooden walls," she said shakily. "That's my home and where my people are."

There was only tonight and tomorrow night to get through, and then she'd be home. *Su-*

vate. It was almost finished.

To Loretta's dismay, the closer they got to her home, the less anxious she was to get there. The time passed too quickly. At dusk the next day they stopped for the night at the base of Whiskey Mountain. During the trip, the men had collected slender willow limbs, and they now sat in small groups to make lances, each of which was marked with the maker's feathers. Loretta was at first alarmed, but after Hunter assured her they had no intention of making war at her farm, she relaxed and sat beside him to watch. His long, lean fingers fascinated her — graceful, yet leathery and strong. She recalled how they felt against her skin, warm and feather light, capable of inflicting pain yet always gentle. A tingling sensation crawled up her throat.

She noticed that each man's feathers were painted differently. "What do your feathers say?"

"They have my mark. And tell a little bit my life song." His full lower lip quirked in a grin. "My marks say I am a fine fellow — a good lover, a good hunter, with a mighty arm to shield a little yellow-hair."

She hugged her knees and grinned back at him. "I bet your marks say you're a fierce warrior, and yellow-hairs should beware."

He shrugged. "I fight the big fight for my people. This is bad?"

Loretta grabbed a handful of grass and ripped it up. Its smell was sharp in her nostrils. "A-are you going on a raid tomorrow after you take me home?"

He glanced up from his work. "With this?" His dark eyes filled with laughter as he peered along the crooked shaft of the lance. "Blue Eyes, a crooked *tse-ak* such as this would kill my friend beside me. This *tse-ak* will say *hi, hites,* hello, my friend."

"To who?"

"To all who pass. You will see, eh?"

"You're sure you aren't planning to attack my home?"

"No fight. You will be easy."

After his lance was finished, she and Hunter made their fire away from the others, then sat near the flames to eat the traveler's fare his mother had thoughtfully packed for them. As Loretta chewed her jerked buffalo meat, her mouth went dry. The meat got bigger and bigger, a gigantic wad she couldn't swallow.

This was it, the last time they would ever eat together beside a fire. *The very last time.* It was insane to feel sad, but she did.

Soon after they finished eating, they arranged their respective beds near the dying fire and retired for the night. Loretta lay on her back, gazing at the stars. Hardly more than an arm's reach away, Hunter slept. At least she guessed he was asleep. She never knew for sure. He could be still as death one minute and on his feet, wide awake, the next. All afternoon he had been quieter than usual. Perhaps he was a little sad, too. Tomorrow they would have to say good-bye.

The word sounded lonely inside her head. And so final. Somehow, God only knew how, she had grown fond of him. Enough to make her wish they might meet again, one day. *Crazy.* It would be best if their paths never crossed. She had her world, he his, and the two didn't mix. Never could, not in a million years.

She remembered his mother thumping heads with her spoon, Blackbird's merry laughter. *Comanches.* The word no longer struck terror in her heart. Would it after he rode off tomorrow? Loretta sighed. Once he left, they would be enemies again. Their truce was tentative. If he came to the farm, Uncle Henry would shoot him. The thought wrenched her heart.

"Hunter?" she whispered. "Are you awake?"

Silence. She pulled her buffalo robe to her chin and shivered, though she wasn't cold. Memories of those first few days washed over her. Of his arm around her while she slept, the heat of his chest against her back, how terrified she had been. Suddenly the stars above her blurred, and she realized she was gazing at them through tears. She squeezed her eyes closed, and hot streams ran down her cheeks into her ears. She *wasn't* crying, she wasn't. Couldn't be. It didn't make sense.

A sob snagged in her throat and made a catching sound. She clamped a hand over her mouth, furious with herself. How could she have come to *like* a Comanche? Could she forget her parents so easily? It was unthinkable. Unforgivable.

"Mah-tao-yo?"

Loretta leaped and opened her eyes. Hunter knelt beside her, a dark shadow against the blue-black, starlit sky.

"You weep?"

"No — yes." Her voice came out in a squeak. "I'm just feeling sad, that's all."

He sat down beside her and hugged his knees, gazing off into the endless darkness. "You will stay beside me?"

"No." The thought was so preposterous that a wet laugh erupted from her. "I was just thinking. Once I get home, we'll be enemies again. My people would shoot you if you ever came around. And that —" She sniffed and swiped at her eyes. "That makes me sad. And sort of scared. What if there was an Indian attack? What if I —" She turned her head to study him. "I might look down the barrel of a rifle someday, and it might be *you* at the other end."

"I will not lift my blade against you."

"But what if you didn't know? What if you went on a raid and I was there, fighting to protect my family and friends? What if I

sighted in on some murdering savage, itchin'
to blow him off his horse, and it was you?"

His eyes were dark pits in his face when he
turned to regard her. After a long silence he
said, "You would pull the trigger?"

Loretta stared up at him, her chest knotted
around a huge ball of pain. "Oh, Hunter, no,
I don't think I could."

"Then let your sadness go the way of the
wind, eh?" His teeth gleamed white in the
moonlight. "If we meet in battle, I will know
the song your heart sings, eh? And you will
know mine."

She swallowed, trying to read his expression, frustrated by the shadows. "What if it
happened? What if you were attacking a farm,
and you saw me at one of the windows? What
would you do?"

"I would salute you. There will be no war
between us."

"There *is* war between us, though. Our
people hate each other, Hunter."

He sighed and peered through the gloom at
her. *"Ob-be mah-e-vah."*

"What?"

"Make room for me." He lifted the robe
and joined her on the pallet.

"Wha — you're not going to sleep with
me?"

"Nei che-ida-ha, I am very terribly cold."

Loretta suspected he was lying, but she
moved over, secretly glad to have him there,

her mind shying away from the enormity of what that meant. He rolled onto his side and laid an arm across her waist. Their faces were scant inches apart. Their gazes locked. His teeth gleamed again in a slow smile.

"Are you sad? About saying good-bye tomorrow?"

"No. You will ride in a great circle back to me. The Great Ones have spoken it."

"In your song?" She sniffed. "That song has caused me enough grief."

He tightened his arm and drew her closer, "Sleep, *mah-tao-yo*. This last time, at my side."

At noon the following day, the Comanches crested the rise above the Masters farm and drew in their horses, well out of firing range. Loretta clutched her horse's reins with such force that her knuckles ached. Hunter sat astride his stallion beside her, his knee brushing hers. Loretta couldn't look at him. Instead she stared at the little house she had thought never to see again. Nothing about it had changed. She wondered what Uncle Henry had done with the fifty horses Hunter had left. They weren't in the back pasture.

A flash of blue crossed the yard. *Amy.* Running to the house to warn Aunt Rachel and Uncle Henry that Indians were coming. It seemed like a hundred years ago that Loretta had done the same.

She saw Hunter reaching toward her out of the corner of her eye. She looked at him as he lowered his medallion necklace over her head. The flat stone was still warm from where it had rested against his chest. She pressed her palm over it.

"You will wear it? For always? And remember Hunter of the Wolf? It is a promise you make?"

"I will wear it." Her fingers curled around the medallion. "I have nothing to give you."

His eyes clouded with warmth. "Your ruffles."

She pursed her lips. "I'm *wearing* them. If you want them, you'll have to come back and steal them."

His gaze ran the length of her. "Maybe so. You will make them nice like flowers, yes?"

She sighed and bent her head. She knew why the memories hurt. They had become friends. It was impossible, crazy, but it had happened. And saying good-bye had a sharp edge. "Well, I guess this is it."

"For this little bit time."

She looked up. "Hunter, you mustn't —"

He leaned toward her and crossed her lips with a finger. "You can read my trail, eh? You can walk in my footsteps and come to me. I will leave you signs."

With a nod, Loretta slid off the horse and stretched the reins out to him. Instead of taking them, he dismounted and walked around his horse to stand with her. She tipped her head back, trying her best to smile. His song had nothing to do with her. Why couldn't he understand that?

"Thank you for bringing me home. My heart will sing a song of friendship when I think of you, Hunter — for always into the horizon."

He gestured toward the stallion. "You will take him. He is strong and swift. He will carry you back to Comanche land, eh?"

"Oh, no! I couldn't. He's yours!"

"He walks a new way now. You are his good friend."

Tears sprang to her eyes. "I will never return to Comancheria, Hunter. Please, keep your horse."

"You keep. He is my gift to you, Blue Eyes."

Words eluded Loretta. Before she thought it through, she rose on her tiptoes and pressed her lips against his in what she intended to be a quick kiss of farewell.

Hunter had heard of this strange *tosi tivo* custom called kissing. The thought of two people pressing their open mouths together had always disgusted him. Loretta was a different matter, however. Before she could pull away, he captured her face between his hands and tipped her head back to nibble lightly at her mouth. To learn the taste of her. And to remember.

As inexpert as he was, when his mouth

touched hers, a wave of heat zigzagged through him, pooling like fire low in his belly. Her lips were soft and full, as sweet as warm *penende,* honey. She gasped, and when she did, he dipped his tongue past her teeth to taste her moistness, which was even sweeter and made him think of other sweet places he would like to taste. Hunter at last understood why the *tosi tivo* liked kissing.

She clutched his wrists and leaned away from him. He drew back and smiled, his palms still framing her face. Her large eyes shone as blue as the sky above them, startled and wary, just as they had so many times those first few days. She was like his mother's beadwork, beautiful on the outside, a confusing tangle on the inside. Would he never understand her?

"Good-bye, Hunter."

Reluctantly he released her and watched her lead the horse down the hill. At the base of the slope she turned and looked back. Their gazes met and held. Then she turned toward home and broke into a trot, the horse trailing behind her. Hunter shook his head. Only a White Eyes would walk when she had a perfectly good horse to ride.

His gaze shifted to her wooden walls. He could only trust in the Great Ones that all would be well for her there. He feared her adoptive father might abuse her, but there was no way he could protect her when she

304

wasn't at his side. His chest tightened. What if the song did not come to pass? What if the great circle of fate never brought her back to him?

He clenched his hands into fists, struggling with himself not to go after her. His woman, yet not his woman. Did she know she took with her a little bit of his heart? With a heavy sigh, he swung onto his black.

"Are you ready?" Old Man asked.

"No. Let her reach her wooden walls, eh? So she has no fear."

CHAPTER 14

Home. Loretta burst through the gates and started screaming. "Aunt Rachel! Amy! I'm home! I'm home!"

The house looked as still as death. Loretta's footsteps dragged to a stop before she reached the porch. She had seen Amy in the yard. Why hadn't anyone come out to greet her? Surely they didn't intend to turn her away. Uncle Henry, maybe. But never Aunt Rachel.

With quivering hands, Loretta tied her horse's reins around the porch post and took a hesitant step. The reality of her world and its harsh judgments came rushing back to her. *A tainted woman.* Aunt Rachel would never willingly turn her away, but Henry had the say here. His fists had a way of carrying the vote.

Panic worked its way up Loretta's throat. Surely she hadn't gone through all she had only to find she had no home here. The doeskin membrane on the left window moved. Loretta peered at the narrow crack.

"My gawd, girl, you've gone and brung death right to our doorstep!" Henry snarled.

Loretta looked over her shoulder at the Comanches on the rise. She hurried onto the porch. "They won't hurt you. Hunter promised. Let me in, Uncle Henry."

Relief washed over her when she heard the bar rasp. Then the door cracked open, scarcely wide enough for her to squeeze through. When she stepped inside, Henry slammed the door closed behind her as if the hounds of hell were outside. Loretta spun and spied Aunt Rachel crouched before the other window, at the ready with a rifle. Loretta flew across the planked floor.

"No need for shooting," she told her aunt, snatching the weapon from her hands to lean it against the wall. Rachel rose slowly to her feet. "Lands, Aunt Rachel, if you aren't a sight for sore eyes. And you smell like sheer heaven. *Rose water!*" Loretta threw her arms around the other woman and swayed blissfully. "Oh, *mercy me,* there were times when I would've given my right arm to do this."

Instead of hugging her back, Rachel drew away and stood there staring, her blue eyes as big as yeast-raised biscuits. Loretta's heart sank. *Not Aunt Rachel.* She could bear rejection from anyone else, but this woman was like her mother.

"I'm okay, Aunt Ra—" Loretta licked her lips, determined to play this out, to believe in her aunt's goodness. "Reckon I'm a mess, but aren't you glad to see me?"

Rachel still seemed struck dumb.

"Did y'all think I was dead?"

Rachel licked her bloodless lips. "Y-you're talking."

Loretta touched her throat and nodded. "Isn't it wonderful?"

Rachel smiled slightly, and tears filled her eyes. "God forgive me, I gave you up for lost. It's a miracle."

"Unbelievable, more like," Henry snarled.

Loretta ignored him. "Didn't Tom tell you he saw me?"

"He said you were starving yourself, that you weren't likely to last more 'n a few days." Rachel caught Loretta's face between her hands. "We figured you —" Her voice broke, and her throat worked as she fought to speak. "We thought you were long since dead. Tom and some others went out searching for you. Couldn't find a trace. I gave up hope." Her mouth began to quiver. Looking a little sheepish, she shrugged and blinked. "I don't know why I'm cryin'. I should be happy."

With a sob, Rachel began checking Loretta for injuries, her hands trembling as she ran them over her niece's clothes. "Are you — did they cut you anywhere? Burn you? Are you all right?" When she spied the medallion, she cupped it in her palm and stared at it. "Lord Almighty, what's this?"

"It's Hunter's. He gave it to me as a remembrance."

"A remembrance!" Henry barked. "Lord help us, she's plumb addled. A remembrance?"

"I — yes. We're, um, sort of . . ." Loretta licked her lips again and glanced around the room, the words to explain eluding her. *Careful, Loretta.* If she said the wrong thing, it could damn her. "I can't believe I'm actually standing here. Home. Really and truly home."

"Are you hurt anywhere?" Rachel demanded.

"No, not a scratch. Just a little grimy around the edges."

"Lands, you are in a tangle. Don't those Injuns have soap?"

"Not a sniff." Loretta laughed, feeling giddy, not quite able to believe Hunter had brought her here as promised. "Maybe that's a bad choice of words. I bet I smell to high heaven."

"Like a little smokehouse." Rachel grabbed her for another fierce hug. "And talking a blue streak, Henry! Isn't it wonderful?"

Henry, who had stepped back to his post, peered out the doeskin membrane and swore under his breath. "Sweet Jesus, here they come!" He threw his carbine to his shoulder. "Rachel, git your rifle! Loretta Jane, you load!"

"No!" Loretta broke away from Rachel and

ran across the room to jerk Henry's rifle off bead. "Don't shoot!"

"Don't shoot? You done lost your mind, girl? They're attackin'!"

Loretta bent to peer out the crack. There they came, forty Comanches, all whooping and hollering, lances raised, a frightening spectacle indeed. Forgetting for the moment that she must guard what she said, she cried, "They *aren't* attacking. He promised."

"Then what the hell *are* they doin'? Get outa my way!" Henry shoved her aside and resighted his rifle. "He promised? She's touched, Rachel! They messed her up in the head, keepin' her all this time."

Loretta ran for the door. "He isn't attacking! I *know* he isn't. Please, don't shoot!" The bar stuck as she tried to lift it. Her heart began to slam as she wrestled with it. A vision of Hunter lying dead in the yard flashed through her head. This was exactly what she had dreaded might happen, what she'd tried to explain to him last night. "Please, Uncle Henry — he promised me. And he wouldn't make a lie of it, he wouldn't, I know he wouldn't!" The bar finally came free. "Don't shoot him, don't!"

Throwing the door wide, Loretta ran out onto the porch. The Comanches were circling the house. She ran to the end of the porch and saw a lance embedded in the dirt fifteen feet away.

Hi, hites, hello, my friend.

Her knees went weak with relief. "Uncle Henry," she cried over her shoulder, "they're marking the property. Protecting us! Don't shoot or you'll cause a bloodbath for sure!" She ran to the window and peered in the crack at her uncle. "Did you hear me? If they were wanting to murder somebody, I'd be dead."

She turned back to watch as the Comanches widened their circle to mark the outer perimeters of Henry's land. Tears stung her eyes. Hunter was leaving a message to every Indian in the whole territory: those at this farm were not to be attacked.

Within minutes the braves had driven all forty willow lances into the dirt and ridden to the crest of the hill. Loretta shaded her brow, trying to find Hunter in the swarm. Recognizing him from the rest at this distance was impossible. Then they disappeared over the rise. Loretta stared at the empty knoll, her chest aching, her knees still shaking.

"Good-bye, my friend," she whispered.

As if he had heard her, Hunter reappeared alone on the rise. Bringing his stallion to a halt, he straightened and lifted his head, forming a dark silhouette, his quiver and arrows jutting up above his shoulder, his shield braced on his thigh, his long hair drifting in the wind.

Forgetting all about her family watching

her, Loretta stumbled down the steps and out into the yard to be sure Hunter could see her. Then she waved. In answer, he raised his right arm high in a salute. He remained there for several seconds, and she stood rooted, memorizing how he looked. When he wheeled his horse and disappeared, she stared after him for a long while.

I will know the song your heart sings, eh? And you will know mine.

The joy of Loretta's homecoming was overshadowed by Henry's rage. Friends with a murderin' savage, was she? A Comanche slut, that's what, kissin' on him in broad daylight, comin' home to shame them all with her Injun horse and heathen necklace. His land looked like a bloomin' pincushion with all them heathen lances pokin' up. He was gonna get shut of 'em, just like he had those horses. Half of 'em stole from white folks! Some trade that was! Loretta listened to his tirade in stony silence.

When he wound down she said, "Are you quite finished?"

"No, I ain't!" He leveled a finger at her. "Just you understand this, young lady. If that bastard planted his seed in that belly of yours, it'll be hell to pay. The second you throw an Injun brat, I'll bash its head on a rock!"

Loretta flinched. "And we call *them* animals?"

Henry backhanded her, catching her on the cheek with stunning force. Loretta reeled and grabbed the table to keep from falling. Rachel screamed and threw herself between them. Amy's muffled sobs could be heard coming up through the floor.

"For the love of God, Henry, please . . ." Rachel wrung her hands in her apron. "Get a hold on your temper."

Henry swept Rachel aside. Leveling a finger at Loretta again, he snarled, "Don't you sass me, girl, or I'll tan your hide till next Sunday. You'll show respect, by gawd."

Loretta pressed her fingers to her jaw, staring at him. Respect? Suddenly it struck her as hysterically funny. She had been captured by savages and dragged halfway across Texas. Never once, not even when he had just cause, had Hunter hit her with enough force to hurt her, and never in the face. She'd had to come home to receive that kind of abuse. She sank onto the planked bench and started to laugh, a high-pitched, half-mad laughter. Aunt Rachel crossed herself, and that only made her laugh harder.

Henry stormed outside to get "those dadblamed Indian lances" pulled up before a passing neighbor spied them and started calling them Injun lovers. Loretta laughed harder yet. Maybe she *had* gone mad. Stark, raving mad.

Aunt Rachel moved the bed to let Amy

come up through the trap. Loretta managed to regain control of herself in time to catch the child in her arms when she cannoned across the room.

"Loretta! Loretta!" Amy clung to her neck, sobbing and laughing. "They didn't kill you. I *knew* they wouldn't!"

"How'd you know?"

Amy pulled back and grinned. " 'Cause I couldn't have stood it, that's how. And I prayed you home. Two rosaries a day, faithful! You can ask Ma."

"No cheating? I don't believe it. You always skip Hail Marys."

"Nary a one." Amy trailed a finger along Loretta's cheek. "The old toad! He gave you a shiner, sure as rain. I hate him."

"Amy!" Rachel admonished.

Loretta ruffled her little cousin's hair. "You don't even seem surprised that I'm talking."

"That's 'cause I ain't. I heard you talk out in your sleep, remember?"

Loretta did remember. She hadn't believed Amy then; she did now. Sighing, she released the child and threw a lingering look at the room. Aunt Rachel's patchwork, Amy's primer, the *Godey's Lady's Book,* the scarred old rocker. *Home.* Even with Uncle Henry to spoil things, it was heaven to be back.

Questions flooded Loretta's mind. How had Tom Weaver fared during his journey home? How many men had gone searching for her? Where were the horses Hunter had left? How were the chicks doing? Had the jerky Loretta had put up dried to a turn, or was it tough?

Rachel answered each question as it came, unable to keep her hands off Loretta as she talked. Tom was fine. About thirty men had tried to track the Comanches, but the Indians had split into groups, making false trails.

"Which explains why Tom wasn't with the same group I was." Loretta frowned. "Who'd think it? Those Indians have more brains than we credit them with."

"The first day there were at least a hundred of them," Rachel replied. "I figure there were sixty when they came back, give or take. The other forty split into groups and led the border patrol a merry chase, dang near all the way to the Colorado River in one direction, toward the Staked Plains in another. The other group rode in circles."

"Well, while they were chasing around, I was right here on the Brazos!" Loretta rolled her eyes. "I prayed and prayed someone would stumble across us, but no one did."

Loretta leaned her head sideways to press her cheek against her aunt's hand, forcing the memories from her mind. "I'm so hungry, I could eat the south end of a northbound mule. What's for supper? And please don't say pecans or buffalo meat."

Rachel laughed and released her. "A bath?"

Loretta stuck out a leg and grimaced at her filthy bloomers. No wonder Hunter had told her to make them nice like flowers. She must reek to high heaven. "A tub bath? You reckon I can? It isn't Saturday, is it? Uncle Henry might get into a snit."

"It's Tuesday, and he won't get in a snit." Rachel handed Amy the bucket to start hauling water. "A bath and a good currying." She lifted a hank of Loretta's hair. "If we can't get those tangles out, I may have to cut it."

Loretta glanced down at the web of curls on her shoulder, once golden, now dull with dust, and wrinkled her nose. *Lilac water.* It would be paradise to soak in a hot tub and scrub until she squeaked. She could scarcely wait.

That night, long after Henry and Amy were asleep, Aunt Rachel came up to the loft and sat on the edge of Loretta's and Amy's cot. Loretta rolled onto her side and took her aunt's hand, thinking how beautiful she was. Fragile, like porcelain, and shimmering in the moonlight like intertwined gold and silver with her white skin and unbound flaxen hair.

Rachel sighed and patted Loretta's wrist, smiling yet not smiling, her expression taut and frightened. "Loretta Jane, we have to talk."

Loretta's chest constricted. "Aunt Rachel, he didn't violate me, I swear it."

"If he did, would you say?" Rachel smoothed Loretta's hair. "It's a terrible, terrible thing that's happened to you, darling. But it wasn't your fault. I love you, you know, like you were my own. You don't have to hide anything from me."

"I'm not."

Rachel sighed. "Loretta Jane, I'm a firm believer in the power of prayer, and God knows Amy and I prayed our hearts out. But, honey, Comanches don't haul a woman halfway across Texas and leave her untouched! You're either lying or you've blocked the horror out of your mind."

Loretta gazed out the window. Memories played through her head, some so bad they made her shiver, others strangely sweet. "He's not like you'd think. He's —" She frowned. "He's not cruel, Aunt Rachel, just different."

"One of the men in the border regiment that rode out with Tom to look for you — he told us some stories about Hunter, stories that'd turn your blood cold. From what he said, the man's a monster. He ran a soldier through with a lance . . . lengthwise. Skewered him, Loretta Jane, and left his — his —" Rachel passed a hand over her eyes. "He left his pride dangling on the lance tip."

"I don't believe it!" Loretta cried shrilly. "How does he know if it was Hunter's lance?"

"He said the lance carried Hunter's mark. He seemed to think it was retaliatory —

vengeance over an attack some U.S. Army deserters and some civilians made on a village a few years back. The murdered man had ridden on that raid. He carried an Indian woman's necklace on him — used it for a watch chain — a souvenir, he called it, taken off a girl in the village. When his body was found, the watch chain was gone. It's only conjecture, but this fellow seemed to think Hunter might have known the girl who had worn the necklace and flew into a rage when he saw it."

"Not Hunter. Trust me, Aunt Rachel, he isn't like that. I was in his tepee for three days! I'd have seen evidence. There wasn't even a scalp!"

Rachel tipped her head back, not speaking for a long time. When at last she did, her voice was strained. "I just want you to know that, for better or worse, I love you, and I'll stand by you. If — well, if you're carrying any baggage from the experience, you don't need to worry. Any child of yours has a home here. I don't care what blood it has. Henry can either accept that or get to packin'."

Though she knew Aunt Rachel's promise was more bluster than fact, Loretta sat up and enfolded the older woman in her arms. "I appreciate that, Aunt Rachel. It's good to know you love me so much. But trust me, I'm not in the family way. Couldn't be."

Rachel returned the embrace. "If the time

comes you need to talk about it, you can share anything you need to with me. I won't judge you — not for anything."

Loretta stiffened. "What could you judge me for?" She pulled away.

Rachel averted her face.

"Oh, Aunt Rachel, not you, too? Is it a crime to live through something like this and emerge unharmed? I *did* starve myself. I chose death, just like any self-respecting woman would. But then he promised to bring me home, and I started eating again. He hadn't harmed me, and I figured —" Loretta broke off. It was clear as rain Aunt Rachel didn't believe her. "Merciful heaven, would you rather I was dead?"

Amy groaned and tossed her head.

Lowering her voice, Rachel replied, "No, I wouldn't rather you were dead!" She lifted trembling hands to her face. "Lord, no. I — oh, Loretta Jane, no. I love you. I just can't understand. You come home looking fit as a fiddle, claiming they didn't touch you? I saw you kiss him with my own eyes. And Tom said you shared the Comanche's bed, that it appeared you were receiving good treatment. I can only wonder what you had to do to survive so you could be here tonight. It's amazing what we women can live through — the things we're willing to put up with just to get by. Look at me. Stuck here in this unforgiving land with a man I despise. Do you think having him touch me is pleasant? But I let him and pretend I like it. Without him, where would the three of us be?"

Loretta couldn't answer. For an instant it was like being mute again, her throat felt so tight. She could understand Uncle Henry's not believing her. He was one tier short of a full cord, anyway, and a body expected him to be an imbecile. But Aunt Rachel? That hurt — a bone-deep hurt that would be a long time in easing. Even if eloquence had been hers, Loretta would have offered no defense. She knew the truth, and that would have to be enough.

Aunt Rachel stood up and wiped her palms on her shift. "I'm here if you need an ear. You can count on me."

With that, she left the loft. Loretta wrapped her arms around her knees and gazed out the window at the moonlit yard, remembering another night, a lifetime ago, when Hunter had sat astride his black stallion there, his arm lifted to her in a salute, his fisted hand holding her stolen bloomers. How could it be that a Comanche understood the song her heart sang and her own aunt did not?

Three days later Loretta still felt bruised from the conversation she'd had with Aunt Rachel. As she bent over the washboard to scrub her badly soiled bloomers, her thoughts weighed so heavily on her mind that she scarcely felt the sun glaring down on her shoulders. Now that she was home, it was almost as if nothing had changed. Yet so much *had* changed.

Amy stirred the steaming clothes in the soak tub with a laundry paddle, chattering nonstop, drawing breath only when she paused to run her sleeve across her sweaty forehead.

"I think it's plumb loco, that's what!" The paddle thunked rhythmically against the sides of the tub, making such a din that it nearly drowned Amy out. "If you marry up with that old man, you'll be suppin' sorrow with a long spoon, mark my words."

"Tom's not so bad," Loretta murmured.

"Not so bad? He reeks! I guess maybe he's nice enough. But, Loretta, he's old enough to be your gramps! Even if his heart's in the right place, how could he raise up a young'n? He'll be six feet under before it learns to walk."

Loretta froze, her arms submerged elbow deep in the sudsy wash water. She stared at Amy. "What young'n?"

Amy's face flushed scarlet, and she glanced nervously toward the house, stirring industriously. "I — don't pay me no mind. I was just runnin' on."

"What young'n?" Loretta repeated icily.

Amy shrugged one shoulder. "I guess I mighta done some eavesdroppin'." The paddle went thunk, thunk, thunk. "I heard

Ma and Pa talkin' to Mr. Weaver. He said he didn't have no care about who the father of your baby might be, Injun or no. He'd love it same as his own."

Nausea clutched Loretta's stomach. She bent her head, staring sightlessly into the soapy water. Never, in the seven years she had lived with Aunt Rachel, had she given her cause to doubt her. Why did she question her now? Maybe Hunter's people weren't the most noble of mankind, but at least they didn't question each other's word. *The words from your mouth say who you are, Blue Eyes.* Such a simple philosophy. Only problem was, not every race of people abided by it, and that gave rise to suspicion when the truth sounded too absurd to be true.

Amy continued her noisy stirring. "Oh, hang," she said softly. "I done it now. I didn't mean to talk outa turn, Loretta. Don't get your feelin's hurt, please?"

Loretta tried to speak but couldn't. She drew one arm out of the water and swiped her hair back from her eyes. Then she bent over her work again, determined to force the unpleasantness from her mind. Amy's paddle clunked, resounding in Loretta's ears. Loretta put words to the rhythmic beat. *It'll all work out. It'll all work out.* Experience had taught her that time usually straightened out most tangles. This one was just worse than most, with Tom Weaver as the solution.

"Por favor," a deep voice drawled. "Thees *caballero* and hees *amigos* beg that you would share your water? A leettle beet, no? For a dry throat?"

Loretta whirled. Her heart slammed against her ribs, then fluttered to a stop. Ten of the dirtiest, most disreputable-looking men she had ever seen stood nearby. The dark-complected man who had spoken appeared to be Mexican, his bull denim trousers nearly black with grime, his shotgun chaps studded along each fringed leg with Spanish-tooled silver that glared in the sun when he moved. His fingernails were crusty with dirt, his knuckles gray.

The men with him were as bad, some gringos, some Spanish, all as mean-looking as buffalo bulls in rut, their eyes glassy and shifty. To a man, they wore six-shooters, and Loretta could tell by the way the guns rode their hips, strapped low on their thighs, that they were quick draws. An unnatural quiet settled over the yard.

Out by the smokehouse, their horses had been left ground-tied. The man who had spoken tipped his sweat-rimmed hat to her and stepped forward, his spurs chinking as they stabbed the earth. His friends moved forward with him. *Ching, ching, ching.* Loretta swallowed, wondering how she had failed to hear them approaching. *Amy's paddle.* Oh, God.

Loretta had never seen Comancheros be-fore, but she'd heard stories, and these men fit the description — ragtag misfits and dirt mean. Whoever they were, they meant trouble, big trouble. She knew they weren't there for water, not with a whole river full such a short distance away.

Keeping her voice as level as she could, Lo-retta said, "Feel free to help yourself at the well."

The leader's swarthy face split in a grin. "You weel not geeve thees *caballero* a cup from inside your *casa?* I do not think that ees very neighborly, *señorita.*"

Loretta rose and gave Amy a little push, praying the child would run for the house, but Amy threw her arms around Loretta's waist and clung to her. "I ain't leavin' you," she whispered fiercely.

Ignoring Amy, Loretta met the lead man's gaze and said, "You're quite right. How remiss of me. Amy, darling, run inside and have Uncle Henry bring the nice man a cup." In a lower voice, her tone promising reprisal later if Amy didn't obey, she hissed, "*Do* it, Amy. *Now.*"

With a push from Loretta to get her started, Amy wheeled into a run. The lead man snaked out a hand and caught the child's arm, laughing at the terrified expression that crossed her small face as he jerked her back toward him. "Not so fast, *muchacha*. Ah, you are very pretty. Such nice golden hair. You weel be neighborly, no, a pretty one like you? We are not so bad."

Loretta prayed her voice wouldn't shake. To show fear would be a grave mistake. "Let go of her."

In her peripheral vision, she saw the other men circling her. *Ching, ching, ching.* As terrified as she was, fear for Amy took precedence. She stepped forward and grasped the girl's shoulders.

"Go inside, Amy. The nice man didn't mean to frighten you. Isn't that right, sir?"

The man smiled and handed Amy to one of his friends. "No, that ees not right, *señorita*. You see, we have come a very long way. We are tired, no? And hungry. But mostly we are needing a pretty *muchacha* and a pretty *señorita* to play weeth us a leettle while. When we see two so fair, we have to stop, you understand? We say to ourselves, 'Eet may be a very long time before we see two such pretty ones again.' "

Loretta opened her mouth to retort, but before the words were born, the man lunged at her. She screamed as she stepped backward and tripped. The next instant she fell rump first into the washtub, her feet stretched skyward, bloomers flashing. Pain shot up her spine from where the washboard jabbed her tailbone. The hot water surged upward to her breasts, scalding, taking her breath. The Comanchero put his hands on his hips and threw back his head to roar with laughter, staggering sideways as he walked toward her. He was clearly more than a little bit drunk.

"Ah, thees ees very good! I like a clean woman."

Loretta wiped soapy water off her cheek with a tremulous hand and stared up at him. Uncle Henry was out in the fields, God only knew where — or if he would even come if he saw what was happening. Hiding behind a bush, more like.

"Aunt Rachel! Aunt Rachel, get the gun!"

Amy screamed. Loretta took her eyes off the leader to see what had happened. Her blood heated to boiling. Two of the other men were wrestling with Amy, one holding her arms behind her while the other groped under her skirts. Amy jerked and kicked the man in front of her, catching him on the shin. His high-topped boots deflected the blow. A shrill cry of anguish ripped up Amy's throat when the man's hand slid inside the waist of her bloomers. Then she let loose with a spray of cuss words that would have done Uncle Henry proud.

"Get your hands off my rump, you no-account wart toad!"

The Comanchero stuck a boot between Amy's feet and viciously kicked her ankles until she accommodated him by spreading her legs. Crimson flooded to Amy's cheeks as the man's hand found a resting place between her thighs. Then she squealed with pain. The man who held Amy's arms behind her had his hands full trying to keep her still. Knifing upward with her knee, Amy caught the other man in the groin. He grunted and retreated a step, the color draining from his face.

"You little bitch!" Drawing back his arm, he slapped Amy so hard that her head jerked sideways and lolled on her shoulder. "Try that again, and I'll tie you out on the desert so the vultures can pick your bones."

Before Loretta realized she had moved, she was up and out of that tub, rage lending her impetus. "Take your hands off her, you filthy animal!"

The Comanchero leader caught Loretta around the waist and shoved her to the ground. The sky spun. She saw several of the other men converging on her. The next instant her wrists and ankles were seized in cruel grips, her limbs jerked wide, her skirts thrown high on her thighs. The leader crouched beside her, chuckling at her futile struggles. She heard Amy screaming. Helplessness welled within her. *Not Amy.*

Then Aunt Rachel's voice rang out. "Freeze, you miserable bastards!"

Loretta wrenched her head around to see Aunt Rachel on the porch, skirts billowing, rifle to her shoulder.

"Move and I'll blow your head clean off. Let those girls up, go get your horses, and ride out."

The man who held Amy's arms pulled his knife and pressed it to the child's larynx. "Shoot, ma'am, and I'll slit this little gal's gullet."

Rachel's lips went white.

"Now, you jist put down that rifle, real slow and easy like. That is, you better, if you don't want her dead."

Loretta tossed her head, trying desperately to get up. "No, Aunt Rachel, don't do it! Shoot him! Shoot him!"

The Comanchero leader slapped Loretta's mouth. *"¡Silencio!"* he hissed.

The taste of blood spilled across Loretta's tongue.

Rachel slowly lowered the rifle to the porch, her eyes gigantic splashes of blue. The moment she was unarmed, one of the men leaped onto the porch, kicked the rifle across the planks, and grabbed Rachel's hair. Dragging her behind him out into the yard, he snarled, "Three! This is our lucky day, Santos! For an old one, she ain't bad. Nice tits."

"Did I not tell you we would have a good time?" The Comanchero leader smiled and leaned over Loretta. Grasping the neckline of her dress in his fists, he said, "And now, let us see what we have here, pretty one."

With that, he ripped Loretta's homespun

from neck to waist, laying bare her chemise. Looking up into his eyes, Loretta knew nothing would forestall him from taking what he wanted. Amy's screams pierced the air. Loretta strained against the cruel hands that held her wrists and ankles, remembering the times Hunter had held her thus, how gentle his grip had been in comparison.

As the Comanchero cupped his hands around the fullness of her breasts, his attention shifted to the medallion she had been wearing, concealed from Uncle Henry under her dress. His bleary eyes sharpened, then went wide. He jerked his hands away and quickly crossed himself.

"*¡Jesucristo!*" He scrambled backward, his gaze riveted to Loretta's heaving chest. "El Lobo!" he cried. "Do not touch her."

As if by magic, Loretta found herself unhanded. She blinked dazedly, not quite sure what had happened. Indeed, the yard had gone deathly silent. She sat up slowly, clutching her ruined bodice. The men who held Amy were studies in motion, their eyes wide with fear. Loretta glanced down. *What in blazes?*

She stared at the crude stone medallion that rose and fell against her bosom. And then it struck her. El Lobo, the wolf. Hunter of the Wolf. Her friend had protected her with something more than just lances in the yard. He had left his mark on her person. *You will wear it for always?*

A hysterical laugh welled in her throat. And then relief swept through her. *Hunter's woman.* They were afraid to harm her! She pushed to her knees. The Comancheros were scattering as if they'd just come face to face with Satan himself.

The Comanchero leader crossed himself again as he staggered to his feet and ran for his horse, spurs chinking. It sickened Loretta to see the likes of him praying.

"Leave the old one. She won't be worth the trouble," one of the men barked.

Loretta turned in time to see Aunt Rachel shoved roughly to the ground. Then she realized two of the men still had Amy and were carrying her away between them. She lurched to her feet.

"You bring her back here!" Loretta screeched. "El Lobo will kill you if you take her! I'm warning you!"

As they dragged Amy closer to the horses, the child's dauntless courage deserted her, and she sobbed Loretta's name. "Let go of me! No, don't take me! Ma!" Her voice rose to a shrill scream. "Ma-aa-a! Loretta! Stop them!"

Her soaked skirts shackling her legs, Loretta ran for the porch. Grabbing up the rifle, she threw the butt to her shoulder and tried to sight in, terrified she might hit Amy. "I'm warning you! Let go of her, or I'll shoot!"

Ignoring Loretta, the men tossed Amy onto a horse. One of the men mounted quickly behind her. Loretta took careful aim at his head. She had no doubt she could knock him out of the saddle. "I mean it!"

"Shoot me and you can bury me with your sister!"

Loretta saw a knife glint and knew the man had the blade pressed to Amy's throat. The little girl was sobbing, "Please, don't kill me. Please don't."

Rachel cried, "Loretta, no. He means it. He'll kill her."

"Damned right I will."

Loretta's legs turned to water. Amy's sobs were testimony to how terrified she was, and Loretta's heart twisted. Amy didn't cry easily. She snugged her finger on the trigger. "Santos! If you take that child, I'll send the Wolf after you." Thinking of Hunter, how angry he would be if he were there, lent Loretta courage. "He and his men marked every foot of this property with their lances, fair warning that all who live here are under his protection. I swear to you, he'll hunt you down and kill you."

Santos smiled. "I think you lie. I see no lances."

"My uncle removed them."

"*Señorita,* I do not take the girl. Thees other man does. And you do not know hees name. I cannot be blamed, eh? El Lobo weel understand thees. He weel also understand that I meant no harm to hees woman. The stone was hidden under your dress, no? How could I see?"

The Comancheros wheeled their horses and rode off in a cloud of dust. Loretta stared after them a moment, her mind racing, and then sprinted toward the barn to get her horse. She had to find Uncle Henry. There was no time to spare. Someone had to round up a group of men and go after Amy.

CHAPTER 15

Loretta held her stallion's reins, listening in frozen silence as Tom Weaver and Uncle Henry discussed Amy's plight. Riding over to the Weaver place had already wasted half an hour of precious time. Now the two men were mulling over the situation as only dirt-farming Texans could — slower than two flies on tack paper. Loretta could have screamed in frustration and fear. Why didn't they *do* something? Every extra minute took Amy farther away from them.

"Ain't no way in hell a small group of men can track 'em." Tom scraped his boot against the edge of his rickety porch to rid the heel of cow dung. "They'll split up and go sev'ral different directions. Without a big group of men, we'll have to split up, too. And divided into small numbers, there ain't no way we can take on the likes of them. Them Comanchero are damned good with guns, Henry. We'd be dead before we ever cleared leather."

Henry ran a hand over his hair. "We gotta

do somethin', Tom. They've got Amy. We have to find 'em before —" He broke off. "First Loretta, now Amy. What'll people think? That I can't protect my own, that's what. Besides that, Rachel's fit to be tied. If'n I don't find Amy, I'll never hear the last of it. You've heard the tales about Santos. He's as mean-hearted as they come. Won't matter squat to him that Amy's only twelve."

Tom's face looked drawn. He leaned a shoulder against his porch post and scratched his scraggly beard, gazing sightlessly at Loretta's stallion. Loretta measured seconds by the wild slamming of her heart, and when he didn't speak she wanted to grab him by the shirt and shake him. She kept seeing that filthy Comanchero groping his hand in Amy's bloomers.

"Ain't no man I know could find a Comanchero camp," Tom said wearily. "I've heard tell that they hole up in the Palo Duro Canyon sometimes, but it's a long shot they'd be heading that direction now. It's a far piece from here, for one, and a long ways to go on a wild goose chase, for another."

Loretta hugged her waist, acutely aware that the shirt Uncle Henry had lent her was damp with his sweat. At least she had something to cover her. Did Amy? Those men might have torn her dress off by now. They might — She cut the thought short and cried, "A long shot's better than doing nothing."

Tom shook his head. "Not so. We could waste a good two weeks of hard riding, maybe three, lightin' off for the Palo Duro Canyon. They'd have Amy clear across the Rio and sold before we got back here and regrouped."

"Sold?" Loretta squeaked.

"Deep into Mexico." Tom didn't meet Loretta's gaze. "There's men down there who'll pay a king's ransom for a blonde with blue eyes. I'm surprised they didn't take you. Thank God they didn't."

Loretta wasn't about to explain why she'd been spared. Uncle Henry would tear the medallion from her neck. She'd never see it again, and it was the only thing that had saved her.

Henry slammed his fist into his palm. "There's gotta be somebody who can find 'em."

"A Comanch', maybe."

Henry snorted. "A lot of good that does us."

Loretta stepped closer. "Comanches could find them?"

"Hell, yes." Tom sucked his teeth, then spat tobacco juice near the sagging stoop. "They trade with 'em, honey. How do ya think they get their rifles and ammo?"

Loretta's pulse increased tempo, the sound a rapid drumbeat inside her ears. "Trade with them? You mean that the Comanches I was with — *they* could find Amy? Hunter could

335

find her?"

Tom's gaze sharpened on hers. "Don't even think it."

Ignoring him, Loretta stepped around her stallion and grabbed his mane to haul herself up. "It's Amy out there, Tom."

Tom lunged off the porch, trying to grab Loretta's horse's bridle before she could ride off. The black reared and evaded Tom's hand. "For Pete's sake, use the brains God gave you."

"I *am*. That's why I'm going!"

"You ain't neither," Tom growled. "You go back, Loretta Jane, and we'll never set eyes on ya again."

"You don't know that." Loretta shifted to keep her seat on the nervous stallion. Hunter hadn't exaggerated. The animal fought having anyone but her touch him. "He brought me back once, didn't he?"

"He won't a second time. I can't let you do somethin' so reckless."

"It's not your place to say," Loretta shot back.

"Maybe she's got something there, Tom," Henry inserted. "He did take a shine to Loretta. He might not hurt her."

Tom reached up and grasped Loretta's hands so she couldn't rein her mount. "Git down, girl, or I swear I'll drag you off."

Loretta met his gaze. "You can't stop me, Tom. If he can find her, I'm going to him."

"Are you crazed? Say he found her for ya? Which is worse, girl, Comanches or Comanchero?"

Henry passed a hand over his eyes. "For God's sake, why not let her go? Loretta's future is done ruint, anyhow."

"Ruint?" Keeping a grip on Loretta's wrist, Tom whirled on his neighbor. "I've met some heartless bastards in my time, but I swear, you take the prize. You got any idea what they'll do to her over a period of time? Any idea at all? *If* she could find them. More'n likely she'd git herself lost out there."

Loretta tensed. This wasn't the time for talking. She watched Tom, waiting for the right moment. When his grip on her wrist loosened, she kicked her stallion's flanks. The black surged forward in a powerful leap, knocking Tom off his feet.

"Loretta Jane, come back here!"

Loretta lay low over her horse's neck, urging him to go faster. She had to get home, gather some things for traveling, and leave before Henry and Tom could round up Tom's horse and get there to stop her.

After throwing together some food at her niece's order, Rachel followed Loretta up to the loft, wringing her hands and weeping. Frantic to pack what she needed and flee, Loretta darted around the tiny room, stuffing things into a satchel. *He'll never bring me back. Never.* The words played inside her head, a warning she refused to heed. She couldn't allow herself to think about anything but Amy.

Loretta jerked open the drawer of the bedside table and scooped out her mother's diamond comb and her father's razor. The comb was almost too beautiful to take along, but she was already sacrificing enough without relinquishing her keepsakes as well.

Rachel doubled her hands into fists at her sides, her blue eyes riveted to Loretta's face. "You aren't going back to him. You can't. I won't let you."

"Aunt Rachel . . ." Loretta closed the drawer. "Hunter never mistreated me when I was with him. That's more than I can say for what those Comancheros will do to Amy."

The color drained from Rachel's face, and she swayed as if she might faint. "Is it? He's a Comanche, Loretta. You can't *know* what he'll do. How could you? You can't predict an animal's behavior. You aren't thinkin' straight."

"Maybe not! But it's something I have to do. You'd do the same. Don't stand there and tell me you wouldn't."

Rachel met Loretta's gaze. "Say you find him —"

"I *will* find him. He taught me how to follow his trail."

"It'll be too late for Amy."

338

"Too late for what?" Loretta cried.

"She'll never be the same. You know what they'll do to her. She'll never forget, never. Even if you bring her back, her future'll be destroyed. No God-fearing man will ever marry her."

Loretta closed the clasp on the satchel and hugged it to her breasts, staring incredulously at her aunt. A picture flashed in her mind of Rachel standing on the porch, sighting her rifle on her. Blessed release? Or insanity? Was a woman truly worth so little that her whole life rode on whether or not she was chaste? They were talking about Amy, sweet, bright-eyed, courageous little Amy.

"You're the one not thinking straight, Aunt Rachel."

Tears streamed down Rachel's face. She cupped a palsied hand over her eyes. "She's my child. No one loves her more than me. It's just — first I lost you. And by the grace of God, you've come home. Now, it's Amy. There's only so much I can take. If I let you walk out that door, I'll have lost you both."

"Oh, Aunt Rachel." Loretta clasped the other woman's shoulder. "Have faith. We'll both be back."

"That animal will never bring you home again. You know it as well as I do. I can see it in your eyes."

Loretta couldn't dispute the truth, so she said nothing.

"You're right, you know," Rachel whispered. "If I could be the one to go, I would. She's *my* daughter."

"And she's my little sister. Maybe not by blood, but in all the ways that count. Hunter — he may be too late to spare her completely. But he can reach her before they take her across the border." Loretta's stomach quivered with fear, fear she refused to analyze. "He's only three days ahead of me. The village won't have moved this quickly. I can find them. And that's exactly what I'm going to do."

"At least take some men with you for protection."

"Against an army of Comanches? They'd all be killed. And Hunter would feel betrayed. He's left me a trail out there to follow. If I show it to his enemies . . ." Loretta started down the loft steps. "No. This is something I must do alone. I can't take time to argue, Aunt Rachel. Tom'll get here any minute. He'll try to stop me."

Rachel tore down the steps after Loretta, her sobs high-pitched and ragged. "At least change your dress. Take a minute to think!"

"I'll change clothes on the trail." Grabbing the pack of food off the table, Loretta slung it over her shoulder and strode across the room. "I've done my thinking."

"Those animals killed your mother! Can you forget that?"

Loretta froze with her hand on the door. For a moment the old fear came washing back over her, paralyzing her. Slowly she turned to look at her aunt. "I'll never forget. And I'll never forgive. But that has nothing to do with Amy."

"You'll be facing an army — you said it yourself. Let someone else go. Why does it have to be you?"

"Because." Loretta searched for words. "I've spent half my life hating myself for being a coward. Now Amy needs me. If I turn my back on her — well, I just can't. I won't. Please try to understand, Aunt Rachel. Isn't it better to risk your life than not to have one?"

With that, Loretta burst out the door and ran for her horse. Glancing in the direction of Weaver's farm, she saw a faint wisp of dust trailing skyward. Tom was headed this way. Riding hard. She secured her satchel and food pack to the saddle, then mounted up. Rachel ran out onto the porch, wringing her hands.

"Good-bye, Aunt Rachel," Loretta said hoarsely. "I love you."

Loretta wheeled her stallion and kicked him sharply in the flanks. The black broke into a flat-out run. She knew no horse of Tom's could catch him. Like his sire, he ran like the wind.

■ ■ ■ ■

The trip quickly became a nightmare for Loretta. The nights were lonely and frightening; the days were even worse. When Hunter had shown her how to track, he'd made it look easy. It was not. He had left markings for her on rocks, trees, pieces of hide and bark. But finding those messages in so vast a land was nigh unto impossible. Mile after mile of plains, with only the sun to guide her. Loretta spent half her time in terror that she was lost, the other sick with fear for Amy.

The second day of the journey, she lost Hunter's trail completely. Then her jug of water ran dry. All too soon her throat became parched. She was afraid to wander too far off course to find water, and none of the signs Hunter had taught her to watch for were apparent. No grass to indicate a spring. No wild ponies to follow. No dirt daubers with mud in their beaks.

At one point Loretta grew so desperate she took a gamble and followed a coyote for several miles, hoping he would lead her to water. No such luck. The coyote had only been hunting, wandering as aimlessly as she. It was then that Loretta began to panic. Then Hunter's voice whispered to her, as clearly as if he were beside her. *If you cannot find water, Blue Eyes, give your good friend his head. He will find it for you.*

Swiping her arm across her forehead, Loretta stared at the heat waves that rippled like molten silver in the distance. Last night her light bedroll had offered scant protection against the chill; today she was cooking. Neither she nor the horse would last long in this heat without water. Desperate situations called for desperate measures. Amy was out here somewhere, and every wasted day decreased her chances of being rescued.

Putting her life in her stallion's hands was not an easy decision, but Loretta had no choice. She gave Friend, as she had come to call him, free rein. He stood in place, as if he didn't know what she expected of him.

"Water. Go to water," she whispered.

Friend looked at her, rolling the whites of his eyes. She wished she knew the Comanche word for water, but she didn't. She felt certain the horse would have understood her if she had.

The words are in your hands, Blue Eyes.

Loretta sighed and lay forward along the horse's neck, forcing her body to relax and go limp. "It's up to you, Friend."

For several minutes the stallion stood in place, but when Loretta persisted in not moving or giving him direction, he at last began to walk. Loretta prayed she was doing the right thing, for her sake and his.

Three hours later Friend lowered his head

to drink at a water hole. In the distance Loretta could see a herd of ponies grazing. As she dismounted she saw a dirt dauber take flight from the moist bank, his beak coated with mud. The spring was surrounded by mesquite and tall, dark green grass. Everything Hunter had told her to watch for was here.

After Loretta quenched her thirst and filled the water jug, she was faced with still another crisis. Where were they? She stared across the endless expanse of country, undulating golden-brown flats. Everywhere she looked things were the same, no landmarks. Her stomach knotted with dread. She knew she was going north, which was the right direction, but if she was off by even a few degrees, she might miss the headwaters of the river and bypass Hunter's village. She would ride into nothingness — hundreds and hundreds of miles of nothingness.

Frightened and horribly frustrated, Loretta sank onto a rock and hugged her knees. *Think.* Amy's life depended on it. And so did hers. *Lost.* The word dripped into her mind, as cold as melt-off ice. Hunter had made it look easy, but he was a Comanche. She was a stupid *tosi tivo.* How could she hope to track Comanches out here when some of the finest scouts in the country had failed?

Loretta sighed and stood up. She couldn't turn back. The Comancheros had Amy. To

344

admit defeat would be like signing Amy's life away.

Friend had wandered to the far side of the water hole, grazing. Loretta circled the pool to fetch him. She had walked perhaps thirty feet when she glanced down. The earth on this side of the pool was torn up with hoof marks. Unshod horses had been here. One of the prints was achingly familiar, a notched crescent.

"They were here!" she screeched.

Friend lifted his head and fastened bewildered brown eyes on her. Loretta started to laugh. She wasn't just any stupid *tosi tivo*. She was a stupid *tosi tivo* on a perfectly wonderful Comanche pony. She ran her hands into her hair and closed her eyes, letting the fear flow out of her. Hunter would never have told her to come to him if he hadn't believed she could find him. Between her and Friend, they would make it.

Loretta mounted up, no longer feeling so horribly alone. As crazy as it was, she felt as if Hunter rode beside her.

Six days later, two full days after her food supplies had run out, Loretta rode onto the plateau that overlooked Hunter's village. She reined Friend to a halt and stared down at the river valley. She had come so far and been through so much, spending all her time praying she would get here in time to save Amy, that she hadn't spared a thought for the danger she would face upon arrival. Comanches. Hundreds of them. A white woman who rode down there would have to be insane. This time she didn't have Hunter to protect her.

Friend nickered and sniffed her foot. Loretta knew he sensed her fear. "What if one of them kills me?" she whispered.

The horse snorted and nudged her.

"It's easy for you! They won't hurt you!"

The horse sidestepped and blew.

"Oh, Friend, you don't understand. You can't."

Three Hail Marys later, Loretta and Friend were still on the plateau, silhouetted against the sky. She began a fourth prayer, scarcely hearing the words, her eyes scanning the cluster of lodges below. *Please, God.* Perhaps Hunter would see her and come out to meet her.

Hunter was sitting under a brush arbor, tossing dice with several men, when Blackbird came tearing up the path between the lodges, screaming, "The yellow-hair! She's back, Uncle! She's back!"

Accustomed as he was to Blackbird's mischief, Hunter ignored her while he finished a throw. Then he swept the child onto his lap and growled like a bear, playfully biting her belly. He knew something was amiss when Blackbird didn't let loose with her usual cackles of glee.

"The yellow-hair! She's come back!" Blackbird caught his face between her tiny hands so he had no choice but to look at her. "She isn't moving. I think she's waiting for you."

Hunter's heart tripped. "If you're teasing me, you little weasel, I'll toss you into a prickly pear."

Blackbird's eyes danced. "She's here! Grandmother sent me to tell you. *Nabone*, look!"

Hunter set the child aside and left the arbor. He shaded his brow against the sun. Up on the plateau, he could see the distinct silhouette of a white woman on a horse. As he walked up the path between the lodges, the breeze caught her hair and lifted it. Gold glinted in the sunshine.

Hunter's throat tightened. He nearly tripped over Blackbird, who danced excitedly about his feet as he walked. A mixture of gladness and dread filled him, one emotion as powerful as the other. His little blue-eyes had come to him, just as the prophecy foretold. He couldn't help but wonder if it would not also come to pass that he would one day leave the People.

Numbly placing one foot before the other, Hunter strode to the edge of the village and stared up at the plateau. Even at a distance he recognized the way she sat a horse, the tilt of her head. He couldn't believe she had come so far and so quickly. Fate had indeed led her in a circle back to him.

Ordering Blackbird back to his mother's lodge, Hunter increased his pace, the dread of leaving his people forgotten. Destiny. A month ago he had railed against it. Now he wasn't certain how he felt. Resentful, yet pleased. And relieved. Deep in the quiet places of his heart, he sensed the rightness.

Fate. Today it had brought him a woman, a woman like no other, with skin as white as a night moon, hair like honey, and eyes like the summer sky. *His* woman, and this time she came freely.

From the hilltop Loretta watched the lone man walking toward her from the village. Relief flooded through her when she recognized Hunter's loose-hipped, graceful stride. She crossed herself quickly and murmured thanks to the Holy Mother for her intercession. A dozen emotions surging through her, she urged Friend down the embankment.

Hunter met her halfway across the flat. As Loretta rode toward him, she couldn't stop staring. Even though she had been away from him only a short while, she had forgotten how Indian he looked. How savage. He moved with the fluid strength of a well-muscled animal, his shoulders, arms, and chest in constant motion, a bronzed play of tendon and flesh. The wind whipped his hair about his face.

Mercy. He wasn't wearing any breeches, just a breechcloth and knee-high moccasins. She drew Friend to a halt and swallowed a rush of anxiety. Aunt Rachel was right. He was a Comanche, first, last, and always. Yet she had come to him.

"Blue Eyes?"

He slowed his pace as he got closer, his indigo eyes traveling the length of her, taking in every detail of her dress, from the high neckline down to the bit of petticoat and black high-topped shoes showing below the hem of her full skirts. His eyes warmed with the familiar gleam of laughter that had once irritated her so much.

She fastened her gaze on his face and, resisting the need to blurt out her troubles, searched her mind for the appropriate Comanche greeting, determined to begin this encounter on the right note. *"Hi, hites,"* she said, lifting her right hand.

He caught the stallion's bridle and stepped close. He was so tall that he didn't have to tip his head back to see her face. With a smile in his voice, he replied, "Hello."

Loretta caught her bottom lip between her teeth to stop its trembling. How like him to remember *her* word of greeting. He *was* her friend. She had been right to come here. If anyone on earth could take on the likes of Santos, it was this man. "I need your help, Hunter."

The laughter left his eyes. He caught her chin and turned her face, his gaze tracing the faint bruise on her cheek. His jaw tightened. "He struck you?"

Loretta had forgotten about the shiner Henry had given her. "No, no, that's not important."

His grip tightened. "He struck you."

"Yes, but that's not why —" She flinched as his fingertips explored the curve of her cheekbone. "It's nothing, Hunter."

"He will sure enough die."

"No! That isn't why I'm here." She shoved his hand away and pressed the back of her wrist to her temple. "You shouldn't even talk that way. You can't *kill* him."

"Yes. Very quick."

"No, I don't want you to. It's Amy, Hunter. That's why I'm here. The Comancheros stole her!" Her voice rose. She had practiced what she wanted to say, over and over. Now the carefully rehearsed words fled her mind. "They — she's just a little girl. And they took her. I was wearing your medallion, so they let me be! But they took Amy!"

His brow pleated in a frown. "Aye-mee?"

"Amy, my little cousin, my sister. You remember her."

"Ah. The *herbi* who shoots holes in the ground."

"Yes. And the Comanchero took her, a man named Santos." Loretta slid off the horse and

350

caught his hand. What she felt at seeing Hunter again, her exhaustion, the Indians below, none of that mattered. "We'll never find his camp, not without your help. Hunter — I didn't know where else to turn."

His eyes took on a dangerous glint. "Santos? He rode past the *tse-aks?*"

"Uncle Henry pulled all the lances up and buried them. He was afraid people would call us Injun lovers if he left them."

His fingers curled warmly around hers. His gaze dropped to his medallion, which she had been wearing on the outside of her dress since entering Comancheria. "Santos did you no harm. He is one smart Mexican."

"He took Amy!" Loretta pressed her free hand to her chest. "My heart is on the ground, Hunter. My uncle can't find Santos. He says no one but a Comanche would know how to find him. That's why I came here — to you."

"It is good you come. It is in the song, eh?"

"No — no, you don't understand. I came to ask a favor." She grasped his hand in both of hers, looking up at him with pleading eyes. "Please, will you find Santos and bring Amy home to me?"

His facial muscles drew taut. "To your wooden walls?"

"Yes, home to me. Please."

His smile died. "This is why you come? To ask this favor?"

351

"Please, Hunter, don't say no. I'll do anything, anything you ask."

All trace of warmth left his eyes.

Loretta stared up at him. She had come so far. She couldn't bear it if he said no. Amy was out there. "Please, Hunter, I'll do *anything.*"

He said nothing, just studied her, his expression stony.

Exhaustion and defeat sent Loretta to her knees. Still clinging to his hand, she bowed her head. "Please, Hunter, please. I wouldn't ask if I had anyone else to turn to. I thought you were my friend."

Hunter studied her blond hair, braided and coiled like a snake around her crown, long curls escaping the combs to trail halfway down her back. He had walked to meet her believing she had returned to him. Now he realized she had come only to ask his aid, that she had no intention of remaining beside him. He felt like a foolish young boy, humiliated and angry. But not so angry that he wanted her on her knees.

It was the first time he had seen her surrender her pride. By that alone he knew how deeply she loved the child that had been lost to her. *I thought you were my friend.* The words cut deep. Perhaps he should feel honored. She had traveled a great distance into his land, trusting him with her life and with the life of the child she loved.

"Stand, Blue Eyes," he told her gently.

She tipped her head back. Tears shimmered on her cheeks. "I'll do anything, Hunter. I'll serve you on my knees. I'll be your loyal slave forever. I'll kiss the ground you walk on, anything."

He disengaged his hand from hers and grasped her shoulders, hauling her to her feet. "I want you in my buffalo robes, not making kisses in the dirt."

Her eyes darkened. "I'll do anything."

Hunter was about to tell her he would find Amy, that she need not beg, but her last words stopped him. He was not a stupid man. He searched her pale face.

"I'll be your woman. That's what you want, isn't it? I'll stay with you. Freely. If you'll find Amy and bring her back to me. I promise, Hunter."

Her desperation made him feel ashamed. She had come to him for help; he couldn't turn her away. He needed no reward for finding her sister. Yet he wanted this woman. And she was here, offering herself to him.

His gaze riveted on the faded bruise along her cheek. If he sent her back to her adoptive father, how many more bruises would she receive? "You make lies of your promises, Blue Eyes."

"Not this time. I swear it, Hunter. I swear it before God, I'll be your woman. Anything for Amy."

353

He caught her chin. "You make a God promise? You will lie with me in my buffalo robes?"

Loretta closed her eyes. The words stuck in her throat. She was sacrificing her self-respect. Her own people would forever scorn her if they knew. But what choice did she have?

"Yes, I'll lie with you."

"You will see into me when you speak."

She lifted her lashes. His eyes burned with an intensity she'd never seen before. "I'll lie with you, I swear to God."

"You will not fight the big fight when I put my hands upon you?"

"No."

"And you will eat? You will stay beside me? Forever into the horizon?"

"Yes."

He brushed his thumb across her mouth, remembering how sweet her lips had tasted. A slow smile creased his dark face. "You will say it before your God."

Loretta blinked and met his gaze. "I swear it before God — I'll eat and I'll stay beside you, forever into the horizon."

"You will not fight the great fight?"

"No, I won't fight."

He slipped an arm around her waist and drew her against him. "Ah, Blue Eyes, it is a good bargain this Comanche has made."

"You'll go find her?"

"I will find her, and I will bring her to you, eh?"

Loretta hadn't realized she'd been holding her breath. She exhaled in a rush, so relieved that she felt weak. Hunter bent his head and pressed his face against her hair. The next instant she felt his lips on her neck. She also felt his hand on her posterior. Frustrated by her high neckline and her full skirts, he made a fist in the calico.

"So much *wannup.* Where are you, Blue Eyes?"

He started to lift her dress. Loretta reached behind her and caught his hand. "Wha—what're you doin'?"

He lifted his head, eyes alight with teasing mischief. "I search for my woman. You are in there."

"I'm not your woman yet. Have you no shame? It's broad daylight. People might see."

"They will see you are my woman."

"They'll see my drawers, that's what they'll see!"

He abandoned his hold on her skirt to run his palm up her back. "No bones. That is good."

Loretta's face flamed when she realized he was referring to the whale bones of a corset. A decent man didn't mention such things. "You haven't brought me Amy," she reminded him. "Our bargain doesn't start until you do."

"I have spoken it. It is done."

"Amy first."

Before she realized what he was about to do, he swept her off her feet and put her on the horse, then leaped up behind her. Cinching an arm around her waist, he bent his head and said, "This Comanche will sure enough find her quick."

CHAPTER 16

Woman with many robes, arms laden with weapons, came racing from Hunter's lodge just as Hunter reined Friend to a halt outside the doorway. Blackbird trailed behind her grandmother, dragging a bulging parfleche. Puzzled, Loretta glanced at the things Woman with Many Robes held. War axes, lances, knives. Her gaze shifted to the parfleche Blackbird hauled behind her. A bit of calico cloth poked out from beneath the flap.

The woman and child looked flustered. Loretta felt Hunter's body tense. He said something to his mother and slid off the horse. The woman turned and went back inside his lodge, shooing Blackbird ahead of her. A grim expression crossed Hunter's face as he lifted Loretta from the saddle.

Circling Hunter's war shield, which sat on a tripod outside the lodge entrance, Loretta was filled with mounting dread. She had the feeling Hunter's mother had been trying to remove certain items from his lodge before she arrived. When she stepped through the doorway, it took a moment for her eyes to grow accustomed to the light.

Woman with Many Robes and Blackbird stood to one side of the room, their faces lined with guilt. Behind them Loretta saw a tall pole laden with scalps and feathers. Her knees turned to water. She looked over her shoulder at Hunter. He moved past her, avoiding her gaze.

"Mea," he barked.

His mother and niece skittered toward the door, throwing apologetic glances at Loretta. After they exited, Loretta stepped closer to the scalp pole . . . drawn to it with morbid fascination. The scalps were too numerous to count. She didn't try. One would be damning enough. She studied the weaponry his mother had tried to spirit away. The parfleche probably held souvenirs Hunter had collected off his victims.

"My mother wished to spare you sadness," Hunter said huskily. "You came this day with no warning."

Loretta remembered the night Aunt Rachel had visited her in the loft. Loretta had defended Hunter that night. What a fool she had been. "Why did you hide these things from me, Hunter?"

He stepped past her to grasp the scalp pole and jerked its tip from the ground. She knew he intended to remove the gory booty from the lodge, and she caught his wrist.

"Please don't. To take it away is as much a lie as saying false words."

His dark eyes held hers. "Blue Eyes . . ."

Releasing him and pressing her hands to her waist, she spun away, sickened by the concern in his voice and so weary that she wanted to drop right where she stood. Dear God, what had she done? He *was* an animal, just like Aunt Rachel said. So many scalps. How many of her people had he mutilated? And she had come running to him for help.

"You *will* go find Amy? *That* wasn't a lie, was it?"

He drove the pole back into the ground with such force that the leather walls vibrated. Loretta closed her eyes. *Amy.* She had to control her tongue, stay calm.

"I fight the great fight for my people. I have never made a lie of that. My mother hid these things to spare you pain."

Loretta wanted to whirl on him. He had presented himself to her as a gentle man, hiding his vicious side. It had worked. She had broken a seven-year silence for him. And she had trusted him more than she ever would have believed possible.

"Does it matter what I think?"

"Yes." He circled to stand in front of her. Folding his arms across his chest, he said, "Your thoughts cannot change my face, but —"

359

Loretta cut him off. "I don't ask that you change, Hunter. All I ask is Amy's return."

"I will bring her to you."

"Nothing else matters to me."

He studied her at length. "Your heart holds great love for her."

"Yes. Those terrible men — She's just a little girl. They've already had her for eight days. I can think of nothing else. Even in my sleep I dream about what could be happening to her, hear her calling for me. I try to find her, and I can't."

He grasped her chin, his touch deceptively gentle, as it had always been. "This night, you will sleep without dreams. I have said I will find her. *Suvate,* it is finished."

With that, he left the lodge.

A few minutes later he returned. After donning a pair of buckskin pants, which he pulled on while still wearing his breechcloth, he gathered his weapons, making several trips outside to his horse. When he had collected everything he needed, he sat on a fur pallet, propped a small shaving mirror on his knees, and painted his face, outlining his eyes with black graphite and striping his chin thrice with crimson.

Loretta sat on the edge of the bed watching him. When he finished he glanced over at her. She was seeing Hunter the killer for the first time. On the one hand, he looked so fierce that he terrified her; on the other, she felt strangely reassured. Such a brutal, grimly determined man would be able to find and rescue Amy when another might fail.

"What does the paint say?" she asked.

"That this Comanche rides for war."

"War?" she whispered.

"Santos will know by the paint that I come in anger."

"Will there be a fight? Amy might get hurt."

"Your Aye-mee will suffer no harm." He rose and put away his paints, cleaning his hands on a swatch of cloth. Turning to face her, he said, "My brother, Warrior, and my good friend Swift Antelope will remain beside you. Their strong arms are yours." He motioned for her to stand. "I take you to Warrior now. You will sleep in his lodge circle. No harm, eh?"

When Loretta stepped out of the lodge, she clasped Hunter's arm. "My horse, where is he? I need to tend him, and I — I want my satchel." She was afraid her mother's comb might get stolen. "It has things I need in it."

Hunter never broke stride. "Your good friend is in the meadow. Your bag is with Maiden of the Tall Grass, in her lodge."

At the edge of the village, Loretta saw a group of men milling, their horses ground-tied and outfitted for travel. "Are those men going with you to find Amy?"

"Yes. I must hurry." Hunter's pace slowed as they approached Warrior's lodge. Outside the doorway he drew to a complete stop and grasped Loretta's shoulders, forcing her to meet his gaze. "You will walk in Warrior's footsteps like a woman behind her husband? Until I am beside you again."

Loretta nodded, casting frightened glances into the shadowy lodge. All around her the village people went about their daily routines. She could smell meat roasting over a fire. A nearby group of women had stopped chatting and looked up from their needlework to stare at Loretta, their dark eyes lingering on her clothing. A group of children ran past, giggling and whispering behind cupped palms. Across the way a very old man sat under a brush arbor, studying her with unblinking intensity.

"Does Warrior mind my staying here? What will his wife say?"

"She welcomes you. It is good. Be easy, Blue Eyes. My mother is close. She will come with her spoon." He steered Loretta through the doorway. "Warrior? She has come."

From out of the shadows Warrior emerged, so dark of skin and hair that for a moment Loretta couldn't discern his features. He was eating something, and before he spoke he pocketed the food in his cheek. She was relieved to see that he wore breeches and wondered if he had donned them in honor of her arrival.

"My heart rides with you, *tah-mah*."

Hunter moved his hands in a light caress down Loretta's arms, then released her. "And mine remains here. *Nei meadro,* I am going."

Loretta felt him move away from her. At the last second she turned. "Hunter —"

He paused in the doorway to look back at her. "It is well, Blue Eyes."

She heard leather rustle behind her and knew Warrior had drawn near. So tense her neck ached, she glanced over her shoulder to find he was standing close enough to touch her. He didn't. Instead he smiled, a gentle, reassuring smile. Outside, Loretta heard Hunter's horse run past the lodge.

Warrior stepped around her to the lodge door and roared something in Comanche. Seconds later a slender young woman wearing a soft doeskin skirt and brightly beaded leather overblouse slipped into the room. She bent her dark head and addressed Loretta in a silken voice.

"My woman, Maiden of the Tall Grass, invites you to her fire," Warrior translated. "You will go. I come soon."

Loretta's feet were anchored to the dirt. She was terrified of leaving Warrior's lodge without Hunter. The woman murmured something, nervously stroking one of her long braids, her slender fingers coming to rest on the strip of ermine that bound it. After a moment she took Loretta's hand, tugging her along.

363

"*Mea,* go," Warrior encouraged. "It is well."

When Loretta stepped outside, the sunlight blinded her. She shaded her eyes, glancing around them. The Comanches here had never dared approach her when Hunter was at her side, but now he was gone. *Gone.* When she had decided to come here, she hadn't thought this far ahead. Being deserted in a village full of savages was more than she had bargained for. The women here didn't speak English. That left her with only Warrior to talk with. Warrior, with the scalps on his horse's bridle.

Maiden of the Tall Grass tightened her grip on Loretta's fingers, her lovely features softening, her dark eyes filled with compassion. *"Keemah, Yo-oh-hobt Pa-pi. Toquet."*

Loretta recognized the words. *Keemah,* come. *Yo-oh-hobt pa-pi,* yellow-hair. *Toquet,* it is well. Searching her mind for their word for "enemy," Loretta replied, "I'm frightened. Your people are *to-ho-ba-ka* to me."

Maiden's cheek dimpled in a smile. *"Ka to-ho-ba-ka!"* She patted Loretta's shoulder. *"Hites."*

No enemy! Friend. Loretta smiled back, feeling reassured as she followed the Indian woman to a nearby tepee. Maybe she wasn't completely alone after all. It was small comfort, but until Hunter returned it was all she had.

Hunter reined his horse to a halt and gazed

at the relentlessly flat, endless expanse of land around him. Short golden grass stretched for as far as he could see. *Home.* This summer, the hunting was better to the east, but even so, Hunter missed the Staked Plains, especially the safe natural fortress of the Palo Duro Canyon. Here, the Quohadie ruled the land, and all who dared enter, even the fierce Comancheros, feared them. His people were never as carefree when they were forced to camp close to the *tosi tivo* settlements.

He shifted on his stallion to look back at the band of warriors who rode with him. Their horses were so weary, their heads hung. The men slouched, exhaustion weighing on their shoulders. Hunter had set a grueling pace these last few days, and it was beginning to tell.

"Santos is here somewhere," he told Old Man. "The horse dung is fresh, and this area of grass is a darker yellow from being trampled. They've been grazing their animals here."

"So why are you stopping?"

"We will rest a while."

Cha-na, Hog, drew his horse up beside Old Man's. He scanned the ground quickly, his dark eyes sharp and assessing. "Why rest now? We're almost upon them."

"One more night will make little difference," Hunter replied. "If there's trouble, we should be refreshed."

Old Man snorted. "You have pushed like a crazy man to get here, and now you worry about tiring us? I'm not afraid of a few Comancheros. I could take on ten of them by myself. Let's get the girl. Then we will rest, eh?"

Hunter gazed at the horizon for a moment. Loretta's voice kept whispering to him. *Even in my sleep I dream about what could be happening to her, hear her calling for me. I try to find her, and I can't.*

Hunter wasn't sure why finding Amy had become so important to him, and he didn't care to analyze his feelings. Was his aim to cement a bargain with a woman he had already bought? Why must he pay twice to possess her? Was her happiness so important to him that he was willing to risk his life and those of his friends to chase the shadows from her eyes? The questions were unanswerable. And troubling.

It was bad enough that his friends sensed his urgency. They must think him *boisa*, becoming so obsessed over a *tosi* child.

"*Mea-dro,* let's go," Hog pressed.

Hunter set his jaw. He had made good choices when he had asked these men to ride with him. Not only were they loyal friends, but they asked no questions. "All right, we'll keep going," he agreed. "But on the way home, we'll take it slower."

Hog scowled. "We may have no choice. The

yellow-hair will be in poor shape after being with Santos all this time."

Hunter's guts knotted. He just hoped the child was still alive.

An hour later the group of Comanches crested a swell that looked down on Santos's camp, situated near an underground spring. The three supply wagons, parked in a half-circle on the west side, blocked the glare of the setting sun.

The Comancheros lay about in the scant patches of shade. Their stench, combined with that of a rotting antelope carcass and fresh horse dung, drifted on the breeze. An unnatural stillness fell over them when they spied the Comanches. One man, who had been scratching his crotch, froze with his hand clamped to his groin. Another had the short butt of a cigarette pressed to his lips. When the ember burned down to his fingers, he yelped and waved his arm. The sudden sound set the others into motion. They sprang to their feet, their voices carrying across the grassland as they yelled for their leader.

The thirty Comanches, shoulders erect, expressions stony, slowed their horses to walks. Hunter riveted his gaze to the third wagon on his right. Something blue and white hung from the rear wheel. As he rode closer he saw it was the girl, her thin arms lashed to the spokes, head hanging to her chest. All that remained of her blue dress was the tattered skirt. The gleam of white was her skin and the remnants of her muslin chemise.

Santos walked out to meet them, his right hand lifted, palm forward in greeting. Hunter advanced on him, his eyes glittering, his mouth set in a grim line.

"Hi, hites," Santos called, linking his forefingers in the sign of friendship. In Comanche he said, "It is good you come, my friend, El Lobo. I have many rifles and cartridges. And trinkets for your women."

Hunter did not make the sign of friendship in return. He saw Santos's eyes widen on his painted face. "We do not come to trade. You have my yellow-hair's sister."

The color washed from Santos's swarthy features. "Your woman's sister? No, not me. I am El Lobo's good friend."

Hunter tightened his grip on the reins. As irrational as it was to be so upset over a yellow-hair he didn't even know, he wanted to kill Santos. He had come to get Amy safely away, though, and he must do that first. "I have come for her."

"I swear on my mother's grave, El Lobo, I had no idea. This is a terrible thing."

Santos was doing an admirable job of acting remorseful. If it hadn't been for his pallor, Hunter might have believed him. Hunter swung off his black. He glanced at Hog and Old Man. They knew he counted on them to guard his back. The Comancheros, their number about twenty, showed the proper respect and moved aside to let Hunter pass as he strode toward the third wagon. His chest tightened as he drew close enough to see the girl clearly.

Rage. It hit him like a well-placed blow to his diaphragm, cutting off his air. He knotted his hands into fists and missed a step, swallowing the roar of anger that tried to crawl up his throat. This was the spirited child who had confronted him with a rifle? Her thin white arms were peppered with black-and-blue marks where cruel fingers had dug into her flesh. Her chemise had been torn away, baring her chest, and through the curtains of her tangled gold hair, her small breasts protruded, swollen and purple. Her tattered skirt rode high, and he saw that the milky skin of her inner thighs was caked with blood and dried semen.

Hunter knelt on one knee, the toe of his moccasin nearly touching her bare foot. In the dust he could see that other men had knelt there. Many times, judging by the disturbed earth.

"Aye-mee?" She didn't stir. Hunter touched his hand to her hair, so like his woman's. "Aye-mee, you will be awake. I have come to take you away."

With a suddenness that startled him, she jerked her head up. Her huge eyes filled with stark terror. Hunter stared into their blue depths, searching for sanity. He found none. She took one look at him and began to whimper, fighting against the rope that held her suspended from the wheel. A two-inch swath of bloody-raw flesh banded each of her wrists. This clearly wasn't the first time she had awakened to find a man in front of her.

"Aye-mee," he whispered, trying to soothe her. "*Toquet,* it is well."

He started to untie one of her arms, but her screams stopped him, shrill and short, interspersed with shallow panting. She shrank against the wagon wheel, digging her heels into the dirt to put distance between them. He realized then that she thought he meant to rape her or kill her, perhaps both.

Hunter backed off and held up his hands so she could see he held no weapons. She glanced around wildly, as if she sought help. Tears welled in her eyes. When she looked at him again, her expression was one of complete despair.

Hunter kept his hands up. "Loh-rhett-ah sent me. To find you. Loh-rhett-ah, your sister who loves you."

For an instant her disoriented eyes seemed to focus on him. "Loretta?"

Hunter nodded. "See into me, eh? You remember this Comanche's face?"

She stared at him, and for a moment he hoped she might trust him. Very slowly he reached again to untie her. The instant he moved, she panicked, screaming and throwing her head.

Hunter knew he must hurry. The sooner he got the girl away from here, the safer she would be. His own men wouldn't make a move, but the uneasy Comancheros were another matter. If they sensed, even for a moment, that Hunter's men might seek retribution for this foul deed, they would throw caution aside and start shooting.

Pulling his knife, which terrified Amy even more, Hunter swiftly cut the ropes that anchored her wrists. She dropped to the ground and curled into a ball, knees hugged to her chest, head tucked. When he touched her she jerked and whimpered.

Hunter had to pry her knees from her chest to lift her. She offered no resistance, just trembled when he swept her off the ground into his arms. Her head lolled against his shoulder. When he glanced down at her small face, his heart caught. She was sure enough Loretta's face upon the water. The same small facial bones and sensitive mouth. The same hair. The same eyes, like large patches of summer sky.

Hunter walked toward his horse, looking neither right nor left, acutely aware of the Comancheros all around him. As gently as he could, he set Amy on the stallion's back, then mounted behind her. She moaned and braced her hands on the horse's shoulders. As carefully as he could, he helped her sit crosswise, supporting her back with the bend of his arm.

Santos came forward again. "El Lobo, you have my word, I did not know this woman was close to your heart. I would not have allowed them to touch her."

"Woman?" Hunter hissed.

Santos shrugged one shoulder, his gaze darting nervously. "She is not the first young girl to be broken to ride. You have done the same, many times."

"I make war on men."

Santos scrutinized the entire party of Comanches before he replied. "That is not true of you all."

"This Comanche leaves one set of footprints," Hunter said softly. "Others walk their own way."

Fastening his attention on the girl, Santos slipped into English. "I meant you no harm, leettle *muchacha*." To Hunter he added, "I am your good friend, El Lobo. Thees ees the truth I speak."

With a snort of disgust, Hunter wheeled his horse and rode off. His men closed ranks behind him to defend his back. Amy huddled in Hunter's lap, arms crisscrossed over her chest, eyes squeezed closed, teeth chattering. Hunter scanned her body. There were a couple of deep scratches on her legs that needed to be cleaned. He hoped that was the worst of it, that her insides were not torn as Willow's had been.

He had promised his blue-eyes that he would bring her the child. He didn't want to deliver a corpse.

An hour later, after the Comanches had stopped and made camp in a ravine, Hunter was no closer to discovering the extent of Amy's injuries. Each time he tried to touch her, she became frantic. Now, with him sitting close by, she lay huddled on her side, knees drawn to her chest, arms shielding her head.

Memories washed over him, memories of Amy coming out alone to face an army of warriors, a rifle bigger than she was held to her shoulder. Amy, biting and kicking, when Swift Antelope tried to hold her on his horse. *Comanche heart.* Spirit like hers was hard to break. What pain she must have suffered that she had been reduced to this.

Hunter didn't want to overpower her again. He should tend her injuries, and quickly, but some wounds ran deeper than the flesh. Gentleness was what she needed. From a woman's hands.

There wasn't a woman within a hundred miles.

Hunter called to Old Man and asked that he and the others move some distance away, so Amy would suffer less distress. After a few minutes, when all grew quiet around the two of them, Hunter crossed his ankles and sat beside her.

Very lightly he grasped her shoulder. She shrank from him and began to sob. He kept his hand on her, knowing that sooner or later she must accept his touch so he could find out how badly she was hurt. Her weeping reminded him of Willow, made him remember things best forgotten. The one thing he recalled more vividly than anything else about that distant night was his dying wife's terror. She had clung to him, afraid of the darkness around them, panicking when anyone else got close to her.

Amy had no one to cling to. He could almost taste her fear. She needed to be held. And there was no one. No one but Hunter.

"Aye-mee," he whispered.

She shrank into herself, trying to escape his touch. Hunter ran his hand down her back, then up to her shoulder again. It looked as if there were fresh blood on her tattered skirt. He touched it to be sure. When his fingertips came away wet, fear chilled his skin.

"Aye-mee? You have hurts. This Comanche must care for you. No harm. It is a promise I make for you."

He grasped her skirt and tried to lift it. She came up screaming and lashing out with her small fists. Hunter rocked back on his heels and raised his hands. She scrambled in the dirt to put some distance between them, then hunched forward over her knees, palms pressed to her lower belly.

"Don't touch me! Don't *touch* me!"

Hunter kept his hands raised, trying not to frighten her any more than he already had. "You have many hurts," he said softly. "This Comanche is your good friend. I will help you."

A sob caught in her throat. She lifted her head and fastened swimming blue eyes on him — bruised, aching eyes. He could see she wanted, needed, to believe him. Her small mouth twisted. "F-friend?"

Hunter started to lower his arms. She flinched and shielded her face, clearly afraid he meant to strike her. "Ah, Aye-mee, do not fear. I take you to Loh-rhett-ah, eh? It is good."

"You're lyin'! Loretta's at home. She couldn't have sent you. You're tryin' to trick me."

"This Comanche makes no lies. Loh-rhett-ah waits for you — in my village. She came to me. She knew this Comanche could find you." Hunter searched his memory for something that might convince Amy he spoke only truth. "She came with a black *sitchel* to carry her White Eyes ruffles."

"A satchel?" Hope sprang to Amy's eyes. "H-her black satchel? The one my ma gave her?"

Hunter nodded. "*Huh,* yes, a black satchel. Her dress, it was blue, with small snakes and pink prairie flowers. Much *wannup,* eh? Many white skirts and breeches beneath."

"Her blue calico," Amy whispered.

"Ah, yes? Callee-cho. My eyes could not see this if she did not come to me. This is sure enough the way of it."

"Th-then why did you stop here? Why aren't you taking me to her?"

"You have many hurts."

Tense and ready to bolt, she watched him as he slowly lowered his hands to his knees.

"You will see into me? Do my eyes talk lies?"

She searched his gaze. Hunter knew better than to move, even to breathe.

"Why would Loretta ask *you* to find me?" She passed a trembling hand over her brow. "You're an Injun."

It was a question Hunter couldn't readily answer. Very slowly, cautiously, he raised one hand shoulder high. "She has seen my Black-bird, a small girl. Your Loh-rhett-ah knows this Comanche understands the pain in her heart because her Aye-mee is lost. She trusted this Comanche to find you, to fight the great fight to bring you back to her."

"You have a little girl? Loretta truly sent you?"

She looked so incredulous that Hunter nearly smiled. "I am here, yes? I have come a

376

very long way. If this Comanche wished to make tricks, I would make tricks near my village."

Her eyes clouded for a moment, then cleared. He could see she was beginning to believe him. The sound of footsteps drew both their attention. Hunter glanced over his shoulder to see Old Man approaching. A cry of anguish tore up Amy's throat.

"M-make him go away!" she screeched. "Make him go away!"

Old Man halted midstride. He held up a gourd canteen.

"He brings water, eh?"

Her face blanched. "No — no. Make him leave! I — I don't want him here!"

Hunter started to stand, intending to go and get the canteen. The moment Amy saw him move, she cried out and launched herself at him.

"No! Don't leave me with him! Please don't!"

Taken off guard, Hunter nearly lost his balance when her small body collided with his chest. She vised her thin arms around his neck, cutting off his breath, her naked, sweat-filmed flesh sticking to his like a river leech. For a moment he didn't know how to react. Then he felt the shivers of fear running through her, and he instinctively wrapped his arms around her. She felt no wider in the torso than Blackbird. Hunter's heart twisted

377

at the desperate way she clung to him.

"Don't let him. *Please,* don't let him hurt me."

"No, no, I will not. You are safe, Aye-mee. You are safe." He ran his hand lightly over her back, taking care because of her many bruises.

She went limp and began to cry. Hunter pulled her across his lap. She didn't fight him. He thought perhaps she was too terrified. Her eyes clung to his, huge and wild with fright, her face so pale it looked bloodless.

"Ah, Aye-mee," he whispered.

"Don't let him hurt me, please, don't let him hurt me. I'll be good. I will! I'll do what you say. Don't let him hurt me."

"No one will hurt you. It is a promise I make for you. No one." Carefully, cautiously, Hunter gathered her to his chest. "*Toquet,* little one. Do not fear. It is well."

As his arms tightened around her, she shuddered. Aware that Old Man stood nearby watching, Hunter dipped his head close to hers and began to whisper, rocking her as he would Blackbird. At first she lay rigid. But when he persisted, she began to sob again, and he knew the battle was won.

He shifted her in his arms so her head could rest more comfortably on his shoulder. Not ceasing the rocking motion, he stroked her hair and continued whispering to her. He wasn't sure what he said, if he spoke *tosi tivo* or Comanche. The words didn't matter. The message was in his voice and his hands.

He wasn't sure when it happened, but at some point she turned and again encircled his neck with her thin arms. She pressed close to him, burying her face in the hollow of his shoulder, the violent force of her sobs shuddering through him. Hunter took his cues from her. When she hugged his neck more tightly, he increased the pressure of his arms around her.

He worried about the blood on her skirt. But there was little hope of investigating its source until he had gained her confidence, so he continued to rock her. Feeling her narrow, almost flat chest plastered against his, he could only wonder how those men could have done this to her. No, woman, this, but a child. Hatred rose like gorge in his throat.

Hunter motioned for Old Man to leave the canteen on his horse. When Amy heard his footsteps she jerked, then clung to Hunter more frantically.

"Don't let them take me! Don't! Please, don't!"

"It is well. They will not take you, eh? I am here." He ran his hand into her hair. "I am here, Aye-mee. I am big and mean like the buffalo, yes? You are sure enough safe."

Old Man left as quickly as he had come. Hunter could only guess what the other men must be thinking. That he had lost his Comanche heart. That he had forgotten how his wife had died. That he was *boisa.* For this moment, none of that mattered. He closed his eyes, conscious only of the child in his arms, of the great gift she had bestowed on him — her trust.

Hunter couldn't be sure how much time passed. The sun sank lower on the horizon, heralding nightfall. Still he sat and rocked her. Now and again, when he opened his eyes, he saw the contrast of his dark arms against her white flesh, the shimmer of her hair. A White Eyes. It no longer seemed of any importance.

The rapidly descending sun at last forced Hunter to straighten. He should tend Amy while he still had light.

"Aye-mee," he said softly, "you bleed. I must see to your hurts. Loh-rhett-ah will be heap big angry if I do not care for you."

She stiffened. "I — I got cut on my leg."

"I will see this cut, eh?"

"No . . . I don't want you to."

"It must be. You will trust this Comanche. A little bit, eh?"

She began to tremble again. "No! I ain't gonna let nobody look, not ever again."

Hunter remained still for a moment, thinking. "I will give you my knife. If I make tricks, you can sure enough kill me."

That suggestion brought her head up. She fastened incredulous blue eyes on his. "You wouldn't."

Hunter pulled his knife from its sheath and pressed the hilt into her small hand. She stared down at the wickedly curved blade. Then, with visible reluctance, she said in a shaky voice, "All right, I'll let you — but only if you do it fast."

Hunter lifted her off his lap and onto the ground in front of him. She propped herself up on an elbow and held the knife before her, ready to swing. Biting back a smile, he met her frightened gaze and touched her left thigh.

"Here?"

She nodded. He felt her trembling and knew what it cost her to let him lift her skirt. The gash on the side of her thigh was deep and still bled. Hunter could tell by the clean line that the wound had been inflicted with a knife. Rage roiled inside him. Still, he was relieved. The cut would heal. Keeping his hand on her leg, he glanced up at her.

"Do you bleed from within?"

Her face flamed, and she bit her lip. Hunter would have traded every horse he owned at that moment to have a woman there.

"You must say only truth, eh?"

Her eyes filled with tears. "I'm gonna die, ain't I?"

Hunter felt as though a horse had kicked him in the guts. The years rolled away, and he remembered his wife's last day of life.

"This bleeding from within — it is bad?"

She shook her head, her face twisting. "It was at first. Just a teeny bit now. Am I gonna die?"

Slowly the tension eased from his shoulders. "*Ka,* no." He released his hold on her and lowered her dress. "You will not die." His store of English failed him. "It is the way of it, no? A little bit blood."

He started to get up.

"No! Please, don't leave me!"

"I only go for water and cloth — to clean and wrap the wound." He inclined his head at his horse. "You will watch."

She considered the distance, then agreed with a nod.

Hunter allowed her to keep his knife while he dressed the cut on her thigh. She seemed calmer now that she believed she could defend herself. He wasn't overly concerned that she would stab him, and even if she tried, he knew he could stop her before she did much damage.

When he finished cleaning and wrapping her leg, he gave her one of his leather shirts to hide her nakedness. She took it gratefully but was too weak to pull it over her head without help. She was also loath to surrender the knife. He bit back another smile and suggested she switch the weapon from hand to hand while he fished her small arms down the sleeves.

When that was done, he made her a pallet beneath a mesquite bush, then sat beside her. Immediately her eyelids began to droop. She groped for his hand. Hunter enfolded her fingers in his own. Gazing down at her, he thought of Loretta.

At last Amy drifted off into an exhausted sleep. Afraid that she might cut herself with the razor-sharp knife she still held clutched to her chest, Hunter removed the sheath from his belt and very carefully slipped it down over the curved blade.

He made certain she was deeply asleep before he left her. As quietly as he could, he fetched his horse and led it some distance away before stopping to check his gear. He opened a parfleche, withdrew his spare knife, and threaded the sheath onto his belt. Next he strung his bow and checked the edge on the blade of his ax to be sure it was sharp.

Old Man emerged out of the gloom. "What are you doing?"

Hunter continued preparing for battle, making no reply.

Old Man glanced toward the girl and stroked his chin. "You are going back? It is dangerous, one man against so many."

Hunter pulled all the extra baggage off his horse. "Better than one small girl against so many."

"Your strong arm is hers?"

"It is the way I must walk." Hunter set his

jaw, avoiding Old Man's gaze. They both knew the implications of such a statement. Hunter wished he could explain, but his reasons weren't clearly defined, even to him. "Santos has stolen her honor. Someone must go back and reclaim it."

"I will ride with you."

"No. If I should fall, you must take her to Warrior and Loh-rhett-ah for me."

Old Man sighed, then nodded. "Consider it done, my friend."

With that, Old Man trotted off to rejoin the other men. Hunter heard voices, running footsteps. A grim smile touched his mouth when he looked up to see several of his friends mounting up to ride with him. No questions, no bitter accusations. If he wished to fight over a yellow-hair, they would stand beside him.

Hog rode up, reining in his pinto so sharply that the horse pranced in a half-circle. "So we go to fight, do we?"

"I go."

"Then we go with you." Hog fastened his gaze on the huddled shape under the mesquite bush for a moment. "You'd do the same."

Hunter mounted up. "You're certain you want to go? I'll understand if you stay."

"I am with you. Do you plan to leave any of them alive?"

"This Comanche will show them the same

384

mercy they showed her." Hunter's lips thinned. "None at all."

Amy was still sleeping when Hunter returned three hours later with Santos's bloody scalp dangling from his stallion's bridle. Her honor had been reclaimed . . . with a vengeance.

CHAPTER 17

Firelight danced inside the tepee, casting golden swaths across the room. Loretta sat in the shadows, quietly plaiting her hair, the satchel open beside her. When she finished her hair, she pressed her back against the leather wall, her gaze fixed on the group of Indians who sat cross-legged near the fire, engaged in some sort of dice game. Their playing board was a piece of soft hide with squares painted on it. Each person had a pebble assigned to him, its surface painted a different color from those of the other players.

Loretta couldn't concentrate on the game long enough to figure out its rules. She had eyes only for Red Buffalo. He had joined Warrior's family for the evening and was displaying a jovial, gentle side that Loretta could not believe. Pony Girl, Warrior's two-year-old orphaned niece, climbed all over Red Buffalo, using his braids for handholds, squeezing his neck from behind until his face turned red, tickling him when he ignored her to concentrate on the game. The warrior put up with her antics, his hands always gentle when he disengaged his hair from her clutches. Loretta could scarcely believe her eyes.

When Maiden of the Tall Grass picked up the dice, Red Buffalo said something to her, and she gave an outraged squeal, elbowing him in the ribs. Red Buffalo laughed and grabbed her braids, looping them into a knot beneath her chin. She rolled her beautiful eyes and shook the dice, tossing them with a flourish. Red Buffalo leaned forward to see what she had thrown, then groaned and thumped his brow with the heel of his hand. Warrior threw back his head and roared with laughter. Turtle, who at the advanced age of five had been allowed to play, began to pout.

The game was over, and Maiden of the Tall Grass had clearly trounced the men. She unlooped her braids and swept them over her shoulders, a smug expression on her face. The gesture reminded Loretta of Amy, but then, these days, everything did. As she watched this family interact, the only differences she could detect between them and white people were their dress and language. Indeed, they seemed happier and more content.

Red Buffalo glanced up. When his gaze collided with Loretta's, his smile died. He looked down at her satchel, his attention caught by the diamond comb twinkling in the firelight. He stared a moment, then averted his face, but not before she saw the hatred he harbored for her. Loretta closed the satchel, determined to ignore him. Hunter would be back with Amy soon.

Maiden's distorted shadow danced upon the walls as she rose from the circle and rummaged in her cooking utensils. Returning to the fire, she suspended a large kettle on the spit over the low flames. Turtle followed on her heels, his face alight with anticipation. After tossing in a dollop of grease, the Indian woman poured something from a parfleche into the kettle and clamped on the lid. Within minutes Loretta heard a peculiar popping noise.

Popcorn. Amy's favorite. The memories hurt — sitting at the table, lips smeared with melted butter, the sound of laughter like music in the air. Loretta averted her face and blinked away a rush of tears. No wonder Turtle was excited. Didn't all children love popcorn? Soon, the smell drifted to her. If only Amy were here with them.

Warrior beckoned to her. "Loh-rhett-ah, you come, eh?"

Loretta glanced uneasily at Red Buffalo. To her surprise, he moved closer to Maiden of the Tall Grass to make room for her. Blackbird dashed across the room and seized Loretta's hand.

"Keemah!" she cried.

Loretta rose and let the child lead her to the circle. She shot a glance at Red Buffalo. He caught the look and smiled. She had the uneasy feeling he did so only for the benefit of Warrior and Maiden of the Tall Grass, and that he had a motive for this sudden turnabout. *Oh, God.* Did he hope that Warrior might leave him alone with her?

"This Comanche will not eat you," he said. "Be easy."

Not sure what to make of his mood, Loretta arranged her skirt around her and sat down, folding her hands in her lap. With Warrior sitting so close, she felt fairly safe. These last five days he had proven himself to be an even-tempered and kind man. Maiden of the Tall Grass, in her sweet, quiet way, ruled the roost. Loretta felt confident no one would harm her with Warrior close at hand.

After the corn finished popping, Maiden removed the kettle from over the flames and set it in the center of their circle. When she whisked away the lid, the smell itself was almost good enough to eat. Once everyone else had helped themselves, Loretta shyly scooped a small handful, trying not to think about Amy and failing miserably. Red Buffalo snorted and dipped his hands into the fluffed kernels, his palms forming a sizable bowl. The next instant he dumped the mountain of corn onto Loretta's skirt where it stretched across her lap.

"Oh, my! I —" Loretta was about to say she couldn't possibly eat so much. She swallowed the words and forced a smile. These people didn't know Amy. She couldn't expect them to understand her somber mood — or even to care. "Thank you."

Blackbird snitched a piece of popcorn from Loretta's mound, and everyone laughed. Not to be outdone, Pony Girl, always on the move, toddled over and helped herself as well.

"You see? It is good you have so much," Red Buffalo said.

His voice sounded so kind that Loretta looked up. With his face so horribly scarred, it was difficult to read his expressions. Was the glint in his eyes simply a reflection of the firelight? A tingle of unease ran up her spine. She glanced away. No matter how nicely he behaved toward her, she would never trust him.

Swift Antelope poked his head around the door flap and called Turtle's name. When he smelled the popcorn he came toward them, his handsome face wreathed in a grin. Loretta leaned sideways when he reached for a handful of the rare treat. Though Hunter had assured her that Swift Antelope's strong arm was hers, Loretta hadn't seen enough of the youth during her stay with Maiden of the Tall Grass to feel at ease around him.

Swift Antelope looked more Mexican than

Comanche, and Loretta wondered if perhaps he wasn't of mixed blood, like Hunter. His features were almost too perfect for a man, a straight, regal nose, large liquid brown eyes, and finely drawn lips that formed a perfect bow. Not that his bloodlines mattered. Whatever his origins, he was an accepted and well-liked member of the village. She guessed him to be fifteen, maybe sixteen, but he carried himself like a man, his musculature well defined, his stance prideful. She suspected he could be as brutal as any in battle.

Stealing another helping of popcorn, Swift Antelope said something to Turtle and winked. Without asking permission from his parents, Warrior's small son leaped up and followed the older boy from the lodge. Loretta gazed after them, wondering where they were going so late in the evening. Warrior and Maiden of the Tall Grass seemed unconcerned. Loretta was learning that Comanche children were given a far freer rein than white, coming and going at will. She had yet to see one of them punished or even so much as scolded.

Blackbird stole Turtle's place beside her father, cuddling up to his side and cooing. Warrior grinned and shoved some popcorn in her mouth. She gobbled at him like a turkey, nibbling at his fingers. Pony Girl, always in competition with the older girl for attention, squealed and dashed in their direction. As she scurried around behind Loretta, she tripped.

Red Buffalo lunged to catch the child, but not in time. She toppled and landed on her back in the fire. Her screams pierced the air.

"Oh, my God!" Legs tangled in her skirts, Loretta couldn't move quickly enough.

Warrior fought to disengage himself from his daughter. Maiden, scrambling to her feet, was on the far side of the circle. Red Buffalo was closest and swiftest. He snatched the little girl from the flames, took one look at her burns, and whirled toward the lodge door, holding her up before him as he ran. Loretta, unable to understand what he shouted, could only wonder where he was taking her.

Warrior and Maiden of the Tall Grass ran after Red Buffalo, Blackbird a streak of motion behind them. By the time Loretta got her skirts jerked free and could rise, she was alone inside the lodge, the sounds of Pony Girl's screams drifting back to her, growing fainter. She couldn't follow them. She was an outsider. Trembling, she gazed at the fire. Poor Pony Girl. Guilt washed over Loretta and she gave her cumbersome skirts a disgusted swat, remembering how gently Hunter had touched the child, how his eyes had warmed when he looked at her.

Popcorn littered the ground at Loretta's feet. Still shaking from fear and concern, she crouched to pick up the mess and tossed it onto the fire. By the time she finished, several minutes had passed.

This was the first time she had been left alone in the village. Those first three days, Hunter had hovered over her, and these last five, Maiden of the Tall Grass had been with her. Loretta sank to her knees, staring into the flames, senses tuned to the noise outside. Other villagers who had heard Pony Girl's screams were talking back and forth, their voices sharp with concern.

Loretta closed her eyes. She prayed the child was all right.

The door flap rustled as someone came inside. Loretta couldn't bring herself to look up. Had someone realized she was alone? Were they coming to torment her? To kill her?

"Warrior and Maiden will return soon. They must cool the fire from Pony Girl's burn — in the river. When it is finished, they will take her to Herb Woman for healing salve. Warrior sent me back to guard you. Swift Antelope is off in the night with Turtle."

Loretta threw up her head to find Red Buffalo striding toward her, his leggings and moccasins dripping wet. She could picture him dashing into the river with Pony Girl, his hands gentle, his voice soothing. Her throat tightened. It unnerved her that she was seeing him, not as a one-dimensional villain, but as a man who loved and was loved in return.

A man with two faces, one human, one monstrous.

He squatted on the other side of the fire, his gaze trailing slowly over her. A mocking smile tugged at his mouth. "Have no fear. No need, eh?"

Loretta bunched her skirt in her fist. "I thought you hated me. Why this sudden change?"

His smile widened. "No change. My hate burns" — he nodded toward the firepit — "like the flames. My heart is glad, yes? You are my cousin's woman. It was your bargain with him. In trade for your sister?" He lifted an eyebrow, watching her like a cruel little boy who had tossed a bug into a hot skillet. She had the uneasy feeling that he was glad of this moment alone with her, that he had been waiting, like a cat watching a mouse, to pounce. "The song will soon be finished."

A kernel of the corn that Loretta had tossed onto the fire chose that moment to pop. The sudden noise made her start. Red Buffalo's disfigured mouth twisted.

Dread mounted within Loretta. She knew that was his intent, to unnerve her. Why allow him to bait her? "You're referring to Hunter's song, I take it?"

Red Buffalo looked surprised. "He has said the words to you?"

"No. What *are* the words?"

His eyes gleamed, and this time she knew it

had nothing to do with the firelight but was evil shining out of him. "You will learn the words — very soon." His expression turned smug. "When my cousin returns. You are sure enough not smart, Yellow Hair. But that is good, the song must come to pass."

"What do you mean?"

He shrugged off her question.

"Tell me," she insisted.

"You will see." He smiled, as if amused by a private joke. He gazed into the fire for several seconds. "Did he not show you how to walk back to him in his footsteps when he took you home to your wooden walls? Did he not mark your ground, so all who passed would know his woman lived there?"

"Yes, what of it?"

He watched her, as if waiting for the implication of that to hit her. When she simply stared at him, he chuckled aloud. "Did he not leave you one of his finest horses? Did he not leave his medallion with you to mark you as his woman?"

A chill slithered up Loretta's spine. "Yes."

"And soon after he left, the Comancheros came, eh?"

"Yes. What are you saying?"

Red Buffalo smiled. "That you are sure enough not smart. He *sent* Santos to find you. The words of the song say you must 'come' to him. Hunter made the path back to him an easy one to walk. And now, stupid woman, you have traded yourself to him. You are his. When he returns, the song will be finished."

The pieces fell into place with horrible clarity. Loretta stared at him, her pulse quickening. "No . . . you're lying."

Another kernel of popcorn snapped. Red Buffalo tossed the charred remains back into the flames. "It had to be. The beloved child stolen to bring you to him, eh? His medallion marked you, so his *friend,* Santos, would not steal the wrong woman. Three golden ones. Santos knew you by the stone my cousin gave you."

"No." Despite her denial, he was making a twisted sort of sense. "He wouldn't do something so despicable. Not to a child!"

"The Comancheros visit your wooden walls often?"

"No, never." Loretta licked her lips, her tongue dry and sticky. "But it's not unheard of for them to be in that area."

His eyes pierced hers. "Hunter leaves you, and, for the first time, they come? They take the child. And his yellow-hair returns to him, sure enough quick."

"You're lying!"

"The song must come to pass. When he returns with the child, he will hold you to your bargain. You came to him, as it was spoken in his song so long ago. You bargained with him, giving yourself in trade, to get the child back. When he returns, he will go to the central fire and announce his marriage to you. Then . . ." Red Buffalo grinned and made a slashing motion across his larynx. "*Suvate,* it is finished."

Loretta's stomach dropped. "No."

He shrugged again, as if in agreement. "Ah, yes, he will play with you a little first." Leaning toward her, so the light from the fire played upon his scarred face, he leered and said, "As will I. Many of us, eh? It will be heap big fun, Yellow Hair. You think he would be so kind to another white woman?" He gave a snort and rose to his feet. "You are a fool. A White Eyes? We spit upon you. You sicken his gut. Your people killed his wife, his unborn child. He has taken you into his buffalo robes? No, Yellow Hair. To find pleasure with one such as you, he must wait and have you *his* way."

As if her close proximity contaminated the air he breathed, Red Buffalo left the fire to sit upon a pallet. Pulling his knife, he tested the blade with his thumb. Then, leveling his gaze on her breasts, he traced a path with the tip of the knife across his chest. "Soon, eh? Very soon."

Nausea welled in Loretta's throat. She couldn't stop watching the path of his knife, imagining it on her body.

"Say my words to Warrior. He will tell you I speak the truth. Watch my cousin when he returns. He will go to the central fire and speak the words to make you his wife. You watch. You will see. Red Buffalo does not make a lie."

A sudden and chilling fear gripped Loretta. Hunter did believe his song must come to pass, and that she was an integral part of it. Had he manipulated her like a marionette, making her dance to the words so his prophecy would come to pass? His wife had been killed by white people? Perhaps he was as consumed with hatred as she, detesting all people with white skin, just as she did Comanches.

Sweat beaded on Loretta's forehead. *I will know the song your heart sings.* She had believed Hunter. She cared for him a little, and thought of him as her friend. Her *friend.* He had understood that, nurtured it. *There will be no war between us. I would salute you and ride away.* Could he be so deceitful? So totally merciless?

She remembered his scalp pole — how his mother had tried to remove it from his lodge, along with the other evidence of his treachery. Dear God, they were all a part of it, all of them, even Maiden of the Tall Grass.

Loretta clenched her teeth, meeting Red Buffalo's evil gaze. Memories of Hunter flowed through her mind. The husky whisper of his voice, the gentle touch of his hands, his indulgent smile. Could a man put on that convincing an act? No, she wouldn't believe Red Buffalo, she couldn't. She owed Hunter that much.

She would wait and pray. If Red Buffalo wasn't lying, if Hunter had indeed manipulated events to make her return to him, then she and Amy were as good as dead.

At daybreak, terror hit Amy the moment she opened her eyes. *They* were all around her. Mornings and evenings, when it was cool, were always the worst. They would come soon, one man, perhaps two, followed by a steady flow until the sun rose high overhead.

She prayed for death to take her before it began again.

As she did every morning when she first awoke, Amy strained against the ropes that bound her. When she realized there were no ropes, bewilderment welled within her. She wasn't tied to the wagon wheel? She was lying on soft fur, covered with a buffalo robe? Her fingers tightened reflexively on the handle of the knife, and the previous day came rushing back to her.

Hunter, the Comanche.

Ma said he was a heartless animal. Maybe he was. But at least he hadn't done *that* to her yet. Amy glanced around. His horse grazed nearby, but Hunter was nowhere to be seen. A sob tore up her throat, followed quickly by another and another. Where was he? Had he left her? The minute those other Indians realized she was alone —

A large warm hand came from out of nowhere and settled on her hair. She snapped taut, swallowing her sobs, terrified to move. *A man.* But who? Had one of the other Indians sneaked up on her? Twisting her neck, she discovered that Hunter lay nearby, the top of his head inches from her own, his feet pointing one way, hers the other.

"Ka taikay, ka taikay," he whispered sleepily. *"Toquet, ma-tao-yo."*

Amy didn't understand the words. She only knew they soothed her in some indefinable way, as did the weight of his hand on her hair. A hard, powerful hand, yet strangely gentle. She *wasn't* alone. He had been with her all night and never once touched her.

Before she thought it through, Amy dug in with her heels and scooted in his direction. When her head rested beside his, he lifted his dark lashes and tried to focus on her. She was so close, his indigo eyes turned inward toward the high bridge of his nose. He moved back and blinked.

Amy held her breath. She was afraid, yet not afraid. His shoulder loomed in her peripheral vision. His brown chest was twice the span of hers, maybe wider, and his muscle-padded breasts made her own look like two little skeeter bites in comparison. He

400

could kill her if he wanted. Snap her neck like a dry twig.

He could also protect her.

When he had fed Amy and given her water, Hunter began making preparations to leave, the first chore on his list to hide Santo's scalp so she wouldn't see it and become frightened. After securing a saddlebag to his stallion's surcingle, he stowed the scalp, then moved to grab another bag and bumped into something. Glancing over his shoulder, he discovered that the *something* was Amy. Her huge eyes shone up at him, so vivid a blue and so filled with fear that he bit back a growl of irritation. Stepping around her, he bent to pick up his traveling pack. As he straightened, his elbow connected with her shoulder. When he walked back to his horse, she came along as if she were attached to him by invisible strings of sinew.

Hunter strapped the traveling pack onto his stallion, then turned to regard her. She was clearly terrified that he meant to abandon her. He knew what the other men would think if he treated her with too much regard. He didn't care. If they believed he meant to take Loretta as his wife, that this child was his new sister by marriage, they would treat her more kindly during the trip, and Amy needed all the kindness she could get.

Resigned, Hunter lifted an arm so she could

step close to his side. He felt her clammy little fingers curl under his belt, as if she feared he might escape her. A smile tugged at his mouth as he tightened his arm around her small shoulders. "You must take care with that knife," he told her softly. "It has a fine edge, and will cut if you take it from the sheath."

She clutched the weapon more fiercely. Hunter regarded her for a moment, then pulled a length of rawhide from his packs. Kneeling before her, he extended his hand for the knife, his gaze holding hers. "For this one moment, yes?"

Loath to relinquish her only means of defense, Amy stared at him. Patiently Hunter waited her out. When at last she handed him the knife, he fished the rawhide through the belt loop on the sheath, then tied the rawhide around Amy's waist, positioning the weapon so that it rode handily on her hip. His reward was a shaky smile. Hunter figured it was a good trade.

CHAPTER 18

Someone was cooking up a pot of dried plums. The sweet smell drifted on the evening air, tantalizing Loretta. Maiden of the Tall Grass had lifted the side flaps on her lodge, allowing a breeze to drift through, which afforded Loretta a view of her neighbors. Funny how, if she closed her eyes, she could imagine she was camped with white folk. There was laughter. Children's voices chimed. In the distance she could hear some man yelling at his wife, just like Uncle Henry at home, except that the wife yelled back. Aunt Rachel never dared.

Maiden, bent over her sewing, glanced up and grinned. With a soft glow in her dark eyes, she lifted the velvety doeskin blouse she was making, turning it so Loretta might admire the style. Watching her, Loretta found it difficult to believe the woman could be involved in a treacherous plot, and if Maiden knew nothing of a plot, there probably wasn't one. Which was why Loretta had decided to reserve judgment until Hunter returned.

Just as Red Buffalo predicted, Warrior had confirmed his story. Yes, Hunter had given Loretta a fine horse and had taught her to walk in his footsteps so she could "come" to him, as it was spoken in his song. Yes, he had given her his medallion to mark her as his woman. Loretta hadn't grilled Warrior for any information beyond that or told him what prompted her questions. If Hunter *was* guilty of trickery, she'd need the element of surprise to escape with Amy.

If Hunter was guilty. In the seven days since Red Buffalo's frightening revelations, Loretta had found that increasingly difficult to believe. If Amy's abduction and consequent rescue by Hunter had been prearranged, surely Hunter would have been back before this. For him to have taken this long, he must have run into difficulties — in finding Santos, in getting Amy away from him. At this point Loretta could only pray that Amy was still alive.

Forcing her mind off Amy's plight and onto the garment Maiden was holding up, Loretta said, "It's beautiful, truly beautiful."

The blouse *was* beautiful, with fringed, elbow-length raglan sleeves and a slit neck, bordered with intricate beadwork. It was the latest in fashion, if Maiden's excited jabbering was any indication.

Loretta leaned forward to touch the blouse.

"You're a wonderful seamstress."

"*Huh, huh.*" Maiden of the Tall Grass bit her bottom lip to stifle a pleased smile. Loretta knew *huh* meant yes, and by that she also knew Maiden understood she approved, even though they couldn't communicate well. "*Ein mah-heepicut,*" Maiden added softly, shyly.

Loretta had heard those words before, but she couldn't recall when or what they meant. She scooped a handful of beads from Maiden's bead bag and began sorting them on the fur pallet into piles, reds, blues, greens, blacks. Maiden of the Tall Grass murmured something and nodded in appreciation. Loretta was glad for something to do. When her hands were busy, she found it easier to keep her fear for Amy at bay.

A shout from outside drew Maiden's attention. She cocked her head and set her sewing aside, rising to her knees. After listening a moment, she began jabbering and waving her hands. Loretta looked outside and saw people rushing along the pathway between the lodges toward the edge of the village. Habbe Esa. When she heard the name, alarm, hope, and something indefinable shot through her. Hunter was back.

Loretta gathered her skirt so it wouldn't trip her and leaped to her feet. She didn't dare leave the lodge, not without Warrior's protection. *Amy.* Had Hunter found her? Loretta's feet moved, carrying her toward the lodge door. Maiden of the Tall Grass hurried outside and bounced about on her tiptoes, trying to see over the heads of the growing crowd. She chortled happily and nodded at Loretta. The words *"yo-oh-hobt pa-pi"* rang loud and clear. Yellow-hair! Loretta forgot about her own safety and ran out of the lodge. Maiden of the Tall Grass caught her arm and held her back with unexpected strength.

"*Ka,* no!"

In an agony of anticipation, Loretta strained to see the large group of men riding in. Then she glimpsed a blond head. That was all it took. She broke away from Maiden and ran out into the pathway, joining the flow of bodies that pressed forward. *Amy.* She shoved her way between two women.

Loretta was so excited, she didn't notice Swift Antelope walking beside her. The next instant she glimpsed a black horse cutting through the crowd, and a familiar, deep voice said, "Blue Eyes?"

Hunter's breath caught when Loretta turned at the sound of his voice. For an instant he forgot about the child cradled against his chest, his entire being focused on the beautiful woman who stood, surrounded by hostile squaws, in a cloud of settling dust. Her eyes shone like the brilliant blue at the base of a flame, dark lashes sweeping to the arch of her honey-gold brows. Her braid had

406

come loose, and rich folds of golden hair spilled to her shoulders. She was so beautiful that he couldn't believe, was almost afraid to believe, she truly belonged to him. Even in voluminous skirts, covered chin to toe in multiple layers of cloth, he could see the feminine lines of her body, the swell of her breasts, the indentation of her waist, the flare of her hips.

Hunter had been proud of few possessions during his life. He had, of course, been proud of his first bow and his first coup feather. And he had certainly been proud of his wonderful war pony, Smoke. But the feeling that coursed through him now surpassed that. This golden woman was bound to him by her God promise, his and only his, forever with no horizon. Desire, hot and urgent, flared to life inside him as he contemplated the coming night. The thought of having her in his buffalo robes, of loving her as he had dreamed of doing so many times, made the trials he had endured to find Amy seem like nothing.

Loretta's gaze shifted to the child he held. Running forward with upraised arms, she cried, "Amy! Oh, Amy! He found you! Thanks be to God!"

Hunter wasn't sure exactly what he had been expecting from Loretta when he delivered the child to her. Gratitude, surely. He had ridden nonstop for twelve days. He had risked his life. He had cared for her sister.

And now she ignored him as if he weren't there? Her *God* had not fought the bloody battle with Santos; Hunter had.

Hunter knew it was bad of him, but he was glad when Amy clung to his waist and hid her face in the hollow of his shoulder. At least *she* knew who had brought her here. He glanced around at the throngs of people. "She fears for her scalp, Blue Eyes."

Loretta placed a hand on Amy's leg. "Honey, it's me, Loretta."

Amy peeked out, saw the strange Indians, and shrank against Hunter, once again hiding her face.

"Amy, darling —" Loretta's voice broke. "What's wrong with her?"

Hunter felt a twinge of guilt. Remembering Amy as she had been before Santos stole her, he could imagine the shock Loretta must be feeling. He had grown accustomed to the child's cowering, and knowing what he did about her ordeal, he understood it. Loretta had not seen her tied to the wagon wheel, defenseless against the filthy men who had abused her.

"Her heart is laid upon the ground." Hunter enfolded Loretta's hand in his and nudged his stallion into a walk, pulling her along with him toward his lodge. He had forgotten how small her hand felt, how fragile the network of bones, how soft her skin. His stomach tightened with delicious anticipation. No brave he knew had a woman such as this.

"It is well, Blue Eyes. She is frightened."

When they reached his lodge, Hunter pried Amy's arms from around him to lift her off the horse. Loretta hovered at his elbow, crooning and smoothing the child's hair.

Amy vised her arms around Hunter's neck. "Don't leave me!" she pleaded shakily.

Hunter carried Amy inside the lodge to put her on the bed. She clung to him and refused to let go. Hunter at last gave in and sat down. She scurried onto his lap, pressing against him as if she wanted to melt and be absorbed, like tallow into leather. Loretta stood nearby, wringing her hands.

Hunter knew he should go directly to the central fire. It was the custom for warriors to give a public recounting after making a trip. His friends would be waiting, anxious to tell of their exploits and brag of their courage in front of their women. Tonight they would reap the rewards for their bravery in loving arms. The more exciting their feats, the better the loving.

Yes, they would be anxious to get the talking done, to give their women the booty taken from Santos's wagons and show off their new rifles. Since Hunter had been the leader on this trip, his presence was required.

But, just as Loretta had her first night in his lodge, Amy needed him. For this little while. *"Toquet,"* he whispered, hugging the child tightly in his arms. "This is my lodge, Aye-mee. No harm here."

Loretta swallowed a lump of hot tears. Watching Hunter, she felt ashamed for suspecting him of having apart in the child's abduction. The way Amy clung to him told its own story.

Staring down at Hunter, she noticed things about him that she hadn't before. Or perhaps it was that she now saw him in a new light. The broad span of his shoulders, knotted with muscle, hunched protectively around Amy, no longer seemed threatening. His large hands, capable of brutal strength, touched Amy with incredible gentleness. Even his voice seemed altered, low and silken, his whispers transcending the language barrier, a blend of English and Comanche that seemed to soothe Amy, tranquilize her, while Loretta could not. Man and child, strength and fragility, dark skin and fair.

Loretta couldn't feel the ground under her feet. A warmth spread through her chest. She tried to remember, a little guiltily, how it had felt when Hunter's hand rested on *her* back like that, on *her* hair. This was no time for such thoughts. Only Amy should matter right now, but Loretta couldn't help herself. *Hunter.* Her hated captor had become her hero, and the backwash of her own emotions swamped her. Hunter, the legendary killer. Where had he gone? Had he ever existed?

"Loh-rhett-ah is here, eh?" Hunter reached to take Loretta's hand, pulling her close to the bed. "Her heart has been laid upon the ground, and she has wailed and wept. You will see into her, yes?"

Hunter joined Loretta's hand with Amy's. The touch was all it took. Amy disentangled herself from his embrace and threw herself at Loretta, sobbing and shaking. Loretta clasped the girl to her, swaying from side to side.

"You're here, Loretta! Really here! I was afraid I'd never see you again!"

"Oh, yes, Amy, I'm here, I'm here."

"They — they did awful things to me," Amy cried. "Awful, awful things!"

Hunter rose slowly from the bed. The time for woman-talk had come, and he was no longer needed.

Seeing that he was about to leave, Loretta worked one arm loose to touch his shoulder as he stepped around them. Their eyes locked. Pausing midstride, he touched his hand to her cheek. Once again Loretta felt curiously detached, disoriented. She wanted to lean toward him, to feel the steely warmth of his arms around her, to hear his voice saying all would be well, to feel safe — as only he could make her feel. She wanted those things with such intensity that she ached, and the realization frightened her. What was happening to her?

Hunter saw the glow of fondness in Loretta's eyes, and it was all the gratitude he needed. He left the lodge, standing a little taller than when he had entered.

Loretta sank onto the bed to comfort Amy, listening to her in shocked horror as she brokenly described her ordeal. The brutality of it sickened her. Fury welled inside her. She wanted to kill Santos with her bare hands.

"When Hunter got there, was there a terrible fight?" Loretta asked shakily.

In a faint voice Amy said, "No. He just walked into Santos's camp and carried me to his horse."

Something quivery and cold fluttered in Loretta's belly. Licking her lips, she turned to stare at Hunter's scalp pole. Her mind reeled with the implications of what Amy had just said. "What do you mean, he just walked in? With guns, right?"

"No, no guns. He put me on his horse, talked to Santos a minute, and then rode off."

A ringing sound began in Loretta's ears. Shock anesthetized her emotions, emptying her, chilling her. "Amy . . . this is extremely important. Did it seem like Hunter and Santos were good friends?"

"Santos said so. 'I am your good friend, El Lobo,' that's what he said." A sob caught in Amy's throat. "You know what, Loretta? I wanted them Comanches to kill him. I truly did. I hoped Hunter'd scalp him, right there in front of me. That's bad of me, ain't it?"

"Oh, no, sweetheart, it isn't bad. The man ought to be strung up for what he's done."

"Do ya think God'll forgive me for wishin' him dead?"

"I know He will." Loretta pressed her face against the child's hair. "Oh, honey, you mustn't torture yourself this way. It's perfectly natural for you to hate Santos. If I understand, don't you think God will?"

After several minutes Amy relaxed in Loretta's arms, her heavy-lidded eyes glazed with exhaustion. Loretta stroked her hair, whispering platitudes that she hated even as she said them. Everything *wasn't* all right. She and Amy were in more trouble than Loretta knew how to get them out of. A horrible quivering attacked her limbs and set her teeth to clacking.

Minutes passed. Loretta's mind raced. *I am your good friend, El Lobo.* Dear God, what should she do? Run? And if they ran, where could they go?

Her thoughts were interrupted when she heard men's voices. Lowering Amy onto the bed, Loretta crept to the lodge door and lifted the flap to peer out into the twilight. Some distance away, a crowd had gathered around a roaring fire. Hunter, astride his black stallion, his body shimmering like oiled bronze in the firelight, was delivering a booming oratory, his arm raised above his head,

413

his fist knotted. He seized a handful of his hair and made a slashing motion across his skull with his other hand. It was obvious he was talking about scalping someone. The crowd roared with approval.

The names Loh-rhett-ah and Aye-mee floated on the breeze. Everyone turned to look toward Hunter's lodge. Another cheer went up. Loretta knew they weren't yelling because she was so well liked.

Dropping the lodge flap, she hugged her waist, her pulse accelerating. Red Buffalo's warning was all she could think about. Part of her wanted to scream a denial, but another part of her gave way to unreasoning fear.

She knotted her fists in her skirt, remembering the oath she had made to stay with him, to be his woman, his slave. She didn't break promises easily. Weakness attacked her legs. Dear God, why was she standing here, worrying about promises made to a man who had lied to her from the first? She couldn't afford to wait and then learn she had been duped. She had Amy to think of.

"Amy!" Loretta ran across the lodge. "Darling, wake up!"

Amy's eyes opened. She stiffened immediately. "What's wrong?"

Loretta grabbed her arm and hauled her off the bed. "We have to get out of here!"

The little remaining color in Amy's face drained away. "Why? I don't wanna leave without Hunter. There's Comanches out there! Hundreds of 'em."

Loretta didn't want to frighten Amy. The poor child had been through enough. "Just trust me, love. We have to leave."

Too agitated to think about food or water for the trip, she grasped Amy's hand and half dragged her to the door. Peering out to be certain no one at the fire was watching, Loretta ducked under the flap, pulling Amy along behind her. As quickly as she could, she circled the tepee so it would block them from view.

"I think that Injun saw us," Amy cried shakily.

Loretta glanced around wildly and spied Red Buffalo walking toward the central fire. If he had seen them, he gave no indication. "We have to reach the horses. It's quite a ways, Amy. Can you make it?"

Amy swayed on her feet, nodding. Loretta struck off, one arm stretched out behind her to pull Amy, her other hand holding up her skirts so she wouldn't trip. After what seemed an eternity, they reached the edge of the village. Loretta sent up a prayer of thanksgiving. Then Amy began to slow her steps. Loretta glanced back to see if she was okay. The child's face was pasty. "Honey, are you all right?"

Amy stumbled and nearly fell. "I just feel funny."

With that pronouncement, Amy pitched forward. Loretta barely caught her in time. With a strength she didn't know she had, she managed to keep Amy on her feet by leaning into her. She had passed out. Frantic, Loretta had no choice but to carry her. Shoving her shoulder against the girl's stomach, she straightened. The dead weight nearly buckled her legs. She staggered, regained her balance, and stumbled in the direction of the horses.

A hundred yards later, Loretta stepped on her skirt and crashed to her knees. Amy rolled off her and flopped on the ground. It took all Loretta's strength to lift Amy again and throw her over her shoulder. She staggered forward, praying. She had to make it to the horses. She just had to. Before Hunter realized she was gone.

The moment Hunter saw Red Buffalo walking toward him, he knew something had happened to Loretta. Nothing else would make him look so smug. In the middle of his speech, Hunter broke off and glanced toward his lodge, his chest constricting around a knot of fear. Red Buffalo drew near, his smile widening.

"Your woman tries to flee," Red Buffalo snarled. "She makes a lie of her promise to you, eh? It is just as I said. She can never be one with the People. Never! She is an *easop*, liar, and unworthy. She has made a fool of you, cousin!"

A hush fell over the crowd. Hunter tightened his legs around his stallion and picked up the reins. "Which direction did she go?"

"Toward the horses. Where else? Whose will she kill this time, eh?"

Hunter kicked his stallion's flanks, biting down on a roar of sheer outrage. She had given him her God promise! Was nothing sacred to the White Eyes? As he rode out of the village, Hunter heard another horse pounding up behind him. He glanced back to see Swift Antelope coming up fast on his sorrel.

Seconds later Hunter spotted Loretta. She was carrying Amy, bent under the weight, scarcely able to lift her feet. He reined in his black, struggling to sort and make sense of his emotions. Anger, yes, but pain as well, a pain that ran so deep he could scarcely bear it. She had used him, and now she meant to flee, her many promises forgotten. From the very beginning she had planned to leave him as soon as he brought her the child. Hunter could tolerate many things, but being made to look the fool wasn't one of them.

Swift Antelope drew up beside him. "Hunter, what are you going to do?"

"Teach her not to make lies!"

Swift Antelope watched the yellow-hair struggling to carry the smaller girl. Seconds later she lost her balance and sprawled in the

417

dirt. He winced. Glancing at Hunter, he raised an eyebrow. Hunter kept his horse reined in, his gaze pinned to the woman. Swift Antelope sighed. That glitter in his friend's eyes boded ill. The woman struggled frantically to lift the girl again. Twice she dropped her. Then, at last, she managed to drape her over her shoulder. She plodded forward a few more steps before her legs buckled and she slammed into the ground.

Swift Antelope leaned forward on his horse, his attention on the younger girl, remembering how fiercely she had fought him that long-ago morning at her wooden walls. A protective feeling welled inside him.

"Ai-ee," he exclaimed. "We'd better stop her, Hunter. If your woman drops the one called Aye-mee again, she may be badly hurt."

Hunter kicked his horse into a run. Swift Antelope had never seen Hunter kick his horse like that, never.

As they rode up behind the two yellow-hairs, Loretta jerked the knife from Amy's sheath. Hunter flashed Swift Antelope a grim smile. "Are you ready for a fight?"

Swift Antelope rolled his eyes. "If she doesn't lay herself open first."

Hunter swung off his horse and strode toward his woman. She stepped between him and Amy, holding the knife high, shaking so badly that he was surprised she didn't drop it. He kept advancing on her, growing more furious by the second.

"Stay back, Hunter! I mean it! She's been through enough! I won't let you hurt her any more, do you hear me?"

Hunter's rage magnified. After all he had done, she dared accuse him of harming Amy? He slowed his pace. He had expected defiance. Instead Loretta was quivering, so frightened that she could barely stand. He drew to a stop, studying her. As angry as he was, he wasn't blind. He had no idea why she had tried to run, but whatever the reason, she was too frightened to see beyond it.

"Blue Eyes —"

"Don't call me that. My name's Loretta. You can't fool me anymore with your pet names and gentle act. I know the truth."

Hunter considered that for a moment. "You will tell me this truth, eh?"

Tears filled her eyes. "Stop it! Stop it, do you hear me? I know, Hunter. I know it all — why you taught me how to track you, why you left me the horse and medallion. How could you? How could you?" He started toward her, and she made a jab with the knife. "Don't do it! I'll kill you. I will!" She swallowed, glancing toward Swift Antelope, then back at Hunter. "You said you were my friend! And, God help me, I believed you!"

Hunter held up a hand. "Do not swing at the air, Blue Eyes. The blade is long. You will gut yourself."

"I'll gut *you,* you miserable bastard!"

Hunter folded his arms across his chest, regarding her with a bewildered frown. "I bring you the child. This is not good?"

"Was it hard finding her?" she cried. "Where did Santos agree to meet you?" Her face twisted. "You let them rape a twelve-year-old. A *twelve*-year-old, Hunter!"

Hunter's gaze slid to the knife, then back to her face. Someone had been making lies to her, and he had a good idea who. "Santos is dead."

"You lie!"

"I make no lie. This Comanche killed him."

"Amy says you took her and rode out. That Santos called you his good friend."

"Those were his words, not mine. I returned — after Aye-mee slept. She does not know, eh? The scalp is in my bags."

He inched toward her, alert to her every move. She lifted the knife higher.

"Stay back!" she cried.

"I come. Choose your mark, Blue Eyes, and drive the blade deep. You have one strike." When he was within arm's reach of her, she made a lunge, arcing the knife at his chest. Hunter deflected the blow, swallowing down cold, mind-numbing anger. She meant to kill him? No matter how frightened she was, he couldn't believe it of her, couldn't believe how much the realization hurt him. He wrested the weapon from her hands and tossed it to Swift Antelope, tempted to shake her until her teeth rattled. After all he had done, how dare she turn on him?

"Take Aye-mee to my mother's lodge, Swift Antelope."

Loretta staggered backward, holding her arms out to keep him away from the unconscious child. "No! Stay away from her. She stays with me."

"Not this night," Hunter snarled. "You have a bargain to keep, eh?"

She shrank from his outstretched hand. "To hell with our bargain, you animal! I'll die before I let you put your filthy hands on me."

"Then sing your death song."

With that, he grabbed Loretta's wrist, jerked her half off her feet, and proceeded to drag her behind him toward his horse.

CHAPTER 19

Loretta's one thought during the ride back to the lodge was to reach Amy. She fought to escape Hunter's grasp and throw herself off the horse, but she soon discovered that fighting him was useless. He guided the horse with his legs, which left his arms free to restrain her, one clamped around her waist, the other engaged in holding her wrists so she couldn't strike him.

When they reached his lodge and Hunter leaped from the horse, sweeping her off with him and somehow managing to keep her clasped firmly in one arm, she knew the battle was lost. Digging in her heels, she strove to slow his advance on the doorway, but the force of his body swept her along before him like flotsam on a wave. Amy's plight took second seat. If Loretta once entered that lodge, she might never emerge, and then both she and Amy would be doomed.

Behind them Loretta heard voices, coming

closer and closer. Were some of those people going to follow Hunter inside? A sob broke from her throat when Hunter ducked beneath the door flap with no more difficulty than if she were an intractable child squirming in his grasp.

Never had she seen him this angry, not even the night she had injured his horse. She knew it was because she had lunged at him with the knife. But what choice had he given her? Was she to stand there and meekly accept whatever fate he visited upon her?

The interior of the lodge had grown darker, the edges shadowy and threatening. Hunter strode toward the bed, his long legs eating up the distance so quickly that she grew frantic. Thinking he meant to rape her, or worse, Loretta twisted in his arms to press a frontal attack, succeeding only in accommodating him when he fell with her in a full-length sprawl onto the furs.

Blanketed by his broad chest, she couldn't move her torso, and before she could gather her wits to kick, he anchored her legs with his thigh. A blow to his face was likewise foiled when he captured both her wrists with one hand. She lay beneath him, chest heaving from exertion, her breath coming in short, painful gasps. He wasn't even winded. She strained against him, praying for strength, finding none.

Seconds passed, fraught with tension. His

dark face hovered above hers, stern and implacable, his features cast into harsh relief by the shadows. She couldn't save herself, and she couldn't save Amy.

He said nothing, did nothing, just stared down at her, his lips drawn into a relentless line. The longer she stared up at him, the bigger and more intimidating he seemed and the more breathlessly frightened she became. When she could bear the agony no longer, she cried, "What are you waiting for? Do it! Do it, blast you, do it!"

His grip tightened on her wrists. With agonizing slowness, he grasped the bodice of her dress, his glittering gaze locked on hers. Her breath caught when she felt his arm tense. He intended to rip the dress off her. One look into his eyes told her that and more. He would show her no clemency this time. And she would plead for none. At least not for herself.

"I trusted you," she cried. "I *trusted* you."

The pain in her voice sliced through Hunter's anger as nothing else might have. His gaze sharpened on hers as he remembered the accusations she had made a few moments ago and his certainty that Red Buffalo had filled her head with lies. Glancing down, he realized just how close he was to behaving like the animal she had accused him of being. "Blue Eyes, you will say to me this great truth you know. *Namiso,* now!"

424

"I'm finished playing your games. Finished, do you hear?"

"It will be finished when I have said it." Loretta had never heard such venom in his tone. He made a visible effort to calm down, gentling his grip on her wrists and easing some of his weight off her. Relief flooded through her when he released his hold on her bodice. "No harm. You will make talk with me."

A wave of uncertainty coursed over her. He sounded so sincere. Only with great difficulty did she recall Amy's recounting of her rescue. She closed her eyes. "Oh, Hunter, why have you done this? Does your hatred run so deep? A *twelve*-year-old."

"My cousin, Red Buffalo, has said false words to you? If this is so, you will tell me."

"As if you don't *know* what he told me!"

"You made a lie of your promise and tried to flee, *this* is what I know! You came at me with a knife, *this* is what I know! You made me look the fool, *this* is what I know."

"Oh, yes, you're the man whose words are drifting on the wind, whispering to him always! The man who never lies! I *saw* you out there at the fire! How stupid do you think I am?"

Grinding out the words between clenched teeth, he said, "Why did you make a lie of your promise?"

"Why wouldn't I? A little girl, Hunter? *Ani-*

mal! Aunt Rachel was right all along. *I* am the fool!"

He made a strangled sound in his throat and rolled off her, turning her loose to throw an arm across his eyes. Loretta tensed, casting a hopeless glance at the door. Even if she made it outside, her chances of saving Amy were slim.

In a taut, barely restrained growl he said, "Do not test me by trying to run, Blue Eyes. I will sure enough beat you."

After a moment he let out an audible breath and eased onto his side, folding an arm beneath his head, his blue eyes so dark they looked black in the dusky light. "You will make an echo of Red Buffalo's words. I cannot fight an enemy whose face is hidden."

Hearing his voice, so silken and close, brought bittersweet memories rushing back to her, and she wanted to cry. "You let me think you were my friend."

Hunter studied her delicate profile, his attention coming to rest on her tremulous lips. Her voice ached with the pain of betrayal, but he felt betrayed as well. "Did I not bring you the child?"

The tendons along her throat became distended, and her voice dripped with sarcasm. "Was it terribly difficult finding her?"

"I knew the path Santos would walk! I have traveled it many times to trade."

She clenched her hands into fists. "You *are*

well acquainted, then? The two of you are friends!"

"*Ka,* no, I did not call him friend."

"He called *you* friend. Amy heard him. She says you rode right into his camp, no guns, no fight, and took her away. How much did you pay Santos to steal her, Hunter? Twenty horses? Fifty? Or did he do it just for the fun of having her there for a few days — to entertain him and his friends?"

The question hung between them, ugly and discordant, an insult to him, a heartbreak to her. Fresh anger surged up Hunter's throat. He swallowed it down. "I paid him *nothing.*"

"Do you deny that your song says your yellow-hair must come to you? You took me home and taught me how to walk back to you in your footsteps!" Her voice rose, turning shrill. "You gave me a fine horse to ride! Do you deny that?"

Confusion welled inside him. "You are angry because I teach you and give you gifts?"

At last she wrenched her head around, her tear-filled eyes sparkling with contempt. "Like your medallion? 'Wear it for always,' you said. But it wasn't as a remembrance! It was to mark me, so your filthy friend Santos wouldn't steal the wrong yellow-hair. You *knew* how much I love Amy. You struck where I was most vulnerable, knowing I'd do anything to save her. I *trusted* you. You spoke of songs in our hearts and remembering for

427

always. And I —"

Her voice broke and trailed off into a squeak. For a moment he thought she might strike him, so deep went her pain, but then her face crumpled and the fight drained from her. She looked so forsaken, so frightened, that all he wanted was to hold her and soothe away her hurts.

"I *believed* you, Hunter. Do you know how difficult that was for me? After what Comanches did to my parents? I betrayed their memory, trusting you. I turned my back on everything."

Hunter's heart caught at the bruised, aching intensity he heard in her voice. Two large tears slipped over her bottom lashes and washed onto her cheeks, trailing in silver ribbons to her chin. He ran his hand into her cloud of tangled hair and drew her toward him, ignoring her resistance, pressing her face into the curve of his neck. She lay rigid against him, shaking violently. He dipped his head, the last traces of his anger dying.

Hunter had always known his cousin was a clever man, but he hadn't known until now just how clever. Red Buffalo had dealt in half-truths, which lent his lies power. No wonder she had come at him with a knife. Would he not have done the same to save Blackbird or Pony Girl? The only difference between him and this frail woman was that he had more strength with which to do battle. A strength he had nearly used against her, just as she had once feared.

"Ah, Blue Eyes." His voice, muffled against her neck, went raw with emotion. "I made no tricks against you. My heart sings only good things. It is the truth I speak."

"I *saw* you at the fire!"

They were back to the fire again? Hunter tried to think what it was she thought she had seen. "I was at the fire, yes. This is bad?"

"You were announcing our marriage and promising your people you would scalp me and Amy! Just like Red Buffalo said you would! I saw you!"

He couldn't help but smile, imagining how it must have looked to her. "*Ka,* no. I told them of my battle with Santos, Blue Eyes."

"But they cheered!"

"Because I fought and reclaimed your Aye-mee's honor. They cheered for my courage, eh? And my victory. There was no talk of marriage. You are a White Eyes."

"Y-you reclaimed Amy's honor?" She stiffened. "But she said you visited with Santos, and then you just rode away. That there wasn't a fight!"

"Santos was very much afraid, eh? He had wronged a fierce warrior of the Quohadie. He feared for his life when he saw me. He called this Comanche his good friend to chase away my anger. After I tended your Aye-mee and she slept, I rode back to San-

429

tos's camp. He will make her weep no more."

She arched away from him so she could study his face. He knew she wasn't aware of how her hips pressed against his, of the effect her nearness had on him.

"Then it was all lies? None of it was true?"

He traced the fragile cordillera of her vertebrae through the cloth of her dress. "Red Buffalo has great bitterness. Many *taum* ago, the Blue Coats rode down on our village when most of our warriors were away on a hunt. Red Buffalo's wife and little son were —" Hunter's throat tightened. His own memories of that attack were almost too painful to bear, and speaking of them didn't come easily. "His wife was shot. His son was trampled, not once, but many times. Red Buffalo's heart was laid upon the ground. After that day, he made fierce war, yes?"

"But I'm not a Blue Coat!"

"His hatred is blind, Blue Eyes. During one of his many raids, Red Buffalo was captured. The White Eyes wished to know where his village was, and they held his face over a cooking fire to loosen his tongue."

"Oh, God." Nausea roiled through Loretta's stomach. "His face — that's how he became scarred?"

"He remained loyal to the People. The *tosi tivo* were determined. When he escaped and made his way back to us, he was ugly, as he is now. So ugly that all women turn from him.

430

There will be no new wife for him, no second son. He stands alone for always, and seeks solace in fighting the great fight."

"But why take it out on me? I've done nothing to him, nothing."

Hunter rolled onto his back, taking her with him. He loved the feel of her slender length pressed against him. Running his hands into her hair, he held her face inches above his own so he could search her eyes. It pleased him to see compassion and pity shining there. She was as golden within as she was without. After all Red Buffalo had done to her, Hunter was surprised she could still feel sorry for him.

"I am Red Buffalo's good friend from childhood, his beloved cousin, as your Aye-mee is to you. He fears that you will steal this Comanche away from him, that my heart will turn against him and he will be left behind. An ugly man, alone forever, with no one. You understand? He cannot see past his hate."

"But I —" She splayed her fingers on his chest, shoving with the heels of her hands to lever herself away from him. Hunter tensed his arm at her waist to hold her. He wondered if she was aware of his hardness. Then he felt her heartbeat accelerate and had his answer. He bit back a tender smile. If only she knew how easily he could see her thoughts, like pebbles at the bottom of a clear pool. "Why would he think *I'd* steal you away? I'm the one victimized, the one who left her family."

"This saddens your heart?"

"Of course!"

"You must not be sad. This Comanche will bring your family to you many times."

"Here? No, Hunter, they will never come here to see me."

"Then I will take you to their wooden walls. I want no sadness in your heart."

He felt some of the rigidity leave her and knew he had said the right words. "Oh, Hunter, I *want* to believe you. You can't imagine how much."

He flexed, as if he meant to set her aside and rise. "I will bring you Santos's scalp and the silver from his breeches."

Her eyes widened, and the color washed from her face. "Mercy, no. I don't want to see his scalp."

"You believe?" He met her gaze, keeping his face solemn, though the horrified expression on hers made it difficult. "The scalp is in my bags. Proof, yes?"

"I — I don't need to see it." The tension drained from her, and she relaxed against him. "I believe you. Why would you bother lying?" Her eyes darkened. "What would you gain?"

"Your ruffles?" He watched her face and knew the moment when she realized he was teasing her. "You said I could steal them, yes?"

"As I recall, we decided you should take them when I wasn't *in* them."

He ran a knuckle along the shadowy contour of her jaw. She tipped her head to press her cheek into his palm, tears spilling in sparkling splendor from her eyes. "Oh, Hunter, I should have trusted you. I'm so sorry. After all you've done for us, how will you ever forgive me?"

"It is finished," he murmured. "No sorrow, eh? Only gladness. Your Aye-mee is yours, so she is mine. It is a very simple thing, yes?"

Through the gloaming, he could see her features softening, her quivery lips tipping up at the corners in a smile. She was not easy with him yet. A sudden move from him would set her heart to pounding again. Her smile encouraged him, though.

He ran his palm up the curve of her back and then removed his arm from around her, amused at how swiftly she rolled off him, fussing with her many skirts to be sure her ruffled breeches weren't exposed. Her shyness baffled him. He could remember how her body looked in firelight, her skin as pale as moonbeams, the tips of her breasts the delicate pink of cacti blossoms. How could such loveliness bring shame?

When she finally grew still, a taut silence settled over them. From the corner of his eye he could see her worrying her lip, her small white teeth sinking into the soft pink flesh.

Remembering how those lips felt beneath his, another surge of longing knotted his guts, making him recall the plans he had made for the evening — plans that were now drifting away on the wind. He wanted her, yes, but not if it meant forcing her.

"I suppose that . . ." Her voice trailed off. She plucked nervously at her skirt, then ran her fingertips up the line of buttons on her bodice. She glanced around nervously, still nibbling her lip. "I, um, haven't forgotten my promises to you."

"This is good." Hunter watched her with gentle amusement.

"A promise is a promise, even when given under unusual circumstances. You kept up your part, and —" She seemed unable to meet his gaze. "I'm sure you expect me to keep up mine." A dark flush crept up her neck. "I, um, guess you had Amy taken to your mother's so we could — so we could . . ."

She looked so distressed that Hunter took pity on her. "Ah, yes, we have a bargain, do we not?" He forced a long and very loud yawn. "My heart is heavy to say these words, Blue Eyes, but I am sure enough weary after traveling so far, eh?"

Her expression brightened so visibly that he nearly chuckled. "Oh, but of course!" she exclaimed in a shaky little voice. "You've ridden a very long way. You must be exhausted."

He yawned again and patted the fur beside

him. "You will lie beside me."

"But what about Amy?"

"Your Aye-mee is with my mother, yes? The woman who is mean like a buffalo. She is safe. You will be easy about her until the sun shows its face." His voice turned husky. "*Keemah*, come."

"I — I'd really like to check on her. She fainted, Hunter. I want to know she's okay. I won't rest until I know that."

"If she were not, my mother would come. My mother has good medicine, yes? And she is very kind. You will trust." He stretched out an arm and watched the myriad emotions that crossed her face as she contemplated the spot beside him. She had slept beside him before, many times, but tonight was different. There was nothing to stop him from taking what he wanted. She had even bargained away her right to fight him. What she didn't seem to realize was that there had never been anything to stop him. *"Keemah."*

When at last she scooted over to him, Hunter experienced a feeling like none he had ever felt. It went beyond satisfaction, beyond contentment. Having her fair head on his shoulder felt perfectly right, as if the Great Ones had hollowed the spot for her long ago, and he had been waiting all his life for her to fill it. He curled his arm around her, his hand on her back.

"It is good, eh?"

She placed a palm lightly on his chest. In a dubious tone she replied, "Yes, it is good."

Another silence settled over them. He measured the thrums of her heart beneath his hand, pleased that the rhythm no longer reminded him of the frantic wing beats of a trapped bird. Staring at the conical roof, he longed for the weariness he had pretended. It didn't come. He was relieved when she broke the silence.

"Hunter, what did you mean when you said you had made no talk of marriage because I'm a White Eyes?"

He brushed his lips across the top of her head, loving the flower smell that still clung to her hair. He would never again smell springtime and not think of her. "My chief wife will be a woman of my own blood." He felt her stiffen and, seeking to mollify her, added, "You can be second wife, eh? Or third?"

To his surprise she bolted upright, shaking again, this time in anger. With an indignant lift of her small chin, she flung herself away from him.

"You are angry?"

Her reply was frigid silence.

"Blue Eyes, what wrong words have I said?"

"What have you said?"

Hunter frowned. "It would not please you to marry with me? Better a wife than a slave, yes?"

"I will *never* play second fiddle, *never!*"

Hunter studied her, trying to figure out why she had switched the topic of conversation from marriage to making music.

"How *dare* you!" she cried. "Of all the — You arrogant, simple — Oh, never mind! Just you understand *this!* Amongst *my* people, a man has *one* wife, *only* one, and he looks at no other, thinks of no other, *touches* no other, until death do they part. I wouldn't marry you if you got on your knees and *begged* me!"

Hunter sat up slowly, feeling a little dazed by her fury and wondering what had sparked it. Would he never understand her?

She leaned toward him, her blue eyes flashing. "Even if I *would* marry you, an announcement by a central fire would not constitute a marriage in my books." She thumped her chest. "I must make my vows before a priest! And furthermore, when I take a husband, he won't be a Comanche. You couldn't be chief husband, second husband, *any* husband, to me. You're a barbarian who treats women like chattel!"

Very calmly Hunter inserted, "You are my woman. You will sure enough marry no other."

"Well, if you think I'm going to marry *you,* you have another think coming! Never, do you hear me?"

With that, she wrapped her arms around

herself and glared at him. Hunter sighed and flopped onto his back, staring upward sightlessly. Minutes passed. When at last he felt her curl up at the foot of the bed, as far away from him as possible, a knowing smile touched his lips. No woman could possibly get that angry over another woman unless she was jealous. And a woman didn't get jealous unless she was in love. Perhaps he wasn't the only one with another think coming.

In the morning Hunter awoke to find his blue-eyes curled up against his side, only the tip of her nose and a tangle of gold hair showing above the edge of the buffalo robe. She had one hand wedged under his backside, the other insinuated between his thighs. He was tempted to wake her, just to see the look on her face when she realized how intimately she was touching him.

He slipped from the bed, finger-combing his hair as he left the lodge. His mother would be awake by now, and he was anxious to check on Amy. As he crossed the clearing between his lodge and his mother's, he spied Swift Antelope and Bright Star, his dead wife's sister, visiting outside his mother's doorway. Bright Star cradled a bark dish in her cupped palms, a gift for his mother, he guessed. Swift Antelope's reason for being there was harder to define.

As Hunter approached, Bright Star lowered

her long lashes and blushed. "Good morning, Hunter. I missed you while you were away."

Resting a hand on her hair, Hunter forced a smile. These last few months, being around Bright Star had become a strain. Comanche men usually married sisters, and because of her relationship to Willow by the Stream, Bright Star clearly expected Hunter to follow custom. She was a lovely girl and sweet-tempered. Any man would find her acceptable as a wife. But, for reasons beyond him, Hunter had been evasive, uncertain about his feelings. Did he want Bright Star as his first wife?

Tension balled behind Hunter's eyes. Gazing down at Bright Star's perfect face, he tried to imagine taking her into his buffalo robes, touching her as a man did a woman. The picture eluded him. Then another image sprang to mind, of a woman with golden hair, blue eyes, and skin as pale as moonbeams.

He blinked and replied absentmindedly, "And I missed you, Bright Star."

Swift Antelope caught Hunter's arm before he could go inside his mother's lodge. "Hunter, about the little yellow-hair."

"Yes, what about her?"

Swift Antelope glanced uneasily at Bright Star, then plunged ahead. "I would like to make arrangements with you — to take her as my wife. Not right away, of course. When

439

she grows old enough." The young warrior straightened his shoulders. "I will pay a fine bride price, fifty horses and ten blankets."

Hunter smothered a grin. After a year of raiding, Swift Antelope had only ten horses. How much horse stealing did he plan to do? "Swift Antelope, I don't think she even likes you."

"Your yellow-hair doesn't like you too well, either."

He had a point. Hunter stroked his chin, acutely aware of a sparrow singing nearby, of cottonwood leaves rustling in the gentle breeze. Such a peaceful sound. He had enough problems without Swift Antelope adding to them. "Can we discuss this another time?"

"No! I mean . . . well, I've heard some other warriors talking. I'm not the only one who wants her. If I wait, you may accept the suit of another. She is very fine, is she not?"

Hunter wondered if they were talking about the same skinny girl. Then he focused on Swift Antelope, who was only a few years Amy's senior. He supposed a younger man might find Amy's coltish prettiness appealing. "I can see your concern. But you forget one thing, Swift Antelope. You have proven yourself my loyal friend. I will not accept the suit of another. Does that ease your mind?"

Swift Antelope still gripped Hunter's arm. "May I visit with her?"

"I don't know about that. She's been through a terrible time. Having a young man around might upset her."

"Old Man told me what happened to her. But someone must help her walk back to the sunshine, eh?"

Again, Hunter had to concede the point. A difficult path lay ahead of Amy, and her way would be made easier if she had a good friend, a young man who could teach her to trust again. "You will take great care with her?"

Swift Antelope grinned. "I will protect her with my life. Your mother says she will be strong enough to go on a walk tomorrow. May I take her?"

Hunter placed a heavy hand on the boy's shoulder. "She won't want to go. You do realize that?"

Swift Antelope nodded. "I can handle her until she gets used to me."

"She's a fighter."

"And I am twice her size."

Hunter almost wished he could go on this walk. It might prove interesting. Little did Swift Antelope know how useless strength could be when tussling with a frightened female. "Come to my lodge late tomorrow afternoon."

Swift Antelope beamed. "I think we should change her name. Aye-mee? It sounds like a sheep baaing. Golden One. That is a good name for her."

Without replying, Hunter swept the door flap aside and stepped into his mother's lodge. Woman with Many Robes knelt by the fire, stirring a pot of porridge. She glanced up and smiled. Amy huddled on the bed, her blue eyes huge with fear. Hunter noted that his mother had found the child a buckskin shift and moccasins, which pleased him. When Amy saw Hunter, she rose to her knees.

He crossed the room and hunkered down beside her. She still looked pale, and he wondered if his mother wasn't hurrying things by telling Swift Antelope a walk would be in order for tomorrow. His mother had brushed Amy's hair into a cloud of gold that rippled around her shoulders. No wonder Swift Antelope wanted to call her Golden One.

"You are well?" Hunter asked in English.

"I'm better." She threw a worried glance at the doorway. "Is that awful boy still out there?"

He had expected questions about Loretta. "Swift Antelope?"

"Is that his name? I don't like him."

"Ah, I see." Hunter pursed his lips. "You have reason?"

"I just don't like him." She gave a delicate shudder and wrinkled her nose. "He stares at me funny."

Hunter guessed that Swift Antelope had

442

been mooning, not staring, but he thought it unwise to tell Amy that. "My mother has treated you well?"

"She's your mother?" Amy glanced toward Woman with Many Robes. "She's very nice. Can't understand a thing I say, though. You talk English so good. Why can't she?"

"She has no need."

Amy pondered that a moment, then asked, "Where's Loretta?"

It was becoming more apparent to Hunter by the moment that Amy didn't recall her wild flight with Loretta last night. "She sleeps in my lodge."

"Why am I here? I want to be with you, Hunter. And with Loretta. Please?"

"You may come to my lodge tomorrow." Hunter glanced at the pot of porridge. "My mother prepares food for you to eat. And medicine. She will make you strong again. I will bring Loh-rhett-ah to see you. It is a promise I make."

Amy caught his arm. "Will you make that boy go away?"

Hunter pried her fingers loose and rose. "Swift Antelope is my loyal friend. It is good that he stands outside. No harm."

Turning to his mother, Hunter slipped easily into his own language, plying her with questions. His mother informed him that although Amy was weak, with proper nourishment and plenty of rest, she would soon recover. The internal bleeding had completely stopped. The cut on her leg was healing nicely.

Hunter explained that he would return with Loretta shortly, then left the lodge, holding the flap aside for Bright Star, who had respectfully waited for him to finish his business before she tried to enter. Swift Antelope inched toward the doorway, stretching his neck to see past Hunter's arm. Hunter tugged the flap closed.

"Swift Antelope, stop staring. You're making her uneasy."

"She is very golden, is she not?"

Hunter had the disturbing feeling that his young friend hadn't heard a word he said. "She's very frightened. Of *you.* She wants you to leave, and I don't blame her. You're drooling like a rabid wolf."

A dimple flashed in Swift Antelope's cheek. "That is a good sign, is it not? That she has noticed me."

Hunter walked away, shaking his head. He found Loretta awake when he entered his lodge. She was sitting up in bed, raking her fingers through her tangled hair. When she saw him, she averted her face, still angry, if the glint in her eyes was any indication.

At first Hunter tried ignoring Loretta's glares. After feeding her a breakfast of dried fruit and some of his mother's flat white bread, he took her to visit Amy. After that he retrieved her satchel from Maiden's lodge and escorted her down to the river. Instead of bathing, which would have required the removal of her clothing in his presence, Loretta washed her hair and scrubbed her face. En route back to his lodge, she refused to look at him and didn't respond when he spoke to her.

When she was still treating him to frigid silence long after the midday meal was over, Hunter's patience snapped. They were sitting in his lodge on buffalo robes, she on one side of the room, he on the other, the silence so thick it suffocated him.

"You can make war with your eyes for a moon and win no battles. I grow tired of your anger, Blue Eyes."

She lifted her small nose in the air and refused to look at him. Her hair had dried in a wild tangle of ringlets that wreathed her head in gold. Frustrated, Hunter clenched his teeth. Whether she realized it yet or not, she no longer feared him as she once had. A frightened woman didn't push like this.

"You will tell me of this anger that burns within you, eh?"

"As if you don't know!"

He propped his elbows on his bent knees. *Women.* He'd never understand them. If she was still angry because he had mentioned taking other wives, why didn't she say the words to him? It wasn't as if he planned on marrying someone else today.

"Blue Eyes, you are my woman, eh? This Comanche wishes for your heart to be filled with sunshine."

She threw him a contemptuous glare. "I may be your woman, but that doesn't mean I have to like it! Besides, why worry about me? With so many wives, I'll be lost in the shuffle. You won't know if I'm happy or not. And you certainly won't care." Two bright spots of color dotted her cheeks. "And that suits me just fine."

Silence fell over them for a moment.

"When will you take Amy home?" she asked suddenly.

"Her father hides behind his wooden walls and lets Comancheros steal her. She stays with this Comanche."

"You can't possibly mean to *keep* her here! Her mother will be worried sick."

"That is a sad thing, yes?"

"You promised!"

"I made the promise to bring her to you. I have."

"She isn't a horse, Hunter! You can't keep her here!"

He lifted an eyebrow. "Ah, yes? Who will take her from me?"

"You are an insufferable, arrogant, bull-headed —"

Hunter gave a snort and rose to his feet. His lodge suddenly seemed too small for the both of them. He would go to visit his father, where women showed proper respect.

Many Horses was putting the finishing touches on a bow he had been making when Hunter entered the tepee. Setting the weapon aside, he fastened his wizened old eyes on his eldest son and pursed his crinkled lips. "You look like you've been eating She Who Shakes's plum pudding and bit into a plum pit."

Hunter was in no mood for jokes. "My woman has my hackles raised." Sitting crosslegged, he picked up the iron poker next to him and began prodding the charred wood and ashes in his father's firepit. "One unto the other, with no horizon, that is what she wants! Imagine her setting up a lodge, tanning hides, sewing, cooking, gathering wood, all by herself. And what if she became ill while I was away? Who would tend her? Who would keep her company? The way she believes, if I was gone for a long while, she couldn't even go to Warrior to seek solace."

"Would you wish for her to?"

Hunter gave the ashes a vicious poke, sending up a cloud of gray that made Many Horses cough. The truth was, he couldn't bear the thought of Loretta with another man. "Right now, I'd give her away to the first man stupid enough to take her."

Many Horses kept silent.

"All my children would be —" Hunter

rolled his eyes. "Can you see me, surrounded by White Eyes?"

"Ah, that is the trouble. She is a White Eyes." Many Horses nodded and, in a teasing voice, said, "I don't blame you there. No man could be proud of a son with white blood. He'd be weak and cowardly, a shame to any who claimed him."

Hunter froze and glanced up. The white blood in his own veins was an unspoken truth between him and his father. Never before had Many Horses alluded to it.

Many Horses sniffed and rubbed the ash from his nose. "Of course, there are the rare exceptions. I suppose a man could raise a child of mixed blood and teach him to be one of the true People. It would take work, though."

The stiffness eased from Hunter's shoulders. "Did I test your patience, my father?"

Many Horses seemed to ponder that question a moment. "I found myself short on patience the time you shot me in the thigh with your first bow and arrow. It wouldn't have been so bad if I hadn't been standing *behind* you."

Hunter laughed softly. "You weren't when I let fly with the arrow. If I remember, I turned around to ask you a question."

"Which I never did answer. I always thanked the Great Ones that you were only knee high. If you'd been much taller, your brothers and sister never would have been born." He sniffed again, then grinned. "Come to think of it, Warrior was even more dangerous with his first rifle. Remember the time he accidentally fired through my lodge and shot a hole in your mother's cooking pot? She was boiling rabbit. The water hit the fire and filled the place with so much smoke, I nearly choked to death before I got everyone outside to safety."

Hunter threw back his head and roared with laughter. "I remember you pulling that rabbit out of the pot and telling Warrior it was a perfect shot, right through the heart. Except, of course, that it was gutted. And would he practice on *live* targets from then on?"

"Speaking of pits in plum pudding, do you remember your sister's first attempt? Your grandfather broke off his only remaining tooth trying to eat it."

"And swallowed tooth, pit and all, so he wouldn't embarrass her in front of Gray Horse, who had come to court her." Hunter placed a hand over his aching midriff and sighed. "It is good I came, my father. You have the gift. Already my heart is lighter."

Many Horses ran his tongue over his own jagged teeth, nodding thoughtfully. "I am proud of all my children," he said huskily. "Of you, most of all. It is a strange thing, my son, but when a man takes a babe into his

449

arms and claims him as son, it becomes a truth within his heart. The blood in his veins is as nothing. The color of his eyes is as nothing. When you took your first step, it was toward my outstretched hand. *That* was everything. White Eyes or Comanche, you were my son. I would have killed any man who said you weren't."

Tears burned behind Hunter's eyes. "What are you saying, my father?"

"I am saying that you must walk the path of your own heart. You came here angry because your yellow-hair is angry, yes? If you love her, it will be the same when she is sad, when she is happy. Have you ever stood where a stream spills into a river? The two become one. They laugh over the stones together, twist through the sharp canyons together, plunge down the waterfalls together. It is the same when a man and woman love one another. It is not always a pleasant thing, but when it happens, a man has little to say about it. Women, like streams, can be smooth one minute and make a man feel like he's swimming through white water the next."

Hunter leaned forward over his knees, brandishing the poker under his father's blackened nose. "I don't understand her. I treat her kindly, yet she still shakes with fear at the thought of being one with me. I try to make her happy and make her angry instead."

Many Horses lifted an eyebrow. "Fear is

not like a layer of dust on a tree leaf that washes away in a gentle rain. Give her time. Be her good friend, first — then become her lover. As for making a woman happy, you succeed sometimes, you fail sometimes. That is the way of it."

Hunter took a deep breath and let it out on a weary sigh. "It's not that I have another woman in mind to take as wife. It's just —"

"That you are bullheaded?"

Hunter smothered an outraged laugh. "A little bit, yes?"

Many Horses shrugged. "One unto the other is not a bad thing for a man. I am sure enough glad I have only one tug rope coming into my lodge. Can you imagine how exhausting three or four wives would be?"

"My mother has been enough for you, but she is a special woman."

Many Horses grinned. "She is a jealous woman. And I'm not a stupid man. I didn't want to live in a wasp's nest all my life." He shrugged. "I like things as they are. Fewer sharp tongues nagging me. Fewer mouths to feed. And only one woman to try to understand. I brought her slaves to help her with the work."

"My yellow-hair does not believe in having slaves."

"Neither does she believe in many wives. Give her a choice, slaves or wives. See which she chooses." Many Horses waved his hand before him to clear the air of ash. "You must also remember the yellow-hair may give you many more children than a Comanche woman. Take care or you could father more children than you can feed. I've never seen a white woman yet who wasn't a good breeder."

A slow grin spread across Hunter's mouth. "You will tell her this, yes? So far she isn't showing the proper enthusiasm."

"She'll come around. Give her time. Be patient. The rewards will be worth the wait."

Hunter tossed aside the poker and rose. "I will think long on your words."

"You sound like a man with eyes going two different directions. What maiden in the village entices you?"

"There is no one."

"Hmmph. Bullheaded, just as I suspected. I used to hope you might outgrow it. I see you never will."

"I have the strongest arm in my lodge circle. Her pouting will not sway me. If that's being bullheaded, then I sure enough am."

Many Horses rolled his eyes.

"You think my arm is not the strongest?"

"I think you should fight your battles with men on the battlefield, my son, where you have a chance of winning. That is what I think. But when have you ever listened to me?" He reached for the bow he was so skillfully crafting. "I suppose you must learn life's lessons your own way."

Choosing to ignore his father's digs, Hunter said, "It's a very small bow. Who is it for?"

"Turtle," Many Horses replied with a mischievous smile. "At my age, there is little pleasure in life. It is time I watched my grandson learn to shoot. I and my friends are placing bets. I have two horses that say he will shoot Warrior in the thigh. Old Man thinks it will be in the rump. Want to wager?"

Hunter's smile turned wry. "I don't think so. If I recall, I told Warrior that *I* would teach Turtle how to shoot."

Many Horses nodded, then quirked an eyebrow. "So it's *your* thigh I'm wagering on, eh? Hmm. Sometime today, bring your yellow-hair by to meet me."

"Why?"

"She may want to bet with us."

"My yellow-hair?"

Many Horses grinned. "If Turtle aims a little high, think of all the grief he might save her."

Hunter gave a snort of disgust and left the lodge.

CHAPTER 20

Patience. Over the next five days, Hunter's became as elusive as dandelion fuzz caught in a high wind. He was living with not one but two angry yellow-hairs, Loretta because he refused to take Amy home and had made mention of the possibility that he might marry more than one woman. Amy because he was forcing Swift Antelope's company upon her. On all counts, Hunter felt justified and carried on with implacable determination, trying to ignore the glares to which he was treated every time he set foot inside his lodge.

By the fifth night his perseverance was rewarded with a smile from Amy after Swift Antelope escorted her home from their daily walk. With flushed cheeks, Amy regaled Loretta with the details of her time spent with Swift Antelope, about the doe and twin fawns they had spied upon, about the flowers Swift Antelope had picked for her, about the birdcalls and sign language he was teaching her, about the silly tricks he played on her. Clearly Swift Antelope was making headway with Amy; the girl was beginning to heal.

Hunter's already low spirits plummeted. It was a sad state of affairs when an untried boy had more luck with women than a grown man. It was especially upsetting because Hunter knew he had paid dearly, not once but twice, for the right to possess Loretta, that he could exercise his rights at any time he chose, yet found himself hesitating because of the shadows in her eyes. Recalling his father's advice, he could only scoff. The way things were going, if he was to become his woman's friend before he became her lover, they might never move on to the second stage of their relationship.

The more disgruntled Hunter became over the situation, the more he glowered, and the more he glowered, the more uneasy Loretta was in his presence. The worst part was, Hunter couldn't blame her. Their bargain hung over them like a dark cloud, her promises binding her to him yet holding them apart. He knew she dreaded the moment when he would confront her, demanding that she lie with him. With each passing day, the prospect seemed to grow more frightening to her. Hunter was perceptive enough to realize that waiting patiently for her to come around wasn't abetting him in his cause, yet he couldn't bring himself to force her, either.

Though she had never spoken of her parents' deaths, Hunter had been on enough raids to know what horrible things she must have witnessed. That alone would have been enough to make her hate Comanches with a virulence to last a lifetime. And it was certainly enough to make her fear men, no matter what their race. To make matters worse, the other males in her experience had been brutish as well — her incestuous uncle, Santos and his comrades, and, whether he liked to admit it or not, Hunter himself. When Hunter looked at the world as he imagined she must see it, his heart twisted. What was there in her experience to commend him?

The nights tormented Hunter the most. He wanted Loretta beside him with an intensity that made him ache, not only to slake his desires, but simply to hold her. For him it was a sweet pleasure to be close to her — a sentiment she clearly didn't share. She went to amazing lengths to avoid sleeping with him, afraid, he was sure, that sleeping wasn't what he had in mind. Each evening she puttered endlessly in the lodge, inventing needless chores until he took mercy on her and pretended to be asleep. When she deemed it safe, she took her rest next to Amy, with Hunter lying only a few feet away, wide awake and frustrated because he wanted her beside him.

By the sixth morning Hunter came to the

disturbing realization that he had never been more miserable. While chewing on a piece of roasted venison, he studied the interior of his lodge, trying to imagine it as it had once been — with no yellow-hair to nettle him. The imagined loneliness that washed over him nearly took his breath. Hunter realized he preferred being miserable *with* Loretta than to live in emptiness without her. That realization sobered him and spurred him into action. He knew he must take steps to be sure she would never leave him.

Hunter found Warrior down by the river, teaching Pony Girl to swim. Sitting beneath a cottonwood, Hunter pressed his back to the trunk and rested his forearm on his upraised knee. "Warrior, I must make a short trip," he began. "Will you watch my woman and her sister while I'm gone?"

Distracted by the question, Warrior forgot to watch his niece and turned. "Another trip? You've only just returned."

Hunter's gaze dropped to Pony Girl, and his eyes widened in alarm. Shooting to his feet, he yelled, "Warrior, she's going under!"

Warrior snatched a handful of the child's dripping hair and pulled her up for air. Giving his head a shake, he moved toward shore. "I don't know. Maybe she's too young. Maiden insists she isn't, but I don't recall the other two being this hard to teach."

"I taught Turtle, and Maiden taught Blackbird," Hunter reminded him.

Warrior squatted in front of the whining, coughing child, trying to comfort her with body-shaking pats on her lower back. Hunter thanked the Great Ones that Pony Girl's burns had healed. "Maybe that's what the problem is, eh?" Warrior mused. "I'm a lousy teacher. Hunter, why don't you teach her?"

"I'm leaving on a journey."

"Ah, yes, a journey. Where are you going?"

Hunter ignored the question. It was one thing to surrender to his woman, but quite another to admit it to his brother. "Maybe I'll teach her when I return. A swap, yes?"

Warrior looked relieved. "That sounds like a fair trade. I'll gladly watch your woman if I can get out of this swimming chore Maiden has pressed upon me. At the rate I'm going, I'll have to change this one's name to Pebble. She sure enough sinks like one."

Hunter swung Pony Girl into the air above his head and grinned up at her. "Pebble? No, I like Pony Girl. Let's teach you to swim, eh, weasel?"

At such a lofty height, Pony Girl forgot why she was crying and burst into giggles. Hunter tucked her wet little body under one arm and strolled along beside his brother toward home. "I'll be gone for a few days. Do you think you can keep Red Buffalo away from my woman that long?"

"After the tales he told when you were gone

last time, *Maiden* will keep him away. She has developed quite a fondness for your Lohrhett-ah. She's even making her a blouse and skirt and moccasins."

"She is?" The thought of Loretta in leathers pleased Hunter. "Tell her thank you for me, will you?"

"Tell her yourself. I'm not too happy about it. *That's* why I'm teaching Pony Girl to swim! Maiden's busy sewing."

"I can't tell her. I'm leaving."

"Right away?"

As they drew to the outskirts of the village, Hunter set Pony Girl on her feet and gave her a farewell pat on the back. "Yes, right away. I have to find a few men to go with me. I'll bring Loh-rhett-ah and Aye-mee to your lodge before I leave."

Hunter gave Loretta no explanation for his sudden departure. One moment he was there, the next he was gone. For the next several days, Loretta and Amy stayed with Maiden of the Tall Grass. Amy, taught by a patient Swift Antelope, was acquiring quite a vocabulary in Comanche, which proved helpful, and before Loretta knew it she was learning words herself. Maiden delighted in teaching Loretta, not just the language but customs as well: never to let her shadow fall across the cooking fire, never to speak the names of the dead, never to turn right when making a formal entrance into someone's lodge. Loretta soaked up the knowledge, eager to learn all she could.

Late the fourth evening, Many Horses visited Maiden's lodge. At first Loretta sensed that Hunter's father was taking measure of her, and she was suspicious of his motives for coming, but soon Many Horses' dry humor had her smiling and then laughing. To Amy's delight, Many Horses regaled them with stories of Hunter's boyhood. By the evening's end Loretta had to admit she actually *liked* him. What was even more unsettling was that he seemed to like her, and she felt absurdly pleased that he approved.

When he departed he placed a gnarled hand on Loretta's forehead, much like a holy man bestowing a blessing, and bade her good night, addressing her as "my daughter." The title took Loretta completely by surprise. When she looked up, Many Horses gifted her with an understanding smile and left before she could gather her composure.

On the eighth day of Hunter's absence, along toward dusk, Loretta heard a distant yodeling sound and glanced up from Maiden's cooking fire to see men riding in. It wasn't difficult to spot Hunter, several horse lengths ahead of the others, leading what looked like a mule carrying a priest. Loretta rose on her tiptoe, frowning. Surely she couldn't be seeing what she *thought* she was seeing. What priest in his right mind would visit a Comanche village?

Glancing around at Maiden's neighbors, Loretta saw her bewilderment mirrored on every face. Then she looked at Warrior, who had been reclining nearby, guarding her. He had leaped to his feet upon hearing the men ride in. He slid a wary glance toward her and cocked an eyebrow. "My brother brings a Black Robe?"

It *was* a priest. Loretta craned her neck to see. Hunter rode directly to the central fire, which had already been lit in preparation for nightfall, and dragged the priest off the mule. After barking a command at the poor man, he spun on his heel and came directly toward Maiden's lodge, his stride purposeful, his jaw clenched in determination. Loretta drew a deep breath. Suddenly, incredulously, she *knew* why Hunter had brought a priest into the village.

His footsteps slowed as he drew close, the muscles in his thighs bunching and drawing the leather of his pants taut. Loretta stiffened at the challenge his eyes issued. Lifting her chin, she waited for him to reach her, riveting her gaze on his broad shoulders, resisting the urge to run. Those long, powerful legs of his would easily outdistance her.

"I have brought you a Black Robe," he said tersely, and nodded toward the waiting priest. "He will pray your God words over us, yes?"

461

With that, Hunter grasped her firmly by the arm and drew her toward the central fire, never breaking stride despite Loretta's attempts to slow him down.

"I won't marry you!" she cried frantically.

He threw her a look charged with martial arrogance. "You will be my wife, little one. My way or yours, in the end, it will be so."

Hunter drew to a stop before the priest. Loretta focused on the poor man, who was trembling so badly that he was about to drop his Bible. At the moment she was too preoccupied with her own plight to concern herself with his.

"Father," she cried in the most reasonable, calm tone she could muster, "would you please explain to this heathen that a marriage cannot take place without a woman's consent?"

The priest's mouth opened, but no sound came out. He slid horrified eyes to Hunter, and his face blanched. "M-my good young woman, perhaps it would be best to proceed. This man seems uncommonly determined, and I, for one, do not relish the thought of angering him."

Hunter turned to regard her, one dark eyebrow tipped upward in a measuring look. Eyes narrowed in defiance, Loretta jutted her chin and leaned toward him. "What have you done to this poor man? He's terrified! Have you no shame?"

Hunter could have reminded her that there had been a time when she had been equally terrified, but he chose to stay on course. Marriage was his goal, not a contest of tongues. He cast a compelling glare at the Black Robe. "Pray your words, old man."

The priest licked his lips and glanced fearfully at the crowd of savages around them. Perhaps it was the stark contrast of black robes against pallid flesh, but Loretta thought he was losing color at an alarming rate. Indeed, he looked as if he might faint.

"Say the God words, old man!" Hunter snarled again.

"Don't you dare bully him," Loretta hissed. "He's a man of God, Hunter! You don't *roar* at a man of God."

"It's qu-quite all right, child, quite all right." The priest, his face dripping sweat, made haste to open his Bible. "Merciful Father," he muttered, clearly praying for deliverance. With a strangled cough, he began leafing through pages, turning slightly so the light from the fire was thrown across the small print. "I beg your forgiveness. I don't usually need to use the book —" He coughed again and waved away smoke. "For some reason, the words have fled my mind. Ah, yes, here we are."

Infuriated, Loretta jerked her arm from Hunter's grasp. "Father, there's absolutely nothing to be afraid of, I assure you."

Hunter reclaimed her arm in a biting grip that made her swing around to face him. Bending his head, he whispered, "Blue Eyes, you test my temper. I will blow hard at you like the wind."

"Blow, then!" She tried to twist her arm free. "You're *hurting* me."

"I will *beat* you. Then you will know a hurt. Now be silent!"

Loretta's eyes flared to a fiery blue. "I'm not going to marry you. Beat me senseless! Go ahead."

Hunter sent her a look that would have scared her to death a month ago. "Loh-rhett-ah, you will be silent and let him say the God words."

"He can say the God words until snowballs melt in —" She broke off and blushed. "I'm the one who has to say the words, Hunter, and I *won't.* Do you understand?"

"My dear child," the priest inserted, "it's not often one of these" — he threw a meaningful glance at Hunter — "*gentlemen* offers to make an honorable woman of a captive. Wouldn't it be wise to accept?"

"I'm in no need of matrimony, Father. I still *have* my honor."

Hunter jerked her to his side and, in an ominously even voice, said, "Your honor will soon go the way of the wind, Blue Eyes. You made a God promise. You are my woman! Now I say you will be my wife!"

Loretta wet her lips, trying to meet his gaze without wavering.

"I brought you a Black Robe, yes? So this will be a marriage in your heart. If you do not say your God words to make it so, I will sure enough marry you my way." He swept his hand in a wide arc. "Your honor will fly away on the wind. *Suvate,* it is finished. You choose."

Her voice hoarse with frustration, Loretta cried, "But I don't *want* to marry you. If I do, it's for *forever!* Don't you understand?"

"For forever is very much good."

"No, it's very much bad. I'll never be able to leave you!"

Hunter threw up his hands. "No Black Robe, no marriage for your God. I am sure enough happy with a marriage my way." With a determined glint in his eyes, he turned toward the crowd, raised his arms, and shouted something. Then he shrugged. "There. *Suvate,* it is finished. I have said *my* words. We are married." Seizing her by the arm, he growled, "*Keemah,* come, wife."

Loretta dug in with her heels. "No! Wait!"

He looked down at her, his vexation evident. "You will say the God words?"

Loretta didn't see as how she had any choice. At least this way her marriage would be blessed by a priest, and she wouldn't be living with Hunter in sin. "Y-yes, I'll say the words." Casting him a sideways glance, she said, "Can I have just a moment with the priest?"

"For why?"

"Just to ask him something."

Hunter's grip on her arm relaxed. "*Namiso*, hurry."

Loretta cupped a hand over the priest's ear and quickly whispered her request, then stepped back to Hunter's side. The priest considered what she had said, then nodded. A moment later he blessed the young couple before him, and the ceremony began. The words bounced off the walls of Loretta's mind, making no sense. Numbly she made her responses when she was instructed to. Then it came Hunter's turn. The priest asked the usual question, adding at the end, "Forsaking all others, taking one wife and only one wife, forever with no horizon?"

Hunter, eyes narrowed suspiciously, shot Loretta a knowing look. For several long seconds he made no response, and she held her breath, her gaze locked with his. Then, with solemn sincerity, he inclined his head and replied, "I have spoken it."

The priest, momentarily confused by the unusual response when he had expected an "I do," sputtered a moment, seemed to consider, then nodded his assent and finished the ceremony. Loretta and Hunter were married, according to his beliefs and hers. Hunter instructed his friends to return the priest to his mission, stressing that he would have their heads if the man didn't arrive there unharmed. Then he sent Amy to his mother's lodge. When everyone had been dispatched, he turned to Loretta, one dark eyebrow cocked, his indigo eyes twinkling with laughter.

"One wife and only one wife, forever with no horizon?"

Loretta's gaze chased off, and her cheeks went scarlet. Clasping her hands behind her, she rocked back on her heels, then forward onto her toes, pursing her lips. "I told you, Hunter, I refuse to play second fiddle."

He smiled — a slow, dangerous smile that made her nerves leap. His heated gaze drifted slowly down the length of her. He grasped her arm and led her toward his lodge. "Now you will show this Comanche how good you play number one fiddle, yes?"

"I —" Loretta's mouth went as dry as dust as she tripped along beside him, her arm vised in his grip. "Surely you don't mean right *now.*" Her startled gaze focused on the lodge door. "It's not even dark yet. People are still awake. You haven't eaten. There's no fire built. We can't just —"

He lifted the door flap and drew her into the dark lodge. "Blue Eyes, I have no hunger for food," he said huskily. "But I will make a fire if you wish for one."

Any delay, no matter how short, appealed

to Loretta. "Oh, yes, it's sort of chilly, don't you think?" It was a particularly muggy evening, the kind that made clothing stick to the skin, but that hardly seemed important. "Yes, a fire would be lovely."

He left her standing alone in the shadows to haul in some wood, which he quickly arranged in the firepit. Moments later golden flames lit the room, the light dancing and flickering on the tan walls. Remaining crouched by the flames, he tipped his head back and gave her a lazy perusal, his eyes touching on her dress, eyebrows lifting in a silent question.

"Do you hunger for food?" he asked her softly.

Loretta clamped a hand to her waist. "You know, actually I *am* hungry. Famished! Aren't you? What sounds good?" She threw a frantic look at the cooking pots behind him. "I'll bet *stew* would strike your fancy, wouldn't it? After traveling so far and eating nothing but jerked meat. Yes, stew would be just the thing."

Hunter's mouth quirked. "Blue Eyes, a stew will take a very *long* time."

All night, if she was lucky. "Oh, not *that* long. It's no trouble, really!" She made a wide circle around him toward the pots. "I make a wonderful stew, really I do. I'm sure Maiden has some roots and onions I can borrow. Just you —"

Loretta leaped at the touch of his hand on her shoulder. She turned to face him, a large pot wedged between them, her hand white-knuckled on the handle.

"Blue Eyes, I do not want stew," Hunter whispered, his voice laced with tenderness. "If you hunger, we will have nuts and fruit, eh?"

Loretta swallowed a lump of air. Fruit and nuts were better than the alternative. Maybe, if she ate one nut at a time . . . "All right, fruit and nuts."

He spread a buffalo robe beside the fire while she put the pot away and dug up a parfleche of fruit and nuts from his store of preserved edibles. Kneeling beside him, Loretta munched industriously, staring into the leaping flames, aware with every bite she took that Hunter watched her. When she reached for her fourth handful, he clamped his long fingers around her wrist.

"Enough," he said evenly. "You will sicken your gut if you eat more."

Loretta's gut was already in sorry shape. She swallowed, trying to avoid his gaze and failing miserably. When their eyes met, she felt as if the ground fell away. There was no mistaking that look in his eye. The moment of reckoning had come.

She had known it would, of course, sooner or later. She had just hoped for later — much later. Clearly that was not to be. In return for

469

Amy's rescue, she had promised herself to him. It was nothing short of a miracle that he had waited this long to claim his reward. It was even more incredible that he had brought a priest here to marry them. She should be relieved, even pleased to know their union was blessed, but she didn't *feel* married. All she felt was fear, sheer, black, mindless fear.

Unfortunately for her, she didn't come to the marriage bed ignorant, as a bride should. She *knew* what was in store for her and how horribly painful and degrading it would be. Even Aunt Rachel hated it. She had admitted as much, and even if she hadn't, Loretta had heard her whimpering enough times through the cracks in the floor to know, beyond a doubt, that coupling hurt. It was bound to be a thousand times worse in the arms of a brutal savage who thought women could be bought and sold like so much baggage.

Brushing her hands clean on her skirt, Loretta stared dismally at the fire. *Light.* Merciful heaven, why had she asked for a fire? He'd be able to *see* her, which somehow made the thought of undressing in front of him all the more horrid.

Her skin prickled. He was staring at her, waiting, like a man expecting his supper to be served. And what was even more awful, she *felt* like his supper. A hundred thoughts raced through her mind, running away from him foremost, but her sense of honor forestalled her. She had *promised* him, and a promise was a promise. She wouldn't break her word. She'd see this through, with her head held high. She *would.*

With trembling hands, Loretta tackled the long line of tiny buttons on her bodice. With each flick of her fingers, her cheeks grew hotter. The firelight cast too few shadows, making the interior of the lodge seem as bright as day. She tried to draw comfort from the fact that he had seen her nude the night of her fever, but that was a century ago and did little to ease her embarrassment as she slid the sleeves of her dress down her arms.

If only he were a white man. He would at least douse the fire. Or maybe have an attack of conscience and realize how barbaric it was to force a virtuous young woman into marriage. But he wasn't a white man, and conscience wasn't a word in his vocabulary. He *owned* her. Now they were married, even in the eyes of *her* people. For forever.

The thought panicked her as she pushed her dress down her hips and stood to step out of it. She would have to go through this disgusting ritual not just once, but thousands of times. Now she wished she hadn't tricked him into promising he would take only one wife. Plural marriage might have its benefits. With several wives he might lose track of her in the shuffle and never bother with her . . .

Watching Loretta, Hunter swallowed an

amused chuckle. She looked like a little field mouse about to be eaten by a great hawk. Her blue eyes were enormous and brilliant with fear. A flush crept up her pale neck, as pink as — His gaze dropped to her chemise. Through the thin muslin, he could see the shadowy peaks of her nipples. His belly knotted with longing. Cactus blossoms and moonbeams. Perhaps she was right to feel like a small creature about to be devoured. He yearned to possess her, to suckle her breasts, to nibble tantalizing paths along her thighs, to find the sensitive places on her body and tease them with his tongue and light caresses from his fingertips until her passion peaked.

As she struggled with the ribbon sash that held up her petticoat, her hands growing more tremulous by the second, Hunter's amusement changed to a tenderness that nearly overwhelmed him. Though painfully afraid, she was going to honor her promise and give herself to him. His throat tightened, nearly closing off his breath. Memories of Willow by the Stream washed over him, of their first time together and how gently he had eased her into lovemaking. Remembering made him feel ashamed. It had been a long while since he had lain with a maiden, too long if he could be amused by such painful shyness.

Swinging to his feet, Hunter scattered the fire so the flames licked feebly at the wood and threw the lodge into gentle shadows. Then he turned to regard his wife, forcing his hands to curl loosely at his sides, his stance deliberately relaxed. "Blue Eyes, come here," he whispered softly.

She threw up her head like a startled doe, her eyes huge and wary. Hunter's guts clenched, and with one stride he closed the distance between them. Catching her by the chin, he tipped her head back and feathered his thumb across her quivering bottom lip.

"I —" Her voice shook and broke. She swallowed and tried again. "I'm sorry, Hunter. I know I promised. It's just that — I'm a little nervous."

Hunter bent his head and lightly pressed his forehead against hers, nudging her hands aside so he could untie the pink ribbon that cinched her small waist. With deft fingers he loosened the petticoat and let it fall in a heap at their feet. "There is nothing to fear," he whispered, "nothing."

Her breath caught when he untied the first small bow that held her chemise closed. He untied the others quickly and feathered his fingers over her shoulders, skimming the muslin aside and drawing it down her arms. Shame washed over her, hot and pulsating, as the evening air touched her bare breasts. She closed her eyes, wishing she could die on the spot. An instant later she opened her eyes again, terrified of what he might do when she wasn't watching.

Loosening the drawstring waist of her pantalets, he crouched before her, tugging the breeches down her legs, pulling off her high-topped shoes as he divested her of the garment. As he stood back up, it was his turn to catch his breath. His memories didn't do her justice. For a moment he couldn't drag his gaze from her, so fascinated was he by the glowing whiteness of her skin, the delicate curves, so long hidden from him by chin-high calico and multiple layers of muslin. Settling his hands on her narrow waist, he drew her toward him, his heart slamming as the pebbled tips of her small breasts came into contact with the flesh over his ribs. In the dim light he could see tears shimmering on her pale cheeks. He bent his head to catch their saltiness with the tip of his tongue.

"Ah, Blue Eyes, *ka taikay, ka taikay,* don't cry. Has my hand upon you ever brought pain?"

"No," she whispered brokenly.

Determined to finish what he had begun, Hunter swept her slender body into his arms and strode to the bed. Lowering her gently onto the fur, he stretched out beside her and gathered her close, his manhood throbbing with urgency against the confining leather of his pants. He half expected her to struggle, and perhaps if she had, he could have continued, his one thought to consummate their marriage, to put her fears behind them and ease the ache in his loins. But instead of fighting him, she wrapped her slender arms around his neck and clung to him, so rigid with fear that she felt brittle, her limbs quivering almost uncontrollably.

In a voice thick with tears, she said, "Hunter — would you do one thing for me? Just one small thing. Please?"

He splayed a hand on her back and felt the wild hammering of her heart. "What thing, Blue Eyes?"

"Would you get it over with quickly? *Please?* I won't ever ask again, I swear it. Just this time, *please?*"

Hunter buried a smile in her hair and closed his eyes, tightening his arms around her. His father's voice whispered. *Fear is not like dust on a leaf that can be washed away by a gentle rain.* The words no sooner came to him than a dozen forgotten memories did as well. For an instant the years rolled away, and Hunter saw himself running hand in hand with Willow by the Stream through a meadow of red daisies, their laughter ringing across the windswept grass, their eyes shining with love as they drank in the sight of one another. He remembered so many things in that instant — the love, yes, but mostly he remembered the friendship he and Willow had shared, the trust, the silliness, the laughter. Ah, yes, the laughter . . . He and his little blue-eyes had laughed together so few times that Hunter had difficulty recalling *when* they had. Suddenly he knew that without the laughter, their loving would fall far short of what it should be. Especially for her.

In a voice that rasped with frustration as well as tender amusement, Hunter said, "You have such a great want for me that we must hurry, yes?"

Her spine snapped taut, and she leaned her head back to look at him. He met her gaze with a lazy smile, trying not to think about how her nipples grazed his skin, how torturous it was to feel her hips pressing forward against him. Working one hand loose, he carefully brushed the tears from her cheeks.

Giving a low chuckle, which he punctuated with a defeated sigh, he said, "Blue Eyes, we have many nights to lie with one another. Forever, yes? Until we die and rot."

"Until death do we part," she amended.

"Ah, yes, until death do we part." He shrugged one shoulder. "A very long time, yes? If I strike such fear into your heart that we must be quick, it is wisdom to wait. It is enough that you will lie beside me. That I can put my hand upon you."

Her expression went from wary distrust to incredulity. "And do nothing?"

Hunter shared her sentiments. It was the most *boisa* idea he had ever come up with. Never had he ached quite so sharply with wanting a woman. "You would like to do something? You say it and we will do it." Hoping to make her feel less self-conscious about her nakedness, he tugged a fur over them and loosened his arm around her, allowing her some room to get comfortable. "Make a story for me, yes? About my Loh-rhett-ah when she was small like Blackbird."

She stared at him, clearly unable to believe he meant it. He forced a yawn, and from the look that crossed her small face, he knew he hadn't been very convincing.

"You're not sleepy," she accused.

"*Ka,* no," he admitted. "I make a lie, yes? To make you easy? My heart is laid upon the ground when you are afraid. Let us be glad, eh? Make me a story."

"Hunter, I don't have a stitch of clothes on," she squeaked.

One of his dark eyebrows flicked upward. "You must have clothes to make stories?"

"No. I guess I . . . well, it might help me think."

He sighed and rolled onto his back, carrying her along with him in the curve of his arm. Pressing her head onto his shoulder, he made a valiant attempt to ignore the feeling of her silken flesh against his and said, "This Comanche wears breeches. *I* will make the story."

And with that, Hunter began talking, smiling to himself every once in a while because he quickly discovered that he had as much trouble concentrating as she did when she didn't have clothes on. In a husky whisper he recited the prophecy to her. When he finished she stirred in the crook of his arm.

"*That* is your song?"

"*Huh,* yes."

"But, it's beautiful!"

With a start, Hunter realized he thought so, too. "Since my boyhood, I had much hate for the words." He twined a length of her hair around his finger, smiling. "And great hate for the honey-haired woman who would one day steal my heart. I wished to kill you, yes?"

"But I'm not the woman in your song."

"Ah, yes, you are the woman."

"The song says the People will call me the Little Wise One. They don't! And they never will. I'm far from wise."

"It will come to pass," he assured her. "It must. All of the words must."

She saw shadows creep into his eyes. "What is it? Why are you so sad?"

The muscles along his throat knotted. "My song says I will one day leave my people. I am Comanche. Without them, I will be as nothing, Blue Eyes."

Loretta stared sightlessly into the shifting shadows, watching the play of firelight. "It's only a legend, Hunter. A silly legend. Hatred going away on the wind? High places and great canyons of blood! New tomorrows and

478

new nations?" She turned her face toward him. "Look into my eyes. Do you see a new morning with new beginnings?"

He searched her gaze, and then, in a husky voice that reached way down inside her, he whispered, "Yes." He drew out the word until it seemed to echo and reecho in her mind.

It was then that Loretta knew. He had fallen in love with her. She stared up at his dark face, so close to her own that they breathed the same air, and her heart broke a little, for him, and for herself. She would never love him in return. A canyon of hatred and bitterness separated them. In that, at least, the prophecy was correct.

"Oh, Hunter, don't look at me like that."

In one liquid movement he rose on an elbow above her, his broad chest a canopy of bronze, his shoulders eclipsing the light so only her face was illuminated. "You have stolen my heart."

"No," she whispered rawly. "Don't say that, don't even think it. Can't you understand? I'll never love you back, Hunter." Her pulse started to slam. "I'm terrified of —"

He crossed her lips with a gentle finger, his eyes clouding with warmth. "Of lying with me? I am not blind, Blue Eyes. Your heart is laid upon the ground with memories. That will pass. You will come to me. You will want my hand upon you. It will be so. The Great Ones have spoken it."

She wrenched her face aside. "I'll lie with you because I promised and because I vowed to before God and a priest. But I'll never *want* to, never." A sob caught in her throat. "Oh, God, what am I doing here? I don't want to hurt you, Hunter, truly I don't."

He lay down beside her and pulled her back into the crook of his arm, pressing her fair head to his shoulder. "*Ka taikay.* Sh-hh, Blue Eyes. Do not weep. It will be well."

"How can it be? I'm trapped here. I can never leave. I've made promises I'm not sure I can keep. I'm frightened, Hunter, of you and your people — even of myself. How can all be well?"

"It will be well. My people will accept. You are one with them now, the wife of a warrior. In time, you will want to be beside me. Your fear will leave. You will see. Until then, this Comanche will wait, eh?"

"Wait?" she whispered. "You mean you won't —" She broke off and looked up at him. "You won't — force me?"

Hunter's throat tightened. "I make no promise for you. I wait now, yes? We will see where our moccasins fall."

To soothe her, he began telling her stories about his childhood, about his first bow, leaving out the part about shooting his father, about his first fight, about his first hunting trip. He had come to the tale of his vision quest when he felt her slender body relax

480

against him and heard her breathing change. His voice trailed off. He stared upward into the darkness, filled with a yearning that couldn't be slaked. It would be a very long while before he followed his blue-eyes into the black depths of slumber. A very long while.

When Loretta awoke the next morning, Hunter and her discarded clothing were gone. Beside her on the fur lay a doeskin skirt and blouse and a beautiful pair of moccasins. With trembling hands Loretta unfolded the blouse, recognizing it as the one Maiden had been making. *"Ein mah-heepicut,"* Maiden had whispered. Now Loretta knew the words meant "it is yours." Tears filled her eyes.

As she lifted the skirt to examine it, Hunter stepped into the lodge, sending her scurrying for cover under the buffalo robe. Flashing her a mischievous smile, he said, "Maiden sent the clothes. Next time, you will not be wrapped in so much *wannup,* yes? It will take us much less time to do nothing."

He turned and left the lodge before Loretta realized he had made a joke. It took even longer before she smiled. There was a promise behind the lightly spoken words. *Next time, it would take them much less time to do nothing.* With a new lightness in her heart, Loretta sprang from the bed and slipped into the beautiful outfit Maiden had made for her. It fit perfectly.

She ran her hand over the soft supple leather that skimmed her chest, her cheeks flaming. She might as well be naked. The tail of the blouse scarcely reached past her waist, falling in a straight sweep from her bustline, loose and airy. Knowing Hunter's penchant for reaching under her clothes, she couldn't imagine herself wearing this around him. And the skirt wasn't much better, hitting her at the knees, with a tease of fringe around the bottom. No underwear, not a stitch! It was scandalous.

A tight little lump rose in Loretta's throat as she gazed down at the graceful cut of the skirt, at the beautifully beaded moccasins. Maiden had worked so hard. Loretta knew her feelings would be terribly hurt if she refused to wear these things. And she couldn't bear the thought of that.

Loretta thought of her mother, how she would feel about her daughter being dressed like a Comanche squaw. The image brought home the fact that, like it or not, she didn't just look the part, she *was* a Comanche squaw, married to the infamous Hunter, his to do with as he wished, whenever he wished, until she died and rotted.

CHAPTER 21

Over the next several days, life in the village settled into a routine that Loretta found to be, if not pleasant, at least bearable. Thus far Hunter hadn't exercised his conjugal rights. Red Buffalo, much to her relief, went on a hunting trip with a group of his friends, so she was spared his unsettling presence, and as Hunter had promised, Loretta found she could come and go in the village as she wished.

Since her marriage to Hunter at the central fire, the attitudes of the villagers had changed. Everyone she encountered went out of his or her way to help her adjust to her new surroundings. With help from Maiden of the Tall Grass and Hunter's mother, Loretta was slowly learning to speak more Comanche, which opened a line of communication with the other women and allowed her to make friends. She Who Shakes, an elderly woman who lived several lodges down from Hunter, took Loretta aside one afternoon to show her how to make pemmican, a mainstay of the Comanche diet, a mixture of powdered meat, fat, and dried fruit. As unpleasant a chore as it had been, Loretta also assisted the women in scraping and curing hides after a large buffalo kill, and now she was making her first pair of moccasins from an old piece of leather Maiden had given her.

Being actively involved in the day-to-day routine of the village gave Loretta a much needed sense of belonging. She was included in the women's nightly sojourns to the river for baths. It was reassuring to look across the way and see faces she recognized, to smile and receive a smile in return.

Another uplifting development was Amy's recovery from her ordeal. Loretta could scarcely believe how quickly the child was regaining her former gaiety, and she soon realized Swift Antelope was the cause. The young warrior clearly adored Amy and spent hours roaming the river with her, forging a friendship that set Amy's cheeks aglow.

Hunter, quite the opposite of Loretta, found this same period of time a trial. While Swift Antelope made steady progress with Amy, he couldn't see himself making any headway with Loretta. She still went to great lengths to avoid sleeping beside him, choosing instead to share Amy's far less comfortable pallet. To complicate matters further, there was Bright Star's campaign to make

Hunter take notice of her.

It seemed to Hunter that every time he turned around, Bright Star hovered nearby, fluttering her lashes and blushing, making such an obvious play for Hunter's affections that he knew it couldn't escape his wife's notice for long. Hunter didn't want to shame Bright Star by scorning her. At the same time, he didn't want Loretta to believe he was encouraging the girl. He already had enough problems.

While he mulled the situation over, trying to think of a kind way to discourage Bright Star, the young maiden intensified her campaign, and, as Hunter had feared, Loretta at last realized what was going on. When she did, Hunter took the brunt.

"Who is that girl?" Loretta demanded one evening.

"What girl?" Hunter felt heat rising up his neck and avoided meeting his wife's flashing blue gaze.

"*That* girl, the one who seems to have something in her eye."

Hunter obliged Loretta by giving Bright Star a bored glance. "She is sister to my woman who is dead." He bent back over the arrowhead he was sharpening. "She is called Bright Star."

"She doesn't *look* very bright. Is that a tic, or does she always blink that way?"

Hunter smothered a snort of laughter. "She

makes eyes, yes?"

"At you?"

He straightened and lifted a dark brow. "You think she makes eyes for you?"

Loretta's spine stiffened. "You think this is funny? Doesn't she realize that you're a married —" The flash in her eyes grew more fiery. "Oh, yes, how remiss of me. I forgot that you can have an entire *herd* of wives."

Hunter sighed and set aside the arrowhead. "This Comanche has no wish for a *herd* of wives. One is sure enough plenty trouble."

"Are you saying I make your life miserable? If that's the case, why did you marry me? Why didn't you marry *her?*"

Hunter knew jealousy when he saw it. Everything else had failed. New tactics were called for. "I could have. Bright Star thinks I would be a fine husband, yes?"

"She can have you."

That wasn't exactly the response Hunter had been hoping for. "*You* have me, one unto the other, forever until we die and rot. It was your wish."

She sputtered for a moment, trying to speak. "I was *forced* into this farce of a marriage!"

He shrugged again. "And you do not want your man. It is sure enough a sad thing." He thumbed his hand at Bright Star, who was still fluttering her lashes. "She wants what you do not. Yet you are angry? It is *boisa,*

486

Blue Eyes."

Loretta flew to her feet, hands clenched at her sides. "It sounds as if you've been cheated all the way around, you *poor* man. Well, let me tell you something!"

"I am here."

She jutted her small chin at him. "As long as you have wandering eyes, *this* woman wouldn't have you in her buffalo robes if you crawled on your knees and begged. Is that clear?" She swung her arm toward Bright Star. "You can have her! You can have every woman in the village! Be my guest. But you can't have me as well, make no mistake in that!"

With that, Loretta spun and ran into the lodge. Hunter sat there a moment, listening to the muffled sounds that drifted from the doorway. *Sobbing.* With a snarl, he picked up the nearly finished arrowhead he had been sharpening and threw it into some nearby brush.

Bright Star looked stricken when Hunter sprang to his feet and turned toward her. By her expression, he guessed she could hear Loretta crying. He walked toward her slowly. Whether it hurt her or not, he had to tell her he didn't plan to marry her. Loretta's feelings were his first concern.

"Your Loh-rhett-ah does not like me?" Bright Star queried shakily.

Hunter grasped the girl's shoulders. "It isn't

you, little sister. She is a White Eyes, yes? The thought of two wives in my lodge circle makes her heap big angry." Hunter chucked Bright Star under the chin. "You are lovely, Bright Star, and you honor me, but now that I'm married to a yellow-hair, I must walk a new way, yes? My Loh-rhett-ah would never accept you. If her heart is sad, my heart is sad."

Bright Star stopped fluttering her lashes and looked more like her old self. "Do you truly think I'm lovely, Hunter?"

Hunter pressed his forehead against hers and looped an arm around her. "You're beautiful. Your face makes me think of my woman who is dead."

Bright Star blushed. "You say those words to make my heart glad. I could never be as lovely as my sister."

"You are her face upon the water."

"Do you truly think so?"

"You should see how the men's gazes follow you."

Bright Star drew away so she could study him. "Even Red Buffalo's?"

Hunter searched the depths of her dark eyes. "You have a fondness for my cousin?"

She nibbled her lip. "It doesn't make you angry, does it? I've never dishonored you by looking his way. I only asked because, well, since *you* don't want me, I didn't think you'd —"

"Bright Star, no! I feel no anger." Relieved,

Hunter laughed and settled his hands on his hips. "Red Buffalo is a very lonely man. I would be pleased if he found a wife." He gave her a thoughtful study. "You little weasel! I never suspected you had an interest in Red Buffalo."

Her small face softened. "He's not handsome, I know. But he's very brave and strong! And always kind. Have you ever noticed how gentle he is with children? He would make a very good husband, I think, if he —" A cloud of uncertainty dimmed her smile. "If only he would notice me. I don't think he even *sees* me."

"Believe me, he sees you, Bright Star. I think he's probably pretending not to notice you because he's so certain you would never notice him."

"But he's wonderful. Why would he think that?"

"Because he's badly scarred." Hunter sighed. "Will you trust me to speak with him? When he returns from hunting?"

"No! He'll think I'm forward."

Hunter lifted a hand. "I won't tell him we talked. I'll just say I think you might be interested in him. If I don't, he'll keep looking through you, and you'll have snow in your hair before he guesses how you feel."

She relaxed and smiled. "Well . . ." Her gaze shifted to the lodge. "Hunter, I think I'd better leave you, yes? So you can make peace with your woman."

With a grimace, Hunter nodded. "Her heart is laid upon the ground."

"Is it me? I will make talk with her."

"I don't think it would be safe," he said wryly.

Angry wasn't the word to describe Loretta's frame of mind. She wasn't just furious, but horribly hurt as well. That terrified her. She wasn't falling in love. She *wasn't*. So what if Hunter wanted a dozen wives? What difference did it make to her? She didn't care a whit. She *didn't!* It wasn't as if *she* wanted him. So why was she crying?

Pain welled in her throat. She picked up a pan, trying to force her thoughts onto dinner and what she should fix, but visions of Hunter filled her head. She imagined his dark eyes warming with laughter, his mouth tipping into that lopsided grin that made her heart catch, his warm hand holding hers. It would kill her to watch him doing those things with someone else. What was happening to her? When had he become so important to her?

It wasn't fair! He had wormed his way into her affections, made her care about him. And now he was out there making over that silly *twit* of a girl! Fresh tears stung Loretta's eyes. If this was how it felt to be in love, she didn't want any part of it. Her insides felt like a wet rag someone was wringing out. And the worst part was, she was afraid to go out there and do anything about it. If she did, it would be an admission that she cared for him. Once he realized that, he'd expect her to prove it. She glanced at the bed, and her stomach knotted, images from the past tormenting her. She slammed down the pot. She couldn't do it, she just couldn't. . . .

The moment Hunter stepped into the lodge, Loretta swiped the tears from her cheeks and began clanging pots so loudly that her ears rang. Perverse though it was, she fell back on her anger to hide her hurt. Her pride wouldn't allow her to let him know how she really felt.

"Blue Eyes, we must make talk," he said softly, pausing to tie the lodge flap firmly closed.

"Go make talk with Bright Star," she sniped, even though that was the *last* thing she wanted him to do.

"I would make talk with you." He moved slowly toward her. "I told Bright Star I would marry no other, yes?"

Loretta yearned to throw herself in his arms and weep, to hear him whisper, "It is well," as he always did when things went wrong. Instead she rounded on him. "And I suppose you made her feel sorry for you in the bargain? Poor, poor Hunter, stuck with one woman!" She tried to glare at him but

491

couldn't quite meet his gaze. "I've been thinking while you were out there *mooning* over her. And I've decided a dozen other wives around here would suit me just fine. You're right! It's *boisa* for me to feel —" She broke off and swallowed, keeping her face averted. "*I'm* not being a wife to you. . . ." Her voice trailed off into a squeak. "And I'm afraid I never can be."

Hunter's guts clenched at the pain he read in her expression. He hadn't intended to hurt her, only to make her face her feelings. Why was it that no matter what he did, it was always wrong? Sitting on the edge of the bed, he leaned forward and braced his arms on his knees. "Blue Eyes, you will be a fine wife in time," he said gravely.

"No, I won't." Her gaze flew to his, brimming with misery and tears. "Oh, Hunter, what's the matter with me?"

Studying her small face, Hunter realized two things: he didn't want her to be like anyone else, and, right or wrong, he had to bring this torturous waiting to an end, for both their sakes. For once, his father had given poor advice. "Blue Eyes . . ." Hunter sighed and interlaced his fingers, bending his knuckles backward, stalling because he didn't want to say the wrong thing. "Can you say words so this Comanche can see into you?"

"I'm *afraid.*"

"Ah, yes, afraid." He studied her beaded

moccasins. "Because I am Comanche?"

She squeezed her eyes closed. "It isn't that, not anymore. That's just an excuse!"

Cautiously Hunter asked, "Then what makes your heart sad?"

She bit her bottom lip and tipped her head back to stare at the smoke hole. After several seconds she sniffed and said, "You're a man."

She looked so forlorn that Hunter had to bite back a smile. He started to speak, then thought better of it. Clearing his throat, he shifted his attention from her quivering mouth to her nervous hands, wishing he knew how to ease her fears. Being patient hadn't worked.

She closed her eyes again and made a strangled sound, whirling away from him. "Marry Bright Star. It's only fair. I can't expect you to wait forever for me to —" She made another angry swipe at her cheeks and took a jagged breath. "She's very lovely. You wouldn't be normal if you didn't want her. And it's clear she wants you. Why should you be tied to me?"

He pushed to his feet and slowly approached her from behind. She jerked when he grasped her shoulders. "I have no wish to marry Bright Star. You are the wife I want. One wife, for always."

"Didn't you hear what I said? I can't *be* a wife to you. I'm —" A shudder shook her, and she hugged her waist. "I'm a coward,

Hunter. As if you haven't figured that out by now! And it's not going to get better. I thought it might, but it's only gotten worse! If only I were more like Amy. After all she's been through, she's —"

"You are not Aye-mee," he inserted gently. "She is a child, with my strong arm to protect her. Many *taum* from now, she will marry and have to face her memories, yes? But today she runs from them. You can no longer run, eh? The years have rolled away, and what happened long ago now walks beside you."

Hunter drew her back against his chest and bent his head to press his face to her hair. "Blue Eyes . . ." He trailed his lips down one of her braids until he found the sweet curve of her neck. "Make a picture for me, yes? So I can see what you fear."

"What good will that do?"

"Fear is a strong enemy. I would stand beside you."

She sighed. "Hunter, *you* are what I fear."

Releasing her shoulders, he slipped his arms around her, placing his palms beneath her breasts. He smiled at the way she gripped his wrists to make sure his hands didn't wander. "I strike fear into you because I am a man?"

"It isn't funny."

"I do not laugh. It is a sad thing, yes, that your husband is a man. A very terrible thing."

She rewarded him with a tremulous laugh, looking at him over her shoulder. "It *isn't* that you're a man, exactly. It's what will happen between us *because* you're a man."

"Many good things." He felt her tense. "Little one, you will trust, eh? I make no lies. What is between us will be very good."

"I try to believe that, really I do. And then I remember."

"Make a picture of the remembering, eh?"

"I can't."

Hunter tightened his hold on her. "It is a memory of your mother?"

"Yes," she admitted. "My mother and what — the Comanches did to her. The memories hit me, and I feel so frightened. I start wondering what it'll be like, you know, between you and me. And then I start wondering *when* it'll happen. And the first thing I know, it's bedtime. And I'm terrified *tonight* will be the night. I can feel you watching me. And I'm afraid you'll get angry if I sleep by Amy."

"And I have blown like the wind, yes? Angry because you sleep away from me?"

"No. But I know you have every right."

"So you wait for my anger, and it does not come." He turned her in his arms and raised her chin so he could look into her eyes. "And the fear grows, until it is big like a buffalo?"

"Yes," she admitted in a quavery little voice.

Hunter sighed and pressed his cheek against the top of her head. "Ah, little one, I am sure enough a stupid man. We must make talk, yes? It was my wish to make your fear small, not big. To become your good friend, not your enemy."

"Oh, Hunter, I wish we *could* be friends again. Remember our journey to my wooden walls? Sometimes — I think about those times, and —" She broke off and gave an exasperated groan. "I felt so close to you then, and I was so sad to say good-bye."

"And now your heart does not sing friendship for me?"

"You're my *husband.*"

"I wish to be your friend." He leaned back to see her face. "Can I not be both? You have stolen my heart from me, Blue Eyes."

"Oh, Hunter . . ."

"You will be my friend again?" he asked huskily. "We will make laughter together, yes? And you will lie beside me when we sleep, with no fear, because my hand upon you is the hand of your good friend."

"I'd like to be friends again — truly I would."

"Then it will be so." He nuzzled her ear.

"But Hunter, don't you see? We're *married.*"

"Ah, yes, married." Hunter's mind circled the word, trying to imagine what images it conjured for her. "And good friends, yes? Trust. This last time. My hand upon you has brought pain?"

"No," she whispered hoarsely.

"I have beaten you?"

"No." She pressed closer to him and encircled his neck with her arms. "Oh, Hunter, what must you think of me?"

"I think there is big fear inside you."

"Without cause. You've never been cruel to me, never, and yet . . ." A shiver coursed through her. In a rush, she told him of the many times she had heard her aunt Rachel whimpering late at night. "I keep telling myself it won't be like that with you, that Henry's mean as sin and that's why she cries, but —" She broke off and swallowed. "What if that isn't it? What if it's as horrible as it sounds?"

Seeing through her eyes, Hunter found himself smiling again. He considered telling her that many women whimpered when their men loved them, but he decided it would be unwise. He ran his hand up her slender back, aching to touch her soft skin instead of leather. He controlled the urge, reluctant to shatter the mood by startling her. "No more fear, eh? If I grow angry, I will bring you my mother's spoon."

She sniffed and laughed. "A lot of good a spoon would be."

In one smooth sweep, he lifted her into his arms and carried her to the bed, pretending he didn't notice her gasp of surprise or the frantic way she tugged her skirt down. He sat with his back braced against a gnarled bedpost, shifting her so she was draped across his lap, her shoulders supported by the crook of his arm. Gazing down into her wary eyes, he toyed with a curl at her temple, fascinated by the way it coiled on his finger.

"Blue Eyes, you must make the picture for me. Of the day your mother died."

A tiny muscle in her eyelid twitched, and her mouth quivered. "I can't talk about it. I can't, Hunter. Please don't ask."

"My heart is sad with memories, too," he whispered hoarsely. "Let us make trade. I will make a picture of my remembering, yes? And you will make a picture for me."

"My memories are so horrible."

Hunter swallowed and tipped his head back to rest it against the post. Sharing his own memories would not be easy. His chest constricted as he forced his mind back through the years to that long-ago night on the bluff when he had sworn to kill this woman he now held in his arms. A flash of pain cut through him, but it quickly dulled. His memories of Willow by the Stream were beautiful and sweet. He would cherish them always. But they no longer had the power to destroy him.

In a coarse whisper, Hunter began a story he had never told to anyone, uncertain once he had begun that he could even finish it. The words spilled from him, though, raw and ugly, painting a graphic picture of the butchery that had occurred that day, of his wife's slow death. When he finished the lodge was eerily silent, the woman he held unnaturally still.

At last she stirred and turned haunted blue eyes on him. "Oh, Hunter, you loved her very much, didn't you?"

He touched a finger to her cheek. "That love is for yesterday."

Loretta turned her face against his chest, inhaling the scent of his skin, loving the blend of leather and smoke and oil that she had once found so abhorrent. *Hunter.* When had he become so important to her? She could almost see him, holding his dead wife, much as he was holding her now, his shoulders hunched with pain. She ached for him, and for the young woman whose life had been cut short by those brutal white men. Without asking, Loretta knew Hunter had hunted down his wife's rapists and avenged her. The story Aunt Rachel had heard was probably true. His wife's necklace, the man who had defiled her and killed his baby. Yes, Loretta could see Hunter filled with rage. She couldn't blame him.

"You will make trade?" he whispered.

Loretta's breath snagged, and she swallowed. As horrid as Hunter's memories were, her own were far worse. They would haunt her always if she didn't purge herself of them. She knew that. But talking about them was impossible. "I can't. So many men, Comanche men, like you. When I think about it, I can't breathe."

"Not Comanche men like me." He repositioned his back against the post. "I should blame you for what a blue-eyes did to my woman who is dead?"

"No, but —"

"I did not lift my hand against your mother, little one. Do not have hatred for me, eh? Hate the men who killed her, but not this Comanche."

"Oh, Hunter, I don't hate you."

"Then you will make a picture?"

"I don't know where to start."

"You saw the Comanches coming, yes? There were many? You were afraid? There was sunshine? Darkness? You will tell me. A little bit, yes?"

Memories slammed through Loretta's head with blinding clarity. She went rigid, her ears clamoring with echoes from the past. In a halting voice, she began. There was a roaring in her temples that made her voice sound distant. At first she wasn't sure if she was actually saying the words that formed in her mind. Then she saw the grim set of Hunter's mouth and knew she was indeed speaking.

His arm tightened around her shoulders. With one large hand he clasped both of hers, squeezing her fingers, rubbing as if to chase away a chill. His strength flowed into her, comforted her, warmed her. She could face anything with him holding her, she thought. Anything . . . even her nightmares.

Hunter's heart twisted as he listened to her. He tried to see her as she had been then and imagined she must have looked very like Amy, a frail child, frozen with horror, witnessing the unspeakable. He found himself wishing he could walk backward to that day and be there with her in the cellar, to hide her face against his shoulder, to cover her ears so the screams wouldn't haunt her. Since that was impossible, he held her more closely, trying in the only way he knew to make the telling easier for her.

The Comanches had not only raped Rebecca Simpson, but had invaded her body with foreign objects, venting their hatred for her and all her kind, mutilating her in accordance with their religious beliefs, so she could not pass from this world into the land of the dead. Hunter had suspected this, had known it, but hearing the story from Loretta's lips took him outside his own skin, no longer a Comanche, but a white child, seeing his world through a haze of horror. In those minutes Rebecca Simpson became real to Hunter, no longer a faceless yellow-hair, but the mother of his woman, someone Hunter would have loved. His people had killed her, not mercifully, but slowly and horribly.

Hunter could only marvel that Loretta had come to trust him as much as she did, enough to let him hold her as he was, enough to have come to him for help when Santos stole Amy. Was it any wonder that Red Buffalo's lies had terrified her? Or that she trembled with dread at the thought of lying with a Comanche man?

"Before she died, she begged God to forgive them," Loretta cried brokenly. "She was so good, Hunter. I can't remember a single time when she was cruel — not to anyone. She didn't deserve to die like that."

"No."

"And she deserved far more from me! I stayed hidden, Hunter. She screamed and screamed and screamed for help! And I did nothing. Nothing!"

Tears burned in Hunter's eyes. He hunched his shoulders around her. "You were a child."

"A coward, I was a coward!" A horrible, tearing sob erupted from her. She slid her arms around his neck and buried her face against the side of his throat. "That's what I can't forget! Hiding down there, hearing her scream. Oh, why didn't I do something?"

"You would be dead, Blue Eyes. The Comanches would have killed you — just as slowly, eh? One small girl against many braves? You could do nothing."

"I could have died with some dignity!"

"Not with dignity — with great pain. You are no coward."

"Oh, yes, I am! Look at me! I'm terrified to

let you, my husband, touch me. You've been so kind to me and Amy. I should've overcome these feelings! And I haven't! I don't know why you even want me!"

A sad smile twisted his mouth as he recalled how she had walked out alone to face a hundred Comanches, one small woman against an army. "You make a smile inside me, that is why I want you. The way a man wants his wife." He ran a hand up her back, kneading her tense muscles. "You will trust this Comanche? As you did when you rode in a great circle back to me? This one last time, you will trust? No hurting after the virgin pain — and no shame. It is a promise I make for you, for always."

Her breath came out in a rush. "Hunter, I'm afraid."

"There is nothing to fear. You will trust, and I will chase your fear away, yes?"

A tremor shook her.

"I have made lies to you?"

"No, never."

"Then you will trust — one last time?"

"What will you do if I say no?"

Hunter prayed she didn't. "I will eat you and pick my teeth with your bones."

She laughed, the sound shrill, nervous, and wet with tears. "Or sure enough beat me?"

"Ah, yes, I will beat you, sure enough." He pressed his lips to the wild pulse in her temple, taking measure of her fear. His body tensed as he waited for her answer. "Blue Eyes, you will say yes to me?"

"Tonight? Now?"

"Yes, tonight. Before this time between us passes."

When she sat, silent, watching, Hunter lifted her off his lap and rose, drawing her up beside him. She studied his every move, poised as if for flight. Hunter's hands shook as he unfastened her braids and ran his fingers through the intertwined strands of gold, combing them into a shimmering cloud about her shoulders. Then he framed her face between his palms and slowly bent his head. He wanted so badly to make a glad song inside of her. In his way, he was as terrified of her memories as she was.

As his lips drew close to hers, Loretta's nerves leaped. This was it, no turning back. His mouth came within an inch, then nearer. Her eyes widened. Then their lips touched, silk on silk, their breath mingling, their lashes fluttering closed. Her mind screamed a warning as her senses spun out of control. Something deep within her belly quickened, sending shocks of longing through her. She twisted her face aside, shivering as his mouth trailed across her cheek to her ear.

"Hunter?" She grasped his shoulders for support, digging her nails into his flesh. "Hunter?"

"I am here. Be easy." He slid a hand to the

nape of her neck and turned her face back to him. "Be easy."

Loretta's legs felt like wet clay. As his mouth again claimed hers, a hundred possibilities ran through her mind, all frightening. Then sensation wiped out everything. There was only Hunter, solid and warm and gentle, holding her in rock-hard arms, his body bracing hers.

Even in her inexperience, she sensed that kissing was new to him, that he was doing it only to please her. But after a few experimental nibbles, he mastered the art, claiming her mouth with a shattering thoroughness, his tongue thrusting deep, the sensuous rhythm he struck as old as time. Loretta leaned into him, sliding her hands into his hair, forgetting for a moment to be afraid. Looping an arm under her bottom, he lifted her against him. She could feel his heart slamming. Or was it hers? It didn't matter. All that mattered were the feelings sweeping through her.

When at last Hunter drew back for air, his dark eyes were cloudy with tenderness. He smiled a slow, thoughtful smile and, sliding her down his thighs, let her feet touch the floor. With infinite slowness he grasped the tails of her overblouse and skimmed the leather lightly up her ribs, grazing her sensitized breasts. Loretta glued her gaze to his, bracing herself.

"I'm frightened," she said shakily.

"I am frightened beside you," he murmured.

"You? But why are you —"

"Because you are sunshine. Because you make a glad song inside me. I have great fear that you will go away from me." He drew the blouse over her head and tossed it aside. Smiling, he smoothed her hair, then lifted its heavy length to resettle it around her white shoulders so it covered her breasts. Skimming his palms down her slender arms, he found the drawstring that held up her skirt and made fast work of untying the knot. *"Nei commar-pe ein."*

She clutched her skirt. "What does that mean?"

"I love you."

"Oh, Hunter."

He tugged the skirt from her grasp and let it fall, then knelt on one knee before her, taking care not to look at her body while he unlaced her moccasins. Slipping a hand behind her knee, he bent her leg to draw her foot from the leather and, before she could guess his intent, dipped his head to kiss the inside of her thigh. She clamped her hands over the triangle of golden hair at the apex of her legs.

"Hunter, don't do that."

Smiling, he removed her other moccasin, stealing another taste of milky thigh, this time keeping a hold on her leg, so she stood precariously on one foot, while he trailed his lips up to her white-knuckled hands.

She jerked and hopped to catch her balance. "What are you — Hunter, *don't!*"

He nibbled lightly at her fingertips, butting her off balance with his shoulder. She squeaked in dismay and hopped again, trying to stay upright. The thrust of his weight against her leg made that impossible. Instinctively she grabbed his shoulders to right herself, leaving the place that he sought momentarily unguarded. Hunter, with the unfailing accuracy of an expert marksman, homed in.

Grabbing handfuls of his hair, Loretta shrieked and toppled backward onto the bed. The next instant she was anchored there by two hundred pounds of bronzed muscle. Her nipples thrust through the curtain of her hair, their tips skidding down his chest as he moved up on her. His arms spasmed, and his breath caught. Heart tripping, she stared up at him. A mischievous grin slanted across his mouth.

"Hunter — don't do that ever again. It's — shameful."

"No shame," he whispered, bending to kiss her neck, his fingertips trailing down her arm, setting her skin afire. "Sweet, Blue Eyes. *Penan-de,* honey. Trust this Comanche."

Following the rawhide string that held her medallion, his mouth began a downward trek

507

toward her chest, his long hair trailing across her breasts, tickling and sending waves of sensation over her. She cupped her palms over her nipples. When he encountered the barrier of her tense fingers, he circled, his lips feathering as lightly as butterfly wings, finding exposed breast where the span of her palms and fingers didn't reach.

"Trust this Comanche, little one."

She quickly repositioned her hands to thwart him, and just as quickly he changed tactics and kissed the newly exposed area she had just abandoned. Shards of fire stabbed through her, warming her skin, taking her breath. Loretta knew what he wanted, and the thought appalled her. She clutched her breasts even tighter, only vaguely aware of the bruising dig of her own fingers because her senses were riveted on the touch of his lips, the liberties he was taking.

They continued to parry until, much to Loretta's dismay, she moved one hand far enough off center to bare a pink peak. Hunter's mouth latched on to it, hot and wet, the drag of his tongue sending jolts through her. She drew in a draft of air, going rigid.

Instinctively she tried to push him away, only to find that he was too strong to be so easily dispatched. By the time she realized that, the delicious pull of his mouth swept her mind clean of all rational thought. Instead of shoving, she made fists in his hair and drew him closer, her body arching against the solid wall of his. He slipped an arm around her waist and drew her even nearer, one large hand splayed on her buttock. The familiarity of his touch and the shocking heat of his skin against hers jerked her back to reality. Glancing down, she saw what was to her unthinkable, a man suckling at her breast, her white body clasped to his bronzed chest.

"What are you — White people don't *do* things like this. I'm sure they don't. Stop! Please?"

Alarmed by her tone, Hunter lifted his head to search her eyes. The last thing he wanted was to frighten her. The *tosi tivo* had strange customs, especially when it came to women's bodies. At this point he wasn't concerned with *how* he made love to her, as long as he got it done. "You say it, and I will do it."

Confusion played upon her face. "What?"

"You say to me how."

Scarlet dotted her cheeks. She nibbled her lip, staring at him. "*I* don't know how. It's just, well, there are certain things I'm sure no decent woman would —" Her pupils flared, turning her eyes dark. "Just get it finished."

Finished? Hunter regarded her for several charged seconds. Then an amused twinkle crept into his gaze. "Blue Eyes, if you do not know the *tosi tivo* way, we must do it the Comanche way."

"Well . . . yes, I suppose. It's just that I —

Hunter?" He bent his dark head and trailed his lips to her other breast, nibbling and nudging her rigidly cupped fingers. "H-Hunter?"

"Be easy," he whispered. "It is well." He dipped his tongue between her knuckles, searching for the sensitive, throbbing nubbin that she guarded so protectively. When his plunging tongue grazed what he sought, she snapped taut. He made another pass and another. A cry crawled up her throat. She couldn't think when he did this.

"It is mine," he whispered raggedly. "Give it to me. No pain, little one. Trust me."

As if of their own volition, her fingers parted. Her rosy nipple popped through, its pebbled peak thrusting upward eagerly to meet him. Hunter seized it gently between his teeth and worried it until she began to shiver and moan. His uncertainty fled. No matter how odd her customs, her body, though more lovely than most, responded like any other.

With no further hesitancy, Hunter drew her aureole into his mouth and took a long, hard pull until it swelled against his tongue. Smiling, he lifted his head and blew softly. When the vulnerable nerve endings there responded to the wash of cool air and her flesh sprang taut, he once again teased her with his teeth, then pulled her into his mouth. He worked her until a glazed look crept into her eyes and she began to writhe against him.

Loretta turned toward him, lost in a swirling haze of indefinable yearnings. With feverish urgency, uncertain what it was she sought, she ran her hands over the bunched muscles in his shoulders, drawing him closer, needing him closer. *Hunter.* The fear was gone, replaced by a fiery heat, low in her belly, that radiated outward in shivering starbursts to ignite her every nerve ending, making her tremble. *Hunter.* Dizzy, her mind reeling . . . only he provided anchor, his hands and mouth lifting her on wave after wave of sensation.

Cautiously, gently, Hunter skimmed his hand down her belly to the golden apex of her thighs. Her abdomen spasmed under his arm when his fingertips dipped into the crevice of her womanhood. She leaped and stiffened, trying to sit up, but he rode her back down to the fur and carefully slid his finger into the throbbing, narrow passage. His guts knotted with urgent longing.

"Toquet, mah-tao-yo." Claiming her lips with his to muffle her protests, he reveled in the sweet taste of her breath, in the way she parted her thighs for him even though she was frightened. He trailed his mouth to her ear, whispering to keep her calm. A pounding began in his temples. He lost track of what he said, whether he spoke in English or Comanche. She seemed to be soothed by

either, responding, not to the words, but to his tone. An aching tenderness welled inside him. Loretta, his bright one. She was as golden as sunshine, warming him, searing him wherever she touched.

Working his hand up to a steady rhythm, Hunter plied her, withdrawing, plunging deep. Her breathing became quick and shallow. Then he felt a spasm in the tight passage of muscle, and a hot rush of moisture welled up from within her. His own breathing ragged, he covered her lips with his. Eyes closed, face shimmering, she whimpered softly into his mouth as passion rocked her for the first time.

Drawing back, Hunter gazed down at her, wishing he could lose himself in mindless abandon as she was, knowing he couldn't. Not this time. He wanted this first experience to be as painless as possible for her, as pleasurable as he could make it, total surrender, total giving. When he finished with her, there would be nothing left for her to fear.

Shifting his weight onto one elbow and knee, Hunter wedged a leg between hers and inched back, trailing kisses in his wake to keep her senses spinning so she wouldn't surface to awareness and grow frightened. He had fear enough for both of them. He spread her thighs with the breadth of his chest, trailing his mouth lower . . . and lower,

512

to the sweet place he had coveted for so long.

She cried out and bucked when his tongue found its mark. Not to be dissuaded, Hunter caught her wrists so she couldn't hinder him. He found the vulnerable flange of flesh he sought and took it, ignoring her startled protests, using his greater weight to keep her hips anchored to the fur. Knowing what he wanted, he went after it with single-minded intensity, until a hoarse moan ripped from her and she arched toward him, her body jerking with every pass of his tongue. His, at last.

Hunter rose over her, his gaze riveted to her flushed face and dazed blue eyes. Skimming his breeches down his hips, he undressed quickly and took off his medicine pouch. Then, positioning himself over her, he seized her hips and drew her toward him. Carefully and with a slowness that was agonizing for him, he pressed himself into her. As he feared, the passage was tight, so tight that he nearly pulled back. His guts clenched, and a tremor crawled up his spine. There wasn't any way he could spare her pain this first time. She was a slightly built woman, narrow of hip. He was not a small man. Sweat sprang to his brow.

She was as ready as he could get her. If he didn't take her now, he never would. Setting his jaw, Hunter eased farther into her, filled with self-loathing because, even now, though he knew how much he was about to hurt her, fire flared in his belly and his body ached for release. Her eyes widened at the pain, and the color washed from her lips. When he met with the resistance of her maidenhead, he hesitated, then drove forward in one smooth thrust, sheathing himself in liquid heat.

She screamed — a shrill, broken cry that cut through him. The next instant she scrambled to escape. Hunter quickly blanketed her body with his and captured her flailing arms.

"*Toquet,* it is well, little one. It is finished, eh?"

She panted, tossing her head. "It h-hurts!"

"It will pass," he assured her huskily. "It will pass. It is a promise I make for you."

She went rigid when he began to move within her, her small face drawing tight. Tears sprang to Hunter's eyes when she reached up to hug his neck, clinging to him even though he was the one hurting her. He had asked her to trust him this one last time. And she had. What if the discomfort didn't lessen, as he had promised her? She would never let him near her again.

Relief flooded through him when at last he felt her relax. Carefully he picked up momentum, nudging deeper and deeper. Only when Hunter heard her cry out in pleasure did he allow himself to seek pleasure as well.

They drifted back to reality slowly, limbs

entwined, heartbeats erratic, bodies shimmering with sweat. Hunter drew her head onto his shoulder, unwilling to let her go. A half smile settled on his mouth. He knew this first coupling had fallen far short of what it could have been, what it would be the second time. He had been tense, and so had she, not to mention the pain he had inflicted. His smile broadened. This small woman filled the empty places inside him, made him feel whole again.

Gazing sightlessly across the lodge at the evening shadows, Loretta listened to the rapid tattoo of Hunter's pulse. She felt boneless and completely exhausted. Her cheeks flamed when she thought of the things he had done to her and the shameless way she had responded. A wave of embarrassment washed over her.

As if he sensed her anguish, he slid his hand over her hip and upward to her ribs. "My heart is filled with great love for you," he whispered.

Tears sprang to Loretta's eyes. She couldn't name the emotion that caused them, didn't want to. Then, like projectiles from a cannon, the words shot from her mouth. "Oh, Hunter, I love you, too."

The moment she said it, she knew it was true. She loved him as she had never loved anyone, with an intensity that made her ache. Hunter, the fierce warrior, the culmination of all her nightmares, had become the most important person in her world.

CHAPTER 22

Loretta didn't realize she had drifted off to sleep until she awoke to the delicious warmth of Hunter's lips on her throat. She opened her eyes slowly, registering his presence beside her. A shaft of moonlight coming through the smoke hole gilded the broad shoulders that canopied hers. His solid chest, warm and silken, pinned her against soft fur. A wonderfully hard arm encircled her, his broad wrist pressed against her spine, his long fingers fanning between her shoulder blades. She let her head fall back to accommodate his caressing mouth.

"Hi, hites," she whispered.

"Hello," he murmured against her ear, sending spirals of longing down her spine.

Coming aware by degrees, Loretta tucked in her chin to glance down, shocked to see her white skin glowing in the moonlight. It was shameless to be lying next to him like this. She tensed, but the brush of his lips along her throat robbed her of the will to

517

move. Not that she could have if she tried. There was an urgency in the way he held her, a tautness in his body. His hips moved forward against hers, leaving her in no doubt that he wanted her, again.

"Hunter . . . what about Amy? It's dark outside."

"I tied the flap closed. She will go to my mother." His voice was husky, throbbing. He slid his hand down her back to her bottom and drew her firmly against him. His hardness jabbed her abdomen, and she flinched. He drew back and looked down at her, his eyes shot with silver in the moonlight. "You hurt?"

Loretta knew he had gone to great lengths to be gentle with her earlier, but she was sore nonetheless. The ache was to be expected, she felt sure, and probably would disappear in a day or two. "I'm fine."

He slid his hand to her belly, his strong fingers probing carefully, his gaze alert on her face for telltale signs of pain. "Ah, Blue Eyes, I think you lie."

His gentleness and concern touched her. "It isn't that bad, truly. If you want to —" Heat flooded her cheeks as the impropriety of what she had nearly said struck her.

His mouth quirked in a knowing grin. "This Comanche has much want, but I will wait."

That pronouncement was punctuated by a flurry of horses' hooves outside. Hunter rose on an elbow and cocked his dark head to listen. The next instant, Red Buffalo's voice rang out.

"My cousin! I bring your yellow-hair a marriage gift."

An incredulous smile slanted across Hunter's mouth, and upon seeing it, Loretta realized just how much it would mean to him if she and Red Buffalo could become friends.

Hunter slipped from the bed and grabbed his breeches to pull them on. Bathed in moonlight, the planes of his body were gilded with silver, its contours cast into delineative shadow. Clutching a fur to her chest, Loretta sat up, pretending not to notice. She did, though, and what she saw set her pulse to skittering. Perhaps beautiful wasn't an appropriate adjective for a man, but it was the only word that came to her.

Watching him, she was, for the first time in her life, appreciative of the male form, the smooth play of muscle in motion, the subtle grace in strength. Lean tendons roped his buttocks and thighs. When he turned slightly she glimpsed his manhood, jutting forth, hard and proud, from a mahogany nest of short curly hair. Her throat tightened, and deep within her there welled feelings she could scarcely credit, longing, tenderness, delicious excitement — and fierce pride. That such a man loved her and wanted her was nothing short of incredible. He could have had any girl in the village, someone supple and dark with liquid brown eyes, a dozen such some-ones if he chose, but instead he had picked her, a skinny, pallid farm girl.

Cinching the drawstring of his pants, he tied a quick bowknot and extended a hand to her. For an instant Loretta was swept back in time to that first afternoon, when he had commanded she place her palm across his. She had been so terrified then, but no longer. His arm was her shield, just as he had promised.

"Come, wife. My cousin brings a gift, eh?"

"Hunter, I'm not dressed!"

Chuckling, he grabbed a buffalo robe and draped it around her shoulders. After envel-oping her in the fur, he drew her from the bed and to the door, untying the flap to sweep it aside.

Next to Hunter's tripod, Red Buffalo sat astride his horse. He leaned forward along his stallion's neck, his teeth gleaming blue white against his dark skin, his ebony hair drifting in the night wind. "A gift for you, Yellow Hair. To sing the song in my heart of your marriage to my cousin."

Loretta's gaze dropped to the leather-wrapped gift he held out to her. Clutching the buffalo robe together at her throat, she stepped forward. "Thank you, Red Buffalo."

As Loretta reached up to take the gift, she noted a glitter in Red Buffalo's eyes. Though she assured herself it was only a reflection of the moonlight, she felt uneasy. Clasping the packet, she turned back toward the lodge and rejoined her husband in the doorway. Hunter said something to Red Buffalo in Comanche and then drew Loretta inside, reclosing the flap.

"You will look, yes?"

Loretta force a smile and stepped across the room to stand in the moonlight. She doubted Red Buffalo had brought her anything much, but she pretended to be excited for Hunter's sake. Through the leather, the contents of the package felt soft. Cloth of some kind? It was too small to be an article of clothing. Ribbons for her hair, perhaps? After untying the rawhide strings, Loretta unfolded the leather wrapping and lifted the contents between thumb and forefinger. She felt a damp, tacky surface on the thumb side, thick softness on the other. Silken strands slid across the backs of her fingers. In the shadows, it took her a moment to identify what she held. *A scalp.*

Loretta stared down, her pulse resounding inside her head, the world tipping crazily around her. The unfolding hair was long, the color very like her own. She swayed, horror washing over her. The tacky moistness was blood, *fresh* blood. The scalp slid from her paralyzed fingers and plopped on the floor.

"What is it?" Hunter asked.

He stepped closer, peering down at the indefinable shape at her feet. Loretta felt as if she might faint. She tried to speak and couldn't. Hunter crouched and picked up the scalp, a low growl of rage rumbling from his chest. Before she could stop him, he shot to his feet and left the lodge, yelling Red Buffalo's name.

Loretta stood there, her stomach heaving, sweat trickling down the sides of her breasts. She heard Hunter yell again, the sound more distant this time. Red Buffalo was crazy, crazy with hatred. If Hunter confronted him, there was no telling what might happen.

Red Buffalo and his friends were gathered around the central fire. In the glow of firelight, Hunter could see scalps hanging from their horses' bridles. He heard Coyote Dung bragging about the coups he had counted during the raids. Rage filmed his vision. Throwing the scalp he held into the flames, he walked up behind Red Buffalo, seized his shoulder, and spun him around.

Red Buffalo flashed a smug smile. "Your woman didn't like the gift? I bestowed a great honor upon her, yes?"

A dozen words bottlenecked in Hunter's throat. They both knew the scalp hadn't been meant to honor Loretta, but to terrify and repulse her. That Red Buffalo dared to disguise his maliciousness by pretending he had given the gift with good intentions was an affront to Hunter's intelligence and their friendship.

Hunter slammed his fist into his cousin's mouth. Red Buffalo reeled, staggering backward toward the fire. Hunter caught his arm, stepped to one side, and hit him again. Red Buffalo fell on his back, shaking his head and blinking.

Legs spread, fists clenched, Hunter stood over him. "Never again make grief for my woman, Red Buffalo. If you do, I will sure enough kill you."

Red Buffalo swiped blood from the corner of his mouth, his eyes glittering with rage. "I am already dead to you. Since you found that yellow-hair, we are *all* dead to you. You chose *her* over me!"

"And you choose your bitterness over me!"

Arrow Maker stepped around the fire and touched Hunter's shoulder. "Red Buffalo meant no harm. She is your wife, yes? One with the People! She should be honored that Red Buffalo presented her with a scalp. A Comanche woman would be."

Hunter shook off Arrow Maker's hand. "My woman is not Comanche. To present her with a yellow-hair's scalp was cruel, and both of you know it."

Red Buffalo sat up. "Did I hear you right? Your woman is not Comanche? But, cousin, how can that be? She is your wife, accepted now as one of the People. Do you say that her loyalty is still in *tosi tivo* land? That your people are not hers?"

Hunter clenched his teeth, struggling to keep control. After a moment he replied, "I didn't come out here to play with words, Red Buffalo."

"Because you have no words to defend her!"

"I must defend my woman to you? My cousin, a man who was once like a brother to me? When I look upon you, I see a stranger." Hunter swung his arm toward the horses. "How many *tosi tivo* have you killed? Did you discuss making war in council? No! You cannot see beyond your hate! What will happen to our people when the *tosi tivo* retaliate? They will *die!* Hundreds of them! The rest of us have a right to choose! To decide if we want to make war or seek peace. Men like you are taking that choice away from us. You don't fight the great fight for the good of our people, you fight for Red Buffalo!"

Red Buffalo lurched to his feet. "The *tosi tivo* attacked us! We had no choice but to defend ourselves. Ask Arrow Maker and Coyote Dung, they will tell you."

Hunter curled his lip. "The *tosi tivo* had women with them! They wouldn't have attacked twenty warriors!"

Red Buffalo narrowed his eyes. "I am no White Eyes lover, like some I can name. Look at you! Angry because a warrior presented your woman with a scalp! Using your fists like an unblooded boy. Already she makes you soft. If you were a man, you would fight me like a man — to the death."

Tamping down the urge to smash Red Buffalo's face again, Hunter unclenched his fists. "You are my cousin. My heart holds great love for you. But not so much I will let you make my woman weep. Stay away from her! If you do not, I will call a death match."

"You forsake all that you are!" Red Buffalo cried. "And for what? A white woman who will turn her back on you? You call me blind? Hate me if you will, cousin. Kill me if you like! I would rather die than stand aside and watch you destroy yourself."

Hunter turned his back on Red Buffalo's impassioned cries and walked away into the darkness.

An hour later he lay awake beside Loretta, staring at the firelight that played upon the walls of his lodge. Red Buffalo's words haunted him. If Loretta had to choose, would she forsake him for her people? He knew she was awake by the sound of her breathing, but her voice still startled him when she spoke.

"Hunter, what's wrong? Surely you're not still stewing over the scalp. It upset me, but I'm over it now."

He turned to regard her. There were shadows in her eyes, and she was as pale as bleached bones. "You lie, Blue Eyes. Many of your people are dead, by my cousin's hand, and their spirits wail and call out to you."

"It wasn't you who killed them. That's all that counts."

Hunter's chest tightened. One day he would ride into battle again — to slay White Eyes. It was inevitable. How would she feel about that? "You are Comanche now, yes?" he said hopefully. "One with us."

Indefinable emotions played across her face. "I'm married to a Comanche. I love him. But I'll never *be* a Comanche."

Hunter studied her features, once so repulsive to him, now so cherished. He ran a finger up the fragile bridge of her nose, then traced the line of her brow, acutely conscious of the small bones that shaped her face. Protectiveness welled within him.

"You are one with me, one with my people. You cannot stand with one foot on Comanche land and the other on *tosi tivo* land."

"Both my feet are here, Hunter, but part of my heart is at my wooden walls. No matter how much I love you, that will never change. You are one with me, too. Does that make you one with the *tosi tivo?*"

An unnameable fear grew within him. He felt very much as he had several summers ago when he had been caught in a flash flood, swept along by the raging water. The Comanche struggle for survival was like that, surging forward, catching up everyone in its path.

Men like Red Buffalo fed its fury.

"I am filled with fear," Hunter whispered. "For my people and for you. Red Buffalo did not go on a hunt. He went raiding. He called no council. Many of the People feel that keeping peace with the *tosi tivo* is the only way to survive. Men like Red Buffalo take the chance of peace and throw it away in the wind. The *tosi tivo* will strike back, yes? And many of my people will die. In this village, in another." He placed a hand on her tousled hair, brushing his thumb through the soft strands. "If they attack, I must ride with the others to avenge our dead."

Loretta swallowed. "And kill my people, you mean?"

"This will make you look upon me with hate?"

Emotions tangled into a knot inside Loretta. Red Buffalo had committed a great wrong. If white men retaliated, she wouldn't blame them. So how could she blame Hunter if he did likewise? Suddenly she found herself in the unenviable position of seeing and understanding both sides. Harder still, she sympathized with both. Would it be any less horrible if white men harmed Blackbird than if Comanches harmed Amy?

"Oh, Hunter, if I rode into this village with the *tosi tivo* and killed your people, how would you feel?"

His face tightened. "You would kill my

527

mother? Warrior and Maiden? The little ones?"

"No. And you wouldn't Aunt Rachel or Amy or Uncle Henry. That isn't the question, is it?"

"This Comanche cannot change his face."

"And I can't change mine."

He traced the hollow of her cheek, his mouth tipping into a sad smile. "I like your face, Blue Eyes. It is carved upon my heart."

"We're caught in the middle, aren't we, Hunter? From the first, we knew it would come to this."

"I will make no war on the helpless," he whispered raggedly. "No women, no children. That will be good?"

Still shy with him, she touched a finger to his bottom lip. "Could you lift your blade against a man with blue eyes and not think of me, Hunter?"

He made a strangled sound and pulled her roughly into his arms, pressing his mouth against her hair. Neither of them spoke. There were no words. They drew comfort from the only thing they could, the warmth of each other's arms.

The next day Hunter and Loretta escaped the tension Red Buffalo had brought with him to the village by taking off with Swift Antelope and Amy to play along the river. Swift Antelope broached the subject of the raid only once. Hunter informed him there was enough talk back in the village, that no one could know for sure if Red Buffalo had instigated the attack, and there was no point in ruining the day by worrying about it.

Loretta was glad the subject was taboo. For the first time in weeks, she felt relaxed. The tormenting questions from last night hovered in the back of her mind, waiting. But for now she chose to forget and simply enjoy being with Hunter.

Over the course of the day, he revealed to her a boyish, mischievous side that she found enchanting. One moment he played the lover, sliding his fingers lightly across the nape of her neck or down her arm as they walked. The next he was a rascal, sweeping her off her feet and threatening to toss her in the water or jumping out at her from the brush, ferocious as a bear.

Loretta's pulse quickened at those times. She knew Hunter was only playing, but he was a little too convincing for comfort when he tried to look fierce. Beneath his gentle facade there lurked a dark side, and at those times she glimpsed it. Though he had become her friend and lover, he was also the epitome of all she had feared these last seven years. Making love with him hadn't completely erased her memories. Sometimes she wondered if the past would haunt her forever.

Hunter disappeared once, returning a few

minutes later with a bouquet of wild flowers. When Swift Antelope and Amy weren't watching, he dragged her behind bushes to kiss her. Several times, on toward evening, he pressed his palm against her belly and raised a questioning eyebrow. Loretta blushed, well aware of what he was asking. She was still tender from his lovemaking, but not so much as the night before. Yet how could she tell him? Ladies didn't speak of such things, not even to their husbands.

At dusk the four of them stopped en route home to sit on the riverbank under a canopy of cottonwood trees. Loretta hugged her bent knees, gazing at the reflection of leaves and fading sunlight on the water, only half-aware of Amy and Swift Antelope's chatter. Hunter stretched out beside her, head propped on one hand, his eyes never leaving her. She was acutely conscious of his gaze, and when it started to unnerve her, she finally turned to look at him. Banked embers of passion glowed in his eyes.

Smiling, he plucked a blade of grass and feathered it along her arm, reaching up under her loose sleeve. Next he directed his attention to her leg, tracing a circle around the top of her moccasin, grazing the curve of her calf, the back of her thigh beneath her skirt. Loretta's belly knotted, and delicious shivers coursed down her spine. She felt a blush creeping up her neck.

He was deliberately calling to her mind the things he had done to her last night, something a white man would never dream of doing, not in the company of others. Hunter had grown up running wild on the plains with other children, boys and girls alike, garbed in nothing but a bit of string and cloth. She had been stifled by rules of propriety and layer upon layer of muslin. To him, making love was as natural as eating when one was hungry or drinking to slake one's thirst. He felt no shame, no shyness, no sense of secrecy. *I want, I take. It is a very simple thing.* It wasn't simple, though. Not for her.

Hunter grew amused, watching Loretta. When she threw him an accusing glance, he noted that her pupils had flared until her irises were almost black. Crimson rode her cheeks, and a rosy flush colored her slender throat. He wondered if her entire body was pink and wished they were alone so he could find out. *Soon.* Tonight he would build a fire so she couldn't hide in shadows, and he would learn every inch of her, slowly.

Her shyness tantalized him. He anticipated the time when she would come to him without reservation, but he intended to savor this stage of their relationship just as thoroughly. Like now, teasing her with a blade of grass and watching the emotions that played upon her face, imagining the moment when he could stake claim to what she guarded so jealously.

"We should get back," she said softly. "It'll be getting dark soon. And I'm tired."

Brimming with the energy of youth, Swift Antelope and Amy leaped to their feet, eager to be gone. When Loretta stood, Hunter grasped her ankle. "We will follow later," he said huskily.

Swift Antelope flashed a knowing grin and took Amy's hand to hurry her along. Loretta gazed after them, her color deepening. When she looked down at Hunter, her eyes were wide with wariness. "Why aren't we going now?"

"You know why." He tightened his hold on her ankle and tugged her closer, rolling over onto his back to avail himself of the view. He knew she wasn't aware of how revealing a knee-length skirt could be when a man eyed it from the ground up, and he managed to keep a straight face so she wouldn't guess. "Come here, little one."

"I want to go back."

He hoped she stood there arguing for a time. "Obey your husband."

She wrinkled her nose. "It's broad daylight."

"*Keemah*, come."

Growing tired of just looking when he could be touching, Hunter cocked his head and let her see him leering. He was awarded a fetching glimpse of slender, creamy thighs and honey gold. She gasped and dropped to her knees as if someone had dealt a blow to the backs of her legs.

Tucking her skirt under her knees, she cried, "Have you no shame?"

His answer was a slow grin. Seizing her wrist, he drew her toward him. "There is no shame. You are my woman."

Pulled off balance, she fell across his chest. Squirming, but halfheartedly, she said, "There's a time and a place for everything, and this isn't it."

"No?" He ran a hand under her blouse. "I say it is a very good time."

She jerked when his fingers scaled her ribs. "That tickles."

Without warning he rolled with her, coming out on top. He kissed her lightly on the lips while he moved his hand from her ribs to her breast. The small mound of warm flesh fit perfectly in his hand, the crest springing taut against his palm. Scarlet flamed on her cheeks. Unable to resist, Hunter lifted her blouse and moved off her to look, one thigh slanted across both of hers to keep her still. He had guessed right; when she was shy, she grew pink all over.

"Hunter!" She tried to shove the leather down. "Someone might come!"

"No one comes."

Fascinated, he touched the rosy tip of her

533

nipple with his dark fingers, watching it harden and thrust upward, begging for attention — attention he was more than willing to give it. Dipping his head, he flicked the tip of his tongue across the peak, then seized it with his teeth.

She gasped and made fists in his hair. "Hunter?"

"Hm?" He moved to the unkissed breast. "What is it you want, little one?"

Her breath caught as his teeth closed on her. "I want to go."

With skillful determination, Hunter continued the exquisite torment until the tips of her nipples throbbed, swollen and hot, against the end of his tongue.

"Hunter, please . . ." She moaned and drew him toward her, arching her hips against him. "Hunter . . ."

He obliged her and at last took her into his mouth. She cried out at the sharp pull, and he gloried in the sound, in the knowledge that he could make her surrender to him. After tending each breast, he started to kiss her lips, but she held tight to his hair, pulling him back to her nipple, arching up to meet his mouth. With a pleased chuckle, Hunter fulfilled the silent request, savoring the sweet taste of her. Then he kissed her parted lips.

Loretta opened her eyes and gazed up at her Comanche husband through a haze of longing. By degrees her pulse slowed, and her senses cleared. A tender smile curved his mouth.

"My heart is heavy to say these words, Blue Eyes, but someone may come. My woman who is without shame must wait, eh?"

She groped to jerk her blouse down. Hunter reared back to let her sit up, his eyes twinkling with mischief. She straightened her clothes, keeping her pink face averted. Taking her hand, he rose and led her up the bank, wishing they were a bit farther from home so he could finish what he had begun without running the risk of company.

"We will go to my lodge, yes? I will make you happy there where no one can see."

She slugged his shoulder. "You did that on purpose!"

He laughed and tucked her under one arm to hold her close to his side as they walked. When they came within sight of the village, she drew away. A guilty flush dotted her cheeks. Hunter threw back his head and laughed. She retaliated by grabbing up a handful of pebbles to throw at him. Her aim was terrible, but Hunter ran out of throw's reach anyway — until her ammunition was exhausted. Then he doubled back, charging, so he could reach her before she gathered more rocks.

She shrieked and fled. His longer legs quickly closed the distance between them. He swept her off her feet and tossed her over his shoulder, clamping one arm across the backs of her knees. Playfully she pummeled his back. Just as playfully he ran his free hand up her skirt and gave her bottom a light pinch.

All in all, Hunter decided, it had been a good day.

Red Buffalo was sitting outside Hunter's lodge when they got home. Hunter set Loretta on her feet but kept a protective arm around her, slowing his footsteps, his gaze locked on his cousin's. Red Buffalo glanced away.

"Hunter, I need to talk to you," he said in a low voice. "Would you come to my lodge?"

In English Hunter told Loretta he would return shortly, then accompanied his cousin in tight-lipped silence. Red Buffalo had a fire burning inside his lodge. The two men entered to their left and made a complete circle before they sat cross-legged by the flames. Bracing his forearms on his bent knees, Hunter hunched his shoulders, watching his cousin and waiting. Red Buffalo didn't offer Hunter his pipe so they could smoke together as brothers. As much as Hunter hated tobacco, he yearned for the gesture to be made.

Red Buffalo tossed another piece of wood on the fire, then stared at the licking flames. His bottom lip was slightly swollen where Hunter's fist had struck him. It was a long while before he spoke. "My heart is laid upon the ground," he said softly. "I want no bad feelings between us."

Hunter set his jaw and fixed his attention on a spiral of smoke. "I find that hard to believe. Last night wasn't the first time you've made tricks. You put the snake in her bed, did you not?"

Slowly Red Buffalo nodded. "I will never again try to harm her. You love her, yes? More than the People, more than anything."

Hunter closed his eyes for a moment. The same question seemed to circle back to him, over and over. "I love her, yes. But more than the People? I *am* the People. Must the love between a man and woman kill all other love?"

"If you had to choose, you would choose her. If she had to choose, what do you think her choice would be?"

Hunter's face drew taut. "Why is that important? I will never make her choose."

"It may not be up to you. She is your enemy, Hunter! Her people slaughter us! Open your eyes and see the truth! In the end, she will destroy you! She will turn your face from all that you are, leave your heart a wasteland, and abandon you."

"Is this why you asked me here?" Hunter hissed. "If so, I'm leaving."

"No!" Red Buffalo reached across the fire to catch Hunter's arm. "Don't go, cousin.

I'm sorry. Forget my words."

"They cut too deep. I can never forget them."

Red Buffalo passed a hand over his brow and sighed. "I'm sorry. I'll accept her as your wife, Hunter. I will."

"Your words are shallow, like a stream during drought. Show me your sorrow. Then I may believe you."

Red Buffalo shot to his feet. "I *will* show you. Look what I have here. A gift, yes? For your woman. A gift like no other."

He pulled something sparkly from a parfleche and palmed it, extending his arm toward Hunter. "Moonlight on water, cousin. A comb for your *tosi* wife."

Drawn by the glisten of bright stones, Hunter lifted the comb and turned it to catch the firelight. For an instant he imagined the look on Loretta's face if he were to give her something so fine. Then he discarded the thought. "You took it off a woman you killed. She would spit upon it."

"No! I traded with the Comancheros for it."

Excitement coursed up Hunter's spine. He wanted so badly to give Loretta pretty things, things a white woman would treasure. He knew his world was vastly different from hers. A comb like this might console her. "How much?"

"It's a gift!"

"Ah, no. Only a woman's husband should give her something so beautiful."

"It will cost you a blanket," Red Buffalo said with a shrug.

Hunter snorted. "Two horses, no less."

"One. I will accept no more." Red Buffalo laughed. "We do this backward, eh, cousin? Some fine traders we are."

Fascinated by the fiery stones, Hunter glanced up. "It's worth far more."

"My sorrow for the grief I've caused makes us even."

Hunter smiled and closed his fingers around the comb, so anxious to present it to his wife that he sprang to his feet. "I'll bring you the horse right away."

"Tomorrow is soon enough."

Hunter clamped a hand over his cousin's shoulder. Locking gazes with him, he said, "My heart is glad, Red Buffalo. The sun does not shine as brightly when you are not by my side."

Red Buffalo's smile faded. "I have never abandoned you, Hunter. We are brothers. If it seems I turn against you, it is out of love."

"That is past." Hunter's voice rasped with emotion. "You walk a new way now, yes?"

Red Buffalo smiled and gave him a friendly shove. "Go home to your yellow-hair."

Hunter hesitated in the doorway. "There's something I've been meaning to talk with you about. Bright Star wants you to notice her."

"Bright Star?" An incredulous expression crossed Red Buffalo's scarred face. "Wanting *me?* You are *boisa*, cousin."

"It is so. If you're interested in her, you'd better claim her before someone else does. She's very lovely."

"Yes," Red Buffalo said rather dazedly. "You *are* talking about your woman's sister?"

Hunter laughed. "She's too shy to approach you, but her eyes follow you when you're not looking."

Hunter found Loretta snuggled on her side in bed when he entered the lodge. His heart sank with disappointment. If she was asleep, he would have to wait to give her the gift. Impatience welled within him. He wanted to see her pleasure now.

"Blue Eyes?"

She pushed up on an elbow and fastened a sleepy gaze on him. "What are you grinning so big about?"

Hunter held the comb behind his back. He sat on the edge of the bed, turned toward her so she couldn't see. "I bring you a marriage gift."

Curiosity brought her wide awake. She sat up and tried to spy what he had hidden in his hand. "What is it?"

"Something fine. Something as bright as my golden one."

She leaned farther to one side. "Hunter-rrr! What *is* it?"

Very slowly, Hunter brought his hand out from behind him. Loretta said nothing for several seconds. Then she lifted questioning eyes to his. "Is this a joke? What were you doing in my satchel?"

His smile seemed to freeze in place, and his gaze shifted, settling on the black bag across the room. Loretta's throat tightened. She, too, turned to look at the bag. Icy dread chilled her skin. Slipping from the bed, she walked across the lodge. As she grasped her satchel, her pulse accelerated. The clasp sprang open beneath her trembling fingers. She stared down at her mother's diamond comb.

Time slid to a stop. Suspended there, Loretta slowly assimilated the fact that, seven years after Rebecca Simpson's death, the missing mate to her comb had resurfaced in Hunter's possession. For an instant the obvious conclusion slammed into her, that Hunter had been the man who took Rebecca Simpson's scalp. Then sanity returned. *Not Hunter.* She had come to know him too well to believe that of him. Even so, pain sliced through her, a wounding pain. Her legs buckled, and she dropped to her knees, unable to speak, to lift her head. From the corner of her eye, she saw Hunter rise from the bed, the comb dropping to the dirt, forgotten.

Like a man approaching a guillotine, he

541

moved toward her. She heard his intake of breath when he peered into the satchel.

"It belonged to my mother," she cried. "She was wearing both combs the day she died. I found this one near her body. The other was stolen by the Comanche who scalped her."

"No." The word came out in a tortured whisper.

Loretta clamped a hand over her mouth to throttle the scream that snaked up her throat. Hunter sank to his knees beside her.

"No," he said again, this time with more conviction. "I did not — The day she died, I was not —" His voice broke, and she saw his fingers knot into white-knuckled fists. "Blue Eyes, I made no lies."

Dropping her hand, she gulped for air, swallowing sobs, struggling to speak. She turned to look at him through a haze of tears. "Red Buffalo gave it to you, didn't he?"

Hunter stared at her, making no reply.

"*Didn't* he?"

"*Huh,* yes," he admitted finally, reluctantly. "He traded for it with the Comanchero."

"He's a liar." Loretta squeezed her eyes closed. Hunter, the man she loved, her husband, the cousin of her mother's murderer. It all fell into place, Red Buffalo's hatred of her, his continued efforts to be rid of her. Images spun through her mind, of her mother, of the lean, agile young Indian who had taken her scalp. *Red Buffalo.* Because of his disfigurement, Loretta hadn't recognized him. "Oh, my God! Oh, my God!"

In that instant Loretta's marriage became a nightmare. At least thirty men had taken part in that raid. All of them were probably from this village. Old Man, Hog, Arrow Maker, Coyote Dung, Warrior, Hunter's father, any or all of them could have been there. Possibly even her husband. Blurred faces swirled, out of the past, into the present. She didn't want to believe Hunter had been there that day, but how could she be positive he wasn't? How many attacks had he made on the *tosi tivo?* A hundred, perhaps as many as a thousand? Would he even remember one dusty little farmhouse and the woman who had died there?

Her gaze shifted to his scalp pole. None of the hair was long, testimony that he made war against only men. That didn't mean he was never present when women were victimized, only that he didn't take part. Did her father's scalp hang in Hunter's collection? Loretta fastened horrified eyes on one swatch of brown hair, then another.

"Blue Eyes . . ." He reached to touch her shoulder.

Loretta shrugged from under his hand. "Don't, Hunter, please don't." She gazed through tears at a tuft of stubborn grass shooting up from the packed dirt floor. The hatred between her and Hunter's people was

543

like that, surviving everything. Within her chest there was an awful emptiness.

"Red Buffalo said he traded for the comb. This may be so, yes?"

"As huge as Texas is, that would be quite a coincidence, don't you think?"

Hunter wasn't sure what coincidence meant, but he got the point. For the first time in his life he was tempted to lie, to say anything that might convince her she was wrong. The training of a lifetime forestalled him. Without his honor he was as nothing.

"Red Buffalo was in that war party, Hunter. You know it, I know it, he knows it. That's why he hates me so."

To prove her point, she dug in the satchel and withdrew her mother's portrait. She handed it to Hunter, watching his expression. "That's my mother."

"Your face upon the water," he whispered.

Hunter stared down at the likeness, remembering that first day when Loretta stepped out from her wooden walls into the yard, her golden hair shimmering, her eyes a blaze of blue in her small face. Almost immediately Red Buffalo had begun urging Hunter to kill her, to put her out of his life. Sweat filmed Hunter's face. During Loretta's delirium her first night of captivity, her screams had revealed that she witnessed her mother's death. Ever since, Red Buffalo's hatred for her had intensified. He must have feared that something would trigger her memory — the way he walked, the sound of his voice — and that sooner or later she would recognize him as her mother's murderer and expose him.

In a hollow voice Loretta said, "Red Buffalo had to have known I was related to her the moment he saw me. I'm not beautiful like she was, but the resemblance is unmistakable."

Hunter lifted his head. Not beautiful? He ached to trail his fingertips over the planes of her features, to draw her into his arms and hold on, never to let go. She was slipping away from him; he could see it in her eyes. He gripped the scrolled frame of the portrait, assailed by a fear more terrible than any he had ever felt. *Red Buffalo, men from this village?* If such a thing was true, and Hunter knew it was, he would once again lose the woman he loved, just as surely as he had lost Willow by the Stream, just as irrevocably. A woman could overlook many things when she loved a man, but never this. The thought panicked him.

Loretta took a jagged breath and let it out slowly. Passing a hand over her brow, she said, "This is Red Buffalo's way of getting even with you for hitting him last night. After everything he's done to prevent it, you've turned against him anyway. He has nothing more to lose." She gave a shrill, hysterical laugh. "From the first, he's been trying to keep us apart." Her body sagged. "He's finally succeeded."

"No." He clasped her chin, forcing her to meet his gaze. "You are my woman, for always. We said the God words, Blue Eyes. *Suvate,* it is finished. You cannot walk backward."

Releasing her, he returned the portrait to the satchel, laying it on the fold of linen with exaggerated care, as if his gentleness might somehow undo the great wrongs that had been committed.

"Men from this village killed my parents, Hunter! Don't you understand what that means?" The words tore at Loretta, every syllable driving the wedge deeper between them. "I can't stay here knowing that. I can't! And if you love me, you won't ask me to."

"You are my woman!" He swept his hand toward the door. "I have spoken it before my people. You must walk always in my footsteps. That is the way of it. A woman does not leave her husband. It is forbidden."

Loretta lifted her chin. "According to your ways!"

"My ways are your ways. My people are your people. I am your husband!"

Echoes of her mother's screams bounced off the walls of her mind. If she lived to be a hundred, she would never forget. "Does that mean my ways are yours as well? That my people are yours?" She met his gaze with unflinching intensity. "Will you avenge my parents?"

His face turned ashen. "And kill my cousin?"

"And all the others who were there! That *is* your way, isn't it? To avenge your people? Just last night, you said so. If your people are my people, then my people are yours."

The look on Hunter's face frightened her. Loretta stared at him, scarcely able to comprehend what she had just said.

"Hunter . . ." She reached for his arm. "I didn't mean it."

He jerked from her grasp and rose.

"I didn't mean it," she cried again. "It would tear the heart out of you. Do you think I want that? There's been enough killing."

Alarmed by Loretta's cries, Amy and Swift Antelope burst inside the lodge. Amy's blue eyes, wide with concern, darted from Loretta to Hunter. "What's wrong?"

Trembling violently, Loretta flung a hand toward the bed. "Ma's lost comb."

Amy stepped across the room. After staring at the glistening diamonds for a long moment, she turned a puzzled frown on Hunter. "You?" she whispered. Then, like a wild thing, she gave a hoarse cry and launched herself at him, kicking and scratching. "You butcher! You murderin' butcher!"

Hunter seized Amy's wrists and quickly looped an arm around her, pulling her against

547

him. Swift Antelope stepped closer, torn between protectiveness of Amy and loyalty to Hunter.

"You killed her ma! You killed her ma! She was wearin' that comb the day she died!" Amy thrashed about, fighting frantically to get free. "You scalped my aunt Rebecca! That's the only way you could have gotten her comb! The *only* way! Let me go! Take your slimy hands off me!"

Amy's accusations hit Hunter like a boulder in the chest. It was small consolation that Loretta hadn't reacted this way. Shoving her toward Swift Antelope, he barked, "Take her to my mother!"

Swift Antelope caught Amy's arm and dragged her out the lodge door. Her screams slowly diminished. Hunter turned back to gaze at his wife. She hugged her waist, her eyes dark with misery.

With a snarl of rage, Hunter spun and ducked out the door, his long legs eating up the distance to Red Buffalo's lodge. Warrior came running to fall in beside him. "Hunter, what's happening? What is it your Ayemee is screaming about?"

Never breaking stride, Hunter explained. "I will kill him for this. Cousin or not, I will kill him."

Warrior grabbed his brother's arm, pulling him to a stop. "He left, Hunter! Just a few minutes ago — with all his friends."

"He left? Why didn't you come tell me?"

"I didn't know!" Warrior threw up his hands. "How was I to know, Hunter? He comes and goes all the time."

For an instant Hunter considered following Red Buffalo, but then an image of Loretta's white face flashed through his mind. He couldn't leave her while she was this upset. Taking a bracing breath, he turned back toward home.

"How is your woman taking this?" Warrior asked.

"Her heart is on the ground."

Warrior sighed. "This is bad, Hunter, very bad. Her mother? Her father? She will never forgive this."

Hunter increased his pace, growing more concerned by the second that he had left Loretta alone. "She has no choice. We have said words, yes? She is my woman."

"But Red Buffalo killed her parents!"

"She is still my woman."

CHAPTER 23

Loretta was stuffing her belongings into her satchel when Hunter stepped into the lodge. He stood in the shadows a moment, watching her. The firelight fell across her, shimmering in her golden hair, flickering across the leather that skimmed her bent shoulders. She was sobbing. The sounds cut through him.

"Blue Eyes?"

His whisper snapped her head around. She sprang to her feet, her eyes huge with shock, her lips pale. "I'm leaving, Hunter."

Hunter stepped from the shadows, his heart catching at the way she retreated. "I was not at your wooden walls that day, Blue Eyes. I have spoken it." He paused by the fire, not wanting to crowd her. "It is a God promise I make for you."

Sparkling with tears, her eyes met his. Her throat worked, and her mouth twisted. "Oh, Hunter, don't you see it doesn't make a difference?" She made a gesture toward his scalp pole. "From the first we knew it could never work between us. Somehow, for a few wonderful days, we lost sight of that. You're a Comanche. I'm a *tosi* woman. We're worlds apart."

"Look into me and say you have no love for me," he commanded hoarsely.

"All the love in the world can never change this."

"Say the words to me!"

"I can't. I *do* love you, don't you see? What I must do has nothing to do with what's between us."

"My heart sang only good things —" His voice caught, and he swallowed. "I thought the comb would bring you great gladness."

"I know that." Loretta swiped at her cheeks and sniffed. "I'm not blaming you. It's not your fault, Hunter, or mine, not even Red Buffalo's. Don't you see? This madness began long before we were born, and it'll go on long after we're all dead. Some things, no matter how sweet, how wonderful, just aren't meant to be."

He took a hesitant step toward her. "Your eyes say you blame me. Your heart whispers that I was there that day."

She stared at him a moment, then inclined her head in a reluctant nod. "All right, you want the truth? I think you may have been. How can you know for sure? Red Buffalo is your cousin. How many raids have you made with him? Dozens?"

"We have ridden together many times."

"And has he killed women on those raids?"

"Many *taum* ago. I am a man now and go the way my father went before me. I make no war on the helpless. The men who ride with me fight the fight my way."

"Many *taum* ago. How many *taum*, Hunter? Seven? Would one dusty farm stand out in your mind?"

"This Comanche was not there!" he ground out.

"Would you say if you were?"

"I make no lies!"

"All right, you weren't there. But we're not talking about you! We're talking about Red Buffalo!" Her voice rose to a shrill pitch. "And the fact that you live and ride with my mother's murderers. Whether you were there or not changes nothing. Men in this village killed my parents, and I can't bear to remain here. Imagine how I would feel. Getting up in the morning and calling hello to one of the men who tortured her to death! I can't do it, not even for you."

Raking a hand through his hair, Hunter shifted his weight onto one foot, a lean hip slung outward, one knee bent. "My heart is laid upon the ground because of your tears, yes? But I cannot walk backward and undo the many wrongs. Your mother and father are dead. *Suvate*, it is finished."

Loretta hugged her waist, staring at him.

"*Suvate?* My father's death was one thing. It was quick, at least. But my mother . . ." She bent her head, falling silent. When she looked up at last, tears shimmered on her cheeks. "You're right. It *is* finished. Everything. Unless, of course, you want to leave with me. We could go away. Just you and I, Hunter. Would you do that? For me? We could be together. We could forget, if we tried."

"I am Comanche. Without my people, I am as nothing."

"And I'm *tosi tivo.* If I stay here with my parents' killers, *I* will be as nothing."

"You are my woman. We are one, forever with no horizon."

"Oh, Hunter, it isn't that easy. I'm leaving," she whispered in a quavery voice. "You can't watch me every second."

"It is forbidden for a woman to leave her husband."

"So is our love."

Hunter's guts knotted. He couldn't blame her for wanting to leave. Oh, yes, he understood. He even sympathized, but not so much that he was willing to let her go. She was reeling with shock right now. Later, when she calmed down, perhaps she would see things differently. Regardless, he needed time to think, to decide what to do, to somehow make things right between them. He loved her too much to lose her. Far too much. Hoping to discourage her, he growled, "If you flee, this Comanche will follow you. Anyone who tries to keep you from me will die. Think long and hard on this. I paid a fine bride price. You are my woman. What is mine, I keep."

"You wouldn't!" She said with a gasp. "My family, Hunter?"

The stunned disbelief that crossed her face nearly made Hunter retract the threat, but he knew if he did, she would run at the first opportunity. If she feared for her loved ones, she would be less likely to do something rash.

Her eyes turned hard and glassy. Raising her chin, she met his gaze with contemptuous disdain. "But of course you would, wouldn't you? All you care about is keeping what belongs to you. In this case, me. Bought and paid for, your *tosi* woman! No better than a horse."

"You are mine. I have spilled my seed within you. Run from me, and I will beat you until you wail and weep. It is a promise I make for you."

"You know what my problem has been, Hunter? I have seen only what I wanted to see." She flung her arm toward his scalp pole again. "The evidence has always been here, but I made excuses for you and saw you the way I wanted you to be. Somehow, I told myself you cared about me, not as a possession, but as a person! And in doing so I forgot one major fact. You're a Comanche, first, last, and always. A murdering heathen! Aunt Rachel was right."

He stepped across the room and sat down on the edge of the bed, watching her.

"If you think I'm going to lie there beside you now, you're crazy," she informed him in a tremulous voice.

"I am sure enough one crazy Comanche," he replied. "You will lie beside me. This night and for always. You cannot run. If you do, death will ride beside you, wherever you go."

Moonlight bathed the interior of the lodge. Loretta wasn't certain if Hunter was asleep. She had been lying beside him for an eternity — waiting. Amy's breathing had become shallow and even. If Loretta didn't make a move soon, it would be too late.

Turning her head, she studied Hunter's dark profile, acutely conscious of the length of his warm body next to hers. For a moment an almost paralyzing tenderness invaded her. She squelched the emotion almost as quickly as it came. Love was indeed blind, just as Aunt Rachel was fond of saying. And Loretta had been blinder than most.

In his world Hunter was a good, honest man, but he wasn't and never could be *her* man. His threat to kill anyone who helped her, including her family, was proof of that. Somehow she had fooled herself, seeing only his goodness, which was considerable, and ignoring those things that were abhorrent to her. That wasn't a small difference, something they could work around. She had known from the first that this other side of him existed, he had certainly never lied about it, yet somehow she had lost sight of it.

Loretta scooted to the end of the bed and eased to her feet. Turning, she held her breath, frozen in place, her gaze riveted on her husband. He didn't stir. She retreated a step, then hesitated, half expecting him to leap up and grab her. If he hadn't been serious when he threatened to beat her, he wouldn't have made a promise of it. Among his people, desertion was a cardinal sin, right up there with adultery. A Comanche adulteress got her nose hacked off. Not a pleasant thought. Kinder than stoning her to death, but horrible all the same.

When Hunter didn't move, Loretta inched back, trembling. Amy slept only a few feet away, but it seemed like a mile — a very long, treacherous mile. When at last she closed the distance, she clamped a hand over Amy's mouth. Amy jerked. Above Loretta's tense fingers, her eyes flew open, large as flapjacks and shimmering like sapphires in the moonlight. Pressing a finger to her lips to stress the need for silence, Loretta gestured to Amy that she wanted her to get up and leave the lodge. Amy sat up, shooting a frightened glance over her shoulder at the low bed where Hunter slept.

Loretta crept to Hunter's parfleches, groping in the dark for his gourd canteen and preserved edibles. She confiscated two bags of food, one of dried fruit and nuts, one of jerked meat. Next she grabbed her satchel.

Opening it, she withdrew her neatly folded bloomers. Creeping to the bed, she laid them on the fur beside Hunter. Tears stung her eyes as she straightened. So many memories. Sadness twisted through her. Hunter, saluting her at midnight, her bloomers trailing behind him. Hunter, lifting them to his nose and sniffing the flower scent, his eyes alight with laughter. One day, when the bitterness left him, perhaps he would look at those drawers and smile at his memories of her. She prayed he would. Surely he would eventually forgive her for leaving him.

She and Amy sneaked outside. Darting between the lodges, Loretta took to the trees, afraid someone might spy them and raise an alarm. Now that she had taken this first step, there was no turning back. Taking a beating wasn't high on her list of favorite things to do, especially not from a man with Hunter's strength. When she felt they had gone far enough to be out of earshot, she slowed her pace.

"We're runnin' off, ain't we?" Amy cried. "All because of that nasty Red Buffalo. Swift

Antelope told me what happened. You can't go blamin' Hunter for what his no-account cousin did!"

Loretta, her nerves strung as taut as a fiddle string, whirled and cried, "Not *just* because of Red Buffalo. My God, Amy, don't you realize what all this means? Men from *this* village killed my ma and pa! There must have been thirty warriors there that day! And we're living amongst them, making friends with them. Merciful heaven, I can't stand to stay here another minute."

Amy clamped her arms around her waist and jutted her chin. "I ain't leavin' without I talk to Swift Antelope first."

"You'll do no such thing."

"I got no choice. Me and him made promises. I can't leave without I tell him why and where I'm goin'. When he finds me gone, he'll be mad as hops."

"You'll do what I say, when I say, young lady. What kind of promises?"

"Marryin' promises, and I ain't budgin' 'til I talk to him."

Loretta's stomach flipped and felt as if it dropped to her knees. "Amy, have you lost your mind? You're only twelve!"

"Old enough!" The moonlight shone on Amy's face, revealing her anguish. "What's waiting for me at home, Loretta? Shame, that's what, for somethin' that ain't even my fault. I'm ruint! Here with Swift Antelope's people, things like that don't matter. Hunter reclaimed my honor, and it's over. Swift Antelope loves me, and I love him. He's the best friend I ever had!"

"He's a Comanche, that's what he is. And you'll marry him over my dead body!" Fear clutched Loretta. Amy had already suffered so much. Loving Swift Antelope would just bring her more heartache. She was too young to realize that now, but one day she'd thank her lucky stars Loretta had taken her away from here. "One disastrous marriage in this family is aplenty. As for you being ruined, that's plumb silly. Do you feel ruined?"

"No! But only because the people here don't make me feel ruint! It's different at home. Ladies'll whisper behind my back. They won't wanna sit by me at prayer meetin'! I'll be shunned, and you know it."

"Then we'll move, just you and me, to Galveston, maybe, where no one knows us. Nothing's to say we have to stay here."

With that, Loretta shoved the satchel at Amy and grabbed her arm, jerking her along behind her as she made a beeline for the horse meadow.

"You're plumb addled, stealin' off like this from a Comanche husband. Don't you got an inklin' of what he'll do when he catches you?"

"Beat me senseless, I reckon, which is why I'm not planning to get caught."

"He'll beat you all right, in front of the whole village. Your leavin' is a dishonor to him. Why, he's liable to be so mad he'll hack your nose off! It ain't like he's white folk, Loretta Jane. You don't go leavin' a Comanche! Hunter'll be so mad, he'll chew rawhide clean in two."

"Shut up, Amelia Rose, before I paddle your hiney good."

"You ain't big enough by half!"

"Wanna bet?" Loretta challenged in a shaky voice.

Amy gasped. "You're scared, ain't you?"

"Spitless."

"Then why leave him?"

"Because I have to. I *have* to. Now get walkin'. I'm the oldest. I know better than you what's best."

Amy did as she was told, albeit reluctantly, describing with every step the dire fate that was in store for Loretta when Hunter caught her.

"He won't cut off my nose!"

"Will so!"

"Will not!" Loretta leaped across the wash and turned to help her cousin. "Now stop with trying to scare me."

"You'd best be scared. He's a Comanche, Loretta! When a Comanche woman shames her man, there's certain things he's expected to do. He has to, to save face."

"Praise the Lord I'm not a Comanche

woman, then, hm?" Loretta nudged Amy into a walk, falling in behind her.

"Loretta Jane, we ain't fixin' to steal their horses, are we?"

"You wanna walk?"

"Hunter's gonna flay us alive." When Loretta merely trudged along in grim silence, Amy stepped closer. "Ah, Loretta . . . it wasn't Hunter who did it. Surely you can't believe he was there."

Loretta pressed the back of her wrist to her clammy forehead. "I don't know for sure that he wasn't. Never will. I'm not sure even Hunter knows." She met her younger cousin's gaze. "Can you say for sure, Amy? Can you?"

Amy turned slightly, gazing at the river. Loretta felt certain the girl was thinking of Swift Antelope and all the hours she had spent with him down there. A breeze picked up, whispering in the cottonwoods. "No, I can't say for sure. He might've been. Red Buffalo *is* his cousin. Like you to me. They were bound to do stuff together. I reckon Hunter might've been there."

"If it had been your ma and pa, and you found out Swift Antelope might've taken part in their murders, would you stay here? Answer me true."

Amy squeezed her eyes closed, trembling. "No, I couldn't stay. I'm sorry, Loretta. I shouldn't have been goin' on at you like I was."

Loretta cast an uneasy glance over her shoulder. Hunter could wake up at any time, and when he did he'd head directly for the horses. "Let's just get. There'll be time for talking later."

Amy struck off, setting a faster pace now that she was convinced they were doing the right thing. When they reached the pasture, Loretta's heart sank. The shadowy outlines of the horses were impossible to identify. Where was Friend?

She called his name. An answering whinny led her off to the left.

"There's a black one!" Amy cried.

Loretta stood on tiptoe to see. By the way the horse watched her, she knew it was Friend. She eased her way through the milling animals to seize his line. After taking a moment to greet him the way Hunter had taught her, she pulled his stake and led him to the outer edge of the herd. Turning back, she picked a sleek gray for Amy. His left ear was notched, which meant he was gentled.

After tying the food pouches to the drawstring at her waist, Loretta mounted up, instructing Amy to do the same. Then she sat back on Friend and contemplated the herd of horses.

"We've got to scatter them," Loretta said.

"We gotta what? There's hundreds of 'em!"

"If Hunter can just run out here and mount up, he'll be on us like flies on honey before we've gone a mile." An image of Hunter's muscular body moving in harmony with his horse assailed her. "You know how he can ride!"

"But we could end up trampled!"

Or caught red-handed. There was no telling how far their voices might travel if they started hollering. There was no help for it, though. Mustering her courage, Loretta shrieked and rode Friend into the herd, waving her arms and slapping horses on their rumps. It took a while, but the animals finally spooked, ripping up their stakes to charge in all directions into the darkness. Loretta and Amy chased after the braver ones who dared to linger. At last, nary a horse remained in sight. Loretta hoped they ran a goodly distance. It wasn't much, but at least it might slow Hunter down.

Amy rode abreast of Loretta, looking back toward the village. "I sure hope they couldn't hear us hollerin'. Every Injun in that village is gonna be hoppin' mad when they find those horses scattered."

The words conjured a picture of Hunter in a rage. Loretta seized Friend's mane. "Come on. Let's ride. We have to get a head start."

The journey home proved a lot easier than Loretta's first trip had been. This time she had a better idea of how to find water, so she wasn't slowed down by scouting expeditions for water holes. The first day out, she and Amy kept one eye on the horizon behind them, terrified that Comanches would appear. The second day, both of them relaxed a little. By the third, Amy was convinced Hunter wasn't going to follow them.

"He must figger it's good riddance," Amy mused. "They can cover twice the distance we can in a day. What else could've took him so long?"

Loretta had no illusions. Hunter would follow her — to the ends of the earth if he had to. "Maybe it's Providence. Just thank God he hasn't caught up to us."

"If he said he'd kill anyone who helped you, where we gonna go?"

Amy had asked this question a dozen times. "Fort Belknap. The border patrol is headquartered there. Even Hunter can't take on a fort."

"And what if there ain't no border patrol there? What if they're off ridin' the ninety-eighth meridian?"

"Then we're in trouble. We'll have to go home, gather some supplies, and ride out."

"For where?"

"Anywhere — until we find someplace safe. Maybe Jacksboro. Maybe another fort. I need a map, that's what."

Amy contemplated the endless expanse of flatland ahead of them. "A map? Loretta Jane, I got me this deep-down feelin' that we've bit off a hunk too big to chew."

"We're fine. Trust me. I rode to Hunter's village, didn't I?"

"With directions from Hunter!"

"Well, from now on I have to follow my nose."

"Enjoy it while you still have one."

Loretta rolled her eyes. "Could you try being a little optimistic? We'll make it fine. I know we will."

Despite her words, a lump of dread rose in Loretta's throat. She prayed she was right.

Hunter's mother stood over him, wringing her hands, while he gathered his gear to ride out.

"My *tua,* your anger burns too hot. I fear for your woman when you find her."

His body tense, Hunter strode past his mother to his horse. "She has dishonored me."

"She does not know our ways. Is it a dishonor amongst her people to leave her husband?"

Hunter slung his bags over his stallion's back, securing them to the surcingle. "It is a dishonor here."

"Hunter, won't you stop and talk with me?"

"No. You talk woman-talk. Why is my father not here? I will tell you why. He knows she scattered the horses of every man in the village, leaving us defenseless against an attack.

He knows she left without permission. He knows she has dishonored me! He sits in his lodge and says it is sure enough a good thing if I find her and beat her."

"He sits in his lodge because he has old knees that ache. Go and talk with him."

"I have no time. I must ride hard to catch my woman." Hunter tried to walk inside his lodge, but his mother barred the way. He sighed and planted his hands on his hips. "*Pia,* you test my patience. I am weary, eh? And very angry."

"The horses have all been found. No harm was done."

"It took us two days to gather them! On foot! I will never hear the last of it! You call that no harm? Whatever punishment I choose, my woman deserves it, and more. Name me one woman you know who has run away from her husband. Just one, *pia,* and I will cool my anger."

Woman with Many Robes shook her head. "Comanche women are different. Your Loh-rhett-ah has cause to be upset. And cause to run. You understand that. While you're riding to catch up with her, you think long on my words. If you learned that the man at her wooden walls had raped your pregnant wife, could you live with him?"

Hunter shouldered his way into the lodge, making no reply.

"Look into me, Hunter. I demand an

answer! For love of Loh-rhett-ah, could you live with your dead wife's killers?"

"Enough!" Hunter swept his mother out of his way, too confused by his own emotions to notice that she stumbled. "Go to your husband, old woman. Nettle him with your tongue!"

Three days later Amy's worst fears were realized: there were no troops at Fort Belknap. Loretta knew that the families there would be put in jeopardy if she and Amy sought shelter with them. Her conscience wouldn't let her stay. She and Amy had no choice but to go home.

The Steinbachs, a couple who lived within the stockade, invited the two girls to share in a big Sunday lunch before they left. Despite ravenous hunger, Loretta declined. "We'd best move on. Just in case they're coming up behind us. Please don't worry. We'll be all right," she assured them as she and Amy mounted up. She hoped she sounded more confident than she felt. Mr. Steinbach struck her as the heroic type. There were a good six hours of hard riding ahead of them, and Loretta was anxious to get started. She sensed Hunter was drawing closer, and the feeling panicked her. "Good-bye, Mr. Steinbach."

Loretta glanced toward the dusty yard, where the little Steinbach boys played kerchief tag. She couldn't put their lives at risk.

■ ■ ■ ■

The farm looked strangely deserted when Loretta and Amy crested the rise. The girls reined in their horses and stared at the house. Despite the dry spell, the corn field thrived. Loretta could see one of the pigs rutting in the pen. Things appeared normal, except that it was nigh onto dusk and cooking smoke should have been trailing from the catted chimney.

"That's right, it's Sunday. Mrs. Steinbach said," Amy cried. "Maybe Ma and Pa went over to the Bartletts' for prayer service. I don't see the buckboard."

Loretta nodded. *Sunday.* The word hung in the air, foreign after so long a stay in Comancheria. Saturday night baths. Wearing her Sunday best. Spending the afternoon reading from the Bible. All that seemed like a century ago. She straightened her shoulders, so weary she wanted to drop. She knew Amy was every bit as tired. "Maybe it's just as well they're gone." She cast a derisive glance at Amy's Indian garb. "If Aunt Rachel sees you dressed like that, she's going to have fits."

Amy looked down at her moccasins, still wet from fording the river. "I *like* dressin' like this. It's a sight better than bein' trussed up and stiflin' in the heat."

Loretta kicked Friend forward, leaning back

568

to equalize her weight as he went down the slight slope. It felt odd riding through the gate dressed like a Comanche. After reintying Friend to the porch post, Loretta climbed the sagging steps and crossed the porch to the door. Lifting the outer latch, she pushed inside. The smell of freshly baked cornbread wafted to her, further proof that today had been prayer meeting. Aunt Rachel didn't bake on the Sabbath otherwise. Amy shouldered her way past Loretta and made a beeline for the pan on the hearth.

Scooping out a chunk of bread with her fingers, she took an unladylike bite and turned, grinning around the bulge in her cheek. "Lands, this tastes good! I'm so tired of jerked meat and nuts, I could urp. Want some?"

"Later. We can't tarry. Let's gather food and light out."

"Without seein' Ma?"

"There isn't time."

"I'm not leavin' until I see my ma. It's not me Hunter's after!"

"He'll snatch you back all the same! He has crazy ideas about family when he marries up with a body. The way he figures, you belong to him now. He doesn't think Uncle Henry watches after you proper."

"He reckons right. Pa don't watch after nobody but Pa."

Loretta took a rifle down from the rack and

fished in the nearby cupboard for cartridges. "Pack that bread to take along, Amy. Then go out to the cool-room and grab anything you see — jerked meat, corn meal, dried fruit. Hurry now! If we drag our heels, Hunter could show up."

Less than an hour later the girls were nearly ready to leave. Amy had just gone out to saddle her horse, and Loretta was about to join her, when Amy burst back inside the house, slamming the door behind her.

"Jumpin' Jehoshaphat, Hunter's here!"

Loretta's heart leaped. "Oh, God, drop the bar, Amy!"

Loretta grabbed the bed and slid it away from the trap. Amy came running to help, her small face pinched with terror.

"Did they see you?" Loretta cried.

"I don't think so. But our horses are out front! They'll know, Loretta Jane! What in blazes are we gonna do?"

"Hide!" Loretta threw the trap wide and shoved Amy down the steps. Grabbing the rifle, she cast a worried glance at the bed to be sure it was sitting straight and the covers weren't mussed. If the least little thing looked odd, Hunter would notice and know the bed had been moved. Once he made that deduction, it wouldn't take him long to think of a floor trap. She no longer believed Comanches were stupid, Hunter least of all.

Hurrying after Amy, Loretta reached back to draw the door closed behind her. A damp, musty darkness enveloped her. She groped her way down the remaining steps. Anemic stripes of light coming through the floor cracks fell across Amy's pale face. The hiding space was tiny, a dugout four feet square, just deep enough for them to stand up. Loretta shoved Amy into one corner and stood in front of her, rifle ready.

The thundering approach of horses filled Loretta's mind. She felt Amy trembling behind her. Hunter's voice rang out, barking something in Comanche. The next instant he yelled, "White Eyes, send me my woman!"

Loretta jumped. The fury in his voice strung her nerves taut. Silence fell — a long, deafening silence. She imagined Hunter staring at the doeskin coverings on the front windows, the expression on his face as he began to realize no one was there.

Wood creaked. Loretta snapped her head around. Someone had stepped onto the porch. Another board moaned, then another. Her eyeballs burned. Stiff with dread, she waited. A heartbeat later the door crashed open and moccasined feet touched softly on the cabin floor. She could feel Hunter's nearness in every pore of her skin. Pressing against Amy, she stared at the trap. *Please, God, don't let him see the irregular planks.*

An airless silence buzzed in Loretta's ears.

She held her breath and knew Amy did as well. Then Amy sobbed. She made only a whisper of sound, but it seemed as loud as a cannon boom. Electrical awareness crackled. A board creaked. A shadow fell across the stripes of light coming down through the floor cracks. Loretta snugged her finger on the trigger, shaking, her skin clammy with sweat. The trap lifted an inch. . . .

Amy jerked and gasped. Not certain from which side Hunter would open the door, Loretta waited until she saw the toe of his moccasin, then swung the barrel of the gun toward him. The door whined, yawning wider. The light blinded her for an instant. Hunter loomed in the opening, his features taut with rage.

"Out!" He snapped his fingers and jabbed a thumb over his muscular shoulder, stepping back so they could come up the steps. "*Namiso,* now!"

Amy leaped to obey. Loretta threw her weight back to hold her in the corner. "Get out of here, Hunter. I'm not going with you."

He placed a foot on the top step. Wondering if it was really her doing this, she waved the barrel of the gun at him. "Don't try it! Just leave. Please? I don't want to hurt you!"

He took another step, his expression thunderous, his eyes sparking anger.

"This is loaded! Don't test me, Hunter! I'm not going back!"

To Loretta's horror, he dared to take another step. She braced herself and tried to tighten her quivering finger on the trigger. The imagined blast of the gun filled her ears. She pictured him crumpling and falling down the steps, his broad chest torn open and bleeding. Blazing indigo eyes locked on hers, held her pinioned. Memories of her parents slid through her mind, but other memories did as well — memories of Hunter, in a hundred different scenes, as her friend, her lover, her protector. She hated what he was, the things he was capable of doing. But she loved him, too. And God help her, she couldn't kill him. He knew that. She read it in his eyes. He came down the remaining steps and hauled Amy out from behind her.

"Go to Swift Antelope," he ordered.

"Hunter . . ." Amy clutched his arm. "You gotta understand. It was her ma! Her ma and pa! How would you feel?"

"Go to Swift Antelope!" he snarled.

With a sob, Amy ran up the steps and out of the house, calling Swift Antelope's name. With slow, deliberate anger, Hunter wrested the weapon from Loretta's hands and tossed it onto the dirt. Then, without a word, he slung her over his shoulder and headed up the steps.

"Hunter, for the love of God, don't do this!" She grabbed hold of his belt, remembering the other times he had carried her this way. "Damn you! I won't go back there. I *won't!*"

He strode across the room to the door, acting for all the world as if he didn't hear her. Furious, Loretta pummeled the backs of his thighs. He kept going. The ground swept under her in a dizzying blur. The next thing she knew, he was tossing her on his horse and mounting behind her. Two other Indians collected the stallions on which Loretta and Amy had made their escape. Friend reared at having his line touched by a stranger, but a softly spoken word from Hunter calmed him.

As Hunter wheeled his horse, Loretta realized he truly meant to drag her back to his village. Her wishes counted for nothing. He would force her to live among her parents' murderers, to look into their faces every day for the remainder of her life, to break bread with them, be polite to them, accept them. The thought spurred her into action.

"No!" she cried, turning on him to press an attack. "I won't go back with you, I won't."

Grabbing a fistful of her hair, he gave her a vicious shake. Pain exploded across her scalp. The very brutality of the act made Loretta freeze and stare at him in shocked disbelief. His eyes glittered down at her.

In a voice that dripped venom, he said, "This Comanche will stop and beat you if you make trouble. You understand?"

"You wouldn't."

"I am Comanche, yes? A *mo-cho-rook,* cruel one. This is what you run from? A heathen. A man who will beat you? Or maybe throw you to his friends? That would be good, eh? *If* I could find a man so stupid he would take you!"

Releasing her hair to cinch a bruising arm around her waist, Hunter fell silent, nudging his horse forward into a jarring trot. His hand on her hip was heavy, the bite of his fingers uncomfortable but not cruel. Loretta leaned against him and closed her eyes.

"Why can't you understand that it's over between us — that I can't stay in that village with you?" she said. "Even if you had nothing to do with my parents' deaths, people in your village did! I can't forget that! And I can't forgive it!"

"This Comanche cares nothing for the song in your heart," he retorted, his voice still venomous. "You belong to me. Forever, for always! Within you is my seed. A Comanche man does not give up his woman."

Those were the last words to pass between them. The miles sped by, long into the night, until Loretta slumped with exhaustion and drifted into a fitful sleep, her head lolling against her husband's shoulder.

Hours later she awoke with a start to the biting grip of Hunter's hand on her arm, jerking her off the horse. Stunned and disoriented, she fell in an ungraceful heap at his

575

feet, then crab-walked to keep from being dragged as he pulled her along behind him, a buffalo robe and stakes tucked under his other arm.

Shoving her to the ground, he spread the robe, then picked up a rock. Loretta peered through the moonlit gloom in stunned silence as he began driving the stakes. She knew he intended to spread-eagle her, but a part of her refused to believe he would do it. He was only trying to scare her, to bully her into submission.

"Why are we camped so far from the others?" she asked, striving to keep her voice calm. A fire had leapt to life some distance away, and she could hear the faint sound of the others talking.

"Your Aye-mee must not see," he replied in a clipped monotone.

"See what?" she asked shakily.

"The games we will play," he said softly.

He glanced up from the stake he was pounding. Loretta took one look at the murderous gleam in his eye and bolted. Before she had taken more than a few steps, he was upon her. Seizing her wrist, he dragged her to the fur. Then, so quickly she wasn't sure how, he flipped her onto her back and followed her down, anchoring her flailing limbs with his weight while he secured her arms. Just as quickly, he bound her feet.

Loretta stared up at him, trying to assure

herself that he was only bluffing. She had run away; now he meant to teach her a lesson. Once he felt vindicated, he would be the same sweet, gentle Hunter he had always been.

She kept right on telling herself that until he crouched beside her and jerked up her overblouse to rudely expose her breasts. Her breath snagged as his fingers plucked the tip of one nipple into throbbing hardness. The moonlight played upon his face, revealing the taut anger in his expression.

"Ah, yes, this is the way of it, eh? A heathen and his woman?" His face twisted in a sneer as he rolled her sensitive flesh between his finger and thumb, sending shocks of sensation shooting into her belly. "Hunter, the one who rapes and tortures? That is me." Abandoning her breast, he rocked back on his heels and jerked up her skirt. "This is very good, Blue Eyes. The animal in me likes having you tied."

With that, he stretched out beside her. Even in her turmoil, Loretta heard an echo in every word he spoke. Looking into his eyes, she knew how deeply her leaving had hurt him.

Propping himself up on an elbow, he planted a hand on her abdomen and lowered his head to brush his lips across her temple. Her belly convulsed as his fingers began a subtle manipulation, charging her senses, making her skin tingle, in a relentless path toward her breasts.

"I will be cruel, yes? And make you weep rivers of tears while I play my games. It will be good, very good."

His mouth touched hers, teasingly light. His hand cupped her breast. Silhouetted against the moon-silvered sky, he was a black outline, his broad shoulders a threatening wall, his long hair drifting in a silken curtain around her.

Nightmare or dream?

He continued to whisper — saying terrible things, cruel things, taunting her with what was yet to come, living up to all her worst expectations. But his touch was that of a lover, as sweet and magical, as patient and gentle, as the last time they had been together. She knew he had tied her only to prove a point, that no matter what the circumstances, no matter how angry he might become, he would never harm her.

"Oh, Hunter, I'm sorry," she said on the crest of a sob. "I didn't mean to hurt you like this. I didn't mean to hurt you."

"You rip my heart out and it should not hurt?" His teeth closed on her earlobe, nipping lightly, sending shivers over her skin. "You spit upon all that I am, and it should not hurt? You abandon me, you dishonor me, and it should not hurt?"

The raw emotion in his voice brought tears to her eyes. "I never intended to dishonor you. . . ."

Loretta longed to put her arms around him but was quickly reminded of her bonds when she tried. His mouth claimed hers, hot and demanding, yet strangely gentle.

What followed was beautiful. Unable to remain passive, Loretta responded to him with a spiraling passion that both shocked and disoriented her. At some point Hunter cut the leather on her wrists and ankles, but she was too mindless to realize. He was like a fire inside her, embers licked to low flames, building quickly to an inferno. There was no fear. And no pain. Just a bittersweet joining, becoming one in a way she had never dreamed possible.

Afterward Hunter drew her gently into his arms and reminded her of the promises he had made her, that she would never experience brutality or shame in his arms, only love. "How can you not hear the song my heart sings, Blue Eyes?"

Loretta knew he was referring to far more than his lovemaking. Sobs built pressure in her chest, then crawled up her throat, gaining force until they tore from her, dry and ragged. "Oh, Hunter, you have to understand. You think only of yourself and your rights. What of mine?"

Hunter drew her head back down to his shoulder and wrapped his arms around her. Her warm tears fell on his skin and trickled, cold and wet, under his arm. He closed his eyes, his mind replaying her words, the whispers a torment, the questions unanswerable. Did he think only of himself? *Yes.* To do otherwise meant losing her. Long after his wife fell into an exhausted sleep, he lay awake, staring into the darkness, searching within himself for a solution.

There was none. . . .

CHAPTER 24

The following day's ride passed in uneasy silence. Only Amy and Swift Antelope seemed comfortable with the situation. That night Hunter once again camped some distance from the others. This time, when he began driving stakes, Loretta felt no fear, only an eager anticipation of his lovemaking. She hated herself for that — until Hunter began his assault on her senses. Then she forgot everything except being in his arms.

When their passions had cooled, Loretta felt nothing but hollow resignation. It was inconceivable that she could respond so mindlessly to Hunter's touch. He loved her, but she saw it as a shallow, self-centered love. He tried to make her happy, but only when her wishes didn't conflict with his. If she ran from him again, he would come after her.

Turning her head, she studied his profile, remembering the night he had given her the comb, how pleased he had been to present her with something so beautiful. A gift of love? Every time she thought of it, she became nauseated. There was no future for them together. Not in his village, and he would never leave the People, never.

Hunter turned toward her and looped an arm around her waist. His eyes were dark splashes in the moonlight. "Blue Eyes, it will be good. Trust this Comanche."

"How can it be, Hunter?"

"I will make it so." He feathered a finger across her bottom lip.

Trust. His voice, his gentle touch, delved deep, turning her warm and liquid, melting her resistance. She closed her eyes. In four more days, maybe less, she would be back in Hunter's village.

"Hunter, why did you tie me to stakes again tonight? How long do you plan to do that?"

"Until my touch is carved in your heart."

"Oh, Hunter, it's already carved in my heart. When I ran from you, it wasn't out of fear."

"You said *hi, hites* with a rifle. You will have no fear again. Anger, maybe much hatred, but no fear." He trailed a knuckle along her cheek. "You made pictures of your remembering. Now I make new rememberings, so they are very much good."

Puzzled, Loretta studied his dark face. Then she realized he was referring to her memories of her mother's death — the Comanches, the stakes, her torturous last minutes. He was deliberately evoking those memories, only to expunge them by gently loving her. When she thought of his stakes now, she thought of shivers running down her spine, of sweet kisses in moonlight, of wonderfully strong arms enfolding her with warmth.

Tears sprang to her eyes. "Thank you for the new memories, Hunter. They *are* very much good."

His face drew close. "This Comanche wants to make more new remembering."

She took a ragged breath. "I can't. Don't you see? To say yes is surrendering all that I am."

He manacled her wrists with his iron grip. "That too is why I tie you." His lips brushed hers, setting her senses afire. "You will make war tomorrow?"

He whispered the question into her mouth, his breath warm and sweet. His tongue touched hers. Loretta's heart caught at the careful way he drew her against him. *Tomorrow.* It seemed soon enough for fighting him. For tonight, she couldn't stop herself from loving him — one last time.

New rememberings that were very much good. Hunter brought dozens of new memories to Loretta over the next few days. By the time they reached his village, she had accepted a great deal. She couldn't be happy about the prospect of living there, and she refused to pretend she was, but she knew she couldn't change Hunter's mind. He would keep her with him, waging war on her senses and her memories, until her past became a blur with sharp edges that pricked her only on occasion.

One such occasion occurred a few days after they returned. That evening Red Buffalo and his friends came back to the camp with a group of warriors from another band. Hunter, sensing trouble, strode to the central fire.

Red Buffalo's disfigured face tightened when he spied Hunter. In a clipped tone he said, "We come to warn of trouble. A group of *tosi tivo* have gathered forces and demand the return of some captives taken in recent raids."

The ground under Hunter's feet seemed to disappear. "Then return the captives."

Red Buffalo dropped his gaze. "We cannot."

"They're dead?" Hunter took a step closer. "Red Buffalo, tell me you had nothing to do with this."

Red Buffalo grasped Hunter's arm. When Hunter stared at him, the guilt etched on his cousin's face condemned him. Red Buffalo tried to speak, failed, and dropped his hand. Hunter knew then that he had finally begun to realize how dire the consequences of his actions might prove to be.

Although Red Buffalo said nothing more to him, Hunter stayed by the fire, hoping to glean information. All he heard was fear talking. If matters were as bad as the newly arrived men seemed to believe, the People were in serious trouble. The *tosi tivo* farmers had hired marauders from the east, from a place called Arkansas, to make war until the white captives were returned to their families.

When the visiting warriors left, Red Buffalo and his friends stayed behind in the village.

"Hunter?" Red Buffalo called.

Hunter turned and waited for his cousin to reach him. "What is it this time? Do you have her mother's scalp? That would be a fine gift."

Red Buffalo blanched and studied the trees. "I have done a great wrong. Spill my blood if you must, but don't cut me out of your heart, cousin."

A lump rose in Hunter's throat. When he looked at Red Buffalo he saw not a killer, but a man who had risked his life for him so many times that both of them had lost count. "I cut you from my heart the night my woman wept over the marriage gift I gave her."

Tears glistened in Red Buffalo's eyes. "I will make peace with her, if only you will tell me how."

Though Hunter dreaded the answer, he had to ask. "You killed her mother and father, yes? No more lies, Red Buffalo, only truth."

The scarred flesh drew taut over Red Buffalo's high cheekbones. "Yes. They were as nothing, Hunter! A *tosi tivo* and his yellowhair. I could not see into tomorrow! How was I to know!"

Hunter clenched his hands into fists, remembering Rebecca Simpson's portrait, her face so like Loretta's. "You did those things to her mother? You? It is not the way our fathers walked."

"It is the way many of the men walk. You've never turned your face from them, Hunter. Why must you turn from me?"

"You tortured my woman's mother. They didn't."

"You think I rode alone?"

Hunter braced himself. "Who else was there?"

"That is my secret. I have wronged you enough. I won't steal your friends from you as well. Does it matter? If we could walk backward in our footsteps, do you think we would make that raid again? You know we wouldn't."

"That may be so, but it changes nothing. You killed my wife's mother."

"I killed a honey-haired white woman! She was as nothing to me. Have I touched the one called Ayemee? I could have. There have been many times when I could have."

"You poisoned my woman's heart against me! Even now she yearns to leave. Why did you give me that comb?"

Red Buffalo began to shake. "I meant to accept her. It was clear you had great love for her. I knew you would turn from me if I kept making trouble. When you left to find the child for her, I meant to treat her with only kindness, to become her friend and hope she never recognized me."

"And then you walked backward in your footsteps? Why?"

"The comb!" Red Buffalo lifted his hands in supplication. "I was at Warrior's fire, playing a game. I looked over and smiled my kindest smile. And then I saw it! Lying there in her black bag, moonlight on water, just like the comb I had taken. I knew that one day she would wear hers or show it to someone. And when she did, someone would remember the comb I had taken on that raid. You would have learned the truth."

"That you had killed her mother?"

"Yes! I knew if that happened, she would turn your face from me. That I would lose you. It was wrong, making lies to you, but I knew she would leave if she found out it was men from this village who killed her parents." Red Buffalo grasped Hunter's arm again. "I gave you the comb so she would go before it was too late, before you got her with child. You would have forgotten her in time and forgiven me. Hunter, I have no brothers. *You* are my brother. My wife is dead. My child is dead. My parents are dead. Must I lose another to the *tosi tivo?*"

Hunter took a deep, jagged breath and slowly exhaled. "Red Buffalo, when my woman takes your hand in friendship, you are welcome in my lodge. Until then, walk a road of sorrow. It is the path you chose."

"I never chose to walk apart from you, never."

Though it took all his strength of will to do it, Hunter brushed Red Buffalo's hand from his arm. "Walk a new way. Take a wife. You don't have to be alone unless you wish to be." With a slight motion of his head, Hunter directed Red Buffalo's gaze toward the maiden who lingered on the far side of the fire, adding wood to the flames. When she glanced up and saw Red Buffalo staring at her, she blushed and grew so flustered that she dropped the logs she held in her arms.

"Bright Star?" Red Buffalo whispered.

Hunter walked away, leaving Red Buffalo to take it from there.

When Hunter returned to his lodge, he sent Amy to find Swift Antelope and set Loretta down by the fire to talk with her. First he told her the grim news Red Buffalo and the other warriors had brought. Then, very cautiously, he broached the subject of Red Buffalo's request for peace. Loretta turned her face from him.

"How dare you even ask? How dare you?"

Hunter grasped her chin and made her look at him. "Red Buffalo has had much grief, little one. He is twisted, like a tree in the wind. His woman, his son, his parents, all killed by the *tosi tivo.* You have wept, he has wept. The tears must stop. Is there no forgiveness in your heart?"

"You ask the impossible." She shoved his hand away. "I am here because you force me to be. I am civil to your people because you force me to be. Red Buffalo is another matter. If he comes near this lodge, I will kill him."

Hunter met her gaze, saying nothing.

The ache in his eyes told Loretta how deeply she was hurting him, that he loved Red Buffalo and would always love him, no matter what he had done. But forgiveness? The thought was incomprehensible to her.

Clasping her trembling hands, Loretta pressed them to her waist. "Do you love me, Hunter? Truly love me?"

"I have great love for you."

"Then take me away from here," she whispered raggedly. "It's the only way for us to have a future together. The only way. Please think about it? If you love me, *truly* love me, you won't torture me like this."

The words of the prophecy returned to haunt Hunter. Lifting his hand, he touched Loretta's braid and lost himself in the fascinating azure depths of her gaze. As the song predicted, she had divided his Comanche heart. Only moments ago he had turned his back on a lifelong friend. Now she asked him to turn his back on his people. "Blue Eyes, I cannot leave."

Tears welled in her eyes. "I love you, Hunter, but my mother's screams call out to me. I'll never be free of that, not as long as I stay here. One morning you will awaken and I won't be here. And I'll make sure this time that you never find me." He started to speak, but she silenced him, touching her fingertips to his lips. "Don't. Empty threats won't keep me here. You won't beat me." She moved her palm to his cheek. "Do you think I don't know that by now?"

He clamped a hand behind her head and drew her against his chest, burying his face in the hollow of her shoulder. "It is not the way of a Comanche to beat his woman," he rasped. "Just as it is not his way to let her go away from him."

She turned her face to touch her lips to his neck. "Make a memory with me, Hunter," she whispered huskily. "One more beautiful memory."

Cinching an arm around her waist, Hunter stretched out with her on the fur. Never before had she initiated lovemaking. His hand trembled as he skimmed his palm down her spine. *Make a memory with me, Hunter.* As he dipped his head to kiss her, he wondered why it was that those words had a ring of farewell. *One more beautiful memory.*

Loretta awoke shortly after dawn, alone in a cocoon of fur. She had only the haziest memory of Hunter carrying her to bed after making love to her last night. She sat up, clutching the buffalo robe to her naked breasts. Her clothing lay neatly folded on the foot of the bed, the rawhide wrappings for her braids resting on top. Her blond hair fascinated Hunter, and he had never yet made love to her without first unfastening her braids. A sad smile touched her mouth. Hunter, the typical slovenly Indian, picking up after his *tosi* wife. She had been so wrong about so many things.

She hugged her knees and rested her chin on them, gazing sightlessly into the shadows, listening to the village sounds. A woman was calling her dog. Somewhere a child was crying. The smell of roasting meat drifted on the breeze. *Familiar sounds, familiar smells, the voices of friends.* When had the village begun to seem like home?

Loretta closed her eyes, searching desperately within herself for her own identity and memories, but white society was no longer a reality to her. Hunter had become the axis of her world, Hunter and his people. Amy lay sleeping on her pallet a short distance away.

Loretta listened to her even breathing. *Amy, Aunt Rachel, home.* Could she return there now and pick up the threads of her old life?

The answer wasn't long in coming. Life without Hunter would be no life at all. Yet to see Red Buffalo, day in and day out, was inconceivable.

Throwing back the buffalo robes, Loretta slipped from bed and quickly drew on her clothes. The only way she could get through the day was to ignore Red Buffalo's existence and concentrate on Hunter. There was a fire to build and breakfast to prepare.

After sloshing a measure of water from the pouch into the washbasin, Loretta scrubbed her face, then brushed her hair and plaited it in a single thick braid down her back.

Outside, the morning air was cool and damp with humidity. Birds trilled in the nearby cottonwood trees, creating a cacophony of sound. Loretta paused just outside the lodge, keeping her face downcast. Only two pieces of firewood lay near the firepit. She would have to gather more as soon as she got a fire started.

Kneeling by the firepit, she unearthed last night's coals and arranged bits of kindling over them, adding dry grass as tinder. Bending low, she blew until the coals flared and caught the grass. Then, straightening, she placed the logs over the licking flames.

A loud clunk resounded behind her. She

glanced over her shoulder, expecting to see her husband. Instead she looked straight into Red Buffalo's black eyes. For an instant her heart stopped beating. She stared at him. He stared back. His arms were laden with firewood. One piece lay at his feet. Very slowly he hunkered down and began unloading the rest.

At last Loretta found her voice. "Get out of here!"

"I bring you wood," he replied softly in English.

Even Loretta knew warriors didn't demean themselves by gathering firewood; it was woman's work. Red Buffalo was humbling himself, making her a peace offering. She didn't care. "I don't want your filthy wood. Take it and leave."

He continued his task as if she hadn't spoken. Rage bubbled up Loretta's throat. She leaped to her feet and strode toward him. "I said get out of here! Take your damned wood with you!"

Just as she reached him, Red Buffalo finished emptying his arms and rose. He was a good head shorter than Hunter, but he dwarfed Loretta. She fell back, startled, wondering if he could smell her fear. Lifting her chin, she cut him dead with her eyes. He inclined his head in a polite nod and turned to walk away.

"I said take your wood with you!" she called

after him. "I don't want it!" Picking up a log, she chucked it at him. It landed on end and bounced, hitting Red Buffalo's calf. He stopped and turned, his face expressionless as he watched her throw the remainder of the firewood in his direction.

Saying nothing, he began to pick up the firewood. To Loretta's dismay, he returned to her firepit and began unloading the logs there in a neat pile. From the corner of her eye, she could see neighbors gathering to find out what all the commotion was about. Heat scalded her cheeks. She couldn't believe Red Buffalo was humiliating himself like this.

"Don't," she said raggedly. "Go away, Red Buffalo! Go away!"

He tipped his head back. Tears glistened on his scarred cheeks. "Hunter has cut me from his heart."

"Good! You're an animal!"

Red Buffalo winced as if she had struck him. "He has forbidden me to enter his lodge until you take my hand in friendship."

"Never!" Appalled, Loretta retreated a step. "Never, do you hear me?"

Red Buffalo slowly rose, brushing his palms clean on his breeches. "He is my brother — my only brother."

"You expect me to feel sorry for you? How dare you come near me? How dare —"

Her voice broke, and she spun away, running inside the lodge. Heedless of Amy, who was sitting up on her pallet, Loretta threw herself onto the bed. Knotting her fists, she stifled her sobs against the fur. Hatred coursed through her, hot, ugly, and venomous, making her shake. *Take his hand in friendship?* Never, not as long as she lived.

Hunter was returning from a bath at the river and witnessed part of the confrontation between Loretta and Red Buffalo. Remembering the ultimatum Loretta had given him last night, he did an about-face and returned to the river, in too much turmoil to face his wife until he had time to think.

Lengthening his stride, he set a swift pace, following the stream until the village was far behind him and he had expelled some of his tension. He sprawled under a cottonwood and braced his shoulder against its silvered trunk, his gaze riveted to the flowing water. He let his mind go with it, to a faraway place. The breeze was brisk, the rose-streaked sky gunmetal gray directly overhead. He inhaled the scent of grass and earth, familiar smells that soothed him. Birds twittered above him, celebrating the new day.

Hunter wished he had gone out with the other hunters this morning. The danger, the ceaseless tension of a buffalo hunt, might have cleared his mind. He had to make a decision about Loretta, and he had to do it soon. Cruel fingers squeezed his heart. His people or Loretta? His mother's and father's faces flashed in his mind. Then others crowded in, Blackbird, Pony Girl, Turtle, Warrior, Maiden of the Tall Grass, and Red Buffalo. As much as he loved them, he had come to love Loretta more. When had it happened?

He had once told Loretta that he would be as nothing without his people, and that was true. He would be giving up all that he was to be with her. Yet how could he live without her? The prophecy had come to pass. Without her, he had no tomorrows. How could a man live without them?

He sighed and closed his eyes. From the moment she had stepped out from her wooden walls, the path ahead of him had been clearly marked, but he had been too blind to see it. A *tosi* woman and a Comanche, their pasts stained with tears and bloodshed, had little hope of coexisting happily with either race. To be as one, they had to walk alone, away from both their people.

Where, that was the question. And Hunter had no answers. West, as the prophecy foretold? Into the great mountain ranges? The thought frightened him. He had been raised in open spaces, able to see into tomorrow, with the north wind whispering, the grass waving, the buffalo plentiful. What would he hunt? And how? He wouldn't know what roots and nuts to gather. He wouldn't know which plants made good medicine, which bad. Did he dare take a woman into an unknown land, uncertain if he could feed her, care for her, or protect her? What if she came with child? *Winter, the time when babies cried.* How would he stand tall like a man if his family starved?

Hunter opened his eyes and sat up, raking his fingers through his damp hair. Looking skyward, he searched for Loretta's Great One, the Almighty Father to whom she gave thanks for her food. At first he had been disgruntled by her prayers. Her God didn't bring her the food; her husband did. Loretta had explained that her God led Hunter's footsteps so his hunts were successful.

Was her God up there in the sky, as she believed? Did he truly hear a man's whispers, his thoughts? Hunter could see his own gods, Mother Earth, Mother Moon, Father Sun, the wind coming from the four directions. It was easy to believe in what he could see. Why did Loretta's God hide himself? Was he terrible ugly? Did he hide only from Comanches? Loretta said he was father to all, even Indians.

Peace filled Hunter. With so many Great Ones, both his and hers, surely they would be blessed. Relaxing his body, he surrendered himself to fate. The Great Ones would guide them. Loretta's God would lead his footsteps in the hunt when his own gods failed him. Together he and Loretta would find a new place where the Comanche and *tosi tivo* could live as one, where Hunter could sing the songs of the People and keep their ways alive.

Rising, Hunter turned back toward the village, his decision made, his heart torn, acutely aware that the prophecy had foretold this moment long ago.

The blast of a gun and a shrill scream brought Loretta up from the bed. Whirling, she fastened horrified eyes on the lodge door, her senses pelted by a barrage of noise, screams, running footsteps, more rifle shots, and the yells of white men. *An attack.* For an instant she was so frightened that she couldn't feel her legs, couldn't move. Then she saw Amy's empty pallet. *Oh, God.*

She moved toward the doorway, her mind screaming hurry, her every movement agonizingly slow. Running, running, inch by inch, toward the screams and the stench of death, to find Hunter and Amy. Ducking beneath the flap, she burst outside, her gaze darting from one lodge to the next, uncomprehending. White men, smoke, careening horses, and blood.

"Hunter! Amy!"

She staggered forward. A woman ran past, screaming her child's name, knocking Loretta off balance.

"Amy! Hunter! *Hah-ich-ka ein,* where are you?"

598

Loretta's voice was lost in the confusion of noise. She tripped over something and glanced down. A little boy lay sprawled at her feet, his chest bathed in crimson, his brown eyes staring fixedly at the sky, already glazed with death.

"Oh, my God!"

Stumbling backward, Loretta clutched her throat, unable to drag her gaze from the child. Four years old, maybe less, slain by a white man's bullet. She whirled, assailed on all sides by more death, unable to believe what she was seeing. White men didn't do things like this. They *couldn't!*

"Amy, where are you? *Hah-ich-ka ein?*"

Loretta ran along the path between the lodges. A horse charged past her, and metal flashed. She threw up an arm and shrank away, expecting the brandishing saber to cut her down. When the bite of the blade didn't come, she inched her arm down. The man, dirty rather than dark, had shoulder-length, greasy hair. He wore tall boots, coated with dust and drawn over bright purple trousers. The handle of a large bowie knife protruded from one of his boots. Attached to his belt were two large revolvers. A border ruffian? Loretta had heard stories about them, but if that was what he was, he was a mighty far piece from home. White trash, more like, which could take root anywhere. His thin, cruel features held her attention, the world around him a spinning kaleidoscope of color.

"A white woman!"

Loretta met his glittering, blue-eyed gaze, shock rendering her mindless. She spun away and ran into the melee of scrambling bodies, men, women, children, all fleeing for their lives. *Tosi tivo* everywhere, the reports of their guns deafening. Ahead of Loretta, a young squaw zigzagged in terror, trying to escape the saber-swinging horseman bearing down on her. On her back she carried an infant in a cradleboard. The ruffian's sword made a deadly sweep, and the woman sprawled facedown. The man reined in, riding the horse in a circle around her body, raising the bloodied blade for another thrust. Loretta screamed and scrambled toward him.

"No! Not the baby! Oh, my God, no!"

Startled by her voice, the man turned his head and fixed his gaze on her hair. Judging by his expression, he was stunned to see a white woman. He hesitated just long enough. She threw herself over the baby, sobbing prayers. The man drew back his saber, staring down at her as she pulled the cradleboard off the dead squaw's shoulders. The baby flailed the air with his tiny fists. Loretta clutched him to her chest and staggered away.

Hide him. The thought became a litany. She darted between the lodges, aiming for the woods. Brush slapped her face. She lunged through it, her arms crisscrossed over the child to protect him. When she came upon a fallen tree, she plunged into the undergrowth behind it. Peeking over the log, she made sure no one had followed her. Then she shoved the infant deep into the foliage, praying that his cries wouldn't lead the white men to him.

There wasn't time to think beyond that. Driven now by desperation, Loretta ran back toward the village, shock numbing her to the horror as she searched for a glimpse of Amy or Hunter. Bodies, everywhere bodies. She skirted a tepee and headed for Hunter's mother's lodge, hoping Amy might have been there when the attack began. As she raced across the central clearing, she saw Many Horses, Hunter's father, running into the fray to grab a little girl who stood in frozen terror, screaming for her parents.

Just as Many Horses reached the child, a rifle shot rang out. A blotch of crimson appeared on the old man's chest. He staggered, clamping his hand over the wound, staring stupidly at the blood pouring through his fingers. Then he crashed to the ground, one arm flung toward the child, who had begun stamping her feet, frenzied. Her would-be rescuer was dead, and his murderer was once again taking aim, this time at her.

Loretta threw herself forward into a race with death, the finish line a helpless little girl. Her mind had stopped assimilating what was happening. This couldn't be real. None of it could be real. Hunter, where was Hunter? Loretta reached the little girl and snatched her up into her arms.

Slaughter. Numb, unable to think, Loretta clutched the screaming child to her chest, turning a slow circle, her dazed eyes skimming the bodies for Hunter, for Amy, for Maiden of the Tall Grass and her children. She heard a shallow moaning sound and realized the sounds erupted from her own throat.

She Who Shakes. She lay before her lodge, a wooden spoon cradled in one limp hand, her eyes staring sightlessly. *Old Man.* Shot in the back. *Hog.* He was running toward Loretta, expression wild, long hair streaming.

"Toniets!" he snarled as he reached her, his voice barely audible above the reports of the many guns. *"Toniets! Namiso!"*

Run quickly! Now! The words entered Loretta's brain and congealed there. "Many Horses! Hog, we can't leave him!"

"Ein habbe we-ich-ket!" he roared. "You seek death! *Toniets,* run! *Nah-ich-ka,* you hear?"

She had to find Amy and Hunter. "Hog, where's Hunter? Does he have Amy with him? I can't find them! I can't find them!"

"The trees! She ran to the trees!" Hog threw an arm in the direction Amy had gone. "Go! *Namiso,* woman! Hunter isn't here!"

Still clutching the child, Loretta bolted. *Toniets,* run fast! *Namiso,* now! The two languages danced in her mind, whirring, jumbled. She didn't know who she was anymore. She only knew she must flee from the monstrous *tosi tivo* who would kill her and the child she carried in her arms.

Halfway to the trees, Loretta was intercepted by a shaky, wild-eyed Amy. "Loretta, where's Hunter? Where's Hunter?"

Breathing a prayer of thankfulness, Loretta snagged Amy's arm and pulled her toward cover. "I don't know! He isn't here, he isn't here!"

As they gained the trees, Loretta scanned the brush for the log where she had hidden the baby. Spying it, she shoved Amy along in front of her, heedless of the branches that tore at their faces and hair. Amy dove behind the log. Relieved to hear the infant still crying in the foliage, Loretta hid as well, clinging to the wailing little girl. Peering through the trees, she watched those less fortunate, running, dying. Their screams rose in the sky, eerie and shrill, to be eclipsed by silence. *Many Horses.* Loretta's heart twisted.

"Loretta! That little boy! He's running the wrong way!"

Loretta leaned forward to see. Beyond the trees, a child raced in blind panic, first one direction, then another. A horseman rode out from between some nearby lodges. At any moment he might notice the child and kill him. Loretta tensed. Shoving the little girl

603

into Amy's arms, she vaulted over the log and sprinted in a crouch through the undergrowth. When she gained the clearing, she snatched the little boy by his arm and dove with him into the brush. He flung his arms around Loretta's neck, sobbing and shaking.

"*Toquet, mah-tao-yo,*" she crooned. "It is well, little one. *Ka taikay,* don't cry. Shh-h, *toquet.*"

The words worked their magic. Loretta closed her eyes, hugging the child, memories of Hunter curling around her like warm, loving arms. Then the loud thud of a horse's hooves jerked her back to reality. She stared at the man on horseback who had ridden out moments ago from between the lodges. He reined in his horse and threw his rifle to his shoulder. Loretta craned to see through the brush. An Indian man sped toward the trees. *Red Buffalo.* For an instant Loretta was glad. He deserved to die, and who better to kill him than a murdering *tosi tivo?* Then Hunter's face flashed in her head, his eyes aching with sadness because she had refused to forgive his cousin.

Setting the child away from her, Loretta sprang to her feet. There was no time to think, only to act. She charged from the trees, running toward the mounted man, her pulse thundering. *Hunter.* He had lost his wife and child, his father, and God only knew who else. Hadn't he suffered enough? Love for him lent her speed, her legs churning, eating up the distance. She saw the white man grow still, sighting in, tensing to pull the trigger. With a screech, she covered the last few feet in a leap and threw all her weight against the horse. The animal lurched and sidestepped, making his rider lose his bead on his target. The rifle exploded harmlessly into the air.

Drawn up short by the gunshot, Red Buffalo whirled and saw the white man struggling to keep his seat on the horse, a golden-haired woman pummeling his thigh. The white man's wavering rifle told the rest of the story. For a moment Red Buffalo stood rooted, his disbelieving gaze fixed on Loretta.

When she saw him hesitate, Loretta screeched, "Run, you damned fool! Run!"

Red Buffalo dove for cover. Loretta staggered away from the horse. The white man, a giant redhead in bull denim trousers and a red flannel shirt, wheeled his mount and rode toward her. Loretta spun and tried to outrun him. He seized hold of her hair, jerking her back. Stowing his rifle, he leaned sideways and grabbed her around the waist, hauling her across his lap. The pommel of the saddle dug into her stomach. The stench of his grimy trousers made her gorge rise.

"Well, now, what have we here? A purty little golden-haired squaw?"

"Let me go!"

"That your man I almost shot? That why

you saved his hide?"

Loretta flung her arm back, hitting his thigh. "Let go of me!"

He laughed and made a fist in her blouse, pressing down on her spine with the heel of his hand. Another man rode up. "Hey, Chet, lookee here what I found!"

Loretta saw a sorrel's hooves churning up dust. In her upsidedown position, she couldn't see the other ruffian's face, only his boots and blood-splattered pants. Then she heard Amy scream her name.

"Let go of her!" Amy yelled. "Let go of her right now!"

"Amy, no! Go back! Go back!"

Loretta felt her captor spur his mount into a run. Craning her neck, she tried to spy Amy and caught only a glimpse of her, running toward the trees, a horse bearing down on her from behind. Then all Loretta saw was the body-littered ground spinning past. *Blood and leather. Ebony hair shining blue-black in the sunlight. Babies, children, women.* No one had been spared. Loretta heard someone screaming and realized the sounds came from her. She grabbed hold of her captor's pant leg and, hand over hand, pushed herself up, turning on him with the only weapons she had, her fists.

"You ungrateful bitch!"

He reared back in the saddle and in the next instant struck Loretta's jaw. Lights exploded inside her head, then everything went mercifully black.

Still preoccupied with his decision to leave his people, Hunter walked at a slow pace, his senses turned to the familiar sounds and smells of the world around him. Then, above the rush of the water, he heard a distant popping noise. He paused to listen, uncertain for a moment from what direction the noise came. *Rifle shots, coming from the village.* Panic shot through him. *An attack!*

Berating himself for having wandered so far from home, he ran through the woods, his heels slugging the ground, each impact jarring through his body, his lungs whining for air. Most of the warriors were away on a hunt. Memories sped through his mind. *Loretta.* He ran faster. *Amy.* It couldn't happen twice. It couldn't. This time, he would get there in time. He had to.

Hunter cut a sharp turn, lunging through the brush, leaping over logs, his gaze fixed on the lodge poles that crisscrossed in clusters against the sky. The gunfire had ceased. He heard horses' hooves thrumming in the distance.

As he approached the village, his footsteps slowed. *It was over.* Hunter stopped to gape, his mind refusing to register what he saw. Bodies littered the ground like scattered firewood. Lodges burned, the stench of leather and flesh searing his nostrils. Somewhere a baby wailed. A dog's frenzied barking carried on the wind. Otherwise there was only silence, a heavy, deathly quiet.

"Loh-rhett-ah!" Hunter stepped over a child's body, scarcely registering what it was, his horrified eyes scanning the stillness. "Loh-rhett-ah! *Hah-ich-ka ein?* Say words to me!"

A woman lay sprawled a few feet ahead of him, a young, slender woman, her black braids wrapped in ermine. A scream of rage welled in Hunter's chest. He ran to her and fell to his knees. As he gathered her into his arms, blood smeared across his midriff and down his arms.

"Maiden! Maiden!"

Hunter grasped her chin and turned her face toward him. Her beautiful eyes met his in a sightless stare.

CHAPTER 25

There wasn't a place on Loretta's body that didn't ache. Still slung over her captor's saddle, her belly, bruised by the pommel, felt as though a man had pummeled it with his fists. Her legs and arms were swollen from dangling. Blood had pooled in her head, making it throb. Hours had passed, Loretta hanging upside down, the stranger's hand riding on her bottom. Amy was nearby. Every once in a while Loretta heard her sobbing. She wished she could go to her, comfort her, make sure she was all right.

Hunter. If he was alive, Loretta knew he would come after her. And he had to be alive. She couldn't bear it if he wasn't. Life without him was inconceivable. She prayed as she had never prayed in her life, ceaselessly, with all her heart — for a man she had once hated.

She implored God to give her just one more chance — a chance to tell Hunter she would stay beside him and love him, forever with no horizon. If he had died in the attack without knowing that, a part of Loretta would die with him.

When at last the group of riders stopped for the night, Loretta was dumped off the horse like a piece of baggage. She hit the dirt in a lifeless heap, her arms and legs numb and useless. Sand gritted between her teeth. She blinked, gazing off into the twilight. *Hunter.* Oh, God, why didn't he come? She knew he could outride these men. He should be here by now, unless he was dead.

"Git up, sweet thing!"

Loretta snapped her head around. Darting her gaze from his tall dusty boots up his blood-smeared pant legs to his soft paunch and broad chest, she focused on the redhead's bearded face. His green eyes pierced hers through the twilight, hard and frightening. When she didn't move, he hunkered down beside her and caught her chin in his hand, the grip of his fingers biting and cruel. The weeks rolled away, and Loretta remembered Hunter holding her this way, his grip firm but painless. She had been frightened then, too, but not in the same way. This man used his strength to intimidate, and violence glittered in his eyes. She was a breath away from being raped.

"You sure are a purty thing," he murmured, his voice husky. "I bet that buck of yours'll be hot on our trail to git you back. That is if he ain't dead."

The stench of the man's body filmed the lining of Loretta's nostrils. She hated the contemplative look on his face. If she admitted she was married to a Comanche, he would consider her fair game and use her himself. His men would follow suit with Amy. The thought made Loretta's stomach roll. She was a woman grown, married to a wonderful man who had given her dozens of beautiful memories. No matter what these animals did to her, she'd survive. Amy might not.

"I don't have a buck who'll come after me, so you needn't worry," she replied evenly. "Luckily, you and your men arrived in the nick of time."

He ran his gaze over her Indian clothing. "You're lyin', sweet thing. What'sa matter? You afraid I'll get too friendly if I find out you've been pleasurin' Comanches?"

Struggling to stay calm, she said, "You're a smart man. I heard you and your men talking. You were hired to *rescue* captives, not abuse them. Touch one of us, and it'll be the mistake of your life. We haven't been pleasuring anyone. And if we end up pleasuring you, I guarantee you'll hang for it."

He didn't bluff easily. Running his fingers under the string of rawhide that encircled her neck, he lifted Hunter's medallion from under her blouse and studied the carved stone. "Appears to me like you hooked up with a chief, honey." He smiled and returned the medallion to its former resting place, trailing his fingers under her blouse, his eyes holding hers. Her skin crawled where his grimy knuckles touched. "A Comanche don't wear a wolf sign unless he's somebody important. The wolf is sacred to 'em, their brother. No woman would have a medallion like that unless her man marked her with it."

"No filthy Injun has put his hands on me," Loretta retorted. The words ached in her throat, making her feel disloyal to Hunter. What if he was out there, hiding, listening? "One of the warriors put the medallion on me before he left on a hunting trip. Since it seemed to prevent the others from touching me or my little cousin, I continued to wear it."

He grinned and rocked back on his heels. "Where you from?"

"A farm along the Brazos."

"Fort Belknap anyplace close?"

"Within a few hours' ride." Loretta sat up and glanced over her shoulder, praying Amy was all right. "Is that where you'll take us?"

"I reckon so. Unless somethin' happens to you along the trail. That'd be a shame, wouldn't it? But then, dead women, they don't tell stories."

"Neither do they bring reward money." Loretta said the words with a bravado she was far from feeling. "I don't think your men would appreciate doing all this with no pay. Do you? Fact is, they might get downright cantankerous about it."

He licked his bottom lip, the tip of his tongue skimming his beard as he ran his gaze the length of her. Loretta hoped Hunter came quickly. Men like these had no scruples, none at all.

Cloaked in sadness, Hunter glided through the woods, following the keening sounds that ricocheted off the trees. A chill slithered over him. After listening to his mother and Warrior these many hours, Red Buffalo's mourning song shouldn't have bothered him, but it did. Not just grief, this, but agony. Hunter eased into a moonlit clearing, his guts convulsing as the wails mounted to a high-pitched scream.

Red Buffalo knelt on the riverbank, head thrown back, fists pressed to his chest. Hunter approached him slowly, his pulse a drumbeat inside his temples, irregular and deafening. He had never seen Red Buffalo like this and wasn't sure he had the strength to lend him comfort. He mourned, too. When reality washed over him, when he allowed himself to think of those he had lost, the pain nearly bent him double.

Going down on one knee, Hunter placed a hand on his cousin's quivering back. "Red Buffalo, will you ride with me?"

Red Buffalo choked on a sob. "If you seek vengeance, Hunter, begin with me! It's my doing, all of it! Your father, Maiden of the Tall Grass, Old Man." He clamped a hand over his eyes and heaved another broken sob. "The children! They died because of me. You tried to warn me, and I didn't listen. Even your woman was taken because of me! I'm not worthy to ride with men."

"What do you mean? My Loh-rhett-ah was taken because she is a *tosi* woman, not because of you."

"No! She ran from the trees to stop a *tosi tivo* from shooting me. He wouldn't have seen her if not for me."

The news eased some of the pain from Hunter's heart. All day long, while he was comforting his grief-stricken family and burying the countless dead, doubts had tormented him. He couldn't help wondering if she had gone willingly with his father's murderers.

Hunter wrapped his arms around Red Buffalo and drew him close. "Red Buffalo, you must put these feelings away from you. I need you, cousin, as I never have before. Will you fail me?"

"No, you don't need me. I am poison, Hunter. Everyone I love dies." His shoulders shook convulsively. "Everyone."

"And now you will let their deaths go unavenged? Warrior and I cannot go without you. Who will guard our backs? The time for weeping is over. Now we must fight. For Maiden of the Tall Grass. For my father. For all who are gone from us." Hunter drew a ragged breath. "The wise ones called council. We cannot remain passive. The whites must be driven out. Now is the right time, while they are at war amongst themselves. Their soldiers are away. They're defenseless. The People must strike."

Red Buffalo's sobbing quieted. "But Hunter, that is exactly what you feared might happen. What about survival through peace?"

"It's too late for that." A heavy ache centered itself in Hunter's chest. "I am a dreamer, Red Buffalo. The land is like a single bone between a pair of starving dogs. There is enough for only one. Peace will never come, never. You were right all along, and I was too blind to see it."

"But your woman! She's a *tosi*. You speak of driving them out. What of her?"

Hunter started to speak, couldn't. He took another deep breath and tried again, his voice strained. "I will protect her as best I can. The others have agreed not to attack her wooden walls. A messenger has already left to tell some other bands of today's attack and our decision to make war. He will also pass the word about my *tosi* woman."

"You aren't going to get her? She's your wife. Her place is beside you."

"A man cannot own a woman, cousin. He

can only . . ." Hunter's words trailed off. A picture of Loretta's face flashed in his mind. "He can only love her. The blood of the *tosi tivo* will flow bridle high. To force her to stay with us while we slaughter her people would be torture. Before this is over, my name will be a curse upon her lips."

Red Buffalo drew away and lifted his ravaged face skyward. "So you have lost her. I'm sorry, Hunter. It's my fault."

"Not yours alone. This would have come to pass no matter what. Red Buffalo, I have to make sure my woman makes it safely to her wooden walls. Only a few men can be spared to ride with me. Warrior needs to be here these next few days, with his children. I must trail the *tosi tivo,* make certain they do not harm her and her Aye-mee. If things go wrong, we may have to attack. I need your strong arm. Can you set your hate for her aside and ride beside me?"

Red Buffalo wiped his cheeks dry with the heels of his hands. "You want *me* beside you? After all I've done?"

Hunter clamped a hand around his cousin's arm. "I'm afraid to go without you. Her life depends on us."

Red Buffalo straightened his shoulders. "Then I am with you."

Hunter nodded. "Once again my brother, yes?"

Red Buffalo pushed to his feet. "Yes — your

616

brother." He clasped Hunter's hand and met his gaze, fresh tears spilling down his face. "About my hate . . ." His mouth quivered. "I will not only set it aside, I will bury it. If I must, I will die for her."

Hunter blinked away tears of his own. "I have lost too many already, cousin. Do nothing *boisa* to prove your loyalty to me. Protect her, yes. But guard your back while you're at it."

Where was Hunter? The question repeated itself in Loretta's mind hundreds of times with each passing day. As the mercenaries escorted her and Amy ever closer to Fort Belknap, Loretta's uneasiness grew. Hunter wasn't dead. She knew he wasn't. Sometimes she would have sworn he rode just behind them, but when she looked over her shoulder, she saw nothing. At other times she felt his gaze on her and glanced up, convinced she would see him, astride his horse, only a few feet away. He was never there.

To avoid the horrible nightmares of the attack that had begun to haunt her sleep, Loretta lay awake at night beside Amy, staring at the starlit sky. Through Amy, Loretta had learned of the death of Maiden of the Tall Grass, and she mourned for her. Losing Many Horses had cut Loretta deeply, but at least he had lived a full life. Maiden of the Tall Grass, with her gentle eyes and sweet smile, hadn't. Loretta prayed that she had gained passage into the land of the dead, that she was now at peace. She also prayed for Warrior and his children, that God would give them the strength to go on without her.

While she prayed, she listened — for Hunter, for some telltale sound that he was indeed out there, as she sensed he was. She knew, as surely as if Hunter had told her, that he was watching over her. She knew as long as the white men did her and Amy no harm, he was content to ride shotgun, watching over them from a distance.

On the last night out, Loretta's faith in Hunter was rewarded. As everyone settled down to sleep, a coyote yipped nearby, his voice lifting in a mournful call that shivered along her spine and made the hair on her nape prickle. She rolled onto her side, back to the fire so she could scan the darkness. A shadow moved beyond the firelight. The coyote yipped again.

Warmth spread through her. As unobtrusively as she could, she linked her forefingers in the sign of friendship. If Hunter was out there, he would see and know the song her heart sang.

A rock jabbed Hunter in the belly, but he scarcely felt it. Pressing low to the earth, he kept his attention on the glow of firelight and the small woman who lay by the flames, her face turned in his direction. In his mind he was beside her, cupping her cheek in his hand, whispering his love to her. He wished now that he had taught her how to recognize his animal calls so she would know he was with her, that he had been for over six days.

Hunter leaned his head back and yipped again, letting the cry trail skyward. When he lowered his gaze, Loretta was smiling. She linked her fingers, her eyes fixed on where he lay. She had recognized his call. Perhaps he had taught her more than he knew. Pain lashed him, a pain so sharp and so deep that he couldn't breathe. *The sign of friendship.* In a few short days her heart would never sing a song of friendship for him again.

Two days later, the mercenaries delivered Loretta and Amy to Fort Belknap. After receiving a letter from Mr. Steinbach, attesting to the girls' safe delivery, the ruffians traveled south to get their reward money. At last, Loretta and Amy, escorted by Steinbach, were able to make the last leg of their journey home.

When they arrived at the Masters farm, Loretta and Amy's journey home was over. They dismounted from the horses they had borrowed from Mr. Steinbach and were swept into Rachel's arms for welcoming hugs and tearful kisses. Rachel, gaunt and hollow-eyed from ceaseless worry, could scarcely keep her hands off Amy and seemed loath to let the child out of her sight. Amy hedged when she was asked questions about her ordeal in Santos's camp, and Rachel seemed content to let the matter slide.

As pleased as Loretta was to see her aunt, she went up the sagging steps with mixed emotions, glancing over her shoulder at the horizon, watching for Hunter. He would come for her now. An inexplicable eagerness filled her. She was anxious to go home — back to the village, back to their lodge, back to his arms. Home wasn't here at this little farm anymore. Home was where Hunter was, anywhere he was, even if it meant living with her parents' murderers. She might never forget. She might never forgive. But she couldn't live her life around the past.

Aunt Rachel and Henry asked Mr. Steinbach, who had escorted the girls from Belknap, to come in for dinner. After seeing to his horses, he accepted happily. Though weary from the grueling trip, Loretta washed up and helped Rachel get the meal on the table, feeling oddly disoriented in the once familiar cabin. The walls and low ceiling seemed to close in on her. She yearned for fresh air and the openness of Hunter's lodge. On hot nights like this, one could lift the side flaps and enjoy a gentle breeze.

"So, young ladies, how does it feel to be home again?" Mr. Steinbach asked.

"I reckon it's nice," Amy replied solemnly. "I'm right glad to see my ma, anyhow."

Rachel turned from the hearth. "Amelia Rose, you sound almost gloomy! Show the proper gratitude. Those brave men risked their lives to rescue you, and Mr. Steinbach made a long ride escorting you home from Belknap."

Loretta clenched her teeth and set a trencher down on the table with more force than she intended. "We appreciate Mr. Steinbach's help, Aunt Rachel, truly we do, but if you expect either of us to be grateful to those mercenaries, get ready for a long wait. Those *brave* men didn't come to rescue us. They came to kill Indians. Women, children, babies, and old men. Most of the warriors were away hunting. I'm sure the mercenaries knew it. They rode in to slaughter people, and that's what they did."

The ensuing silence clapped like thunder. Henry fastened appalled eyes on Loretta. Rachel pressed her fingertips to her lips. Mr. Steinbach looked uncomfortable.

Amy, who was sitting with the men at the table, blinked back tears. "They killed Many Horses, Hunter's father, Ma. And Warrior's wife, Maiden of the Tall Grass. She made the outfit Loretta's wearin'. They were our friends."

Henry flushed. "I hope you'll excuse my girls, Mr. Steinbach. They been through a tryin' time. They'll come right here in a few days."

Steinbach cleared his throat. "No need to apologize. There may be a lot of Indian haters in Texas, but I'm not one of them. I've never seen a more disreputable group than those men from Arkansas. Looked like border ruffians from up Kansas way to me. Whoever hired them was plumb loco."

"Comanches took their kin," Henry retorted. "You ever seen what they do to a captive white woman? If you ask me, them Injuns got exactly what was coming to 'em."

Mr. Steinbach lifted a quizzical brow. "You ever see how some white men treat a squaw?"

"It ain't our doin' that Injuns sell off their women to no-accounts."

"*Marry* them off," Steinbach corrected. "Indians don't sell their women, Mr. Masters. They accept a bride price, which is entirely different. The gifts are taken in good faith, and the woman is, according to their beliefs, taken as an honored wife. They expect her to be treated as such."

"Bride price!" Henry snorted. "Same thing as sellin'. Heathen animals, ever last one of 'em."

Steinbach smiled. "Perhaps. But then they would say the same of us and the dowry a woman brings into marriage. The way they see it, we pay to get rid of our daughters, which is just as heathenish and doesn't say much for our women." He took a slow sip of coffee, then shrugged. "It's apparent your girls received kindly treatment with Hunter's band. It's a shame the good Indians pay for what the bad ones do."

Amy threw a rebellious glance at her stepfather, then eyed her mother, who was placing a pot of stew on the table. "It ain't finished yet. Hunter'll settle up with them mercenaries. Just you watch. They'll die. Ever' last one of 'em. And I hope Hunter takes his time killin' 'em."

Rachel quickly crossed herself. "You mustn't say such, Amy. Surely you wouldn't wish a fate like that on anyone."

Amy shot up from the bench. "I wished it on the Comancheros! Was that wrong?"

"That was different."

"No it wasn't. They hurt me, and Hunter killed them. Are you sayin' he shouldn't have?"

"No." Rachel pulled the lid off the kettle with a shaking hand, her eyes searching Amy's, her face draining of color. "If Santos and his men —" She broke off and touched her daughter's shoulder. "Amy, darling. What did they —"

"What they did to me ain't important! What's important is that Hunter came and got me, Ma! And then he fought for me. And you're sayin' he was wrong?"

Rachel let her hand fall to her side. "No. If

Santos and his men — if they —" Her eyes darkened. "They would've been hung. I reckon it's no worse that your friend Hunter punished them for us."

"But it'd be wrong if he punished those mercenaries?"

Loretta stepped forward. "Amy, love, this subject might be better left for later."

"No! I want to talk about it now!"

Rachel's face had blanched chalky white. "Who have the mercenaries harmed, Amy? They're on *our* side."

"Our side? They killed babies, Ma! And little children! Are you sayin' Indian babies ain't the same as our babies?"

"No, of course not."

"Then what are you sayin'?" Tears welled in Amy's eyes. "You weren't there! You don't know! But I was! I saw what those men did. I saw their faces while they was doin' it. I hope they die. I hope they die slow and horrible!" She whirled away. "I wish I was back with Swift Antelope, that's what!"

With that, Amy flew up the loft ladder, her sobs echoing throughout the tiny house. Loretta found herself the object of three accusing stares. Licking her lips, she said, "Amy has been through a trying time. It's gonna be a while before either of us forgets, if ever."

Rachel turned toward the stairs.

"No, Aunt Rachel, don't. Leave her be for a bit. Give her a chance to settle in."

624

"But she needs me. She needs to talk it out."

"She'll talk to you when she's ready," Loretta said gently. "She needs time. She knows you love her."

"Amy talks about that bastard Hunter like he's reg'lar people," Henry hissed.

Loretta walked over to the window and unfastened the doeskin membrane to gaze out into the twilight. She curled her fingers around the windowsill, digging her nails into the wood. Gazing up at the rise, she remembered Hunter's gentleness with Amy when he brought her back to the village after her ordeal with Santos. "Uncle Henry, you may as well know. That bastard you hate so much is my husband." Wood splintered from under Loretta's fingernails. "I married him before a priest, and I — I love him. I'd appreciate it if you wouldn't speak ill of him in front of me."

Behind her, the cabin grew so quiet that Loretta could hear the others breathing. Rigid, she waited for the explosion. It wasn't long in coming.

"Say what?" Henry cried.

"Hunter is my husband." Repeating the words lent her courage. She turned from the window to face her uncle, who had lurched to his feet. "We're married, and our union is blessed by the church."

"He forced you?"

"Unlike some I know, Hunter has never

forced me to do anything." She met Henry's gaze, well aware her meaning wasn't lost on him. "He's never mistreated me in any way, never intimidated me. I'm proud to be his wife. When he comes for me, I'll be going with him."

"Jesus Lord, she's lost her mind," Henry whispered. He sank onto the bench, looking like a billows that had just been emptied of air. "Go with him? Back to the Comanches? Rachel, talk sense to her. I never heard of such."

Making a visible effort not to follow Amy up the stairs, Rachel searched her niece's eyes, then sighed. "I reckon if she loves him, Henry, all the talkin' in the world won't change it. Loretta? Are you sure of this?"

"Yes. I love him, with all my heart."

"You'll go with him over my dead body," Henry blustered.

"That can be arranged," Loretta replied softly.

Henry's face flamed. He started up from the bench again, fists doubled, then remembered they had company. But even if Mr. Steinbach hadn't been there, Loretta wouldn't have been afraid.

"Does this mean I'll never see you again?" Rachel asked in a thin voice.

Loretta tamped down her fear that she might be living too far away to return home. "I'll come see you here. Hunter promised he'd bring me often, and he never breaks a promise."

"Over my dead —" Henry bit the words off, his neck swelling. "If you cross that doorstep to leave, Loretta Jane, don't never let your shadow fall across it again. Any woman who takes up with them animals ain't fit to be around decent folks."

Loretta straightened her shoulders. "If that's how you feel, then I'll wait for my husband outside." Turning, she moved toward the door.

"You're mighty sure of yourself, ain't ya?" Henry barked. "I mean it, young lady. Walk out that door and you ain't welcome back. What if he don't come?"

"He'll come."

Loretta lifted the bar, stepped out onto the porch, and closed the door behind her. She sat down with her back pressed against the well to wait.

Over an hour later Aunt Rachel brought her a trencher of stew. Loretta accepted it, trying not to show her unease. Hunter should have been here by now.

"Loretta Jane, if you'd like to come back in, Henry said you could. All you gotta do is apologize."

Loretta glanced toward the rise again. Hunter would come. "Thank you, Aunt Rachel, but no. I've made my choice. Besides, he'd only say more things about Hunter, and

I'd be out here again before I knew it."

"You truly do love him, don't you?" Rachel bunched her skirts in her fists and sat down, settling her back against the well. "Tell me. Help me understand."

Loretta smiled. "Why I love him, you mean?" Her smile faded, and she sighed. "Oh, Aunt Rachel, how do you explain love? Hunter says it springs up from a hidden place, and I think he must be right. I sure didn't set out to love him or even like him." She shot Rachel a sidelong glance. "I hated Comanches worse than Uncle Henry, remember? But Hunter's a *good* man, a wonderful man. What more can I say? If only you could have seen him with Amy after — Has Amy talked to you yet? About what happened with the Comancheros?"

"Words aren't necessary. I'm her mother. It was there in her eyes. So much — hate, and fear. I didn't know what to say to her, she took me so off guard. They raped her, didn't they? The whole bunch of them?"

"Yes."

Rachel took a steadying breath. "And Hunter killed them all?"

"To a man."

Curling her hands into white-knuckled fists, Rachel averted her face for a moment. "I'm likin' him better by the second."

"Hunter was so good with Amy." Loretta's voice grew husky as she related the story.

628

"Amy will never be truly over it. I reckon what happened will be with her forever. But Hunter gave her back her pride, Aunt Rachel."

"I reckon." Rachel turned haunted eyes on Loretta. "Who is Swift Antelope?"

Upon hearing the name, Loretta smiled, and a feeling of warmth spread through her. "Amy's special friend."

"Special?"

"Her beau." She cleared her throat, reluctant to reveal too much. "Amy's right fond of him. And he's been wonderful for her. I reckon that's all I should say. The rest must come from Amy."

Rachel seemed to accept that. "Is he —" She broke off and heaved a ragged sigh. "Lord, I can't believe I'm askin' this, but is he a nice young man?"

"As fine as you'll find anywhere. But what counts most, Aunt Rachel, is that Swift Antelope doesn't care about what the Comancheros did to Amy — not in the way a white boy would. He's sad she's suffered, of course, but in his mind she's still chaste and sweet and wonderful. That counts for a powerful lot with Amy, especially now, while she's healing. You shouldn't talk against Swift Antelope. You understand? Let things take their natural course. The Comanches believe yesterday is gone on the wind. Amy's ordeal is gone with it. She needs to believe that."

"Yes." Rachel's mouth turned down and quivered. "I'll say nothing against her Swift Antelope. God knows she needs a special friend right now." She leaned her head back and closed her eyes. After a long while she seemed to come to grips with her thoughts and sighed. Clasping Loretta's hand, she asked, "You think this Hunter of yours'll like me?"

Loretta set her trencher aside and gave her aunt a hard hug. "Oh, Aunt Rachel, I love you. It makes me so glad to have your blessing."

Suddenly Rachel stiffened. "Speak of the devil, there he comes."

Joy surged through Loretta. She leaped to her feet and ran toward the gate. Up on the rise she could see horses and riders outlined against the darkening sky. The Comanches reined in, forming a sparse front rank, a few others pulling in behind them. Loretta's footsteps dragged to a stop. Even at this distance and with poor light, she could see the men wore war paint. Her heart plummeted. Surely Hunter didn't believe she had willingly left with his people's murderers?

"Go into the house, Aunt Rachel," Loretta called.

"Why? What is it?"

"I'm not sure. He comes in anger."

"You come with me, then!"

Loretta swallowed an upsurge of fear. One

Indian was taller on horseback than all the rest, broader across the shoulders and chest. *Hunter.* She kept her gaze on him. A month ago she would have fled in panic. She would never run from him again. "Go to the house, Aunt Rachel. Pull the shutters. Do as I say!"

Loretta began walking again, afraid yet not afraid. A war party of Comanches was an intimidating spectacle, even to her, but the man she loved rode with them. Before she reached the gate, the warriors urged their horses forward. Instead of attacking, though, as she had feared they might, they rode the perimeters of the property, driving lances into the earth every few feet. Once again Hunter had come to mark her home.

Loretta no sooner realized that than she also realized that Hunter wouldn't mark the property if he intended to take her with him. *He was leaving her.* She bolted into a run.

"Hunter! Hunter, please . . ." She gained the gate and watched in helpless despair as the warriors sped past on their mounts, sending up such a cloud of dust that she couldn't tell which man was Hunter. "Hunter, at least talk to me!"

If Hunter heard her, he paid her no heed. Moments later the war party withdrew and rode over the rise. Loretta stood there, staring. Was Hunter divorcing her because of the *tosi tivo* attack?

As hurt as she was, Loretta could muster

no anger. It was her own fault he was leaving her. The night before the attack, she had vowed to leave him if he wouldn't go away with her. She had insisted he choose between her and the People. He had done just that. His father and countless others had been killed. His honor demanded that he avenge them.

She pressed her hand to her chest, over the medallion that bore his mark. Throwing back her head, she screamed his name, praying he would hear her and return. She waited, and she prayed. But he didn't come.

"Loretta! Get back in the yard," Rachel called.

Loretta turned, hugging her waist, her body bent slightly to contain the sobs that tried to escape her. "Aunt Rachel, he's leaving me. He's leaving me!"

Rachel came running. Wrapping both arms around Loretta, she cried, "Oh, honey . . ."

"He's leaving me!" Loretta once again threw back her head. "Hunter-rrr!"

The cry carried on the wind, shrill and mournful. Suddenly he crested the hill, a lone figure on horseback, etched in black against the sky. For a moment Loretta thought she was imagining him because she had wanted him to return so badly. Then he lifted his arm in a silent tribute, saluting her as one warrior would another. *Honoring her.* Loretta jerked from Rachel's grasp, staggering toward him, drinking in the sight of him. She wanted to be beside him. She had to make him understand that. He needn't choose between her and his people. She had been wrong, so horribly wrong.

"Hunter! Take me with you! I love you!" she called. "I didn't mean it! I didn't mean it!"

He remained there, his arm still lifted, for several heartbreaking seconds. Then he wheeled his stallion and disappeared from sight. Hollow-eyed, Loretta stared after him. She had asked him to choose, and she had lost. Her legs buckled under her weight, and she fell to her knees, the pain inside her so excruciating that she couldn't breathe.

"Hunter-rr-r!"

The wind brushed her cheeks, catching his name and carrying it away from her. She crossed her arms over her breasts and sobbed, her gaze fixed on the rise. She would never again look at the horizon without seeing him outlined there.

Hunter's name drifted to him on the wind, the call barely discernible yet shrill, like the whisper of a lost soul searching for solace. He reined his stallion to a halt, bracing himself against the sound, teeth clenched, eyes closed, his trapped breath searing his throat. *Hunter.* His woman still called for him. When he began killing her people, would she ever call for him again?

It took all his strength not to go back for her. The last thing he wanted was to hurt her like this. Yet how could he not? He had to fight the great fight for his people. He had no choice. While he was away fighting, he wanted Loretta someplace safe. After the attack on his village, there was no question she would be safer here with her own kind. He had no control over the *tosi tivo* and their attacks, but he could see to it none of his own attacked Loretta's wooden walls.

Another cry shivered through the gloaming. *Hunter.* He opened his eyes, peering at the cloud of dust up ahead. His honor lay before him, his heart behind him. Nudging his stallion into a run, he leaned low against the animal's neck, using the wind against his face to filter out her voice as he raced to catch up with the other warriors.

CHAPTER 26

Over the next few weeks, the Comanches attacked with a vengeance. News came that the mercenaries, en route to attack another village, were all killed. Tales of Hunter filtered to the Masters farm, some horrible, some heartbreakingly familiar. As fiercely as the Indians waged war, Hunter still spared women and children. Loretta's eyes filled with tears when she was told by the border patrol from Fort Belknap that somewhere along the Red River, Hunter had ridden up to a yellow-haired woman and saluted her. Loretta knew Hunter hoped she would somehow hear the tale and understand the message he sent to her.

She did understand, and she grieved for what might have been. With every Indian attack, the chasm between her and Hunter grew wider.

When the horror of it became too much, she found herself justifying the Indians' actions by remembering the attack on the village. She recalled Many Horses, a frail old man, trying to rescue a child and dying as a result. She thought of the terrified young squaw, running for her life and her child's, cut down from behind. She realized now that there was no good or bad, no right or wrong, just people fighting for their lives. Wonderful people, who lived and loved and laughed.

She thought of Red Buffalo often, finally accepting what Hunter had tried so desperately to explain, that good men can be driven to do horrible things. Red Buffalo had committed some unforgivable acts, but at long last Loretta could look deeper into the man and come closer to understanding why. She thanked God that she had saved Red Buffalo's life during the *tosi tivo* attack, knowing that Red Buffalo guarded Hunter's back against the *tosi tivo* with the same ferocity that he had once tried to guard Hunter's future against one *tosi* woman.

Nearly two months after Hunter's farewell salute to her on the rise, Loretta went to the privacy one morning and became violently sick. After repeated vomiting, she was too weak to return to the house, so she sank to the ground outside, bracing her back against the outhouse wall. Clammy sweat filmed her face. She closed her eyes, wondering if she might faint.

"Mercy, Loretta Jane, what's wrong?"

Loretta opened her eyes to see her aunt

636

picking her way through the patchy grass, trying to avoid stickers with her bare feet, her voluminous nightgown drifting in the morning breeze.

"I'm ailin'. Do you have any bee plant? I need some of your tea. My stomach's in a bad way."

Rachel crouched, pressing a palm to Loretta's forehead. "No fever. When did it come on?"

Loretta frowned. "This morning. Come to think of it, I was queasy a few mornings ago."

Rachel frowned, staring hard at Loretta. "Any dizziness?"

"Yesterday. I thought it was this insufferable heat."

"How long since you got your curse?"

Loretta leaned her head back, trying to remember. "I reckon it was —" Her eyes widened, and she clamped a hand to her abdomen.

Rachel sighed. "I'm afraid bee plant tea won't help." She fell silent a moment. "Loretta Jane, normally I'd never ask a woman this. You want me to go pick you some tansy?"

"For what?"

Rachel fixed her gaze on the barn. "In the early months, a few doses of tansy might rid you of the problem."

Problem? Loretta stared at her aunt, still trying to assimilate the fact that she might be pregnant. She didn't *feel* pregnant. But if she

637

was, she would never even consider aborting the child.

"Aunt Rachel, how can you even ask me such a thing?"

"God'll probably strike me dead. But I had to. It's not good tidings, darling. It'd be bad if it was a white child, you with no husband and all. But to be in the family way out of wedlock with a Comanche's baby? It's a disaster."

"It's *not* out of wedlock! I'm married, right and proper!"

"Honey, you got no ring, no paper, no witnesses, not even a last name! And no man beside you. Who'll believe it?"

"I don't care who believes it. I know. That's enough."

"For you, maybe. How's that child going to feel about being a bastard breed?"

Loretta felt as if she had been slapped. *Bastard breed.* The words had such an ugly sound. She wrapped her arms around her waist, a sudden and fierce feeling of protectiveness welling within her. *Hunter's child.* She'd love it with all her heart.

"Oh, Aunt Rachel. A baby. Hunter hasn't left me, after all."

Rachel threw up her hands. "Say that to me when you're tryin' to feed it in dead of winter. Henry's such an ass, he'll probably leave me if I let you stay here. The three of us gals on our own won't have an easy time trying to make it."

"I'll leave, then."

"You'll do no such thing. I said it wouldn't be easy, not that it'd be impossible." Squaring her shoulders, Rachel gazed off into the distance a moment. When her eyes slid back to Loretta's, there was a glint of determination in their blue depths. "Watching you and my daughter, seeing how you've survived things other women couldn't —" She licked her lips. "That steel in your backbones came from your bringin' up, from me. I've taught you to stand up and fight back. I've raised you proud. Lately, I've been staring into my looking glass, wondering where the old Rachel has got off to."

"Oh, Aunt Rachel, you've only done what you felt you had to for me and Amy."

Rachel nodded. "Yes. But there comes a time when a body must draw the line." She sighed and rolled her eyes, a reluctant smile tugging at her mouth. "If it's a draw between a baby and Henry, I'll kick his ornery butt all the way to the fancy house in Jacksboro and tell him to stay there this time."

Appalled and uncertain how to react, Loretta said, "Fancy house?"

"You don't *really* think he goes there to get tobacco and coffee and the *Godey's Lady's Book* for us, do you?" Rachel touched Loretta's shoulder. "Don't look so woebegone. He leaves me alone for nigh on a month after.

639

I consider it a blessing."

Loretta threw back her head and gave a weak laugh. "Uncle Henry visiting a fancy house? Oh, Aunt Rachel, I bet those ladies double their rates when they see the likes of him coming!"

"No doubt," Rachel said grimly. "A lover, Henry ain't. I've wasted a lot of years kow-towing to him. I don't plan to waste any more. I can make it without a man. Just you watch me." She pushed to her feet and extended Loretta a helping hand. "Come on, little mother. I'll fix you some remedy for that rolling tummy."

"Oh, Aunt Rachel, do you think it's for sure?"

"Sure enough that we'd best start cutting out nightshirts. I got flannel tucked away in my barrel. That'll make up nice."

Loretta smiled, and taking a deep breath, she passed a hand over her brow. "I am powerful pleased, Aunt Rachel!"

"Just keep thinkin' that way until I get Henry told."

"Do we have to tell him right now?"

"Honey, if you go to upchucking of a morn-ing before you can reach the privacy, he's gonna know anyway. May as well light his fuse when we're expecting the explosion."

There was no such thing as being prepared for Henry's temper when it blew. Though Loretta was braced for it, she still jumped at the first roar.

"You're *what?*"

"I'm in the family way."

With one suspender up and one down, his shirt partially untucked, and both feet bare, Henry was ill prepared for throwing a tantrum. His face mottled, the spots an alarming shade of purple. Eyes bugging like blue marbles, he croaked, "With that bastard Comanche's get?"

"He isn't a bastard. I met his father."

Henry worked his mouth like a beached catfish. Leveling a finger at her nose, he hissed, "I done told you what I'd do if you threw an Injun brat. I'll swing it by its heels and bash its brains, that's what."

Loretta's stomach twisted into a knot. Fear for her unborn baby made her retreat a step.

"Shut up, Henry."

Rachel's voice was so soft, the words so calmly spoken, that for a moment neither Loretta nor Henry turned to look at her. Then Loretta registered what she had heard. Her aunt stood by the rifle rack. She had the Spencer in her hands; the barrel was pointed at the floor, but she was ready, if her stance was an indication, to throw the butt to her shoulder.

"What did you say?" Henry grated.

"I said *shut up,* Henry." Rachel's voice was still soft, but the glint in her eyes was fighting mean. "I've put up with your cussedness for nigh on nine years. No more. You apologize to Loretta Jane this instant."

"Or you'll do what?"

Rachel lifted a challenging brow. "Well, I reckon you're too big for me to grab you by the heels and *bash* your brains. Guess I'll have to blow them out. Now apologize. I won't have that kind of talk in my house."

"*Your* house?"

"That's right."

Henry did an admirable job of trying to appear amused. Placing his hands on his hips, he bent one knee and eyed the rifle. "Rachel, darlin', you have a gun right now. Here shortly, you're gonna have to put it down and cook. And when you do, I'm gonna beat the sass plumb out of you. Now I suggest *you* be the one to apologize. If you do it convincin' enough, maybe I'll forgit this ever happened."

Loretta figured the bluff would probably work. Aunt Rachel had never been long on guts, and Loretta didn't see her getting a goodly supply in the space of ten minutes. Rachel surprised her, though. Instead of apologizing, she set her jaw and raised her chin.

"Henry, if you touch me when I'm cookin', I'll rip you from stem to bow with my butcher knife. I've had it up to my gullet with you."

"Give me that gun!" Henry stomped toward her.

Rachel took quick aim. The explosion of noise nearly scared Loretta out of her skin. Henry jumped straight up, clearing the floor by several inches.

"Holy Mother, you near shot my foot off, you damned fool woman!"

"Next time I won't miss."

Henry sputtered, so mad he looked fit to bust. "Rachel, I swear, I'll give you the hidin' of your life for this."

"Touch her, Uncle Henry, and I'll knock you senseless with a chunk of firewood," Loretta inserted.

"And if she don't do a good job of it, I'll finish it for her!" Amy yelled from the loft ladder. "Good for you, Ma! Give the old wart toad what for!"

Rachel returned the Spencer to the rack. "Well, Henry? It sounds like three to one. You gonna apologize to Loretta Jane or not?" She shrugged. "I reckon you can leave, if that strikes your fancy. But if you're stayin', you'll apologize before you have your breakfast."

Henry doubled his fists, trembling. Loretta moved toward the hearth and grabbed a chunk of wood, just in case she needed it. Amy swung off the ladder, ready to do the same.

"I swear, I don't know what the world's comin' to," Henry rasped. "Women lippin' off and threatenin' a man like they don't got good sense! I could take on the three of you and roll a smoke while I was at it."

"Then make like a frog and hop to it," Amy challenged. "Otherwise, you tell Loretta you're sorry like Ma says."

Henry hesitated, as if he were considering his options, such as they were. "As if I'd really hurt a baby!" he snorted. "If Loretta Jane don't got the sense to know better, then I surely do apologize."

"Accepted," Loretta murmured.

Henry jerked up his left suspender and raked his hand through his hair, looking at the hole Rachel had shot in the puncheon. "What in hell you gonna tell people happened to your floor, missy?"

Rachel smiled. "Why, I'll tell them how quick you got in and fixed it, Henry. We can't have holes in the floor, can we?"

Late that evening Loretta went outside and sat on the top rung of the fence near the front gate, swinging her feet and gazing at the rise. Rachel had won the first round with Henry, but she was still afraid for her baby once it was born. She considered trying to find Hunter, but how? He might be anywhere in a vast radius — if he had survived the battles since her last word of him. *Please, God, let Hunter be alive. Bring him back to me.* An ache of yearning centered itself in her chest.

Lances, leaning like drunken soldiers standing guard, lined the perimeter of the property, feathers fluttering, their slender shafts black lines in the moonlight. Henry had learned his lesson after the Comancheros' visit. This time he had let the lances be. Loretta wondered which was Hunter's. If she knew, she could take it inside and keep it in the loft. *A keepsake for her baby.* The child might never have anything else.

Tipping her head back, she studied the moon. Mother Moon, Hunter called it. The wind caressed her cheeks. Loretta closed her eyes, thinking of the four directions. Below her was Mother Earth. Come morning, Father Sun would show his face in the east. A primitive man's gods? Loretta smiled. Hunter worshiped the creations of God, the visible signs of His greatness. One God with many faces, whom they each addressed in different ways.

Was Hunter out there somewhere, looking up? She wondered. Was he praying? *Please, Mother Moon, let him be all right. Lead him in a great circle back to me.* Aloud, she whispered, "I love you, Hunter. I need you. Your child needs you." She hoped her words would float on the wind and speak to him. Tomorrow, when the sun rose, she prayed the golden light would remind him of her, his bright one. *Come back to me, Hunter.*

Climbing off the fence, Loretta sank to her knees and made the sign of the cross. Then she began to pray, to her God, to Hunter's. Peace filled her. He would find his way to her.

Loretta pulled her thread taut, checked the edges of the seam, and then took another bite of cloth with her needle. The flannel felt soft beneath her fingertips. She imagined a tiny body warming it and smiled. Giving another push with her feet to keep the rocker going, she glanced up at her aunt. "You know, I should start thinking on names. I have to be over two months gone. A name is important. Especially for this baby."

"Why especially this one?" Rachel asked, looking up from the bread she was kneading. "Names are important for everybody."

Loretta sighed. "Well, with Hunter as the father, I have to think of names he'd approve of."

"You call that child Running Water and I'll disown you."

Loretta giggled. "I don't know. After hemming all those diapers, maybe Running Water wouldn't be so far off mark."

Rachel rolled her eyes, then shook her head, her eyes sad. "Unless this baby's papa comes straggling back to collect his baggage, the child's gonna be stuck in white society. Being a breed is bad enough. A nice, *normal* name is a must."

Amy flipped the page in her spelling book.

"What you need is a nice white-folk name with an Indian meaning that'll make Hunter proud."

Concerned about her child's future, Loretta forced a smile. "Why, Amy, that's a champion idea!"

Rachel paused in her kneading and frowned. "I'm quite a hand on names. Let me think on it."

"Something impressive for a boy, Ma." Amy pursed her lips. "You know — like Mighty Fighter. Or Wise King. You gotta remember how Hunter thinks. They give boys grand names."

"Swift Antelope, for example?" Loretta grinned.

"Makes him sound like he oughta have a tail to wag, don't it?" Amy dimpled her cheek. "Of course, he hates the name Amy, so we're even. He says it sounds like a sheep baaing."

"The way he says it, it *does* sound like a sheep baaing."

"How about naming a boy after his papa and his uncle Warrior?" Rachel asked. "Chase Kelly. Chase means hunter, Kelly means warrior."

Loretta lowered her sewing to her lap, her gaze dreamy. "Chase Kelly — Chase Kelly. It has a nice ring, doesn't it?"

"Be nicer with a proper surname," Rachel commented.

"Wolf!" Amy cried. "That's as close to a

last name for Hunter as you'll get."

"Chase Kelly Wolf." Loretta rolled the name off her tongue a few times, warming to it. "I like it. What do you think, Aunt Rachel? Wolf as a surname isn't too strange, is it?"

"Sounds like a wonderful name to me. And if Hunter comes back someday, he can't complain too much. Hunter Warrior is a sight better than Leaky Drawers."

"Running Water," Loretta corrected.

"Whatever." Rachel smiled. "For a girl, how about Nicole? It means a girl who's victorious for her people."

"Oh, I like that," Loretta whispered. "Hunter would *love* that."

Rachel smiled. "Nicole Wolf. If she has her daddy's eyes, Indigo would go perfect with it. Nicole Indigo Wolf."

"Doesn't sound right," Amy argued. "Indigo Nicole Wolf! That, I like."

"Indigo Nicole." Tears burned behind Loretta's eyelids. A girl victorious for her people. "Yes, that's beautiful, for both worlds."

"Your own name isn't half-bad. Bet you don't know what Loretta means." Rachel folded the dough over, then glanced up with a teasing grin. "Your momma and me picked it, mainly for the meaning."

"It's a variation of Laura, isn't it? Laurel wreath or something?"

"That's the common meaning. But in your ma's name book, there was another."

"Well? Give over." Loretta waited, watching her aunt. "What's it mean? Flat-chested and scrawny?"

Rachel threw back her head and chuckled. "Flat-chested and scrawny? Loretta Jane, I swear, no one can say you have too high an opinion of yourself. It means little wise one."

The color washed from Loretta's face, and she planted her feet on the floor to stop the chair from rocking. "It means what?"

"Little wise one." Rachel's smile faded. "You feelin' peaked? What's wrong?"

Loretta set her sewing aside and pushed to her feet. "Nothing, Aunt Rachel. N-nothing." Glancing dazedly around the room, Loretta pressed the back of her wrist to her temple, a feeling of unreality surrounding her. "I, um, think I'll get a breath of air."

After hurrying from the house, Loretta struck off across the yard to lean on the fence, her favorite spot because it afforded her a view of the rise. *Little wise one.* Still numb with shock, she stared off into the distance, remembering the night Hunter had recited his song to her. *The People will call her the Little Wise One. . . .*

She studied the rise, truly believing, for the first time, that she and Hunter were destined to be together. She tried to remember all the words to his song. They came to her in snatches. *Between them will be a great canyon that runs high with blood.* A silly legend, she had once called it. Now she knew better. Too much of it had already come to pass for her to scoff. A canyon of blood. Loretta curled her hands into fists. Hunter *would* return to her. She didn't know when, or how, but suddenly she felt certain the song, once the bane of her existence, had become her greatest hope.

The smell of burning hay seared Hunter's nostrils. He moved slowly through the thick brush, cautious, the skin along his back prickling, his senses alert, as they always were when death walked beside him. A *tosi tivo* had run from the barnyard to hide in here. Hunter had seen him. He might leap out at any moment, knife slashing. Pausing, Hunter controlled his breathing and listened, his ax gripped tightly in one hand.

A twig snapped. Hunter homed in on the sound and glimpsed a flash of blue denim through a stand of yellow grass. Dropping to his belly, he slithered forward. Suddenly the white man jumped up, throwing his rifle to his shoulder. Instinctively Hunter rolled. The lead plowed harmlessly into the dirt. Bounding to his feet, Hunter launched himself through the air before the white man could reload or draw his knife.

The man screamed as he fell backward under Hunter's weight. After a moment's

650

struggle, Hunter gained the advantage, straddled the white man, and lifted his ax. In the instant before he brought his blade down to split the white man's skull, Hunter's vision sharpened on his enemy's face, pallid with fear, his eyes gigantic spheres of blue.

Could you lift your blade against a man with blue eyes and not think of me, Hunter?

Hunter's body tensed. He stared down into the man's blue eyes, trying to block out the echo of Loretta's voice. The white man returned his stare, his throat whistling, his skin shining with sweat.

"Hunter, hurry up! We must meet up with the others!"

Warrior's voice jerked Hunter from his trance. Straining, he tried to bring his arm down. But it was as if an invisible hand clamped his wrist. The crashing sound of Warrior's feet in the brush resounded. Hunter's breathing became quick and uneven. He couldn't look into this man's eyes and kill him. It was like turning his blade on himself.

When Warrior burst through the tall grass and saw Hunter straddling the white man, he slid to a stop. "Kill him! Be quick! I see smoke coming from the other farm. They're finished there. We have to meet them and get out of here!"

"I can't," Hunter rasped.

"What?"

Warrior's question hung in the air, laden with accusation. Hunter stood, his gaze locked with the *tosi tivo's*. Disbelief spread across the white man's face.

"*Mea-dro,* let's go," Hunter snarled.

Warrior didn't budge, his face lined with contempt. Hunter swallowed. There were no words to explain. He wasn't sure Warrior would understand, even if there were.

"You're leaving him alive?"

"Yes!"

"Why?"

Hunter shoved his way past his brother and broke into a trot. "His eyes."

Hunter reached his horse before Warrior did. Mounting up, he wheeled his stallion and looked at the little farmhouse, where he knew a woman and two children hid. Warrior rode up. The two brothers locked gazes, strangers to one another for the first time in their lives.

"Maybe it's because we're so close to your Loh-rhett-ah's wooden walls, yes?"

"Maybe," Hunter replied in a hollow voice.

He and Warrior nudged their horses forward, joining ranks with the other braves who had helped them wage the attack. Red Buffalo fell in beside them. Above the trees they could see black smoke billowing. For several days Hunter's men had been riding with another band. Today the two groups had separated, Hunter's band attacking here, the other a farm nearby. From the looks of the smoke, the other warriors had set fire to more than just the outbuildings.

When Hunter's band burst from the trees along the river onto the cleared land of the second farm, they reined in their horses. The house had been torched, along with everything else, which meant no one had been spared. Hunter's attention shifted from the roiling black cloud of smoke to the treetops beyond. Loretta's wooden walls were only a few miles downstream.

Heavy of heart, Hunter rode with his men toward the razed buildings to rejoin ranks with the other Indians. As they approached the yard in front of the flaming house, Hunter slowed his stallion to a walk, fixing his gaze on the scattered bodies. He brought his horse to a halt when he spied a flutter of calico. Anger slid up his throat, prickling the back of his tongue. He started to shake. *A woman and two little girls.* Hunter knew without riding closer that their deaths had not come quickly.

Still trying to recall all the words of the prophecy, Loretta sat on the top rung of the fence, feet swinging, studying the worn toes of her shoes. They were an old pair, ones she had kept on hand as spares. Her good hightops were in Hunter's village. She missed her moccasins and the free feeling her buckskin skirt and blouse had given her, but such clothing raised eyebrows now that she was home. The August sun beat down on her nape, hot and relentless. She probably should go inside. Double-wrapped in muslin, with calico over all, a woman could stifle in this heat if she didn't stay in the shade. Besides, Aunt Rachel would be putting the bread in to bake any time now and would need help starting supper.

Sighing, Loretta tipped back her head. For several seconds she was so preoccupied with thoughts of Hunter that she didn't register what she was seeing. Then her gaze sharpened on the billowing black cloud. *Smoke.* Something had happened over at the Bartletts'.

Leaping off the fence, Loretta raced for the barn. "Uncle Henry! Uncle Henry! Something's wrong over at the Bartletts' place. I see smoke!"

Henry ran from the squat building and shaded his eyes against the sun. "Hot damn! Looks like the whole place is afire."

Fear lumped in Loretta's chest, icy and suffocating. "Oh, my God!" She clamped a hand to her bodice. "Oh, my God! Not the Bartletts!"

Henry ran around the barn to saddle Ida. Loretta followed him to hold the colt while her uncle tightened the saddle cinch and adjusted the stirrups. "Go get me the Sharps and a pouch of cartridges, Loretta Jane. I'll meet ya out front."

"Don't you think you should go get Tom? If it's Indians, you might run into trouble."

Henry gestured toward the outer perimeters of the property. "I'll take along one of them damned lances. That'll protect my hide from Injuns better'n Tom can."

Loretta whirled and ran to the house. By the time she finished telling Rachel about the smoke and had gathered Henry some ammunition, her uncle was waiting out front. The three women crowded onto the porch.

"You be careful, Henry," Rachel cautioned.

"From the amount of smoke, I'd say the fightin' is over."

Rachel threw a frightened glance at the blackened sky. Grim resignation lined her pale face. "If it's bad, come back for us. You'll need a hand shoveling."

Henry returned two hours later, his face smudged with dirt, his eyes haunted. The women ran out to meet him. He rein-tied Ida to the post and stepped up onto the porch, his shoulders slumped, his feet dragging. It wasn't necessary for him to speak. Loretta bent her head. *The Bartletts.* All of them. If there were survivors, Henry would be hurrying Rachel so she could get over there to tend them.

"I reckon I'd better go hitch the mules to the buckboard," Loretta said hollowly.

"I'll come help." Amy jumped off the end

of the porch, then turned to wait. When Loretta caught up to her, she fell into a walk beside her. "Comanches again, I bet."

"Not Hunter, though," Loretta retorted. "Mrs. Bartlett and her girls. Uncle Henry didn't say, but they must be dead."

Amy sighed. "No, not Hunter."

Heat from the dying fires warmed Loretta's face, drying her eyes until it felt like her lids were stuck open. Smoke burned the back of her throat. A breeze came up and caught Mrs. Bartlett's calico skirt, fluttering the blue print around her plump white thighs. *Raped and murdered.* The years fell away, and for a moment Loretta was standing over her mother again. She blinked and swayed. The Bartletts' yard undulated like a turbulent body of water, rising, falling, rippling. Loretta turned away, so sickened she had to gulp air and walk for a moment to keep from retching.

After marking the Bartletts' yard with several lances so they needn't fear another attack, Uncle Henry chose a spot under a nearby cottonwood for the graves. Amy was spelling him with the shovel. It was up to Rachel and Loretta to prepare the bodies for decent burial. Balling her hands into fists, Loretta turned back to the job at hand.

Mercifully, her mind went blank while she helped Rachel perform the necessary tasks.

The house was a pile of rubble, so they couldn't dress anyone in Sunday best, as was proper. Loretta taking the feet, Rachel the arms, they half carried and half dragged each member of the family to the tree. It would take hours to get six holes dug. Long, endless hours.

After one turn with the shovel, Loretta couldn't hold her gorge down another minute and staggered away, seeking privacy at the far perimeter of the yard. Falling to her knees, she braced her hands in the dirt and retched. Waves of dizziness washed over her. When her nausea eased, she sat back on her heels and stared ahead of her blankly, one question circling ceaselessly in her mind. How could anyone do that to another human being?

Still too queasy to return to the digging, Loretta pushed to her feet and walked, taking deep breaths in hopes of settling her stomach. Then she spied a hoof mark in the dirt that turned her legs to water. *A notched crescent.*

A loud pounding began in her ears. Only one man could have been riding the stallion that had left that mark. Hunter had been here. Loretta swayed and reached out for support, her groping hand finding empty air.

"Ma's worried about you and the baby. You gonna be okay?"

Amy's question made Loretta leap. She whirled and staggered back a step, fastening horrified eyes on her little cousin's pale face.

"Amy. Oh, God, Amy, Hunter was here."

"Oh, go on! Not Hunter! He wouldn't."

Loretta pointed to the deformed hoofprint. Amy bent low to examine it. She had been pale before; now her skin washed absolutely white. Loretta averted her face and stared at the charred framework of the farmhouse. Not Hunter, she thought disjointedly. Not the man she knew, the father of her child. He couldn't have done this. Not to Mrs. Bartlett and the girls.

"Maybe —" Amy broke off and licked her lips. "Somebody might've stole his horse. That's it, Loretta Jane. Somebody stole his horse."

Loretta pressed her hand over her waist. "No one would steal Hunter's horse — not a Comanche, anyhow. There must be some other explanation. We both know Hunter too well to believe he'd do this."

"At least we thought we did."

Loretta lifted a stricken gaze to Amy's face. "We can't judge him like this. He deserves better."

Amy threw a meaningful glance at the hoofprint. "Maybe he was here and things got outa hand. Maybe he couldn't stop them. Afore he knew it, the womenfolk was dead."

Loretta nodded and turned away, her body quivering. From the looks of things, Mrs. Bartlett and her daughters hadn't died that quickly.

With a feeling of unreality, Loretta moved toward the cottonwood. The graves wouldn't dig themselves. As she passed the spot where Mrs. Bartlett had lain, she paused, scanning the earth for moccasin prints. Had Hunter stood here? At the question, something within her shriveled and died.

Mercifully, Tom Weaver had seen the smoke, and he showed up with another shovel to help finish digging the graves. When the Bartlett family was buried, Tom rode shotgun behind the Masterses' buckboard back to their farm. While the men put up the animals, Rachel and Loretta set out fresh bread and preserves on the table, but no one had an appetite when they finally sat down to eat.

Looking weary to the bone, Tom ran a grimy hand over his hair and sighed. "Pete Shaney and a couple of other neighbors rode over to my place this afternoon when they saw the smoke. Seems most everyone down through here is packin' up and movin' in closer to Belknap. Leavin' in the mornin'. They figger there's safety in numbers."

Henry's brows shot up. "They leavin' their harvests?"

"I reckon a harvest ain't much good to dead people." Tom shrugged. "These last few weeks, the Indians have gone loco. It appears to me they're launchin' a full-out campaign to drive white settlers plumb out've this territory. I hate to say it, but with all our armed forces off fightin' the north, the Indians have the upper hand. They're attackin' farms farther east all the time. We're so far from neighbors out here. That makes a family mighty vulnerable. The border patrol does a fine job, but they're spread thin."

"You leavin'?" Henry asked.

"I told Shaney I was stickin' tight. But after seein' what happened over to the Bartletts', I'm thinkin' maybe movin' out isn't such a bad idea. At least until this damned war's over and we got some infantry to ride the ninety-eighth and hold 'em at bay." Tom cast a quick glance at the women. "Give it some thought, Henry. I know you got them lances out there to protect ya, but, bein' frank, you're ridin' an awful lot on faith. Them Indians could turn on you, just the same as on anyone else."

Henry deferred to Rachel. She gave an almost imperceptible nod. "They travelin' up together?" Henry asked.

"Yep. We could tie up with them at dawn on the trail to Belknap."

Henry pondered that a moment. Glancing at Rachel, he said, "I reckon you'd better start packin', woman. Pick and choose careful. The buckboard'll only hold so much."

Late that night, after everyone else was asleep, Loretta knelt on her bunk and gazed out the window, memories of Hunter churning in her mind, his laughter, his gentleness, his courage. She had believed the worst of him before and wanted to kick herself later. But not this time. The man she knew would never have taken part in the murder of three women.

Tears welled in her eyes. She lay down beside Amy, staring at the moon. A sob worked its way up her throat. Stifling herself with her palm, she began to weep, for Hunter, for herself, and for their child.

CHAPTER 27

Lying on his back, head pillowed on his folded arms, Hunter stared at the full moon. A *Comanche moon.* Good light to kill by. His thoughts turned to Loretta. One thing loomed in his mind as a certainty: he could no longer ride in battle against the *tosi tivo.* The men he fought beside could no longer trust him. He could no longer trust himself.

Every time Hunter closed his eyes, he saw that woman and her little girls lying dead in the dirt. It was a memory that would haunt him forever. He had argued against launching an attack in this area, but with over a hundred men from two different bands riding together, one man's protests had gone unheard. *So close to Loretta's home.* She would have seen the smoke. The slain people might have been her friends.

Taking a deep breath, Hunter forced his eyes closed, punishing himself with the pictures that flashed. Survival or madness? He loved the People, and he prayed they prevailed, but for him the war must end.

As the prophecy had foretold, he was a warrior with no people. There was a place within him now that was not Comanche. How could he lift his blade against Loretta's kind? She had become a part of him. Today, looking into that white man's blue eyes, he had tried to deliver the death blow. *Blue eyes, Loretta's eyes.* If he had killed that man, he would have killed far more than just an enemy; he would have destroyed part of himself.

"Do you sleep?" Warrior asked.

Hunter jerked and peered at his brother through the silvery gloom. "No, *tah-mah,* I do not sleep."

Warrior spread his buffalo robe and sat down, bracing his arms on his bent knees. Contemplating the darkness, he said, "You are no longer one with us."

Something hard and cold turned over in Hunter's stomach. Was his turmoil so apparent? "I love the People, Warrior."

"I know that. But you are no longer one with us." Warrior toyed with the fringe on his moccasin. "Perhaps that is not a bad thing. The People will soon go the way of the wind." He sighed and grew pensive. "We're outnumbered, Hunter. Though we fight with all our strength, we'll never win. When the war between the *tosi tivo* ends, their soldiers will return and drive us back into the wastelands. Hundreds and hundreds will be killed, until only a few of us remain."

Hunter knew what Warrior said was true, but admitting it wasn't easy. "For now, Warrior, the People prevail."

"For now." Warrior swallowed and lowered his gaze. "I have great love for you, *tah-mah*. If you leave me, my heart will be laid upon the ground. But it is time that you fulfill the last part of the prophecy."

Hunter's mouth went dry. He fixed his attention on the stars.

"Someone must preserve the ways of the People," Warrior rasped, "someone who will sing our songs and teach our ways. Unless you do that, all that we are will be lost. You must go get your woman and take her far away into the west lands where this war does not reach." Warrior's voice shook with emotion. "To a new place, Hunter. You know the words of the song."

"Warrior, you make it sound so simple. You saw what happened near her home today. She will spit upon me when she sees me." Hunter angled an arm over his eyes. "I left her and rode into battle against her people. How many have we killed since the attack on our village?"

"She won't turn from you."

"How can you know? You say I should fulfill the last part of the song? How? Where is the high place the Great Ones spoke of? Where is the canyon filled with blood? And how will I ever reach across so great a distance to take Loh-rhett-ah's hand?"

"You must have faith. The high place will be there, as will the great canyon." Leaning forward, Warrior clasped his brother's shoulder. "Courage, *tah-mah*. Have courage."

Hunter clenched his teeth. "I feel so alone. I can't see into myself and find my face, Warrior. I lifted my ax to kill that man today, and I couldn't do it. Our father lies dead. Your woman lies dead. Where is my hatred? When I search for it, it isn't there. Just emptiness and sorrow that runs so deep it aches in my bones."

Warrior's grip on Hunter's shoulder tightened until the bite of his fingers was almost painful. "The hate has gone from you to a faraway place you cannot find, as it was spoken in the prophecy. That's why it is time for you to walk your own way. You must fight the last great fight for the People, yes? And you must fight it alone. I have to stay here. For our mother, my children. You're our hope, our only hope."

"You call it hope? I call it running away."

"No! When we run, we find someplace familiar and safe. Winter will be upon us soon. You will face uncertainty and great danger when you go west." Giving Hunter a small shake, Warrior cried, "You *are* our hope, Hunter! Why can't you see that? When the last Comanche puts down his weapon, when the last chief says it is finished, we will know it is *not* finished. We will know that the People live on — far away from this place — that our songs are being sung, that our ways are being honored. I know you feel great fear, but fear has never stopped you. You mustn't let it stop you now."

"I will go wherever the Great Ones lead me," Hunter whispered. "You know I will. It's just that I can't see the path they want me to follow. There is no one to lead me."

"The path will be there. When you turn your face westward you will *know,* deep within, where to place your feet." Warrior's voice rang with certainty. "I would ask one thing of you, *tah-mah.* Ride beside me one last time into battle. It will be our final memory of each other, yes?"

Once again Hunter remembered looking into that white man's blue eyes. *The battles shall stretch before him with no horizon.* When would it ever end? But his brother had made this request of him. "I will ride with you," Hunter whispered. "One last time."

Straightening his pallet, Warrior stretched out on his back, so close his arm brushed Hunter's. After a long while he said, "You will tell your sons and daughters about me, yes?"

Hunter wished he could weep, but the tears were dammed behind his lids, aching and burning. "Yes. And you will tell yours of me?"

"I will tell them." Warrior's voice cracked. "Of you and your golden one and the song that led you west. Love her well, *tah-mah*. The days together are brief."

"Yes." Hunter knew Warrior was thinking of Maiden of the Tall Grass. In a husky voice, he added, "Far too brief."

The next morning the Masters family joined the wagon train of fleeing settlers heading for Fort Belknap. Since the wagons were already brimming with possessions, every fit person had to walk, which gave the women an opportunity to exchange terror stories. Everyone, it seemed, feared for their lives.

Two hours out, the Shaneys' wagon broke a wheel, and the group had to delay traveling until the men got it fixed. The settlers pulled their wagons into a circle and set up temporary camp. The women immediately began preparations for the midday meal. Loretta's and Amy's contribution was to gather fuel for the cooking fires.

"Buffalo chips!" Amy grumbled. "Fine way to spend the mornin', gatherin' pooh for fires. Why us?"

"Because we aren't so old we get crinks in our backs or so young we'll get lost." Loretta bent over, picked up a dried pie, and stowed it in her gunnysack. Since their ordeal at the Bartletts' last night, Amy hadn't once smiled. Loretta couldn't help being concerned. "You never complained in Hunter's village."

"That was different. You *expect* to do things like gathering Buffalo pooh when you live with Indians." She sighed. "It's flat as a flapjack out here. Who could get lost? We've walked a mile and can still see our buckboard."

"There's one high spot over yonder."

"Only one. A body could walk for miles and use it for a landmark."

Loretta found another pie. In the hopes of teasing a smile out of Amy, she grinned and waved the chip under the child's nose. "Wanna rub a little in our hair?"

"Lands, no!"

No smile. Poor Amy didn't have much to be lighthearted about these days. Keeping up the banter, Loretta said, "That's what you told me once, remember? That Comanche women rubbed dung in their hair."

"Maybe they do." Clearly determined to stay in a foul mood, Amy frowned and picked up a pie, adding it to her bag. "Probably in winter. We ain't never been around 'em then. Dumb Indians, anyway." She bit her bottom lip, looking miserable. "How can you be cheerful? The Bartletts ain't cold in their graves. And Comanches did it! You been listenin' to what everyone's sayin'? Callin' them murderin' animals. And I reckon they're right!"

"Because Hunter's horse was over at the

Bartlett place?"

"Yes!" Amy glanced up, her eyes glittering with angry tears. "He tricked me into thinkin' he was somethin' he wasn't. I *hate* him."

Loretta sighed. "Did he trick you, Amy? Hunter's fighting a war. Bad things happen in war, things beyond our control. If you're going to condemn Hunter, then I say he deserves a trial. Let's list our evidence against him, shall we?" Loretta held up a fist. "What did Hunter do when Santos took you?"

"He came and got me."

Loretta uncurled her thumb. "That's one piece of evidence. What did he do after he got you away from Santos?"

"He took care of me," Amy replied in a thin voice, her mouth trembling. "Oh, Loretta, I *know* all the good things about Hunter! You don't have to make me count 'em."

"That's a relief, 'cause I'm not sure I have enough fingers to keep track." Loretta smiled faintly and touched Amy's arm. "Don't discount all those wonderful things Hunter has done, Amy, not over one hoofprint. Hunter is your friend. And he's been a very good friend. You owe him your trust."

"How can you explain that hoof mark?"

Loretta shook her head, feeling suddenly old and drained. "I don't need to. I did a lot of thinkin' last night. About Hunter, about all the things I *know* about him. There's an old saying that you should believe none of what you hear and only half of what you see. I figure that hoofprint falls into the half I shouldn't believe. I know Hunter. So do you. He wouldn't have done that to Mrs. Bartlett. He wouldn't!"

"You're makin' me feel guilty as sin for doubtin' him."

"Hunter wouldn't want you to feel guilty. So don't. Just have faith in him."

As she reached to hug Amy, Loretta heard someone shout. She glanced back at the small cluster of wagons and saw a woman waving her arms and beckoning to them. "Something's up."

Amy squinted into the sunlight. "Do they want their dung or not? Addlepated woman. If she thinks I'm gonna run all the way back over there, she's got another think. What's she sayin'?"

Loretta cocked an ear but couldn't make it out. "We'd best get back. Maybe the wagon's fixed and they're ready to —"

Loretta froze, the rest of the words caught in her throat. From the corner of her eye she saw Comanches, well over a hundred of them. She forced her head around. Mounted on horses, the warriors formed close ranks, knee to knee, three rows deep. At a glance, none of their faces were familiar. "Oh, my God, Amy, run!"

Dropping the bag of dung, Loretta grabbed Amy's arm, her legs scissoring across the short, curly grass toward the wagons. Until that moment she hadn't realized how far afield they had gone. There was no way they could make it. *No way.* Visions of the Bartletts' farm spun through her head. Her heels slammed against the earth, the impact jarring up her legs.

Amy's skirts tangled around her ankles, and she sprawled belly first in the grass.

Loretta hauled her up, sobbing for breath, "Hurry, Amy! Oh, God, *hurry!*"

A rifle shot sliced through the air, the sound so loud that Loretta felt the repercussion in her ears. Amy dug in her heels, eyes huge, mouth working.

"Amy! Come on!"

Another shot rang out, this one from the wagons. The Comanches let loose with high-pitched battle cries. Their rear line fanned out, riding in a huge sweep to flank the formation at each end. Loretta cranked on Amy's arm, hauling her forward. *The wagons.* They had to reach the wagons. They were defenseless out here.

The ensuing volley of shots lent Loretta speed. She wasn't sure now from which direction the firing came. She only knew a full-scale Indian attack was about to erupt, and she and Amy were *between* the braves and the wagons. *Please, God. Please, God.*

Screams filled the air. The ground under Loretta's flying feet began to vibrate. She threw a horrified look over her shoulder to see horses bearing down on them. The next instant her toe caught on a clump of grass, and she stumbled, losing her grip on Amy's arm.

Staggering to keep her balance, Loretta screamed, "Keep running!" And Amy did. In a blind panic. Not toward the wagons, but toward the Comanches. Loretta veered after her. "Amy! Come back! They don't know you! Come back!"

Amy kept running the wrong way, as fleet as a deer. Loretta made a dive for her, trying to grasp her arm. Her fingertips barely grazed her sleeve and fell away empty. Fastening frightened eyes on the advancing Indians, Loretta faltered and missed a step. *Swift Antelope!* Little wonder Amy was running toward the Indians. Swift Antelope rode in the front lines, and Amy must have seen him. In her terror she was heading for someone she knew would protect her.

Staggering to a stop, Loretta clamped both hands over her mouth, watching Amy as she dashed toward the racing Comanche horses. What if Swift Antelope didn't see her? What if some other Indian rode out and killed her before Swift Antelope could stop him?

Hunter, who rode in the left flank, glimpsed a flash of movement and swung his rifle around, drawing bead on the figure that raced toward them. *Honey-gold hair.* Instantly his mind exploded with fear. *Amy.* The thought no sooner registered than he saw Loretta running behind her. Wheeling his horse, Hunter lunged across the front line. Cut off with no warning, the other charging warriors were forced to rein in. Their mounts reared, striking the air with their front hooves. Comanches coming up from behind were caught in the crush and fought desperately to control their mounts.

In the confusion, Amy lost sight of Swift Antelope. She reversed direction and ran toward the wagons, covering an amazing amount of ground before Hunter could check his horse. Strangling fear surged up his throat. Amy, skirts flying, blond hair a gleaming target, was running in a straight line for the wagons, Loretta right behind her. *Between the opposing forces.* The whites, spying the women, had stopped shooting, but in his peripheral vision Hunter saw a brave aim his rifle.

"*Ka,* no!" Hunter zigzagged his mount into the man's line of fire. "No!"

With a vicious kick, Hunter sent his black into a mighty forward lunge, gaining several yards on the advancing warriors, many of whom were from another band. They wouldn't recognize Amy or Loretta. Unless Hunter could stop the shooting, his woman and her little sister would be killed. When he felt certain everyone in the formation could see him, he wheeled his horse to face them and lifted his rifle high overhead, signaling a cease-fire.

Still trailing Amy, Loretta spotted Hunter the moment his horse drew out in front of the others. Heaving for air, she stumbled to a stop and glanced over her shoulder. Hunter, broad back to the wagons, sat tall on his stallion, waving his rifle above his head.

As if in a dream, she whirled. The sight of Hunter making a target of himself would be painted in full color across the canvas of her mind for the rest of her life.

The sounds around her were eclipsed by her terror. There was only the blood swishing in her ears, the agonized rasp of her breathing, and Hunter's name, echoing in her thoughts like a litany as she broke into a run toward him. Time slid to a crawl. She felt as if she were slogging through a river of cold molasses, her legs straining, her feet weighted to the ground. *Hunter.* Like an image trapped under glass, he loomed before her, every detail cast into stark clarity by the sunlight, but beyond her reach. *Hunter.* The white men at the wagons would kill him. To them he wasn't a person, but an animal. Though she was still a good fifty feet away, Loretta reached out, his name a silent scream on her lips.

When the shot rang out, she jerked as if the

ball had plowed into her own body. The blast echoed and reechoed, loud and reverberating, punctuating her worst fear with a cutting finality. Running, running. She saw only Hunter, sitting on his horse one second, beautiful and proud, then thrown forward, as if a mighty hand had slammed into his back. He pitched sideways off his horse. Falling, falling, forever falling.

Hunter, shot. Loretta couldn't think beyond that. The other Comanches were a blur. Hunter was her only reality, and the cold fingers of death were curling around him. The events of the last three months spun through her head like the acts in a play. Her fierce captor, her trusted friend, her gentle lover. She couldn't lose him like this.

"Hunter! Oh, please, dear God, not Hunter!"

Loretta reached him and dropped to her knees, trying to gather him into her arms. *Dead weight.* She couldn't lift him. *Blood, everywhere blood.* A tortured moan worked its way up her throat. *Not Hunter.* With a trembling hand, she cupped the side of his jaw, sobbing his name. *This Comanche cannot change his face.* She touched the scar that slashed his cheek, the lifeless lips that had so frequently whispered comfort to her. If her face was carved on his heart, his was carved on her soul.

675

"Don't die! Hunter, please, don't die! I love you! Hunter —" A sob tore the words from her guts in ragged spurts. "I love — you. *Nah-ich-ka,* you hear? I love you! You can't die and leave me. Please, don't leave me!"

As if her voice had somehow reached him, he stirred ever so slightly and moaned. Hope flooded through her. Focusing on the wound for the first time, she saw it was in his shoulder. *Not fatal if the bleeding was stopped, if he got the proper care.* On the tail of that thought, a different kind of fear assailed her. Throwing a frightened glance at the wagons, she threw herself across his body.

"Don't shoot!" Her scream pierced the air. "Don't shoot, damn you! Don't shoot!"

A hush fell over the flats. The whites had already ceased firing, afraid of killing one of their own. The Comanches, even those who had never seen Hunter's golden-haired wife, had been told about her and lowered their rifles. Swift Antelope leaped off his horse and ran out. Warrior, at the far right in the front line, rode forward as well.

The two men didn't waste a second. With gentle hands they pulled Loretta away from her husband. Lifting Hunter's limp body between them, they slung him across his horse. Loretta pushed to her feet, watching in helpless misery as Swift Antelope led Hunter's stallion in among the others and

Warrior ran back to his pinto.

"Warrior! Don't leave me here! Please don't leave me!"

Before he rode off, Warrior turned to look at her, his dark eyes piercing, his face stricken. Then he disappeared into the ranks. As quickly as they had advanced, the Comanches retreated.

Loretta, buffeted by the wind, stood alone on the flats until they rode from sight. When she could no longer hear the tattoo of their horses' hooves, she held up her hands and stared at the smears of crimson that stained her skin. *Hunter's blood.* The ultimate sacrifice. And he had made it without a second's hesitation, out of love for her. The pain that knowledge caused her ran too deep for tears.

That night after supper, Loretta sat by the fire, using an overturned bucket as a stool, a mug of gritty coffee cupped in her palms, her gaze fixed sightlessly on the shifting flames. The other women around the fire spoke infrequently, some, Loretta guessed, because they were afraid of another Indian attack, others undoubtedly because they resented her presence and wanted to make sure she knew it. *A Comanche's woman.* After the spectacle she had made of herself that morning, everyone knew.

Loretta was beyond caring. There was an ache inside her chest the size of a boulder.

She didn't know if Hunter was alive or dead. She might never know. He was her husband. She loved him. Why couldn't these women understand that? Instead they acted as if she were some kind of vermin in the flour sack.

Maybe they were right. She didn't belong here now. She wasn't sure if she would ever fit in anywhere again, even with the People. *Warrior's eyes.* She would never forget how he had looked at her before he rode off. She hadn't fired the rifle, but she had been the cause of Hunter getting shot. The accusation had been written all over Warrior's face.

Sighing, Loretta tipped her head back and studied the stars. The settlers, fearing another attack, had pulled their wagons into a tight circle. Practically everyone had been frantic about the delay in getting the Shaney wagon fixed, terrified to spend a night here in the open. They had ignored Loretta's assurances that the Comanches wouldn't come back. As if Warrior would let the others attack a group of wagons when he knew Hunter's woman was there!

A coyote wailed, the sound sending a shiver up Loretta's spine. She cocked an ear, listening.

"I hope that's what it sounds like and not an Injun," Mrs. Cortwell whispered.

"It's likely a coyote," Mrs. Spangler replied. "Look at that there moon, would ya? Of course, it's a good moon for killin', too. A

Comanche moon, my man calls it."

The fire popped, and Mrs. Shaney leaped. "Lawzy, my nerves is frayed."

The coyote yipped again, his cry trailing skyward, mournful and lonely. Loretta stood up, her heartbeat quickening.

"What is it?" Mrs. Spangler cried.

Mrs. Cortwell pressed a hand to her throat. "Oh, Lord. It *is* Injuns!" She jumped to her feet. "Matthew! Matthew Cortwell, where'd you git off to? There's Injuns out there!"

"They won't hurt you," Loretta said softly. "Just stay calm, Mrs. Cortwell."

"It's fine for you to say, you Comanche slut!"

Loretta spun on her heel and left the fire. Alerted by Mrs. Cortwell's cries, Uncle Henry came out from the buckboard and intercepted her. "Don't even think it, Loretta Jane."

"That's Hunter out there, Uncle Henry."

"You don't know that. You wanna part with your hair, girl?" He seized her arm. "Not only that, but you gotta think about us and how it looks."

Several other men gathered around. Loretta glanced at their taut faces, feeling trapped. She heard the coyote again. *Hunter.* "I'm going. He's out there calling me, and I'm going."

Mr. Cortwell moved closer, his hat pulled low, the brim casting his face into black shadow. "You go, woman, and you ain't comin' back. Just you understand that."

"That's right!" another man agreed. "We don't want no damned Injun lover amongst us. Go to him, by God, and there's no changin' your fool mind later."

Loretta stared at first one man, then another. They glared back at her with hate-filled eyes. She knew in that instant that if she stepped beyond the circle of wagons, the decision would be irrevocable. Suddenly she was afraid. Beyond the firelight Comanches waited, possibly the same Comanches who had killed Mrs. Bartlett. *A war party.* These men around her were her own kind and representative of her world. If she turned her back on them, she was turning her back on everything familiar and dear to her, including her family. Hunter had left her once. What if he had come now not to take her away with him, but only to let her know he was all right?

Loretta, paralyzed with indecision, swallowed and shot a frightened glance into the darkness beyond the wagons. If she didn't go to Hunter now, he might never approach her again. She was carrying his child. He had a right to know that. If she went to him, he wouldn't leave her. Not if he understood she couldn't return to the wagons. Yet fighting for his people was important to him. Her people had spilled so much blood in his village.

Trust. It was easier said than done. For a moment Loretta struggled, unable to make up her mind. *Chase Kelly Wolf. Indigo Nicole Wolf.* Her child had the right to know his or her father. And the chance would be lost unless she found some courage. Did she want to spend her life peering into her looking glass, as Aunt Rachel had, searching for herself, berating herself?

Loretta pulled her arm from Henry's grasp. If she was going, she had to hurry before Hunter gave up and left. She shouldered her way through the men, ignoring the insults they hurled after her.

Amy appeared out of the darkness. From the look on her face, Loretta knew she had overheard. Loretta broke stride, then threw her arms wide to catch her little cousin in a fierce hug. "I love you, Amelia Rose. Don't ever forget that."

Amy's shoulders shook with sobs. "I won't. I'll miss you, Loretta. A powerful lot."

Loretta hugged her more tightly. "Maybe one day we'll be together again. You've got to hold my baby!"

"Maybe after Swift Antelope comes for me." Amy gulped and pulled away. "You'll tell him, won't ya? That I ain't forgot my promises to him? That I'll be waitin' for him?"

"I'll tell him."

"You'd best go." Amy rubbed her cheek with her fist. "Go on! Before Hunter leaves!"

Loretta threw a regretful glance toward the buckboard. "Tell Aunt Rachel that —"

"She knows, but I'll tell her anyhow."

Loretta touched her hand to Amy's cheek, trying to smile but too frightened to manage. "Good-bye."

"Good-bye, Loretta Jane. Good-bye!"

The word followed Loretta into the darkness. *Good-bye.* As she left the wagons far behind, she felt more alone than she ever had in her life. Moonlight bathed the flats. Loretta turned in a slow circle but saw no one. If Hunter was out here, why didn't he show himself?

The call of the coyote trailed skyward again. Loretta whirled toward the sound and ran toward the rise. As she crested the slope, Hunter loomed up out of the shadows, tall and dark, his hair drifting in the wind. His upper chest and shoulder were crisscrossed with torn strips of cloth. Calico and muslin.

Slowing her footsteps, she walked toward him a ways, then stopped. Did he even want her as his woman now? So much had happened since they last saw each other. So much pain and grief. His face was in shadow, so she could read nothing in his expression.

When Loretta drew to a halt several feet away from him, Hunter's heart skipped a beat, then started racing. Peering at her through the silvery darkness, he saw a *tosi* woman in *tosi* clothing, her pale skin and golden hair illuminated by the light of the Comanche moon. Just as the prophecy had foretold, they stood on a high place, she on the land of the *tosi tivo,* while he, Comanche to his bones, stood on the land of the People. A great distance divided them, a distance much harder to bridge than the few feet between them.

Hunter ached with things he longed to say, but none of them seemed enough. He realized then that the great canyon filled with blood wasn't a chasm in the earth but one in their hearts. There was an ache in Loretta's eyes that cut clear through him. He knew the same ache was in his own. His father, Maiden of the Tall Grass, her parents. So many were lost to them.

"Are you all right?" she asked.

Hunter was weak from loss of blood. His shoulder felt as if it had a red-hot coal buried in it. "I am well. You *came,* yes? There is much we must talk about."

"I saw your good friend's hoofprint at the Bartletts' farm," she said in a tremulous voice. "A woman and two little girls were killed. I know you were there."

Hunter closed his eyes. If only he could close the distance between them and hold her in his arms, but fear of rejection held him back. "Little one, I —"

"Don't!" She threw up a hand. "Don't say anything, Hunter." Her arm quivered as she lowered it to her side. "I don't want you to explain, really I don't. There's no need."

There was great need. Hunter studied the ground, searching his heart for the right words. None came to him. "I went to the farm after. It is the truth I speak."

Lifting his gaze to hers, Hunter tried to read her thoughts. What if she didn't believe him? When he tried to picture what his life would be like without her, he saw only emptiness. She *had* to believe him.

Afraid as he had never been, he reached out to her, his hand palm up and open. For an endless moment she stared at his outstretched fingers; then, with a strangled cry, she ran toward him. As her hand met his, Hunter caught her slight form to his chest with his uninjured arm and hugged her until he feared her bones might break. *Flowers in springtime. Soft as rabbit fur. Warm as sunshine.* A sob caught in his chest.

"Your shoulder. You'll hurt yourself."

"It is as nothing." It wasn't a lie. The pain seemed distant now, like a hawk hovering and circling. Later it would descend to tear at his flesh, but for now he could ignore it. Hunter buried his face in the curve of her neck, his favorite place. So many nights he had dreamed of this, yearned for her. Tears filled his eyes, and a tremor coursed through his body. "I have such great love for you, little one. Such great love."

"I love you just as much, Hunter. I thought I'd die when you left me."

"You will go from this place with me, walk in my footsteps?"

A strained silence settled between them.

"Oh, yes, Hunter, yes."

"Do not make a promise of it quick. We must go west. Alone, Blue Eyes, leaving all that we are behind. All those we love, your people, my people."

Loretta caught his face between her hands, shaking with the intensity of her emotions. "Hunter, *you* are my people. I'll follow you anywhere."

"I do not know the way." His voice was gravelly, the words he spoke halting. Admitting his own vulnerability didn't come easily. But this was no time for pride. If Loretta chose to follow him, her life could be at risk. He wanted her to know that. "The song says we will make a new nation, but this Comanche fears he cannot feed even two. If you walk behind me, you follow a man who is lost."

Loretta encircled his waist with her arms and pressed her cheek against his chest, inhaling the scent of his skin, loving it. Her gaze settled on the gigantic moon that shone down on them. *Mother Moon, watching over them.* "You aren't lost, Hunter. The words in your song will guide you. And when you falter, your Great Ones will lead you — to the place we're meant to find. We will sing the People's songs to our children. The Comanche and *tosi tivo* will live as one forever. Don't you see? You and I are the beginning." She arched her back to see into his eyes. "Hunter and his yellow-hair, together as one."

"You believe?" Hunter studied her, more than a little amazed. "The words of my song are inside your heart?"

Smiling through tears, Loretta told him the meaning of her name. "Yes, I *do* believe. I believe in your Great Ones, I believe in your song, but, most important, I believe in you." She touched her fingertips to the scar that lined his cheek. "I'm not afraid of anything except being without you. This morning I thought you'd been killed . . . I've never been so frightened. Never."

Red Buffalo emerged from the darkness, leading his favorite war pony. Loretta and Hunter, arms looped around one another, turned to face him. When Red Buffalo reached Loretta, he grasped her hand and curled her fingers around the horse's line.

"Red Buffalo, I can't take your war pony!" This horse, she knew, was Red Buffalo's most prized possession, precision trained, his greatest edge when he rode into battle. It was a great honor he was bestowing upon her, perhaps the greatest honor a warrior could bestow on anyone, but she couldn't in good conscience accept. "Please, keep your horse."

"My cousin's fine Comanche wife must

have a fine horse to carry her. You will never make it into the west lands on a scrawny, poorly trained *tosi tivo* horse."

Red Buffalo extended his hand to her. *In friendship.* She had vowed once that she would *never* take his hand in friendship, *never.* For a moment she hesitated. Then the last hard little knot of hatred within her disintegrated, and she placed her palm across his. Loretta knew that her mother would approve. For Loretta and Hunter, the war between their people had to end. There was no room for the past in their lives, no room for bitterness.

Red Buffalo smiled, inclined his head to Hunter, and turned to leave.

"Red Buffalo, would you give Swift Antelope a message for me? Tell him Amy hasn't forgotten her promise, that she'll wait for him."

Red Buffalo lifted his arm in farewell. "I will tell him."

As Red Buffalo disappeared into the darkness, Hunter's hand, which was riding Loretta's thickened waist, tightened. He glanced down, his brows lifting in question. With a wondrous expression on his face, he placed his other palm on her slightly swollen abdomen. "Blue Eyes, what is this?"

Loretta looked up at him through tears. "Our child, Hunter."

His warm fingers flexed and curled protectively. A slow smile spread across his mouth. "A child . . ." The words were a reverent whisper.

"*Our* child."

Loretta placed her hand over his, so filled with love for him that she felt she might die of it. The future was filled with uncertainty. The way ahead might be fraught with danger. And they would be completely alone. Two people, against a world of hostility.

None of that really frightened her, though. Theirs was no ordinary love, and she knew the course of their lives would have a far greater purpose than that of simply being together.

They would find their way west, just as the prophecy had foretold. She *knew* they would. The Comanche nation was doomed. There was no stopping the tide of white settlers that washed over their land. An entire race of people would eventually be conquered and all but destroyed.

She and Hunter were like a seed floating on the wind. Somehow, somewhere, they would find a fertile place, where they could put down roots and grow strong. Through them, the People would live on. The gods had sent her and Hunter a sign to help them believe, to give them faith, and she no longer had a single doubt that all the words of Hunter's song would somehow come to pass.

Within her grew a child, both *tosi tivo* and

Comanche, the child of the great warrior with indigo eyes and his honey-haired maiden. A child who brought new hope for the People and tomorrow.

ABOUT THE AUTHOR

Catherine Anderson lives in the pristine woodlands of Central Oregon. She is married to her high school sweetheart, Sid, and is the author of more than twenty bestselling and award-winning historical and contemporary romances. Visit her Web site at www .catherineanderson.com.

The employees of Thorndike Press hope you have enjoyed this Large Print book. All our Thorndike and Wheeler Large Print titles are designed for easy reading, and all our books are made to last. Other Thorndike Press Large Print books are available at your library, through selected bookstores, or directly from us.

For information about titles, please call:

(800) 223-1244

or visit our Web site at:

http://gale.cengage.com/thorndike

To share your comments, please write:

Publisher
Thorndike Press
295 Kennedy Memorial Drive
Waterville, ME 04901